# Readers love the Warders

*His Hearth*

"Mary Calmes has once again struck gold. Her latest well plotted release is filled with passionate, charismatic characters that left me begging for more."—Fallen Angel Reviews Recommended Read

"…a worthy afternoon read…"—Literary Nymphs Reviews

*Tooth & Nail*

"…an action-packed love story so absorbing I could not put it down."—TwoLips Reviews

"…drew me right in from page one."—Whipped Cream Reviews

*Heart in Hand*

"Ms. Calmes has balanced this personal part of the story with the creepy… and she's done it with great creative flair."—Literary Nymphs Reviews

*Sinnerman*

"This is such a good story and such a fantastic series!"—The Romance Studio

"…full of intrigue, romance, excitement and hot steamy sex!"— Dark Divas Reviews

*Nexus*

"I loved every minute of this emotional roller coaster…"—Queer Magazine Online

"…a well written story with a great round-up of characters…"— MM Good Book Reviews

*Cherish Your Name*

"…what the Warders series is all about: hot sex, hot men, action, and romance."—Joyfully Reviewed

By MARY CALMES

NOVELS
Change of Heart
Honored Vow
Trusted Bond

A Matter of Time Vol. 1 & 2
Bulletproof

Acrobat
The Guardian
Mine
Timing
Warders Vol. 1 & 2

NOVELLAS
After the Sunset
Again
Any Closer
Frog
Romanus
The Servant
What Can Be

THE WARDER SERIES
His Hearth
Tooth and Nail
Heart in Hand
Sinnerman
Nexus
Cherish Your Name

Published by DREAMSPINNER PRESS
http://www.dreamspinnerpress.com

# WARDERS

## VOLUME ONE
# MARY CALMES

*HIS HEARTH*
*TOOTH & NAIL*
*HEART IN HAND*

*Dreamspinner Press*

Published by
Dreamspinner Press
382 NE 191st Street #88329
Miami, FL 33179-3899, USA
http://www.dreamspinnerpress.com/

The Warders Collection, Vol. 1

Cover Art by Anne Cain   annecain.art@gmail.com

ISBN: 978-1-61372-491-0

Printed in the United States of America
First Edition
May 2012

His Hearth (July 2010), Tooth & Nail (November 2010), Heart in Hand (May 2011) were previously published individually in eBook format by Dreamspinner Press.

Thank you to all my wonderful fans
who asked when the boys would be in paperback.

# his hearth

# 1

IT WAS supposed to be my night. Well, maybe mine *and* my best friend's, but definitely I was in there somewhere. When the stars aligned and you got your dream, nothing was supposed to get messed up. But since there was no such thing as perfect, I shouldn't have counted on it.

"Julian," she said before her arms wrapped around my neck. "Honey, where's Channing?"

Here was the crux of the matter. I turned on the barstool and looked at my best friend's wife. Phoebe Vega was a stunning creature. Waiting expectantly, breathless from dancing, her pale jade eyes focused on me, she was as close to a goddess as I would ever see.

"God, you're beautiful," I sighed.

The scowl came fast. "What's wrong?"

"I can't just give you a compliment?"

"No."

I couldn't contain my grin; it was just too stupid to even have to explain. "I need a drink."

"Oh no, what happened?"

This is the problem with having good friends; they know you well enough to interpret your mood from the expression on your face with simply a look.

"Jules, where's your date?" she demanded, her voice rising.

I emptied the shot of Patron in front of me, refocused my vision since it was the third one I'd had, and looked at her. "Having sex with Peyton Wilson in his office."

She was silent, stood there just looking at me for several moments, blinking, absorbing what I had said. "I'm sorry, what?"

I cleared my throat. "My date, the guy I've been going out with for the last six weeks? Well, the last time I saw him, he was taking care of Peyton Wilson in the production office." And I could have been much more graphic, even more crass, but this was my girl, the wife of my best friend, and she was seven months pregnant. I didn't want to upset her any more than I had to. So I just took in her sweet face.

There was a long pause. Maybe we were having a moment of silence to grieve.

"Ohmygod!" she shrieked, startling people around us, her voice high and shrill. "Are you kidding me?"

"Oh." I nearly choked on my beer, trying not to laugh. "We're doing loud."

"This isn't funny!"

I really had way too much alcohol in me for it not to be funny. My date giving another guy a blowjob when he was supposed to be with me when the CEO of the company came to offer me his congratulations on my promotion... *oh hell yeah, it was funny*! And yes, it was more funny sad than funny ha-ha, but still... funny.

"Julian Nash, what the hell are you talking about?"

"Twenty minutes ago, Channing was on his knees in the—"

"Ohmygod!"

"Sorry."

She swatted me hard. "Not you. Ohmygod! *Channing, ohmygod!*"

"Oh," I grunted before lifting my glasses, settling them on top of my head for a moment as I rubbed my eyes.

"Julian!"

She was upset enough for both of us.

"Ohmygod!"

"Can you stop saying that?" I chuckled, rubbing the bridge of my nose before putting the rimless glasses back on, settling them comfortably on my face. They were my favorite pair and made me look much smarter than I was in real life.

"What'd you... how'd you...?" Her mouth opened, but nothing came out. "Julian, for fuck's sake, what did you do?"

I shrugged. "It seemed rude to interrupt."

"Julian!"

The woman was pregnant and scary hormonal, and as a result, she was much more emotional than I was. I was pragmatic, because it made sense. Channing Isner had obviously needed to have sex, and Peyton Wilson was the hottest guy, correction, hottest *gay* guy in our office after himself. Cash—Carlos Vega, my best friend and Phoebe's husband—was hotter than both of them, but the man was married and straight, so he really didn't count when Channing was looking to get laid.

"It's okay, Phoeb," I soothed her.

"No, it's not!" she snarled at me, picking up one of the empty shot glasses in front of me as I lifted my finger to order another. "How many of these have you had?"

"Only three."

"Ohmygod," she said yet again, yanking on my arm until I slid off the barstool, tugging me after her through the crowd. I was dragged across the floor to where Cash stood in a group of people. When he saw me, his brows furrowed instantly.

I put up a hand to calm him. "I'm fine."

He excused himself from those around him, grabbed hold of my bicep, and gave my arm a solid yank to get me moving. When we were out of earshot, he spun me around to face him. Normally, when I wasn't buzzed, it would have been impossible for him to manhandle me, as we were close to the same height and build, but as I was a little out of it, he had the leverage.

"What's wrong?" he demanded.

"Nothing. Everything's fine," I soothed him. "When are we eating? Your wife's starving."

"I'm not starving," Phoebe chimed in, coming up beside him, rubbing her seven-months pregnant stomach. "I'm not always starving, you know."

"Jules," Cash snapped at me. "What the hell's going on?"

"He's got no date," his wife answered for me.

Cash squinted at me. "What are you talking about? Isn't Isner coming?"

So I explained to him how I had gone to Channing's office early to pick him up and passed by the production office on the way.

"Wait, now," Cash said, staring at me, "you're telling me that your boyfriend and one of my account reps were having sex in the production room?"

"He's not my boyfriend," I corrected him.

"They were dating," Phoebe insisted, glaring at her husband, daring him to contradict her, "but he wasn't Julian's boyfriend. No boyfriend of Julian's would ever cheat on him."

I tipped my head to Phoebe. "Hopefully."

She scolded my lack of faith. "Julian Nash!"

"Are you kidding?" Cash half yelled.

What would be the purpose of that? "No, I'm not kidding. Why would I be kidding?"

"Did you kick his ass?"

I shot him a look.

"You want me to do it?"

"Who are you gonna beat up? Channing or Peyton?"

"Both of them," he said, and I heard the irritation in his voice. "Goddamn it, Jules, this is why I told you to never shit where you eat. Now how in the hell are you supposed to be able to work with either of those fucks?"

"Easily," I assured him. "I promise there won't be any weirdness from me."

"Shit."

"It's fine. I promise you."

"God, you're so calm," Phoebe growled. "I say we go bitch slap Channing 'til he cries."

We both looked at her.

"What?"

I grabbed her and hugged her tight. "It's okay, love. Just lemme get another drink, and I'll meet you guys back there in the big room."

"Aww, Jules," she sighed deeply. "What a way to celebrate your big night."

And that was the part that stunk. It was the culmination of five years of work, and I had wanted to share that with someone special.

We had both just been promoted, my partner and I, Cash to marketing director, and me to creative director of our division. It was a huge step up the corporate ladder, especially since at twenty-eight and twenty-nine respectively; we were the youngest division heads in the company. In celebration of the promotion, our CEO had made a special trip out to congratulate us. Kelly Davis, who had made the decision to reward us based on the revenue our office generated and the quality of our ideas, had told Cash on a phone conference the week before that he was really looking forward to talking in person. Video conferences and phone conversations aside, he wanted to shake our hands and meet us face to face. It was very flattering, as the man seemed to be taking a special interest in both of our careers. He was also looking forward to meeting the people we shared our lives with. It was probably lucky that Channing had decided to show me what my true value was to him so early on. I would have hated to have my heart involved along with my pride. As it was, I would survive this blow to my ego. The timing was the only horror.

"He doesn't know what he's missing," Phoebe said, interrupting my thoughts.

"Oh yeah?" I sighed, meeting her loving gaze. She was crazy about me, and it was there in her soft expression.

She took a quick breath. "Yeah. You have the best heart, you never take yourself too seriously, and you always, always keep your word."

"Aww, sweetie," I teased her.

Cash squeezed his wife playfully. "Quit, honey, you'll make the boy blush."

I grinned at her.

"Mmmm, gotta love that smile," she sighed. "You've got that down pat."

"Stop flirting with my partner," Cash scolded her, and then he looked at me. "Go get a drink and meet us at the table. I'll save you a seat."

As I turned back toward the bar, I had to wonder about my judgment.

I had thought that Channing Isner and I were getting along great. After six weeks of talking and laughing, listening to jazz in the park, and driving to Napa, things seemed like they were going well. We'd had a few dinners during the week and long phone conversations where he shared the pitfalls of his day working as a junior media buyer at our firm. How had we gone from a progressing romance to him having sex in the production office with someone else? What had I missed?

"Jules."

I looked over my shoulder at Cash.

"Hurry up!"

The man lived to order me around. I was still chuckling when I reached the bar. I was waiting for my drink when I felt a hand on my shoulder. Turning, I was stunned to find my date—my ex-date, the guy I had thought was going to be my date, the guy who had just been sweating and panting with somebody else—standing in front of me. It was surreal.

"Julian, where were you? You were supposed to pick me up at my office, and we were gonna take a cab over here together."

I just stared at him. Seriously, the balls on the man… Christ.

"I looked everywhere for you."

But I had not been down Peyton Wilson's pants, so what was he doing looking for me there? The thought, because I have an overactive sense of the ridiculous, made me stifle a laugh.

"Julian?"

He was standing there, lying to my face, and it was hard to wrap my brain around it.

"Are you all right?"

I leaned around him to grab yet another shot of Patron and the bottle of Corona the bartender had just put down for me.

"Jules?" he said, his voice rising.

I threw back the shot before taking a long swallow of beer. If he had not barred my path when I moved, I would have walked away. As it was, he cornered me.

"Julian? What's going on?" he asked fast, worried suddenly, his hand flat on my chest.

"Move your hand," I ordered, turning to face him, my voice hollow and cold.

"Why? Why can't I touch you all of a sudden?" He sounded scared.

I took a deep breath. "I saw you in the office with Peyton."

The bright blue eyes that I had found so lovely got huge and round. "What?"

I took another long swallow of my beer.

"Julian?"

Looking at him, I realized that he was trembling. "Just go home, Chan, or go meet Peyton, or do whatever the hell you want… I don't care."

"Are you kidding?" he asked breathlessly.

*Why did everyone keep asking me that?*

"Who told you I was in the office with Peyton? Was it Cash?"

I squinted at him. "No one told me, Chan. I saw you myself."

"Jules, I need to explain."

"No, don't, just… go. We don't hafta have a whole big blowout. We weren't together long enough. You can just walk away, so g'head."

"I don't wanna walk away."

"Fine, then I will," I said, slipping by him.

Before I could take more than a step, he was back in front of me, his angelic face suddenly a mess, like I had hurt him.

"It's all your fault, you know. What kind of man doesn't have sex?"

Of course it was my fault; why wouldn't it be? The blame just came faster than I thought it would.

"Julian? Tell me, explain it to me."

"I did," I assured him.

"Do it again. Why didn't you have sex with me?" His voice was sharp, attacking.

Heavy sigh. "Because I wanted to have more of a connection than just a physical one," I told him. "And for the record, I thought you enjoyed the time we spent together."

"I did," he gasped out. "But being around you and not having sex is… because the way you kiss should be followed by fucking. You're the biggest goddamn cocktease I've ever met."

"Okay," I said flatly, putting the half-empty beer on the bar before brushing by him to go join my friends for dinner.

"Julian!" he almost screamed. I would have kept walking, but I was afraid his volume would only increase. I had been humiliated once already. I was not ready for a second go-round. Pivoting, I was surprised that he was right there in front of me.

"I'm sorry, all right? Just forgive me already."

Already? The whole mess was not even an hour old. And furthermore, I had no idea what was with the tortured look on his face. I wasn't the one who had ended close to a two-month-long relationship on my knees in the production office.

"You're not actually going to say no to me, are you?"

The reasoning was there in his voice. He was young and hot and was I crazy to even be thinking about calling it quits with him? Who the hell did I think I was?

"Julian?"

"I'll see you at work," I said, stepping around him, making clear the new parameters of our relationship.

He stepped into my path, hands on my sweater, fisted there, holding on. "God, Jules, just… don't do this."

"Don't do what?"

We both turned to look at the man standing beside us. It took me only a second to process who I was looking at.

"Ryan Dean." Channing breathed the name out quicker than I could. "Holy shit."

Everyone always reacted that way, and I understood why.

Ryan Dean was a household name in the bay area. His show, *Ryan's Rundown*, was on Channel 5 and came on every night right after the local news. He had been approached to take it national, to have it make the next big splash on Bravo, but as far as I knew, he had not signed a contract to make that jump to cable. At least, he had made no announcement on his show. And I would have known because I never missed watching him if I was home. It was pure pleasure just looking at him. The man was drop-dead, stop-traffic, catch-your-breath gorgeous. I, with everyone else, understood how he had made a pile of money modeling.

He used to be huge. Magazine editorials, runways all over the world, high-profile advertising campaigns—he was the guy the big fashion houses called, the one who made booking agents lose their minds. He had worked for all the big names: Valentino, Hugo Boss, Dior, Hermès, Calvin Klein, Gucci, Prada, Versace, and so many more. Even though his name was elusive, his face, body, rippling abs, and golden skin were ingrained forever in your mind.

"Hey," I said, my voice low, husky. "How're you?"

I was given an appraising look. "I'm good, Mr. Nash," he said softly, his voice low, seductive, the grin hinting at evil before he turned to look at Channing. "You're standing in my spot."

Channing moved fast, stepping away from me so that Ryan could take his place.

"Thanks," he said before he took hold of the hem of my sweater. "You can go."

When Ryan Dean dismissed you, you went, and Channing Isner was no exception. The man was far too beautiful to disobey.

"That was mean." I chuckled, looking at him, unable to see anything or anyone else. Dressed as he was, the man could have walked off the cover of a magazine. In his black boot-cut jeans and a short-sleeved lime green shirt that pulled tight across his chiseled chest and biceps, he looked like he was ready to be the center of attention at a photo shoot.

"Like I care." He shrugged. "And if you cared, you would have said something. It's one of the many reasons I enjoy working with you. You're never afraid to tell me anything, even if it's to go to hell."

"I've never told you to go to hell."

"No." The look on his face made me feel like prey. "But you could."

We had worked together many times over the past two years as my company, Miller Freedman, did all of his publicity work. And just like everyone who had ever met the man, I had been mesmerized.

Whatever word you wanted to use wasn't enough. He was more. Ryan Dean was a little over six feet, with blond hair that was always artfully messy. It was thick, streaked bronze and wheat, and fell down the nape of his neck to his shoulders. He had hazel eyes that changed color constantly, and his skin, which he showed off quite a bit of at any opportunity, was smooth golden perfection. He had a lean, sculpted, muscular physique and moved fluidly, like a dancer, with a walk that was more strut than anything else. The man was, without a doubt, a walking, talking wet dream come to life. The blond stubble of his beard, tawny mane of hair, long golden lashes, and thick dark brows—you just *thought* sex when you saw him. I understood how he had made an incredible living as a model, but even more alluring than that, to me, was the man's attitude.

During the times we had worked together on the publicity for his reality show, Ryan had made every day fun. One of my favorite times with him had been a charity event for the homeless. It had been a huge party, very exclusive and wildly successful, raised a ton of money, and he had shown his happiness with how everything turned out by inviting everyone who worked on the event to attend it as well. I had watched him hold court, seen all the gorgeous men who trailed after him, and felt thoroughly intimidated. I had left early; there was no way to compete with other models for his attention.

*Ryan's Rundown* had been on the air for three years and was about all the things you could do in San Francisco with your partner to keep the zing in your relationship, from attending cooking classes together to having a picnic at the beach to getting dressed up and hitting the town for a night of dancing. It was fun to watch, and he never took himself too seriously. His audience was as addicted to his personality as they were to his face. People, especially men, threw themselves in his path wherever he went. His conquests were legendary, his sexual appetite consuming. I never stood a chance of capturing his interest, but it was always flattering that whenever he saw me, he remembered my name.

"How are you?" he asked, stepping closer to me, his head tilting back just a bit to look into my face. As I was six three to his six feet, he had to look up at me just a little.

"I've been better," I sighed, taking in the sensuous lips, how full and dark they were.

"Why? What's wrong?"

I realized I was staring and stopped, looking away, but then had to look back or be rude. His eyes were so beautiful, the different colors in them, flecked with gold and copper, the brown, gray, and an ever-changing green that sometimes caught the light and almost glowed. Funny that Ryan Dean never failed to bring out the poet in me.

"Nothing. How've you been? I saw you on a lot of stuff, lots of guest appearances, and you did one of your shows from New York during Fashion Week, very cool."

"Yeah, that's great," he said dismissively, his gaze not moving from mine. "But I was doing too much and the show took me away from home. I don't want that."

"Why not? Don't you want your show to get picked up by a network?"

"No."

"No?"

He gave me a wicked arch of eyebrow. "You sound surprised."

"'Cause I am. Why don't you want a syndicated television show?"

"Just don't."

"Why?" I pressed him.

"It's not my dream."

"But you could be a household name."

"No thanks."

"That doesn't make any sense."

"Not to you," he said. "I need my show to be just big enough to keep me and my crew employed, help the station, still be current, and actually provide a public service. Any more than that is excessive."

He could conquer the world if he wanted. Wasn't that what he wanted?

"There are things I hope to get a chance to have."

"Oh." I didn't want to pry. "Okay, so—"

"But none of that matters tonight," he said, and I watched him bite his bottom lip. I wondered if he even realized he'd done it. "Why didn't you call me?"

It took me a second. "I'm sorry?"

"You were supposed to call me."

"When? We finished all the work for your—"

"No," he cut me off, placing a hand over my heart. "I told *you* to call me."

I tried to think back to the last time I had seen him. We had wrapped the spring campaign for his show, and then there was the press release and the launch... what was I missing? "Wait. Why would you have needed to talk to me?"

"You really have no idea, do you?"

"No." I racked my inebriated brain. "The only reason for me to call would have been if something went wrong, and as far as I know, that event went off flaw—"

"Something getting messed up was not the only reason to call," he assured me, and I saw him swallow hard, saw the muscles in his jaw clench.

"Yeah, but—"

"You didn't even show up to my spring cotillion fundraiser, the one you planned."

I raked my fingers through my hair. "Yeah, well, it turned out that my friend Melina had her baby that night, and I was her coach."

He nodded. "Well, then, I guess I'll forgive you."

"Thanks," I said, my mouth dry, my voice failing me. I could feel the heat radiating off the man as he stepped even closer, his thigh brushing mine, his breath ghosting over my face.

"You're a hard man to get ahold of. Every time I call your office, your assistant tells me you're busy. You never answer your cell, and apparently, my e-mails are going to the wrong guy."

Note to self: kill Conner. My assistant had turned away Ryan Dean? Was he high? "I had no idea you were trying to get ahold of me."

"Well, now that we've got everything cleared up, how 'bout I drive you back to my place and make you some dinner?"

I squinted at him from behind my glasses. "I'm actually here for dinner."

"Oh? With who? Not the guy I just got rid of?"

"He was supposed to be my date."

"Supposed to be?"

"Yeah," I sighed, "I found him at work giving another guy a blowjob."

Unlike both of my friends, who had been livid, his snort of laughter was instant.

"It's not funny," I scolded him.

His low chuckle filled me with warmth. "No?"

"Hell no," I said with no conviction whatsoever.

One gold eyebrow arched as he studied me.

I shrugged. "Anyway, it's my fault, I guess. I must not be all that interesting."

"It's not you, Mr. Nash," he told me.

"What're you doing here?" I ignored the compliment, looking around for the people who normally trailed after him. The man was never alone.

"I came by myself."

"You sure? You can tell me if you're on a date. I promise not to leak it to the tabloids," I teased him.

"I don't date."

"Why not?"

"Everybody bores me."

I chuckled softly. "I see."

"Except you, Julian Nash. You don't bore me one bit."

He was trying to give me a heart attack. "How'dya know? We've never been on a date."

"And I'd like to remedy that, so… come home with me."

"How is that a date?"

"I dunno. I don't care. Just come home with me."

I sighed deeply. "God, I wish I could."

"Why can't you? Just blow off your dinner."

But I couldn't, and when I explained who the dinner was with, his face lit up so fast that I could barely breathe. He was a vision of heat and sex, and the way he looked at me with his narrowed cat eyes was enough to turn me into a human torch. The man was trying to kill me by lavishing me with all his attention.

"I have an idea."

"Let's hear it."

"I'll be your date for dinner. Then afterwards you have to come home with me."

"Are you serious?" I squinted at him.

"Very."

"Well, as nice as that offer is, you don't have—"

"I'm not placating you; my motives are completely selfish, I assure you. I've waited more than long enough."

I didn't believe him for a second. He was taking pity on me because I must have looked like hell. "You know I appreciate what—"

"Oh." His voice rose. "Was that guy going as your friend or your—"

My laughter cut him off. "Everybody at work knows I'm gay, if that's what you're thinking. I don't keep secrets."

"Well, okay, then, you have no reason to turn me down."

And he was right, I didn't. "Okay, Dean, you're on. What am I, stupid?"

"Should I answer?" His eyes glittered, wicked with humor. "'Cause you didn't call me."

I grunted, taking his hand and leading him through the crowd toward the back. When he stopped suddenly, I looked over my shoulder at him. "What? Changed your mind already?"

He shook his head. "No, I just…." He lifted our joined hands. "This is nice. Nobody ever just holds my hand."

"Why?"

"I usually just fuck," he said matter-of-factly.

I nodded, smiling. "Well, can I hold your hand first?"

"Smart-ass," he muttered. I tightened my hold on him and tugged him after me.

As SOON as we walked into the private back room, all eyes were on Ryan and me, and I felt a flush of pride that not only was there a smart, funny, and gorgeous man with me but more importantly, one who was apparently kind of into me. No matter what happened, Ryan Dean was there with me and my best friend and my best friend's wife on one of the most important nights of my life. I would remember it always.

The best part of the evening for me was that our big dinner was taking place at a high-end steakhouse, but with all of us in casual clothes. Suits and ties would not have been us. Me in jeans and a sweater, Cash in corduroys and wingtips, his wife in downplayed elegance—that was us.

Given the level of casualness Cash and I had requested, I was surprised by how many people had turned out to join us for dinner. I felt slightly uncomfortable being the center of attention and so made a beeline for my boss, Miles Teruya, the managing director of the San Francisco office. After he shook my hand and squeezed my shoulder, he told Ryan how good it was to see him again. Miles remembered my date just as well as any of the rest of us. Before I could say another word, my boss turned to speak to Mr. Davis, drawing his attention.

The owner and CEO of the company I worked for rose from his chair and offered me his hand, just like it happened every day. "Such a pleasure," the man addressed me kindly.

I felt the sincerity rolling off him. "Mr. Davis, this is Ryan Dean."

He held out his hand instantly, no hesitation, not a second of lag time. "Pleasure, Ryan."

"And you, sir."

"Julian, I'd like you to meet Brian Santos, our new head of strategic marketing in New York." I extended my hand to the man. "And this is Ryan Dean. Ryan, Brian Santos."

"Hey." Ryan shook his hand as well.

"Please sit. Let's get you two something to drink," Mr. Davis said quickly.

I looked over at Cash, saw him waggle his eyebrows at me. The delight on Phoebe's face was transparent, and I watched Ryan respond to the siren call that was my best friend's wife. She was too adorable to resist. He went around the table fast. Cash watched his wife rise to offer her hand to my date.

"It's so nice that you could join us," she gushed. "I never miss your show."

"Thank you." He reached out to touch her cheek. "God, now I get the whole glowing pregnant woman thing, huh?"

She sighed deeply, staring at him. "I knew you'd be a dream in person."

His eyes glittered, and I saw her melt right there. "And may I say that Cash is a very lucky man to have a goddess on his arm," Ryan told her.

I glanced at Cash, and he looked at me. Both of us were waiting for her to laugh or tell him he was full of shit or smack him or something. Certainly she wouldn't let him get away with such a cheesy line.

"Oh," she purred as she reached for him. "Aren't you wonderful?"

I looked at Cash, and he mouthed the word "hormones" at me.

Their hands were a tangle as they started talking almost frantically. She wanted to know everything about him, down to the smallest detail. He wanted the same from her. You would have thought they were twins separated at birth.

We ate, drank, and talked. Ryan had sparkling cider with Phoebe, which I found charming. Cash was surprised that Ryan was an avid soccer player; Ryan couldn't believe Cash had been to Graceland nine times. We laughed and laughed, and Ryan bet Phoebe five dollars she wouldn't drink the little shot glass of dressing that came with her salad. She had to drink it with a straw. He ordered her more after she did, and he paid up.

Mr. Davis watched us all with the most amused expression on his face. When someone tried to bring up work, he ignored them until they quit pressing the issue. He just wanted to visit; business could be done anytime. Laughing was for the moment.

Halfway through dinner, I leaned in close and told Ryan how much I appreciated him being there. I noticed the tremor that ran through him as I lifted my lips from the hairsbreadth they were from his ear.

"No thanks needed," he whispered back, his eyes absorbing my face as his hand moved under the table, fingers lacing with mine. "I'm having a great time. Your friends are amazing."

"How so?"

"They actually want the best for you. Cash and you work at the same place, but he's not jealous of you at all."

"He's my best friend and my partner; he's the one watching my back."

"And he actually will," he said, like it was weird. "You can count on him."

"Do you have people in your life you trust?"

"For some things," he answered vaguely, "not all."

"I'm sorry, baby."

He caught his breath. "That's okay," he got out, "and you just called me baby."

I'd gotten familiar way too fast. It always happened when I liked someone. "Crap. I'm sor—"

"Don't be," he cut me off, tightening his fingers that were entwined with mine so I couldn't pull my hand away. "You wanna talk like I belong to you… it's fine with me."

*Which was a dangerous statement to make.*

"Julian?" He was studying my face. "Are you okay?"

"I dunno."

He bumped me with his shoulder and gave his attention back to Phoebe. I realized that I wanted his eyes back on me. The fact that he had not let go of my hand, forcing me to eat with my left, filled my stomach with butterflies. When was the last time I had felt like this?

"Oh, look," Christine Abrams, one of the account managers from New York, gasped across from me. "That's Kevin Winters. He just closed that deal with the military to build the circuitry for something or other."

"That's right," Brian said slowly to anyone who was listening. "Did you see in *Forbes* they're calling him the sixty-million dollar man?" It seemed to be a rhetorical question because he didn't wait for an answer. "His business would be nice."

"Yes, it would," Christine said flatly.

"We already have it," Miles assured her and Brian. "Cash and Julian did all the PR for his first merger with Ramsey Software."

"Really?" Brian commented. "Well, that's excellent. Cash, please invite the man over."

"Not me," he said, leaning over his wife and slapping my leg hard. "He doesn't know me. Stand up, Julie, so he can see ya."

I suggested that maybe Mr. Winters was busy and shouldn't be interrupted, but Brian was insistent. I stood up and walked around the table at the same time Mr. Winters glanced around the room. His face brightened when he saw me, and he immediately started across the floor.

"Oh shit," Brian breathed, clearly surprised at his own reaction as well as the fact that the man actually knew me. The way he looked up at me was funny.

Kevin Winters was in a Hugo Boss suit that looked great on him, the cut showing off his wide shoulders and narrow waist. I noticed what always struck me about him, the way the man seemed so comfortable in his own skin.

"Hey," he called over.

I tipped my head at him as he walked up to me, hand held out.

"How the hell are you?" I asked as he grabbed my hand and put his other on my shoulder.

"I'm doing really well, haven't you read the news?"

"I see your wardrobe is improving." I teased him.

His face showed his ease in my company. "Yeah, whatever— don't hate the player, hate the game."

Tall and muscular, he wasn't what most people had in their mind as a stereotypical software developer. He had told me that because he was African-American, he still sometimes he ran into prejudice. I hadn't believed him, and he had given me a funny look. We'd had a long conversation about human nature. I enjoyed his company and the fact that he was very bright. It was nice when someone could follow your train of thought.

"What are you doing here?" he asked, looking over all the people at the table. "Looks like you're celebrating something."

"We are. Cash and I just got promoted, and our CEO Kelly Davis is here. Lemme introduce you to everyone."

He reached out and put a hand back on my shoulder. "You're not leaving, are you? I mean, now that you're moving up the food chain, you're not going to be relocated or something?"

"No."

"And you and Cash will still handle my events personally?"

"Of course. We're not—"

"Oh, hey, Cash!" Mr. Winters walked around the others to hold out a hand to my best friend, who stood and shook it. "Good to see you."

"And you." Cash's voice was warm, and I knew he was pleased that Kevin was genuinely happy to see him.

Mr. Winters turned back to look at me. "So tell me, what now?"

I introduced him to Mr. Davis and Brian Santos, walked him around the table to Miles, and then had him shake hands with all the sales reps, including Christine Abrams. Finally, I walked him around the table to meet Phoebe and Ryan. He was really pleased to meet both of them, praising Cash to his wife and me to my date. It was nice of him, and let me know how much he really valued me and my partner.

"You're very lucky to have Julian and Cash," he told Mr. Davis after turning his attention from Ryan. "They're really good. Nobody else had a clue what to do with my account when I was shopping for a PR firm. And even at your place it didn't look good until I met your boys here. All those people flew in from New York, and it was such a waste since the winning idea was right here the whole time."

"The Moxie campaign was phenomenal," Mr. Davis told Cash and me, "but the product demanded it," he finished, looking at Mr. Winters. "We could do no less for you."

It had been a big campaign. Not the largest in Miller Freedman history, but it was up there in the top ten.

*We had been cornered, Cash and I, on the way out of a meeting that a hundred people had attended. Mr. Winters had sat through presentation after presentation, clearly bored out of his mind, committing to nothing, and on a whim, he called out to us as we exited the huge amphitheater-style meeting room.*

*"What do you two think?"*

*I just looked at him, and Cash did his patented squint.*

*"Nothing, huh?" he teased us, chuckling, ready to dismiss us with the rest, making his way to the door. "Big surprise."*

*"Actually, we do have this one thought." I took a breath, smiling wide.*

*He stopped and took the sketch pad I handed him, the one I had been doodling in for the past two hours. Cash and I had passed it back and forth while everyone was talking earlier, droning on and on about the software that Mr. Winters's company manufactured.*

*"We"—I indicated my partner and I—"heard you say over and over that the software you were launching would presume to know what was best for all the inventory needs of your clients."*

*"And that made us think," Cash chimed in, "maybe the software was like a wise guy and would have the guts to tell you sometimes what you wouldn't want to hear. So then we were thinking, what's a nice way to say smart-ass?"*

*Kevin Winters, who was no longer trying to leave, seemed to have stopped breathing. He had basically frozen where he stood and was staring at us. I was vaguely aware that the room had gone quiet around us.*

*"So we thought, 'moxie', " I explained.*

*The CEO looked away from me, at someone else, and then returned his gaze to me.*

*"Moxie, right." Cash's resonant voice drew Mr. Winters's attention from me. "Like 'that kid's got moxie, lotta balls'. So we thought," he said, pointing to my sketchpad in the software mogul's hands, "that you make the word with a capital M at the beginning, put a fedora on it, and call the software 'Moxie'. Moxie because it*

*knows what's right, and it's gonna tell ya. Your business system's got Moxie, kid."*

"You gotta have the Edward G. Robinson accent," I added. "Very, ya know." I cleared my throat. "'Your inventory's low, see?'"

"That sucked," Cash assured me.

"Yeah, but you were thinking Bogart."

Cash grunted, nodding. "I was, yeah, but you're right. It's more Edward G. Robinson."

Kevin Winters was staring openmouthed at Cash.

"It's simple and memorable," I said as he turned his head slowly to look at me, "and you can have all kinds of fun with the commercials." I waggled my eyebrows at him. "But it's just a thought, since you asked and all."

He nodded slowly, looked back and forth between me and Cash before he offered me his hand. "This is going to work, gentlemen."

It had been the beginning of a very satisfying business partnership, one that had benefited Miller Freedman both financially and professionally.

"I appreciate your business, Mr. Winters," Mr. Davis said, offering the software mogul his hand.

"I appreciate Julian and Cash, Mr. Davis," Mr. Winters said to the CEO of our company before taking his hand. After a minute, he turned back to look at me. "So now what? Everything's the same with you guys except new titles or whatever?"

"Yep, all the same," I told him, appreciating the fact that he wanted to make sure Cash and I weren't going anywhere.

"Good, because I need you. I need to throw a party for my shareholders, and I want you and your partner to make it happen."

"Of course," Cash assured him. "I can call—"

"I'll call you next week. I'll take you and Jules to Donatello's. I'm dying to see if the new lasagna is as good as everyone says."

"Sounds great," Cash agreed, offering the man his hand.

He gave Cash the guy clench and then walked me a few feet away from the table.

"So I'll call you," he said, "is the number the same?"

"Yeah," I answered.

Mr. Winters pulled his phone out of the breast pocket of his jacket. "And your cell number? That's still the same too?"

"Yep."

His eyes flicked to mine. "Then I've got that already."

"Good."

"Okay, I gotta go." He glanced around before looking back at me. "Unless you wanna come?"

"Oh no, I'm good here."

"You're sure?"

I nodded. "Yeah, thanks, though."

"Okay, I'll see ya. Later, Cash," he called back to my partner.

"Later."

I got the hard shoulder pat, and then he was gone. Taking my seat beside Ryan, he leaned into me. I had no idea what I had done to deserve the familiar action, but I wasn't about to question him.

"I don't remember him being so hot," Phoebe was saying. "He doesn't look like that in the magazines... I would have remembered."

Everyone laughed.

"What a compliment that was," Ryan whispered, his hand sliding up my back to my shoulder. "That man really trusts you and your creativity."

The attention, combined with the sultry tone of his voice, the way his fingers sank into my hair, the pressure of him massaging the back of my head... all of it made me dizzy. I could get used to having the man around very fast if I wasn't careful.

Half an hour later, Mr. Davis stood up from the table.

"All right, everyone, we need to call it a night before I have to call cabs for all of you. Monday morning we'll all meet at nine sharp to go over the budget and the profit and loss statement from last year. I want to meet your team, the shining stars and the people we're looking to develop. I want a deep bench, especially here, because with the numbers you're both putting up, I feel that, eventually, we will need to call you to New York." Cash tried unsuccessfully to interrupt him. "Your results put you in a very exclusive club, Mr. Vega. You and Mr. Nash are the future of this firm, and I plan to make it impossible for you to say no to me." Neither one of us said a word. "We'll go over everything on Monday."

We both gave him the agreement he was looking for, the *yes sir* of acknowledgement. Outside the restaurant, we all said our good-nights. Ryan and I walked Cash and Phoebe around back to the parking lot. Once they left, we were alone.

"So," he said. "You ready to come home with me?"

I cleared my throat. "Ryan—"

"Thank you for introducing me to Kevin Winters. You didn't have to."

I squinted at him.

"Well, you didn't." He shrugged.

"But you being here with me was a huge deal."

"I know." He cleared his throat. "You showed me. I've never been to a work function with anybody else. It means more than you know."

"Really?"

"Yes, really." He nodded and closed the rest of the distance between us, his hand reaching for me, his fingers sliding over my jaw then down to my throat. "And now I believe you need to come home with me."

The way he said it, the exhale of breath, I felt my stomach knot.

"Please, Julian."

"Why?" I asked sincerely, wanting to know.

"Because," he said, his voice hoarse, wetting his lips, "I want to talk to you."

And I realized as I stared into those gorgeous cat eyes of his that I desperately wanted to go home with him. His hands felt good on my skin, his breath was warm on my face, and he seemed content standing close to me. It was nice, and I was very flattered. But no good could come of me wanting Ryan Dean. He wasn't serious, and I was nothing but. There was no way to win.

"What're you thinking?" he asked, staring up into my eyes before he reached for and took off my glasses. "Can you see without these?"

"Yes." I told him as he put them on top of his head. "You plan on keeping them?"

"I do like the style: very cool, the metal, the screws, very sleek and clean, but I dunno. Now tell me what you're thinking?"

"I'm thinking that you're way outta my league." I was honest. "You know you are."

"I think it's the other way around," he said, grabbing hold of the lapels of my pea coat, making sure I couldn't walk away from him.

God, he even smelled good.

"Come home with me."

"And do what?"

"Lemme make you dessert," he said gently. "Please, Jules."

How was I supposed to say no?

"Julian?"

I had not had sex with Channing Isner, and now Ryan Dean wanted *what*?

"Come home with me; I'll make you something amazing."

But what I hoped for and what he wanted had to be two completely different things. And I had a process that I went through: friend to lover, lover to boyfriend, boyfriend to partner. I didn't work any other way; I never had. "I'm not how you think I am," I told him.

"How do you know what I think?" he asked, his hands opening my coat and sliding over my abdomen. Just that much contact made my jaw clench.

"You know, I should probably just go home," I barely got out as his hands slipped up under my sweater and T-shirt to touch bare skin.

"Oh yeah, I knew your body had to be something under your clothes, Mr. Nash."

No one had touched me since my last boyfriend, Mitch Carmichael, and six months of celibacy was tough on the libido. At twenty-nine, I had just as healthy a sex drive as the next guy.

"You're shaking." I closed my eyes. His lips brushed over my throat. "Come home with me... please."

The idea of casual sex was exciting, the reality simply not me. I took a deep breath, opened my eyes, untangled myself from him, and took a step back. "I can't. I don't just fuck for fun."

"Who said anything about fucking?"

I arched an eyebrow, and his smile, which made his eyes sparkle, took my breath away. The man was truly the most beautiful thing I'd ever seen in my life. I was in no way prepared to trade snappy banter with him.

"I know that's not you," Ryan breathed. "Is it, honey?"

Could he read my mind? And what was with calling me "honey"?

"You're serious and smart, and you don't go to bed unless you mean it," he said, reaching out and slipping a finger through one of the belt loops of my pants, easing me close to him, his eyes never leaving mine. "Well, I mean it, too, so come home with me."

"Ryan, I—"

"Just come with me," he insisted, and I saw how serious he was. "And we'll see if I can convince you that I'm serious too."

He was messing with me, I thought, a second before he stepped forward and wedged his thigh against my groin. Hand on the back of my neck, he pulled me close. I slowly parted my lips, and then Ryan's mouth was on mine, his tongue darting inside, the kiss hard and urgent. His hands were on my face, making sure I didn't move. He had no idea about what kissing could be, how hot and consuming. I changed my stance, straightened, and decided to show him what he was missing. I tipped his head back, stilling him completely under my hands before I exhaled. He shivered just once before I sealed my lips down over his.

Being taller than he was, even by inches, gave me the leverage I needed. I slid my tongue over his, slowly, deliberately, tasting him, going deep, back and forth, stopping for just a heartbeat before starting again, drinking him down as he pressed himself to me. I kissed him as though he belonged to me, like all I had was time. I felt him tremble when my teeth touched his bottom lip, tugging gently, sucking it inside my mouth before I stepped back away from him.

The muscles in his jaw clenched tight, I had all of his attention. I stared at him as he looked back at me, his chest rising and falling, swallowing hard. One thing I knew: I was a world-class kisser. Sometimes, when I was really concentrating, moving slow, letting the heat build, being playful and dominant at the same time... sometimes, for my lovers, the kissing had been enough.

"Julian," he whispered, his hand lifting, coming to rest gently on my throat, stroking my skin as his eyes narrowed in that way they will before you go to bed. It was very sexy, and the man himself irresistible. I leaned in, and he met me more than halfway. The second kiss was even better than the first.

His lips parted instantly as he submitted to me. I put my hands on his face, my mouth slanting over his, kissing him thoroughly, deeply, making sure I didn't miss anything: the bumpy roof of his mouth, his teeth, the inside of his cheeks and his tongue. I kissed him until I heard the sweet whimper I was after, the telltale sound of surrender. I felt his hands on my waist, his thighs against mine. I slid my tongue around his, letting him feel me move back and forth, the motion hinting at more. And I wanted more, because if it felt this good just kissing him, the way his mouth fit mine, his uninhibited, sensual response, I could only imagine what he would be like in bed. I wanted to feel his bare skin under my hands, be buried inside of him.

I didn't want to stop, he tasted so good, but I made myself before I did something stupid and let myself touch him again. When I pulled back, he came with me for a second, leaning hard before he recovered and straightened up. His eyes were deep olive green, heavy-lidded, and his lips were swollen. I found myself just standing there staring at him, unable, unwilling, to step away. I really wanted to take him up on his offer. I wanted to go home with him.

"How 'bout this?" he asked softly as he dragged in air. "How 'bout we go next door to Dante's and have a drink."

I waited.

"And then," he said huskily, "when you're ready, you let me take you home."

He was being so accommodating, moving slow instead of attacking me. His reputation was that he moved fast: he slept with you and discarded you, usually in the same night. I didn't want to be another notch in his bedpost; I wanted to mean more or never be anything at all.

"Okay?" he pressed me.

"You really think I'm gonna go home with you?" I was watching him intently, studying him, and so did not miss the sudden shiver, the quick constrict of his chest, or the pursing of his lips. The man looked nervous, and I was at a loss as to why.

"Oh yeah."

And the way he said it, so matter-of-fact, the way he was holding my gaze, none of it flirty, just honest, was surprising.

He took my hand, his fingers sliding into mine. "Come on."

The way he was touching me was nice, like he cared. The way his eyes sought mine, the way he bit his lip, took a quick breath, it was all very telling. He wanted me to go with him. When he tugged gently on my hand, I followed after him.

"Shit."

"What's wrong?" I asked gently.

"Nobody makes me nervous like this," he confessed, releasing a quick breath even as he tightened his hand on mine.

INSIDE Dante's, a Latin jazz club I liked, he pointed at an empty table toward the back, and I made my way toward it while he kept going toward the bar to get drinks. I was relaxing, waiting for him, my legs stretched out in front of me, when a guy walked up beside me. I watched as the man squatted down so he was at eye level with me.

"Hi." I greeted him.

"Can I get you to come sit with me?"

"I'm actually here with someone," I told him. Handsome man, older than me, brown eyes, beard, mustache, tall, broad-shouldered, he was the kind of guy I would have loved to talk to. I hadn't been cruised in a long time. The timing was funny.

"I don't see anybody." He openly stared at me as he put his hand on my knee. It was funny; I could not even remember the last time anyone had approached me at a bar, or anywhere else, for that matter. I was not the kind of guy most men noticed. With brown-black hair, dark blue eyes, and glasses, it was easy to lose me in a crowd. My mother has always said that I had striking features, but from living in my own skin, I knew the truth. I was plain, and that was all. I was built long and lean, covered in muscle that came from being an athlete in high school and college, lots of swimming, since I was eight, that I still did daily. I ran and lifted weights, but my body was not the chiseled piece of art that Ryan Dean's was.

"He's right here," I said, tilting my head at Ryan as he closed in on me, reaching for the glass he held out once he was there. "But I appreciate the offer; it's very flattering."

"Oh," the guy said, getting up, looking down at me. "Well, maybe after you're done here, you can—"

"He won't be done," Ryan interrupted, taking a seat in the chair beside me, his legs sliding under mine.

The guy nodded, gave me a last look, and left.

"Can't leave you alone for a second, huh?" Ryan said quickly, his smile forced. I could tell the difference between the real ones that fired his eyes and the fake ones that never made it there.

"Doesn't usually happen," I assured him as he leaned forward.

"Oh, I think it does. I think you just don't notice."

But I actually was a very observant man. For instance, I noticed everything about Ryan Dean. "Yeah?"

"Maybe you're just radiating happy right now."

"And why would I be doing that?"

He looked uncertain, almost floundering. "I dunno, what would be making you happy right now?"

There was no question that being around Ryan Dean probably made me glow.

His expression changed, grew thoughtful, like he was trying to figure me out.

"What?"

"You have no idea what you look like, do you?"

I knew exactly what I looked like, and me, any time, any day, would not have made any man stop and talk. I was the guy you got to know and then noticed. It never worked any other way. Men saw me after they knew me, not before.

"Hey."

My eyes returned to his. As I had been lost in thought for a few moments, when my mind had drifted so had my focus. But Ryan wanted my attention and I would give it back to him.

"You're not drinking." He pointed at my glass. "I want you drinking."

"Sorry," I said, the response automatic, looking at his glass. "What is that?"

"Cranberry juice."

"With what in it?" I asked, picking it up and tasting it.

"With nothing in it."

And there wasn't any alcohol at all. "Why?"

He just shrugged.

I took a sip of my scotch and water. "I shouldn't drink anymore; I'm already not as clearheaded as I should be."

"Drink up."

I chuckled, and he waggled his eyebrows at me. He was very cute, and I was having trouble not just leaning forward and tasting him. The wicked look let me know he could read my mind. When some fans came over, claiming his attention, I was almost relieved.

A while later, as I was listening to the music, I realized suddenly how relaxed I was. That never happened when I was with somebody new. Usually, "anxious" was the word to describe me, because I was never really sure what to say or do. When I glanced at Ryan, I found him looking at me.

"What?"

"Nothing," he sighed, "just content."

Which was a scary word. There were a million casual words to use. "Content" was not one of them. "Content" was reserved for that peaceful feeling that comes with having everything you want. Maybe his definition was different from mine.

"Content?"

He leaned forward and patted my leg gently. "Yeah." I got half a grin.

Nope. He and I had the same personal dictionary. He was happy right where he was, just like I was. It was scary as hell.

"You know, your eyes are amazing," he said slowly. "I have never seen such dark blue eyes before."

I stared at him.

"What?"

Most people assumed that my eyes were black. That Ryan Dean had looked long enough to tell that they were, in fact, blue was amazing. I had to tilt my head a certain way or the light had to catch them for anyone to see that they were midnight blue. He had to have really been studying me. The thought filled my stomach with butterflies.

"Julian?"

"Yours are too," I said quickly, because the changing colors of brown, green, and gray were really something to see. The deep dark shade of clear olive they were at the moment was truly beautiful.

"They turn dark green when I'm happy."

"Really," I said, making sure I was breathing.

He nodded slowly.

I had to swallow down my heart.

"Julian," he exhaled.

I got up so fast I almost spilled my drink. I had forgotten for a second that he was not an option for me. "I gotta go, I—"

"Wait," he ordered, getting up.

I turned to leave, and his arm slid down over my right shoulder, his palm flat against my chest. He held me tight against him, keeping me there. I felt his nose rub over my shoulder. "Why do you wanna run away from me?"

"C'mon, Ry, I—"

"Ry is good," he said, his lips brushing across the back of my neck before he inhaled deeply, breathing me in.

Without even thinking, I'd shortened his name, like we were friends. What was with me?

His hand slid up my chest so his arm was around my neck, his breath warm on my ear. "Come home with me so I can talk to you."

But how smart was that? If I was alone with Ryan Dean, could I trust myself?

"You need to let yourself go, Julian. You worry too much about what could happen instead of just living in the moment. Sometimes it's all you have."

"Like you know me at all," I mumbled, because I liked having him wrapped around me. I would like it even better if he took off all his clothes. I leaned back a little, relaxing, and when he felt my weight shift, heard my slow exhale of breath, his left arm went around my waist, his mouth against my ear.

"You have no idea how long I've waited."

I smiled because the familiar heat was sliding up my legs to my groin. No doubt about it, I was warming to the idea of doing all kinds of carnal things to him. "Yeah?"

"Yeah." He held me tighter, his voice gravelly and deep, his lips brushing the side of my neck before he bit down gently, tenderly, just a nibble, just enough to taste my skin. "So please just stay here with me." He squeezed hard for emphasis. "Please."

I let out a breath and closed my eyes. He was solid against me, stronger than I would have guessed, and he was clutching me close.

"Why do you wanna leave me?"

I just concentrated on breathing because it was getting harder to do.

"I feel good, right?" His lips were featherlight behind my ear.

He did. Why lie? "Yeah."

His hand slid up under my T-shirt, flat on my stomach. "I asked around about you, but no one I know has ever been in bed with you. Word is you just hook up for the night."

"Oh yeah? Is that what everyone says?"

"Yep. My friend Marcus says that you turned him down at a party even though you were drunk and he was naked."

I chuckled. "Marcus Grant is a whore."

"People say the same about me."

"Yeah, but maybe they just don't know you. Maybe you sleep around 'cause you're looking for the right guy, not because you're a cock whore."

"Spoken like a true romantic."

"Is that bad?"

"No," he breathed. "I've just never met one before. Now let's go already."

I tried to turn my head so I could see him. "You don't know anything about me."

"I know enough," he murmured, and I felt it more than I heard it. The sound slithered right through me. "And I want to know way more, which is new for me. I mean I don't like anybody. Nobody makes me curious, but you... you, I have never been able to get out of my head. I think there's a reason for that, one that I almost missed."

His confession made my knees weak. Ryan Dean had been thinking about me. How amazing was that?

"I always enjoyed working with you on all my projects. You're great with people, cool under pressure, and watching you walk around in your jeans is a religious experience." He sighed, pressing a kiss into the crook of my neck. "How do you not get that you're gorgeous?"

But I wasn't; he was. I knew exactly what I looked like, but if he thought I was beautiful, why would I correct him?

"You know you wanna sleep with me. Everybody wants to sleep with me," he said as he kissed my jaw, then my ear.

I put a hand on the arm that he had around my neck. "Oh yeah?" I teased. "Everybody?"

The impatient half growl made me grunt before he pushed me forward so I was out of his arms. I turned around to face him and saw the look of naked need on his face.

"We can do whatever you want, Jules; I just want the chance to spend some time with you."

"Why?"

"'Cause I do," he said flatly.

I looked at him, and his smile shifted, became more intimate, his gaze hot, definitely carnal.

"Now what?" I asked him.

"Oh, you're asking now?"

"Yeah."

"Well, now you come with me," he said, moving forward, throwing an arm around my neck and leading me toward the door.

There were more people in the club the later it got on a Friday night. As we threaded our way through the thickened crowd, I realized I didn't want to get separated even for a second. As we were bumped and pushed from every side, I reached back for his hand and felt him grab it tightly. Somehow, I ended up having to yank him out of the bodies crushed together at the edge of the dance floor. He banged into me, but instead of letting go after he steadied himself, he wrapped both arms around me.

"Julian," he said as he kissed the side of my neck, his breath hot and wet in my ear, "come home with me, all right?"

I didn't answer as he pushed me out of the club ahead of him. When we were outside, I turned to look at him.

"What?" He laughed softly, finishing with a sigh.

I gave him a look.

"C'mon," he pressed me. "You know you're coming home with me. Why are you even pretending to think about it?"

"I had a really good time with you tonight," I said, letting out a breath, knowing full well the teasing was over. I was much too serious for casual sex. Even as attracted as I was to the man, how aroused I got just looking at him, and how much I wanted to do bad things to him, I couldn't change the fact that I was hard-wired for long-term, promised monogamy. "You should go back in and pick somebody up."

His smile was slow and lit his eyes. "I appreciate the offer, but no."

I stared at him, and he looked right back. "You're different from how I thought you were," I said.

"And you're exactly like I knew you were."

"That so can't be good." I was sarcastic because I was at a loss.

"Oh yeah, it can," he said, and his voice was soft. I looked away because all his attention was a little overwhelming. "Come on," he said, taking hold of my hand, tugging me after him.

The direction we were walking was strange because there was nothing there but a Jeep.

"Wait."

"What?"

"Are we riding in that?" I pointed.

"Yeah," he said, looking closely at me. "Why? You too good to ride in my baby?"

"Seriously? This is your Jeep?" I asked as we walked up to it.

"Yeah, why?" He was scowling now.

"Nothing." I was pleased with his ride, actually, because it was so real. Nothing pretentious about a ten-year-old Jeep covered in primer. "What's with the Bondomobile?"

He looked uncomfortable suddenly, squirmy. "It gets banged up a lot, and I was painting it all the time, so I stopped."

"Why? Are you a shitty driver?" I baited him. "Should I ride with you?"

"I'm a great driver," he said quickly, "and you should definitely ride with me."

"Then what's with the story on the Jeep?"

"It gets beat up when I'm working."

Vague answer from a man usually so forthcoming, but it was his car. How much did I really care? "I think cherry red would be hot."

"I'll consider it," he said slowly, giving me a wicked grin and a quick wink. I smiled back. He was irresistible. So easygoing, so aware of how sexy he was with his dazzling smile, gorgeous body, and clear, shining eyes. Used to getting whatever he wanted because he could.

I nodded, trying to keep myself breathing. "So," I said, standing there, looking down at the floorboard of the Jeep. I wasn't sure if getting in was the best course of action; it seemed like the frying pan into the fire.

"Are you gonna get in?"

I looked up at him. "I'm thinking."

"Why?"

"'Cause I want to."

"That makes no sense."

"If you knew me better, it would."

He nodded. "You think too much. Get in."

"You know I—"

"I'm just gonna feed ya," he told me. "Swear."

I got in.

# ||

RYAN'S apartment was close to the Marina District, in a security building with a doorman. He greeted the man by name, and they exchanged some small talk.

"What?" he asked me when he caught me smiling.

"Nothin', Mr. Dean."

He clipped me with his elbow. "Shut up."

I followed him down the hall to the end unit, and he held open the door for me. He brushed by me to flip on the lights.

I glanced around quickly as I followed after him. "Oh, it's nice in here."

He looked at me funny. "You thought… what? That I lived in some studio apartment all grunged out? You figure that the life of an ex-model is what, glamorous on the outside but like a ghetto inside?"

"Well, yeah," I assured him. "It's how the rest of us deal with all you beautiful people. We tell ourselves that you must have empty, wasted hulls of lives."

He rolled his eyes like I was stupid before he walked out of the room.

I looked around, checking the titles of his books, his DVD collection. The patio door was open and a light was on, so I wandered outside. I was surprised to find a large, thriving herb garden. I would have never guessed he had one.

"There's an awful lot of plants out here on your lanai, Mr. Dean," I called out to him.

"I mix stuff." His voice reached me from the depths of the apartment.

"Medicinally?" I raised my voice so it would bounce back.

"Sort of," he answered, walking back into the living room at the same time I did.

I studied him. "What are you? A witch, a warlock, whatever? You make potions?"

"No." He made a face. "I'm not a witch."

"You sure?" I taunted, because he actually seemed annoyed that I was accusing him of some nefarious plot with eye of newt.

"I'm not a witch." He was emphatic.

"But you do make potions?" I asked to make sure he knew I was listening.

"You know, for someone who drank quite a bit tonight, you're awfully clearheaded and inquisitive."

"That was hours ago, and that drink at the club was more water than anything else."

He grunted.

"Are the plants poisonous? Are you brewing up poison on your stove?"

He muttered something under his breath.

"What was that?"

"Nothing."

"Something about guys you just fuck?" I chuckled.

He growled at me. "I said that guys I bring home just to fuck never take the tour and ask questions."

I laughed at how disgruntled he looked.

"Shit."

"I can go," I offered lightly.

"You're not going anywhere," he said, shoving me back toward the large bay window. "Go check out my view of the city—it's nice."

I had no interest in the view. Him being evasive about the plants growing in his herb garden was infinitely more interesting. What proved an even greater discovery was that there was not one framed picture of anyone anywhere in his apartment.

"Look at all the shiny lights," he said playfully before leaving the room again.

"What's growing in the herb garden, Dean?" I called after him.

"Give it a rest already!"

I could see being evasive about something illegal, but I knew what I was looking for, and there was nothing a member of law enforcement would have a problem with growing in his house. It was funny that he was so prickly about it. Also funny was the lack of photographic evidence of family or friends. I found that really odd.

"What?" he asked as he walked back in, having shed his leather jacket.

"No pictures?"

He gave me a weird look. "No."

I nodded and walked over to the walls, looked at his artwork. "These are nice."

"Yeah… yeah, they're great," he said absently, grabbing my arm and pulling me over to the barstool. I sat down at his kitchen counter while he walked around to the fridge.

"So what kind of dessert do ya want?"

My elbow went down on his counter, then my head on my hand. "I dunno, whatever, as long as you don't sprinkle something from the herb garden over it."

"You're funny."

I smiled at the dripping sarcasm.

He made brownies from scratch. Who did that? He talked to me as he worked, smiling, telling me stories that were by turns funny and gross and eye-opening. The day-to-day life of a model was fascinating.

"You should write a book."

He grunted as he prepared the plate he was going to put the brownies on. I had no idea that anywhere but at a restaurant did people concern themselves with presentation. And he used raspberry glaze. How did he just have that in his kitchen cupboard?

"What? It's a raspberry and cream cheese swirl brownie. You have to have the glaze on the plate. It all goes together."

"Uh-huh," I agreed. "Pass it over here. I just wanna eat it."

His face scrunched up like I was a heathen as I gestured for him to hurry up and give me my dessert. "Try and savor the flavor of the… uh…." He ended with a groan.

"What?" I asked around the brownie in my mouth.

His grin came fast as he wiped my face. "You want some milk?"

I nodded because I was chewing.

When I finished with the second one, I told him I was in love.

"Don't tease," he said, his eyes flicking to mine, liquid with heat.

I would have licked my plate clean, but he made a face at that suggestion, so I washed it because I wasn't raised in a barn. He had done all the other dishes while the brownies baked, talking to me the whole time, so the last of the cleanup was minimal. As I stood at his sink, he came up behind me and pressed a kiss to the side of my neck. Something about the constant physical contact was almost as intimate as the kiss we shared earlier. It was like he had to touch me, and I liked it a lot.

We talked for a long time more in the kitchen, about so many different things, finally ending with how well his show was going and my promotion. Afterward, as he looked through his DVD collection for a movie, I noticed a cabinet that I had missed on my first walk-through. It was big, but dark wood and metal, so if you weren't looking, it blended in with the wall, tucked into a corner. I reached for the handle to open it.

"Can I look in here?" I called out to him so I couldn't be accused of snooping.

"Wait!" Ryan barked out a warning, but it was too late.

The door popped open, like the handle was spring-loaded, and I found myself looking at two beautifully etched swords, one long, one short. They looked like they belonged in every samurai movie I had ever seen.

"Shit," he said under his breath as he stopped beside me, having almost leaped across the room.

"What is this?" I asked, like Vicki Vale in Bruce Wayne's inner sanctum.

He wet his lips nervously.

"They're beautiful, Ry." I tipped my head at the swords. "What are they called?"

He pushed his fingers through his thick hair. "Informally, the long one there is a katana, the shorter one is a wakizashi."

I nodded. "Can you use them, or are they just for show?"

"No." He coughed. "I can use them."

"Really?" I was surprised. It was hard to imagine the gorgeous man with the delicate, fragile features I saw before me being able to wield the weapons I was looking at. "Do you cut people up in little pieces with them, Ry?"

"Not people," he said quickly, pushing in front of me, closing the doors together, pulling both handles down and then pushing them in. They disappeared into the wood, flush, not a chance for me to open it again without him there, which was perhaps his intent. It was almost as though the cabinet had been left open accidentally.

"Go sit down in the living room, willya, please?"

"Stop taking the tour?" I suggested playfully.

"Just… I'm trying to be romantic and seduce you, and you're killing my vibe."

"Sorry." I smiled at him, walking back to the living room and flopping down on his red leather couch. "Huh."

"What?" He seemed surprised.

"It hardly gave at all."

"You don't like it?"

I didn't, but that was rude to say. In fact, I liked nothing about his place. It was cold and sterile and did not reflect the man's warmth at all.

"Julian?"

I looked around and felt nothing. "You know, if I didn't know better, I would say that you were messing with me about this being your apartment." I finished by looking up at him. "It doesn't feel like you in here."

His eyes locked on mine. "It doesn't?"

"No."

He trembled slightly. "How so?"

"You're warm, and this place is cold."

"You mean I'm hot," he teased, bending toward me.

I reached up and caught his face in my hands, stilling him. "Yeah, you're plenty hot, but that's not what I mean," I said, tracing his cheek with my thumb. "You're like... home."

He caught his breath and jerked away from me.

"Sorry," I said softly, ready to stand and walk out of his apartment. We could tease and play, but that only worked up to a point. I had the worst timing sometimes, and my words got heavy with meaning. "I didn't mean to make you—"

"No," he cut me off, his hands on my shoulders, holding on, the movement itself, and not the power exerted, keeping me in my seat. "I love what you said."

My eyes searched his. "Ry—"

"How come you never have any fun?" he asked as he took a seat beside me.

He was deliberately changing the track of the conversation. We had been headed down a serious path, but he wanted to keep things light, breezy. He was giving me no reason to run from him. He was taking no chances. Little did he know that the more serious the conversation, the more interested I would be.

"Jules?"

"I have fun," I said slowly, taking the bait, not wanting to scare him, either. I wanted the ease from when we were in the kitchen together back.

"When?"

"All the time."

"You think so?" he asked, stretching his arms out across the back of the couch. "Because I think you're full of crap."

"Do you."

"Yeah, I do. When do you have fun? I never see you out, and believe me, I've looked, and like I said earlier, the guys that do know you—not one of them has ever slept with you."

"So having lots of sex, that's fun? I should sleep around and that would show everyone that I know how to have a good time?"

"No. I dunno. You're so hard to figure out. I mean, it took me so long to even see you." I snorted out a laugh as he groaned. "Shit, that didn't come out right at all."

But I understood what he was saying. I sort of faded into the background if you weren't watching, and if you weren't looking for me… no one ever noticed me right away. It wasn't who I was. I tended to be the quiet guy surrounded by loud, beautiful people. My best friend was a prime example. Hot, magnetic, in-your-face Cash Vega was balanced out by me and the quiet I offered.

"Julian—"

"I get it." I chuckled.

"No, you don't. On one hand, you're gorgeous, and I, along with everybody else, just want to get you in bed, but then you're so cold and reserved, it's scary to even try and talk to you."

I was a lot of things, but cold wasn't one of them. "Aww, c'mon, cold? Really?"

"You don't know what you look like, Jules, with your deep, dark, scary blue eyes and the way you carry yourself. You're so unaffected by everyone and everything. I thought you were a conceited asshole until I realized that you're just shy around new people, especially men."

"I'm not some head case, ya know. I—"

"I know. You just need to loosen up."

"By being a slut."

"That's not what I said," he corrected. "But you do need to get laid."

I couldn't argue with that.

"I can take care of that if you want."

"No," I assured him, even as I let him slide his hand up the back of my neck into my hair. Something about him soothed me instead of putting me on guard.

"Why not? Think of the fun."

Could he be any cuter?

"Can I ask a question?" he asked, shifting closer to me so we were shoulder to shoulder, his knee against mine.

"'Course," I told him, rolling my head sideways to look at his profile.

"You get tested?"

"For what?"

"You know for what," he said pointedly, serious now. "Don't be an idiot."

I chuckled. "Yeah, you?"

"Every six months." He was matter-of-fact about it.

"And?"

"Clean, of course. You?"

"Please, I've never had anything."

"Why're you smiling at me like that?" He grinned back at me.

"'Cause I bet you're the kinda guy that carries condoms in his pocket when he goes out, huh?"

"Yessir." He nodded, looking at me, fingering the hem of my sweater. "Can I ask you another quick question?"

"Yeah."

His gaze was heavy on me. "Can I see your glasses again?"

He had returned them in the Jeep and was now asking for them back. I nodded. Reaching out, he was very gentle when he took my glasses off and put them carefully down on his coffee table. When he looked back at me, I heard him catch his breath.

"Why didn't you call me?"

I let out a deep breath. "I had no idea you wanted me to, I swear to God."

He nodded and bit his bottom lip.

"You're adorable."

There was quick head shaking. "No. No... hot, sexy, gorgeous, whatever you want, but not adorable. That's no good."

"It's good," I assured him, my hand on the back of his neck, leaning in, pulling him close at the same time. "Everything about you is very good."

The second my lips touched his, he opened for me, drawing me inside, sucking my tongue into his mouth. He climbed into my lap, his folded legs clamping around my hips, his groin pushing into my abdomen. His firm, round, muscular ass was sliding back and forth over the bulge in my jeans as he moaned low in his throat. It was very sexy, his want, his need.

He breathed out my name before his mouth covered mine again, and he was all over me, pressing, straining, his hands on my belt buckle. It felt like it was going to be fast and frantic, and I didn't want that.

Reaching up, I cupped his face in my hands and slanted my mouth over his. I kissed him deep and hard, my tongue making love to his, letting him know without benefit of words that he had me. I wasn't going anywhere. I slowed him down, sucked and licked and nibbled his lips, my hands never moving from his face. There was a deep, primal groan before he pulled back, gasping for air.

"You taste good," I told him, my voice low and full of heat.

He inhaled deeply as he looked at me, his eyes wet and glazed, heavy-lidded, his lips swollen from my attention.

I reached for him, but he leaned back, his jaw clenching at the same time his hand flattened on my chest.

"What's wrong?"

He shook his head. "I know you don't just fuck, Julian. Everybody told me how you are. You've got this whole good-boy reputation going on."

"You make it sound so bad."

"No, it's not that... I just mean that if you're staying, then maybe you wanna see me and spend time with me, 'cause you don't just pick up some trick and follow him home."

"No, I don't," I said, my hands sliding up the muscular thighs on either side of me. The man was toned and cut and hard, and I wanted him naked under me. "I'm not built like that."

"But I am," he confessed sadly, his voice hitching. "It's all I am."

"No, it's not," I assured him, staring into his magnificent eyes, shifting him in my lap. "And I think that's why you wanted me to call. Maybe sleeping around isn't so fun anymore."

"Julian," he gasped, pushing down into me as he unbuttoned his short-sleeved shirt slowly, never once taking his eyes off mine as he peeled it off.

The sculpted chest, the rippling abs, all the smooth golden skin begging to be touched, it was all I could do not to attack him. Head tipped back, I watched his eyes close. "Put your hands on me. You know you want to."

And it was just stupid at that point to deny myself anything. I wanted him; he obviously felt the same. Senseless to say no. I had always been attracted to him, and finding out, over time, that he was not the materialistic, brainless but beautiful creature I had thought he was, was humbling. I made snap judgments about people, and it was a terrible flaw. The man was sarcastic, gorgeous, funny, and sexy, and he had the sweetest mouth... how could I say no? But the whole little seduction scene he had going was not going to work for me. He wasn't allowed to treat me like all the others.

"Ryan. You need to look at me," I told him gently, but with a thread of warning, my voice dropping dangerously low.

His head snapped up, and his eyes opened wide. It was the tone of my voice that demanded immediate attention. He was surprised, I could tell, staring deeply into my eyes.

"I'm not some trick you picked up and you're gonna fuck and forget." His breath caught, and I saw the muscles in his jaw cord. "Don't take your eyes off me," I ordered him, my voice firm. There would be no argument.

"No, Julian." He trembled just slightly. "I won't."

I slid my hands up his collarbone to his neck, over his jaw to his face, my fingers gently exploring, tracing his brows, his cheeks, sliding over his skin. "You have to trust me," I told him, my voice a husky growl. "Do you?"

"Oh, yes." His eyes were glazed, the pupils huge.

I smiled lazily, then pulled him forward and ran my tongue slowly over the seam of his lips before he opened for me. I kissed him deeply, slowly, my mouth sealed to his. I inhaled him, the suction strong, his bottom lip mauled before I saw how far down his throat my tongue could go. The whimpering noise he made, the surrender I was waiting to hear, went right through me. I put my hands on his skin and pushed him down hard under me on the couch. He fought me for a second, testing my strength, so I was rough with him and heard his breath catch.

He moaned when my mouth touched his skin, trembling when I bit him. "Julian... I want you so bad."

Which was good since the feeling was mutual.

"I—" Ryan began.

I stood up with him still wrapped around me and walked down the short hall to his bedroom. We fell together on his bed, him under me when we hit the mattress. Standing up, I grabbed one foot, divesting him of one motorcycle boot and then the other before turning my attention to the skintight boot-cut jeans. I had his fly open seconds later, leaning over to place wet kisses on his abdomen to distract him from the slow slide of denim off his hips. When they were gone, wadded up and thrown into a corner, I admired the long muscular legs I had uncovered. There was no part of him not drool-worthy. After I pulled off my sweater and T-shirt, I realized that he was staring up at me.

"What?"

"You're so beautiful," he breathed, his eyes all over me. "Why do you hide that body under all those clothes?"

"Clothes are a necessity," I told him, leaning down to peel off his thong. It was very sexy, but his skin was better. The first view of his long, beautiful cock made my mouth go dry. "But, Christ, they shouldn't be for you." He whimpered in the back of his throat, and it was the sexiest sound, rolling through me, making me catch my breath. When I took his cock in hand, his groan was deep and hoarse. "Look at you needing me."

"Julian," he panted, trembling under me, the rippled abs contorting, his engorged shaft jerking in my hand, the beads of pre-come already leaking from the flared head.

I smiled down at him. "I bet you taste like dessert."

He pointed to his right, to his nightstand. "I just got tes-tested two weeks ago. I have the results right there for you to—oh God!"

I stopped his rambling when I bent forward and swept my tongue around his shaft.

Only my name alone escaped his lips.

"Oh, he likes that."

"Julian—I… Julian."

My smile, if he'd opened his eyes to see it, was evil. Leaning over, I sucked the length of him down my throat. He nearly came off the bed.

"Julian," he gasped, his hands in my hair, fisting, holding tight. "What are you... I... I'm clean, I swear. I have the paper right fuckin' there if you... I have... ohmygod!"

It was my tongue; I knew it felt like heaven sliding over hot, sensitized skin. That, combined with the sucking and laving, the way my gag reflex was nonexistent, how much I loved to give head—I had Ryan Dean. He was at my mercy. He was mine.

"Julian... Julian." He chanted my name, the fingers in my hair tightening and loosening, his body convulsing, his back bowing as he arched up off the bed. "You gotta stop... I'm gonna come, and I don't wanna... Julian!"

I swirled my tongue over the flared, swollen head, then down each side, gently but also using my teeth, making him yell my name, clutch my head, the fingers buried in my hair, splayed on my scalp. I traced the thick vein, licked hard, loving his smell, the feel of his skin, the sounds he made. He was panting as I made everything wet with saliva, stroking him, finally pumping his cock with the hand fisted around the long, hard, velvet length of him.

"Julian... baby... I...."

But I wasn't going to stop, I wanted to know what he tasted like, suck every drop out of him, leave him drained and spent and completely at my mercy. His body that was to die for would be mine to do with as I pleased. As he thrust upward into the back of my throat, writhing under me, bucking up off the bed, I sucked hard.

He screamed my name as he came, his orgasm rocking him as he filled me, his cock swollen as the fluid rushed from him into me. I swallowed him down, holding him inside until he went soft, waiting as he rode out the aftershocks of his bliss, licking him clean, leaving nothing.

When he was still, his spent, flaccid cock finally slipped from my lips, and I rose over him.

"God," he whimpered. "You're fucking amazing."

I arched an eyebrow for him.

"Kiss me, fuck me... please... Julian... please."

I bent, and his arms wrapped around me as he lifted for my kiss.

Our tongues tangled, and he tasted himself on me, just the thought sending a wave of heat through me. He shoved me back, pointed at the nightstand, and when I opened the drawer, I saw the bottle of lube. There was also the biggest box of condoms I had ever seen in my life.

"Do not go near those condoms," he warned me. "All I want to feel is you inside me, and when you come, I want it in me... deep in me." His eyes were liquid as they locked on mine.

"Have you ever done it without a condom?"

"No. I-I never have."

I was overwhelmed, only me, ever, and my resolve faltered. "You don't have to."

"I want to—I never wanted to before, but now... I want you buried in me now," he said, arching up off the bed. "I'll beg if you want."

"You never have to beg me for anything."

"But I will if you need that to bareback."

He was the sexiest man I had ever met, and I had never hoped to hear him say the things that had just tumbled from his lips. I wanted more than anything to be inside of him with nothing between us, but the reality of it had never even crossed my mind. For me it was one of the great perks of monogamy and one of the many reasons the idea of a committed relationship was so appealing. You didn't have to have safe sex. You could have unsafe sex whenever you wanted, however you wanted. The fact that he wanted me to be even closer to him than I would normally be touched me deeply.

"Julian."

"It means a lot. That you trust me....that you know that I'm a good guy." I choked up because I was frankly overwhelmed.

"Then grab the lube, Julian, and come here."

When I moved back to him, kneeling above him on the bed, he spread his legs, bending them at the knee, and lifted up so I was presented with his pink, fluttering hole.

"Fuck me," he whispered as his eyes drifted closed.

I squinted down at him.

After a second, he opened his eyes and looked up at me. "Julian?"

"Baby, what gives you the idea that any part of us being in bed is ever gonna be just about me?"

He was stunned; it was all over his face. "But that amazing, spine-tingling, ohmygod-I've-never-had-a-better blowjob was all about me."

I snorted out a laugh. "I enjoyed the hell outta that, watching you burn up, watching your eyes roll back in your head, listening to the sounds you make when you're about to blow your load. Uh, yeah, I got off on that big-time."

"But—"

I crawled off the bed fast, and before he could protest, I yanked off my wingtips and socks, my jeans and briefs, until I was naked before him. His eyes locked on my shaft.

"Jesus, Julian, you're huge."

But there was no worry in his voice as there had been with others, only awe and genuine appreciation.

"Could you... can I suck that, please?"

"Nope," I told him, climbing back on the bed, grabbing the lube and coating my hands. The second I wrapped my fingers around his semi-erect cock, he hissed in his breath.

"What are you doing?"

"Feel good, baby?"

"Jules...." His moan sounded strangled, and he slowly started to lower his legs.

I stopped him. "No, hold them there. I can't reach you otherwise."

"Reach what?" But he understood the second I slipped a finger inside him. "Julian!"

I slid my finger out, then in, swirling around the entrance before sliding in deep, passing the inner ring of muscle, but not far enough to hit his prostate, interested in getting him ready for me, stretching him, loosening him.

"Jules... please...."

When I added a second slick finger, he yelled my name, his voice hoarse and raspy. The stroking of his shaft, from base to tip, was driving him crazy. Combined with the fingers, three now, plunging in and out, he was trembling with his need for me.

"Julian," he panted. "I get it. You're a goddamn saint. You're not selfish in any way. You want me hot and throbbing and begging, so I'm begging, please… if you don't fuck me, really… I'm gonna die." I withdrew the fingers from his ass to a hiss of sucked-in breath but continued stroking the rock-hard shaft. "Jules," he whimpered.

Leaning back, I lubed my cock until it gleamed in the faint light and then pressed myself gently to his entrance. "You tell me if—"

But I didn't have time to finish before he surged up to meet me, impaling himself, his body opening up and taking me in, swallowing the length of me. The unbelievable heat, his muscles clenching around me, holding me, how tight he was… I was certain my heart stopped.

"Move," he begged me, "please, move."

I slid slightly out and then rammed back into him, hard and deep, sheathing myself to the hilt. "You're so hot inside, Ry. You feel so good."

He cried out, his hands digging into the bed, the sheet bunching as he clawed at it, and his legs wrapped around my hips as I thrust into him.

Normally I went slowly. I checked. I was gentle. I was "that guy." But with Ryan—and it made no sense—it was like I wanted to claim him, mark him, and make sure that he would never want or need anyone else. The way he rose to meet me as I pounded down into him, the two of us pressed together so that there was no ending and no beginning, was a revelation.

"Julian." His voice was a throaty rasp. "Please… don't stop."

I was sheathed in his hot, wet channel, held impossibly tight and buried to the balls in his ass. Stopping was not even possible. I plunged in and out of him, stroking deep, the writhing and the fingers digging into my skin letting me know, without words, that I had found the perfect spot, the perfect angle, to bring him bliss.

When his orgasm finally roared through him, triggering mine, my name became a prayer as he coated my abdomen. Semen caught between us as I fell on top of him, pinning him under me to the bed as I came deep inside his body.

I tried to roll off, but he held me tight, his face buried in my throat as he trembled.

"Ry?"

"I don't want to let you go." He shuddered hard.

I wrapped my arms around him and rolled over so that he was draped over me, the cum and sweat sticking us together. "Then don't," I said with a deep chuckle. "Keep me."

He lifted his face from the hollow of my throat and looked down at me. "You can't... I... just don't say things like that if you don't mean it."

"I always mean what I say," I said honestly, reaching up to touch his face, frame it with my hands, and move the mane of hair back so I could see the shining eyes. "Now go and get me some water."

He gave me an impish grin as he lifted off my spent cock before rolling off the bed. I had a moment of perfect peace, lying still in his bed, staring at the ceiling. My epiphany came at that moment. I wanted to be the only man sleeping with Ryan Dean for the rest of his life.

"What are you thinking?"

I had not realized he was back, standing beside the bed, a glass of water in each hand. He had obviously guzzled some down before returning, as there were drops sliding down his chest.

"That I need my damn water," I teased, holding out my hand for the glass.

He didn't move. I just looked my fill of him.

"What you said before, did you mean it?"

"What's that?"

"That if I want, I can keep you?"

My heart was suddenly in my throat. "Yessir."

"Okay, then," he said, leaning toward me. "Now you get water."

I drained the large bar glass, and he offered me the rest of his. When I was done, he took it from me before crawling back on the bed. He moved slowly, fluidly, moving until he was hovering over me, his eyes glinting in the light. I had the definite impression that I was food and realized that I would willingly be consumed by Ryan Dean.

I took a breath, infusing my voice with calm. "So you're thinkin' maybe you want me?"

"Want, need, having, keeping." His expression changed suddenly, darkening, no more playing. "God, I hope I can. I hope I can keep you."

"You can, you'll see," I told him. "Now ride me, I wanna fill you up again."

The whimper of need from the back of his throat was very sexy. He rose above me fast, studying my face as he straddled my hips, his eyes narrowing in half as he lowered himself over my shaft inch by inch, so I could feel it all, until I was buried in him. He looked so beautiful above me, and he felt like heaven. Between the lube from earlier and my semen still coating him inside, I slid in easily.

"You feel so good," I confessed, reaching for his cock, my hand stroking him lazily.

He shivered hard, rising and lowering. "So do you... Julian, I—so do you."

Already we had found our rhythm. Just in a short time, I knew where to push, and he knew to move slowly and let everything build. My thrust upward, my fingers tightening on his hard, throbbing cock at the same time was too much for him and sensory overload for me. As I found my release, he followed me seconds later, my abdomen once more coated with him. When he demanded I never, ever leave him, I didn't second-guess his words.

# III

HIS hands were everywhere, and I smiled into the pillow. I shifted, and there was pressure exerted between my shoulder blades, gently stroking to keep me from getting up.

"Don't move."

"Yes, Ry," I sighed, loving the whispering.

He cleared his throat. "How do you feel?"

"Pretty damn good." I could not contain my grin. "How 'bout you?"

"I'm fine," he said distractedly, "but could you—is it okay if I turn on the light?"

"Why?"

"Please."

"If you must," I teased him, closing my eyes, wondering vaguely why it was so important but not enough to really care.

I heard the click of the light, felt his hands run over my skin, pressing, touching, almost like he was checking me for injuries.

"What're you doing?" I chuckled, rolling over onto my back, opening my eyes a crack, squinting up at him.

His eyes were huge as he stared down at me. "Julian, your skin is... your hair... you're... can you look at me?"

"I am looking at you."

"No, could you...?" He trailed off, his breath catching, shivering suddenly. "Julian, look at me. Open your eyes wide and look at me."

I did as I was asked, breaking into a smile seconds later when he caught his breath. "I am so not this interesting, by the way."

"Oh." His eyes filled as he stared into mine.

Shit. "Honey, what's wrong?" I reached for him, worried suddenly.

"Julian," he barely got out, "you're fine. You look the same."

"Not glowing in postcoital euphoria, ya mean?"

"No, you just—" The way his voice hitched, how he had to bite down on his trembling lower lip, was almost funny. "You're fine. You're perfectly fine."

He had not taken the bait of the sarcasm; instead, he was completely engrossed in my appearance. "What's going on, Ry?"

His smile a moment later was breathtaking. "I wanted it to be you so... I hoped." He swallowed hard.

I was confused, but the question died on my lips when he leaned over and snapped off the light, plunging the room back into darkness. His head pressed to my chest.

"What're you do—"

"I'm listening to your heart."

"Why?" I asked, inhaling the scent of his hair.

"Be still."

He was acting weird, off-the-chart weird, but his warm skin felt so good next to mine that the reason for the contact hardly mattered. He had to touch me, *had to*, and the knowledge ran through me and warmed all the hard to reach places.

"I knew it. I should have just listened to... but I don't trust myself anymore," he said more to himself than to me.

"Knew what?"

He let out a deep breath, almost a sigh, slipping his leg over mine and pressing into my side. "Julian, I'm keeping you," he said matter-of-factly.

I snorted out a laugh. "I thought you already were."

"God," he said, leaning into me, "you're so amazing. Anybody else, I would be freaking them out." He lifted up, moving over me so he could straddle my thighs and stare down at me in the semidarkness. "I knew it was you, Julian. I just knew it."

The moonlight streaming through the window illuminated him above me. I saw the way he was looking at me, possessively, watching his own hands as they slid over my chest. I had never been this riveting to anyone before.

I wanted to pull him down, because I was getting excited. Just the way he was touching me, slowly, so intimately, like he owned me, was heating me up all over again.

"You're mine, you know," he growled. The daring in his tone, the way he had marked me with bites, it maybe should have scared me, but none of it did.

"Am I?"

"Oh, yes," he assured me, pressing his ass against my cock, which was already straining for him.

"And does that go both ways?"

The startled expression, how big his pretty eyes got, it was adorable.

"Ry?"

"I just... I thought I would have to—"

"What?" I cut him off, shifting under him, leaning up to ease him close. "You thought you'd have to convince me?" I smiled as I rolled him over onto his back. "Why would you need to do that? You're a gift, Dean, a fuckin' gift."

"Julian." His voice hitched, and the moan that escaped when my stiff cock slid over his own velvety hardness was very sexy. "Just lemme hold you."

"I don't think I can do that yet," I said, bending to him, burying my tongue in his mouth, tasting him again. He stretched his arms wide, then let them fall down onto the bed. I smiled and sucked on his bottom lip. "You're giving up?"

"For once, yeah, 'cause I finally can. Just do whatever the hell you want to me."

I stared down into his beautiful eyes. I promised him I'd be gentle as I shifted on the bed, back to his nightstand, where he kept his condoms and lube.

"Are you worried?"

I smiled over my shoulder at him. "About what?"

"That you fucked me without a condom."

"No, you told me you're clean."

"And you believe me."

"Why would you lie to me?"

"I wouldn't... ever. And I didn't." He took a quivering breath.

"I know." I smiled back at him. "So no, I'm not worried. Are you worried about me?"

He closed his eyes, his grin wide. "No. You don't sleep around, Julian."

"How do you know?"

"I know," he breathed out. "Come here."

When I slid my slick fingers inside him, he moaned low, the sound torn from him, and wrapped his legs around my hips. I was gentle with him, opening him up, and then couldn't stop and buried myself in him, hard and deep. He was so tight and so hot, and I felt him tremble under me. When I fisted his cock in my hand, he arched up off the bed.

"Julian," he cried out, and he gasped when I drew myself out only to pound back down into him a moment later. "Oh, baby, please."

So sexy, the deep smoky voice, his head thrown back, his back arched, completely consumed with what I was doing to him, his legs tightening to keep me close. I leaned forward to kiss him, and his hands went to my face, holding me there, swallowing my tongue.


HOURS went by the way they do when you're not paying attention to anything but your lover in your arms. I rolled over, and he came with me, wrapped tight, tangled together. The bed was a sweaty, sticky disaster, only the fitted sheet still in place.

"I didn't hurt you, did I?" I asked him gently.

"No." His voice was soft, his breath warm against my throat, his mouth on my skin.

"You like it rough." I grinned, my eyes drifting closed.

"I like you."

"Made for me," I said, leaning my cheek against his forehead.

"What?" he asked sleepily, and I knew he was testing to see if I'd say it again. Not a game, just fishing. Making sure I was for real.

"You heard me," I said, my voice husky, letting out a deep contented sigh. "We fit, and you know it. Like you were made for me."

He kissed up my throat to my mouth. "Julian," he whispered before his lips covered mine for a moment. "We are so much more than you could even know."

"Oh yeah?"

"You have no idea," he murmured as he shifted against me, over me. I put a hand on the back of his neck and pulled him down so I could kiss him again. "Let me explain it to you."

Whatever he wanted.

# IV

I WAS thinking about Cash on my way home because I wanted to tell him about Ryan. The stunning new development in my love life would not seem real until I bounced it off my best friend and heard what he served back. Sometime over the course of five years, Cash Vega had become the person whose opinion most mattered.

*There had been no fanfare. At our regular Monday morning meeting, Miles Teruya, the managing director at Miller Freedman San Francisco, had announced that Vega would now be working with Nash, and Reynolds and Tyge would form the other new team. It had been fine with me as Eric Tyge and I had not hit it off, and looking at Cash Vega all day was going to be a treat for me. I would have been his partner any day of the week.*

*With his thick, jet-black hair and dark, chocolate-brown eyes, Carlos Vega, nicknamed Cash by his father, was the kind of guy who other guys just hated on sight. He had a profile that belonged on coins, with his aquiline nose, full lips, and square-cut chin. His eyebrows were thick and looked like they'd been painted on, perfectly arched, quick to raise or furrow with his mood. The deep bronze tan stayed year-round, and when he wanted to show off, he could wear everything tight to flaunt his broad chest, flat stomach, and bulging biceps. He looked like some gorgeous Aztec god come to life. But what inspired the most jealousy from other men was not his beauty, but his voice and how he used it. He spoke English with the warmth of Spanish haunting it, and the tone was so smooth that sometimes people would keep him talking just because they enjoyed listening. Women—and men—could not be trusted to keep their hands to themselves when he was looking into their eyes and speaking at the same time.*

*That first day, Cash had come into the new office that we would be sharing and asked me what I was doing.*

*"I do this sometimes to get the blood rushing to my head,"* I had explained from my position. *"I think it helps with getting the creative juices flowing."*

*"I see,"* Cash said as he crouched down beside me. *"You want me to stand on my head too?"*

This was one of the many things I did that had driven Eric Tyge apeshit crazy.

*"Only if you want to."*

*"Okay,"* he agreed, and I smiled wide. I got excited thinking that maybe my new partnership was going to work out. *"But I don't sing karaoke or do Outward Bound bullshit or do trust exercises. This is as much of this bonding crap as we're gonna do."*

*"I agree,"* I assured him.

He did a headstand next to me, his wingtips on the wall beside mine.

*"Right on."* I smiled at him, and he grinned back crazily. *"What?"*

*"You said right on,"* he clarified.

*"Eric probably told you I wasn't well."*

*"He wished me good luck,"* he said honestly. *"He thinks you're manic."*

*"Huh."*

*"How come no one likes you around here, Nash?"*

*"I dunno. I think they just don't get me?"*

A quiet grunt greeted my statement.

I had known I was getting a difficult reputation, but I hadn't been sure how to go about fixing it. I just wanted ideas that were unique and fresh. New spins on old themes seemed like cheating, and in my opinion, it was just lazy. I wanted to think outside the box, and everyone else was happy to be where they were inside. The flip side of the argument was that while I was striving for perfection, I was also the only one not bringing in any money. None of my ideas turned into actual campaigns because I needed a partner, someone to bounce thoughts off of, to take them from the development phase to the presentation phase. Someone needed to help me translate what was in my head.

*"Well, it's doing something," Cash told me after another minute. "I think I know why this is actually a form of torture in some cultures."*

*But he didn't get down. He remained standing on his head as long as I did and then took me to lunch. That Friday night I met him and his wife Phoebe for drinks. Sunday they invited me to barbecue with them and a few other friends. At the following Monday morning meeting, I put a steaming cappuccino down in front of him, and he drank it like it was expected. We traded notes back and forth until Mira Towne, the senior partner, told us to knock it off. A week later, the firm got a shot at the Dunbar account because Crandall Media missed a deadline for Stella Verity's new fragrance, Velvet Steam.*

*Cash and I had stayed up all night, but there was no way to make Velvet Steam not sound stupid. At nine in the morning when everyone came back, we were still there playing hoops in our office with the Nerf ball and the trash can.*

*"Are you two going to the meeting?"*

*We turned with the ball, Cash draped over the top of me as he was defending his goal. Stella Verity stood in our doorway looking just as stunning as she had when she had appeared on* Legacy *for all those years. I remembered my mother watching the nighttime soap every Thursday.*

*"Hi." I smiled at her.*

*"Hey." Cash smiled, too, his voice low.*

*"Well," she purred, sliding into our office, pouring herself into Cash's chair. "Aren't you two the prettiest of the bunch?" We straightened up, and her smile deepened. "Disheveled, sleepy, and unshaven. Did you know that's my favorite?" We both just stood there, grinning at her like idiots. She looked at me hard. "I've got a soft spot for hot boys with glasses and that mouth... lovely." I could only stare. My brain had actually switched on. "And you," she purred, looking at Cash. "Are you that gorgeous color all over?" She meant the deep bronze tan of his skin.*

*He nodded lazily. "Yes, ma'am."*

*She smiled and then looked back at me. "What are you thinking, darling?"*

*"How about just 'Steam'?"*

*"'Steam'?"*

*"For the name of the fragrance."*

*"Yes, love, I got that part." She smiled demurely. "Go on."*

*"It could mean so many things. There's the sex angle, of course, but there's also anger or heat or—"*

*"Power," Cash offered, following where I was going. "We could have more than one ad, and it would appeal to different people in different ways. The print material would be amazing."*

*It had been the first time we were in creative sync. We talked out our ideas in one voice, finishing each other's sentences, building one idea on another, the shared vision exactly the same. It was like I could read his mind. I understood the value of a great partner at that moment and knew I had found mine.*

*Stella was staring at us as Miles poked his head in our office, with Todd Joplin right behind him.*

*"What's going on in here?" he asked pointedly as Stella swiveled around in my chair to look at him.*

*"I like what these two have," she informed them and put up her hand as they began to argue. "I'm not saying I won't hear the other pitches. I'm just saying they'll need to be exceptional to change my mind."*

*She was as good as her word. We had heard later that she sat still and listened to every other pitch before getting up and announcing that the two cute guys in the glass office by the water cooler would get her backing. The firm had the account as long as Cash and I were on the creative team. It had been the first account the two of us had ever worked together and landed at Miller Freedman.*

It had been seamless from that time forward, five years of another person totally getting me. Cash could always follow my fractured train of thought, no matter how far off the rails it went, and do improvised brainstorming with me at all hours of the night. He knew how my brain worked and wanted to keep track of me not only professionally, but personally as well. So it was not surprising that when I got home at eight in the morning I found him waiting on the stoop of my brownstone drinking a cup of coffee. There was a similar-sized cup for me.

"Hey." I yawned, flopping down beside him.

One eyebrow rose quizzically. I knew already: he needed to know what was going on with me and Ryan Dean. He had to know how that would affect me and therefore him.

"Screw you, Vega," I grumbled, getting up, taking my coffee with me, and walking toward my front door.

"I'm just asking." He chuckled behind me. "I mean, c'mon, it's not every day you find out your best friend is sleeping with a hot model."

I looked at him over my shoulder.

"That's what my wife says."

I grunted.

"So," Cash said as he followed me into my apartment, "what's your deal with him? You guys gonna date now? Do gay men date or just fuck on the first date and move in together and live happily ever after?"

"That one." I smirked at him.

"I figured," he said. "Oh, nice watch."

I looked down at Ryan's blue Rolex on my wrist. "Yeah."

"Yeah," Cash gave me a look. "Really nice."

I shrugged.

"So whose watch is it?" he asked, smiling evilly.

"It's Ryan's."

"Is it?"

"Jesus, when did you turn into such a girl?"

"I'm just asking."

"Why?"

"Maybe we could have dinner tonight," he suggested casually. "Me, you, Phoeb, and Ryan."

"I dunno if that—"

"Why not? You got other plans already?"

I had no idea what I was going to be doing, but whatever it was, it would involve Ryan Dean.

I had tried to leave silently that morning, but when I was dressed and walking by the bed, Ryan had reached out and stopped me with a hand in mine. I had let him pull me down beside him on the bed, my fingers raking through his hair, pushing it back from his face so I could see his eyes.

"Go back to sleep," I soothed him. "I'll see ya later." I wasn't looking forward to catching a cab at seven in the morning, but it had been more than worth it.

"I'll drive you," he said, not really awake, his voice full of gravel.

It would be evil to make him do that when he could stay there and sleep. "No, at least one of us should be warm in bed."

"Why are you even up?"

"I gotta meet Cash and go into the office for a little while."

He reached over to his nightstand, picked up his watch, and passed it to me. "Here, take this with you, okay?"

"Why?"

"Just take it, okay? Just wear it."

"Ry, I have my own watch. I just forgot to—"

"I want it to go with you."

"Listen, I'm gonna see you later whether I've got something of yours or not."

"Okay," he said, but he didn't sound convinced.

"Ryan, I—"

"I just want you to wear something of mine, all right? What's the big deal?"

"No big deal," I assured him, snapping the Rolex onto my wrist. "Kiss me."

He sat up, and I leaned in and kissed him. I meant to just give him a quick peck, but he tasted too good and went all willing and panting on me, and before I realized what I was doing, I had him flat on his back with my tongue shoved halfway down his throat. When I pulled back, I saw how clouded his eyes were, how heavy-lidded, how full of me.

"Kiss me again."

I smiled slowly. "I gotta go."

He grabbed a fistful of the front of my T-shirt. "Stay."

"I hafta go. If I don't see Cash today, Monday's gonna be hell."

He made a noise in the back of his throat. I kissed him again, slower, with more of my tongue.

"God," he groaned when I pulled back. It was obvious he was excited.

"So I'll see ya later."

"Okay." He nodded. "You'll call me, tell me where to meet you?"

"Yes."

"What time?"

"Six," I said without hesitation.

His smile was lazy. "Okay. Call me and give me directions."

"But I need to get your—"

"I programmed my number into your phone last night."

"Oh yeah?"

"Yeah."

"When?"

"While you were sleeping."

"When was I sleeping?" I asked because it couldn't have been for long.

He reached out and grabbed my T-shirt again, holding tight. "For the little time I could let you."

"Why weren't you asleep?"

"I was watching you," he said, grinning sheepishly. "You look good next to me."

"Yeah?"

"Yeah." He swallowed hard, taking a quick breath, his eyes searching mine, checking for hesitation. "So for sure, I'll see you later, right?"

I heard the worry in his voice; he was unsure of me, as if I would walk out of his apartment and never call. Like "that guy" could ever be me. I leaned down close to him, my mouth hovering over his. "You'll see me later," I promised him.

His eyes closed for a second, and I watched his jaw clench tight. "Julian, please just stay here and—"

"You want me back inside you?"

His body jerked in reaction to the question I had asked as I licked up the side of his throat.

"Please...."

I didn't make him beg me.

"*Hey!*"

I looked over at Cash, blinking away the memories.

"What's with you this morning?"

I shrugged. "I don't know."

He crossed the room to stand in front of me. "I think the gym first and then work."

"Fine, I think that'll help clear my head anyway."

"Why isn't it clear?"

"I dunno. I think I need to sleep."

"You didn't sleep last night?"

*No, I had sex all night with a man who couldn't seem to get enough of me.* "Lemme grab my stuff, and we'll go."

He reminded me not to forget my laptop.


AFTER working out and showering, Cash and I were having lunch at an outdoor café we both liked. He was answering e-mail on his phone while I was working on layouts on my laptop when my knee was nudged under the table.

I looked up at Cash, and his eyes flicked behind me.

Turning in my seat, I was stunned to see my ex, Mitch Carmichael. I had not seen him in more than six months, and suddenly, there he was.

"Julian," he said quietly, stepping closer to the table.

I rose, smiling at him, shoving my hands down into the pockets of my jeans. I never knew what to do with my hands when I couldn't touch people, and I could not touch Mitch Carmichael... at least not in public. It was the reason we had broken up. Since we were more than friends, I had wanted people to know that, and because of his family, it was out of the question.

"I was going to call you," he said defensively, his eyes moving from me to my best friend. "But I never could quite get up the nerve. Hey, Cash, how are you?"

"I'm great." Cash forced a smile. "Did you know Julian's dating Ryan Dean now?"

I shot Cash a look.

"What?"

I rolled my eyes and walked around Mitch, moving inside fast, making my way to the bar. Once he joined me, I turned to face him.

"Sorry about Cash."

"He hates me," Mitch said, his eyes roaming all over me, up and down, not missing anything. "But he has a right to. The way I left... I had no choice, Julian."

"Sure."

He stepped in close to me, leaning on the bar. "Like I said, I was going to call you, but I just... and I remembered us coming here a lot and how much you liked it, so I figured sooner or later if I was here that you'd show up." It was a long, rambling, nervous explanation. "I should have called."

"It's fine," I assured him. "Everything's fine."

He lifted his hand like he was going to touch me. It hovered close to my cheek, but then he glanced around and dropped it.

"So you've been back for a while, then?" I asked politely, not caring at all.

"Yeah... no, I... Ryan Dean?"

I found that I couldn't suppress the smile. "Yeah."

He nodded. "So is it serious?"

I scowled at him. "What do you want, Mitch?"

The muscles in his jaw corded as he stepped closer to me. "I miss you."

There had been a time when his words would have meant something to me, but it felt like years had passed instead of a pile of weeks. Five months of him being gone before I started dating Channing Isner, six since I'd laid eyes on the man.

"Julian?"

"I'm sorry."

"What are you sorry about?"

"That you still care."

His eyes locked on mine. "You're saying you don't?"

"I'm saying that if you wanna hang out… we can try, but any more than that, I don't want to do. You didn't want us to be more than friends, and now I don't, either," I finished, turning to go.

"Wait," he said, reaching out to put a hand on my bicep. "I never said I didn't want to be with you. What I said was that I needed time for my family to accept me being gay."

But time was not the issue. There was no way for him to ever live as a gay man with a partner instead of a wife. His family could not accept him that way, and they were not only the people who loved him but also the people he worked with. He was in business with his father in one of the largest commercial construction companies in northern California. He had pledged his heart to me at the same time as making sure we were never seen together in public even once. I had wondered where my self-respect had gone. I was just too healthy to be anyone's dirty little secret. I wanted to be on the Christmas card with somebody. I deserved to be.

"Would you come by my place?" he asked under his breath.

"No." I gave him a slight smile, raising my head, looking into those pale blue eyes of his. They were so big and expressive. It was the first thing I had ever noticed about him. He was staring at me, his jaw set, his body rigid.

"C'mon, Jules, don't make me beg."

"I won't," I said flatly. "I'm not coming over."

"Can I come over to your place?"

"No."

"But I want to talk to you in private," he said, his hand tightening on my arm, holding on. "I could stay the night."

I rolled my shoulder and stepped back at the same time so he had no choice but to let go. "I gotta go; me and Cash have got a shitload of work to do before Monday. We both got promoted, so we're excited but buried, ya know?"

"Oh, sure, I just thought—"

"So as soon as I come up for air, I'll give you a call." I wanted him to hear me, hear the buddy vibe I was giving him, the overture of friendship.

"Julian," he said softly, "I just want to spend some time with you—I need to—"

"Hey," Cash said as he stepped in beside me. "I hate to cut the begging short, but we've got a shitload of work to do today so we can get off in time for our double date."

"You know, Cash," Mitch began, "you don't have to be a prick all the time."

He shrugged. "To you I do. What kind of a friend would I be if I wasn't?"

"The thing with me and Julian is more compli—"

"It isn't complicated," I cut him off. "I get it. You can't be gay, and you have your reasons, and I would never judge you for that. I would never ask you to come out for me, Mitch, but you can't ask me to be in for you. You understand?"

"Asshole," Cash said under his breath.

I looked at him. "Go back to the table."

"No, let's go." He scowled, gesturing at Mitch. "This is done. You don't need to make everything better all the fuckin' time. Sometimes shit just ends, and it's bad, and that's how it is, Jules."

"Charming."

"You love me," Cash teased, waggling his eyebrows. And I did, even though he was kind of an ass.

"Julian," Mitch said, "can we just talk?"

I looked back at him. "Let's wait awhile, maybe down the road, but not now. I'll call you, all right?"

"He'll call," Cash closed for me. "Bye, Mitch."

And as Cash and I walked back to our table to collect our things, I had the overwhelming feeling that I would never see Mitch Carmichael again. And it was sad but also inevitable. Mitch needed someone to be in the closet with him, and I had never even seen the inside of one.

I CALLED Ryan around two and told him to meet me at my office that night. He didn't pick up, but I got his voice mail and left a message. I got a text back fifteen minutes later saying that he would be there. When Cash and I were walking out at six, we found Ryan in the lobby of our office sitting on one of the couches, head back, eyes closed, looking like he belonged on a photo shoot instead of waiting to have dinner. He had on dark brown plaid pants with shiny brown boots, a dress belt, and a brown and black cashmere turtleneck. A tight black leather-racing jacket completed the outfit. I took a deep breath when I saw him, that possessive feeling hitting me hard. Like: *that's mine. He belongs to me.*

"Hey," I said, deliberately using a low voice, rousting him.

His head came up, and I realized he'd been asleep. It took a second for him to focus. "Oh, hey." He smiled, and his eyes glowed as he stood up. He raked his fingers through his hair before he walked over to me. He stopped just short of touching. There were other people walking around—not just Cash and I worked weekends—and I watched his eyes take them all in.

I leaned forward, put a hand on the back of his neck, and pulled him close to give him a quick kiss on the mouth. When I stepped back I saw how huge his smile was.

"So, we're gonna go eat," I said simply.

"Okay." Cash smiled wide, offering Ryan his hand.

"Cash," Ryan said, clearing his throat, taking my partner's hand but having trouble looking away from me. "It's good to see you again."

"And you."

"You ready to go eat?" I asked Ryan. He nodded like he was in a daze. "Thanks for being here like you said ya would."

"You don't have to thank me for that," he said seriously, looking me straight in the eye. "That's a given."

"So, hey," Cash said, grabbing hold of Ryan and me, one of his arms draped over each of our shoulders, "you like Mexican, Ry?"

He turned to look at Cash. "I do."

"Great," he said, leaning on me, "'cause Jules and I have a favorite place."

"Well, then, take me." That he wanted to be included, that he liked Cash, meant a lot. "I can't wait to see Phoebe again." And I saw Cash's smile, the real one, because Ryan was crazy about the person Cash loved more than anything in the world.

"I think this is gonna work out just fine," Cash said, giving me his blessing as he dropped his arm off me when we reached the elevator.

He didn't let go of Ryan, and that was nice. When Cash liked you, he touched you. It was the way he was raised. I liked him liking Ryan.

I got stuck sitting in the back of Ryan's Jeep, and when we stopped at Cash's condo, we had to wait outside for him to collect his wife. Over the phone, Phoebe had forbidden Cash from bringing Ryan in. Once the place was immaculate, he could visit.

"You know we didn't have to do this tonight," I told Ryan from the backseat.

He turned around to look at me. "Are you kidding? Your partner, his wife... are you high?"

I smiled at him. "I'm not following you at all."

"Oh, man, c'mon, that's gravy. Women love me. I mean love-love-love-love-love me! So once Phoebe is crazy about me and after that little display a second ago—I'm golden."

I grinned at him.

"Don't look at me like I rode the short bus to school. I've got this wired."

"I still don't—"

"You just kissed me where you work in front of your friend. No one has ever done that before. I could never be around long enough to... and you—you didn't even think about it; you just did it, like it was the most natural thing."

I shrugged. "I guess I'm not getting the significance."

"No, you're not, but that's okay."

"Ry—"

"Last night when I was with you and your friends and your boss, and then just now... why was I even worried?"

"Why were you worried?"

His eyes were locked on mine. "You don't get it right now, but you will."

"What does that even mean?"

"Nothing." He shook his head, his bottom lip trembling. His eyes, I noticed, were sparkling in the light. "So you wanna maybe gimme a kiss? I missed you today."

I patted my thighs. "Come sit in my lap."

"Don't tease." His eyes narrowed in half.

When I leaned forward, he met me eagerly, his lips parting under mine, my tongue sweeping inside his mouth, tasting him. Phoebe's greeting made me ease back, and I smiled against his mouth when he leaned with me, whimpering, wanting to prolong the contact.

"Julian," he breathed, his eyes unfocused like he was drunk.

"I missed you too," I told him.

It was nice that just my words made him catch his breath. I could get used to Ryan Dean wanting me.


THE stroll after dinner was nice. As I walked beside Cash toward the ice cream parlor at midnight, we looked ahead at Ryan and Phoebe, arm in arm, whispering, leaning against each other as they walked. The way Phoebe looked up at him, the way he tilted his head down to listen to her, it was nice. They had instant chemistry, and they both liked chocolate ice cream with strawberries. It was a very good night.

Ryan drove me home and got out, grabbing my laptop bag from the back seat, slinging it over his shoulder. I noticed that he had a small duffel as well.

"What's that?"

"My clothes for the morning."

"You just assume you're coming up?"

"Oh yeah," he said quickly, his smile wicked. "I'm sleeping in your bed tonight."

My apartment was a cluttered mess compared to his, but in a lived-in way, not in a scary, reality TV kind of way. And with a few hours' work, it always looked good. He liked that the floors were wood, that I had only a radiator for heat, that I had a hurricane lamp in the living room, and that there were framed pictures everywhere you looked. The black burlap couch in the living room, vintage bullfighting posters on the walls, the exposed red brick wall by the front door, the mermaid mural I had painted in the bathroom, the Chinese lantern in my kitchen, the hammock on my fire escape, my black teak wood furniture... he told me he liked all my things. He sat in the rocking chair that used to belong to my grandmother, an Adirondack chair that never ceased to look out of place, and took a look at my computer.

After a moment he rendered his verdict. "It's a Mac. Who owns a Mac?"

"Us creative types," I teased.

He looked at all the framed photographs on the shelves with all my books, checked my fridge's inside for food and outside for more photos. I had several pictures of my brother Frank, my folks, Cash and Phoebe, and all my friends' kids, and postcards from my ex-boyfriend Evan, who was backpacking through Europe. There were clippings and my horoscope and a recipe for pot roast that I hadn't gotten around to trying, and everything was held on just barely with poetry magnets. If you slammed the door too hard, things always fell off.

"You know you're supposed to create haikus and sonnets with these words. You're not supposed to just use them to keep stuff up."

"How's a haiku go again?" I asked.

He laughed and continued his walk-through. "You have more stuff framed than anybody I know. What is this?"

I walked up behind him, looking over his shoulder. "Oh, it's a doodle my friend Melina did on a Post-it note."

"And it's framed?"

I defended it. "It's a good doodle."

"What's it of?"

"You can see it's a church."

"I can?"

"Sure."

He pointed to something else. "And that?"

"It's the first leaf I found when I came to the city."

"A leaf?" He chuckled.

"Yeah. I asked for a sign that I was supposed to stay here, and a green leaf fell on my head." He just looked at me. "A green leaf," I repeated, so he'd get the significance. "Why would a new green leaf fall from a tree?"

He smiled at me. "I don't know, but I'm sure you do."

"To show me that my life was supposed to grow here."

"It's not green anymore."

"So not the point."

He nodded. "Yeah, you're nuts."

"Maybe." I shrugged, yawning, walking back to the kitchen. "You want something to drink?"

He shook his head, looking at everything else on my wall. "I love all this crap."

"Crap?" I asked before drinking orange juice from the carton.

"Gross, man, get a glass," he said, walking out of the room.

I smiled after him. When I didn't see him for a minute, I went looking and found him standing in my bedroom.

"What?"

"Nice."

"Antique brass bed."

"I know," he said, and then he turned to look at me. "Ask a question?"

"Sure."

He pointed at the bed. "Why?"

"I like stuff you wouldn't expect."

"Okay."

I shrugged. "I know my place is kinda weird. I—"

"I love your place," he said, cutting me off, taking a quick breath like he was nervous "It's got a nice feel in here. It feels like home."

Good that he was comfortable, since my plan was for him to spend a lot of time with me. I told him that, and then I reached for him.

"Yeah? You wanna spend time with me?"

"I do." I smiled at him, and he shivered once as I hugged him to me, my hands sliding up and down his back. "Is that what you want, Ry?"

The noise he made in the back of his throat, part whimper, part sigh, clutching at me so tight, answered over and over that it was all he wanted. And the fact that he was honest, holding nothing back, made me want him even more.

I had thought that maybe the first time was a fluke. That so much ease and chemistry wasn't really possible with a brand-new lover. Usually there was the fumbling and awkward moments of the learning process, getting to know what the other person liked or didn't. But with him, there was ease right away, and lots of laughter and enthusiastic encouragement. I felt free to just be myself, let him see that I was a big dope, and tell him that everything about him was heaven. And I didn't just hear him when he said I felt good in his arms, I actually listened. Because when he looked at me, I knew he meant it.

He had to be close to me. My skin next to his, he said, was a necessary thing. His words were halting, his eyes searched mine, and his breath caught when I kissed him. There was no mistaking that he wanted me, his hands on me constantly giving him away. It was terrifying to think of us being in the same exact place, wanting the same things. I was more excited than I'd ever been. I couldn't wait to see what was going to happen next.

# V

WHEN I rolled over onto my back on Sunday morning, I was surprised that I wasn't mauled. I wanted to be mauled, so I opened my eyes to figure out why I wasn't. The piece of paper cut into the shape of a heart taped to the lamp on the nightstand stood out right away. He had gone to get coffee and bagels and lox and eggs and apples. All this was on the note in his big, fluid handwriting, along with a promise of all kinds of carnal pleasures as soon as he returned. I hoped he was already on his way home. I was getting used to having him around. I was looking forward to a long, leisurely morning when I thought I heard something shatter.

"Ry?" I called out.

No answer.

I raised my voice, making it carry. "Ry?"

The bang shook my wall, and I gasped. It sounded like something heavy had hit it. A second later, frames rattled loose from their hooks when something slammed against it from the other side. Family photos hit the wooden floor and cracked, sending pieces of metal, frame, and glass in every possible direction.

Moving fast, I reached under my bed, grabbed the baseball bat there, then rolled to my feet, and charged out into my living room. The second I recovered from my shock, I yelled, "What the hell is going on?"

Two men held Ryan against the kitchen wall, and two more clustered around them, but that wasn't the scary, weird, or upsetting thing. The freaky part was their eyes when they turned to look at me.

They all had eyes that looked like they were filled with blood. And not simply pupils that were red like an anime character, but the entire eye filled with wet, welling gore. It was gross and disturbing and twisted my stomach into knots. Had I not seen it for myself, I would have never believed it was possible for people to be alive and look like that. I had no frame of reference for what I was looking at.

My intrusion allowed Ryan to twist free, leap up onto my counter, and then dive over the hands that reached for him. I just stood there, frozen, watching as he rolled to his feet in front of me, grabbed the bat from my hand, and turned on the men charging toward him.

He shoved me back and swung. I had never seen anything like the blur of speed that he was. The leap up into the air and the spinning kick that threw the first man across the room, crashing into the kitchen table, backed me up several feet. The way Ryan moved, fast, inhumanly fast, like a coiled snake, a blur of motion lost to the eye, was terrifying. And when the men fell, they didn't stop at the floor—but disappeared, as though sucked into the floor that, for just a second, turned into almost an open airlock. I heard the howling wind, saw how fast and hard they were pulled, the suction fierce, their cries and screams drowned out.

The second the room was clear, Ryan was in front of me. He wasn't even breathing hard.

"Jules."

I took a step away from him, taking in everything I had just seen, gauging my senses, making sure I was awake, sane, whole.

"Julian." His voice cracked as he took a step forward.

I lifted my hand, holding him where he was.

"Julian," he repeated my name.

My eyes flicked to his.

"I have to go right now, but I want to come back. Can I come back?"

I had no idea what to say to him.

"Please."

After a moment, I nodded.

He winced. "I don't want to go, but I have to let them know."

I wanted to ask a question, the first of many, but suddenly there was thunder in the room. The floor dropped out from beneath my feet. I was standing for seconds before I was falling into a funnel of wind. I was surrounded by sound, like a jet engine, and the air was hot, scalding, burning my skin. I was tumbling, spinning, rolling, terrified of what was going to happen when I stopped.

Then arms around me, warm, solid, strong, and when I focused my eyes, there was Ryan. Tears were swept from his face, his hair blown back in the gale. He was trying to speak, but I couldn't hear him.

"I don't understand," I yelled, not even hearing my own voice in the wind.

He let me go suddenly, releasing me fast, and I was surprised that I didn't just fly away, instead remaining just as close as we plummeted together. The ringing in my ears that became a pulse of overwhelming sound hit me hard, pounding me into unconsciousness.

MY EYES drifted open, and when I turned my head, I saw the man... men. There were five of them there, one sitting on the coffee table close to me, the other four standing.

"Julian Nash," the man closest to me said.

I scrambled to sit up, staring at them all and taking in the tailored suits and dress shoes, as well as the fact that none of them were wearing ties. I felt strange there on my couch in only sweatpants.

"I am Jael," the man told me, "sentinel of the city. The men with me are Jaka, Marot, Malic, and Leith, my warders."

Warders. I had no idea what that was. More to the point, I was actually awake. Really, truly, awake.

Leaping to my feet, I walked backward until I hit the front door. The cool wood against my back was comforting.

"Julian," Jael began, "I—"

"Jesus Christ," I gasped, trying really hard not to hyperventilate. "When I woke up before, and I came out of the bedroom and there were-were those things, and-and what the fuck were those things?"

"Verdant demons," they all answered at once.

"Verdant demons, right." I took a breath, dragging my fingers through my short wavy hair. "Okay, so like I said, the first time I figured, bad chicken or something, ya know? I'm dreaming or having my stomach pumped somewhere, or God knows what, but now—" I looked up, my eyes roaming the room, seeing Ryan first and then the other five men. "Now I'm thinking I'm not dreaming, and I'm awake, and I had demons in my kitchen."

"You're very much awake," Jael soothed. "And your sanity has not deserted you, Julian Nash. You're not mad. Sentinels and warders exist to protect man from all the creatures from the pit. We stand between you and the abyss."

"Dramatic," I said, coughing, "and I'm normally up for that, but—why the hell were there demons in my kitchen?" I finished with a roar.

"They followed Rindahl to your home."

Rindahl.

"You call him Ryan."

My eyes flicked to the man I was crazy about. I saw how wounded he looked, his eyes wet and pleading.

"Look at me."

I had to turn back to Jael, who I realized now was just massive. With him sitting down, we were almost eye to eye. Standing, he would have towered over me. "What's a verdant demon?" I asked.

Jael frowned. "I don't understand. What class of demon?"

I made a noise in the back of my throat; I had no idea what I was even asking.

"Verdant demons cluster together in one place. They have an almost hive mentality. They are as vicious in battle as they are well-trained and synchronized." He looked at me intently. "What else would you like to know?'

I had just received the Wikipedia answer to my verdant demon inquiry. Christ, the whole thing was absurd. "That's not what I meant," I scoffed, hovering between yelling until I felt better and thinking I was dreaming. Everything I knew had been changed in an instant.

"Julian—"

"I'm losing my mind," I said, closing my eyes, concentrating on breathing, counting. I needed things to be normal just as I had an inkling that they never would be again.

"Listen to—"

My eyes snapped open. "Who the hell are you? Why are in my house? And what the hell is a sentinel?"

Jael's eyes glinted, but there was nothing else. "Rindahl has chosen well."

I put out my arm, braced myself on the wall to my right, and focused on taking deep in-and-out breaths.

"Mr. Nash?"

"Every city has a sentinel?" I asked him, breath in, breath out.

"Yes," he answered softly.

"And every sentinel has five warders?"

"Like the fixed points of a pentagram, yes."

"Warders do what?"

"The same thing as a sentinel. We all fight creatures, demons, but the sentinel is the oldest, has seen the most action, and so is in charge."

I absorbed what he'd said, added it to things I knew, facts, trivia, names. Every city had a sentinel; a man who made sure that creatures like verdant demons didn't get me. Okay.

"Jules?" My eyes flicked to Ryan. "Can I talk to you now?"

"Are you all right?" I asked, and even I could hear the worry in my voice.

His eyes locked on mine, but he didn't move. He looked like he was in pain.

"Come here," I demanded.

"Julian, I—"

"Now."

He rushed across the room to me. When he was close enough, I grabbed him and pulled him into my arms. I hugged him tight, letting out a deep breath.

"Christ, I thought those guys were gonna kill you," I said, leaning back to look at his face. "Why didn't you tell me you're like a ninja or something?" The gasp of air, the stunned look on his face. I had to smile. "Now I get the swords and the weird herbs and your Jeep all beat to shit all the time. Can't paint your baby if it's just gonna get scratched up."

"God, Julian, you're amazing."

"I need a second to process this, okay?"

"You're not frightened?"

"I don't know what I am yet," I confessed, feeling Ryan's warm hands slide over my back. "You gotta let me think."

"Jules."

"Wait."

"Julian, you—"

"Wait," I snapped, before chuckling at how absurd everything was. "We'll talk as soon as we're alone."

I heard his quick intake of breath. "You're not sending me away?"

"Why would I wanna do that?" I scowled automatically, turning to face the men, tucking Ryan behind me. It was stupid, considering he was fresh from having subdued four men, but he brought out every protective instinct I had. He belonged to me. "Put your hands back on me so I know you're there."

He didn't just touch me; he leaned into me, pressing against my back, his arms wrapping around me tight. I felt his stubbled cheek between my shoulder blades and the shudder that tore through him.

"Listen to me, Julian Nash."

My eyes returned to the man who rose and rose from the coffee table, huge, easily seven feet tall, dark green eyes staring at me.

"I am Jael Ezran, and as I said, these are my men. We hunt and kill things that if I told you about, you would think I was nuts."

I tracked him with my eyes, watching as he walked around the couch only to stop a couple of feet away.

"A sentinel"—he put his hand on his heart—"that's me, has a team of five warders who hunt with him, or sometimes on their own, in teams. Normally, things like the creatures you saw earlier would not come to the home of a warder, as our homes are sealed, but your house, as it is not Rindahl's—Ryan's—house, it is not sealed. He is not supposed to remain overnight anywhere but his own home, but I suspect he was distracted by the discovery of your new bond and so neglected his own safety as well as yours."

"Our bond? You lost me."

He nodded, gave me a slight smile. "Every sentinel, every warder, has to have a hearth: a home, a channel for safety, peace, love, whatever you want to call it. A warder must have a hearth or eventually they die. We have found over the centuries that all power and no hearth will kill a warder. There has to be balance between the emotional and the physical. Without balance, there's chaos within. Do you understand?"

"I don't think so," I told him honestly.

"All right," he sighed, "think of it like this. I fight evil. I kill horrible vicious things, but to do that, I have to be prepared. I have to be ready physically, emotionally, and mentally to take life every single day."

I realized suddenly how he looked tired but determined at the same time.

"I can train myself, as well as my men, to be strong physically and be focused mentally, but the heart—that's not in my power to do for anyone but myself."

"'Course," I agreed. I was mostly following. I wasn't sure why I was receiving the explanation, but if he felt the need for the exposition, I would hear him out.

He nodded, rubbing at his thick dirty-blond hair. "We all protect each other. We are all dependent for our very survival on one another. If one of us is distracted and their thoughts are on what they want or need instead of on the fight... someone could die."

It made sense. Men in battle had to be focused on the task at hand. "I don't understand why you're tell—"

"My men protect me and each other, and to do that, they need a balance in their lives. For a warder, their hearth—home—is vital and necessary." I stayed quiet not wanting to interrupt. "A hearth makes a home for the warder. There are very few men or women that can be a hearth to a warder as the warder's energy drains the life force of most humans."

"So what you're saying is that the bad has to be offset by the good, by the love of the hearth."

His smile made his laugh lines crinkle and elicited a heavy sigh. "Usually after the first time a warder and a human share a bed, the warder wakes to find their partner withered, years burned away in a single moment of shared bliss."

"It ages people, sleeping, having sex with a warder."

"Yes."

Which was why Ryan had so thoroughly looked me over after the first night we made love: he had been checking to make sure he hadn't hurt me.

"If the warder leaves, then the partner will recover their years, given time, but if the warder remains, even out of love, the woman, or man, will die."

"Sounds like a succubus."

"There are both female and male warders, so stories of incubus and succubus, a night hag, all of these myths can be attributed in some way to warders."

"What if the warder chooses to stay with the person they love, but they just never have sex again?"

"Just their presence alone would drain their partner once they're joined for the first time."

I flashed him a grin. "It's a helluva excuse to sleep around: gotta look for your hearth and all. It's not a one-night stand, it's just research." His eyes narrowed, and I chuckled. "Sorry, go on."

"You're very odd."

Pot to kettle in my opinion, but I shut up since he was much bigger than me and a whole hell of a lot scarier. "But what does any of this have to do with me?"

"Don't you know?"

Before I could respond, Ryan tugged on my hand, prodding me to follow him. "C'mon," he urged, pulling me after him out of the living room and into my bedroom. He shoved me down hard on the bed.

Looking up at him, I saw all the emotions swimming across his face, and his jaw muscles were cording hard. "So? I guess the other night, when I held you down, you really—"

"No," he cut me off, sounding pained, his eyes a mess. "Don't look at me like I'm scary."

"But you are."

"Not to you."

I was having so much trouble wrapping my brain around him as a monster killer. He looked the same, like Ryan.

"I need, I want—you have to be the… the one who says, who does."

I wasn't stupid; it just took me a second because my day had been a little weird. "Why would you submit to me? Why would you want to?"

"Because then I have no power, and I can just be." So he didn't have to think if he was surrendering up all his control to me. He just had to feel. "Don't send me away," he whispered. "Please, Jules. I just"—he took a sharp breath—"realized it was you."

And I understood. He had always liked me, but something had changed, and he had really seen me for the first time.

"I'm sorry I was stupid. My instincts have been wrong before, and I've hurt people. I don't trust myself like I should. Jael hates it."

He had to be ready on a moment's notice to make a life or death decision and not wonder if what he was doing was right or wrong. If I were Jael, I would have been just as frustrated.

"Please don't send me away."

I stared up into his beautiful eyes. "Ry—"

"I want to be the one you take. I need to be the guy you dominate and hold down. Don't," he almost yelled, and I heard the panic in his voice. "Don't let it be anybody else."

He was trembling, and it sunk into me then, that for him, this was much more than us deciding whether we were going to keep seeing each other. He had bigger concerns.

Wounded eyes locked on mine. "I'm so sorry for all this. I never thought I would be tracked. I'm not as valuable as the others."

But Jael hadn't mentioned any hierarchy; he had said *his* warders, like they were all equal. I was betting that Ryan's enemies saw them all the same way.

"Is it really Ryan, or do you prefer Rindahl?"

He cleared his throat. "When I was made a warder at fifteen I was given that name. I hate it. It's not who I am. Ryan, Ry… that's who I am."

The age stuck in my head. "Where are your parents?"

"I never had any; my mother died in childbirth and there's no father listed anywhere. Her last name was Dean, and she told a nurse she wanted to name me Ryan before she went into labor. It's the story I was told. I don't even know if it's true or not."

"And the others?"

"We're all the family any of us have. Jael said that's how it's always been."

"That's why you all need a hearth to come home to."

He nodded. "I want to come home to you, Julian, if you let me."

I opened my arms for him. "Come here."

The tears in his eyes came fast, welling up as he dove down into my arms, face buried in the hollow of my throat.

My fingers sank into his thick blond mane as I felt his mouth open on the side of my neck. "So how does it work, reality talk show host by day, scary kick-ass warder by night? When the hell do you sleep?"

He smiled. I felt it as he kissed my skin. "I don't wanna sleep. I wanna make love to you. Please, Julian."

"Tell me."

"Okay, yeah." He nibbled down the side of my neck to my collarbone. "I live two complete and separate lives that need to be connected. That's the part Jael left out, the connection. If you're not grounded in the real world, the day-to-day existence of a regular man, you lose your mind. I've seen it happen to a lot of warders over the years."

"So this team is not your original one."

"No."

"Because sometimes a warder just freaks out," I clarified.

"Yes."

"And you avoid that by having your hearth make a home for you, provide a life for you that has nothing to do with hunting and killing creatures of the night."

He snickered at my wording. "Exactly."

"So you really do need a hearth."

He leaned back to look up at me. "I need you, Julian."

"It's like Buffy."

The scowl was instant and dark. "I'm sorry?"

"You're like Buffy the Vampire Slayer, ya know, Buffy. She patrols. She kills things. She's hot. She wears cute clothes… you're Buffy."

He exhaled fast. "I will give you a half a second to—"

"And the guys are like the Scooby Gang," I teased, patting his ass. "Huh, honey?"

His growl was loud as I dissolved in a fit of relieved laughter. He sat up, yanked the pillow out from under my head, and smacked me hard across the face with it.

"You shit!" he yelled. "Here I am thinkin' you're making a life and death decision for me, and you've already decided that you're gonna keep me! What the fuck?"

I could not have stopped laughing if my life depended on it.

He came back down on top of me, pinning me to the bed, his mouth sealing over mine, breathing me in and kissing me hungrily. I rolled him to his back and broke the kiss, sitting up, straddling his hips. His eyes were heavy-lidded as he gazed up at me.

"We get along, I think."

He ran his hands up and down my thighs. "We more than get along."

"You realize that between the two of us, you're the domestic god, right? Not me."

"It's not about cooking or cleaning or anything else but having a home, Jules. It's being with you, knowing that you know everything about me and want me anyway. It's acceptance and unconditional lo—safety," he finished haltingly.

I smiled down at him. "Nice save. You can say 'love'. I won't freak out." He trembled beneath me. "I think I could fall in love with you pretty easy."

"Julian, God, my body is… I need—"

"Whaddya need?" I asked, bending to brush my lips across his.

He wriggled under me, the whimper of want sending a pulse of heat straight to my slowly filling cock. "God, you feel good."

"You too," I said, shifting over his groin until he caught his breath.

"Your legs are so hard," he marveled, his fingers digging into my thighs.

"So is there a secret handshake or some scary ritual? Do you hafta drink my blood or something?" I asked him.

"What're you talking about?"

"Becoming your hearth, what's the process of that?"

"You say: Ryan, I agree to be your hearth."

"That's it? That's really anticlimactic."

"You want pageantry?"

"Maybe not quite that big, but something."

His smile was radiant. "You are so great. Do you have any idea how great you are?"

I grunted. "So listen, I want to go with you." He was distracted, biting his bottom lip, reaching up for my neck. I brushed his hands away. "Promise I can come. I want to see you do it so I know what it's like for you. I want to know."

"Mmmm," he breathed out, hands on my thighs again. "Kiss me."

"Ry—swear."

He took a quivering breath. "You know you've got a lot of clothes on." His voice was husky and deep. "Maybe you should take some of them off."

"You want me to be your hearth, right?"

"Your skin makes me crazy."

"Do you?"

"Oh, yes," he barely got out. His eyes glazed, the pupils dilated and round.

The way he was looking at me, I wouldn't be able to be logical too much longer. The man burned me up, and we had been together too short a time to be anywhere near sated with each other. I felt my body start to heat. "Ry—"

"Nice piece," a voice said from behind me.

Whirling around, I was off Ryan and standing beside the bed seconds later. I had not heard the door open, so I was surprised to see the man in the black Armani suit and the Prada boots standing in my bedroom. He was tall, with white blond hair and ice blue eyes. He looked as though he had been carved out of porcelain.

"Get the hell out of my home!" Ryan barked at him, rolling up off the bed, growling.

"It's not your home," came the crisp accent, not English, something else. "It belongs to the stud. If it was yours, I, along with everyone else, wouldn't have been able to get in here, now would I? Jael was right; you're acting really stupid."

"What the fuck do you want?" Ryan hissed at him, walking around in front of me, shielding me even though I was bigger than he was.

He smirked, fiddling with his silver cufflinks. "Jael said I had to go out with you tonight. He wants to make certain you don't neglect your duties."

Ryan scowled at him. "That's bullshit. You're the only one who doesn't trust me. I'm supposed to have Jackson this week, not you."

"Jackson's too trusting. He would just expect you to give him backup, and then he'd end up dead."

Ryan moved fast and had the other man pinned to the far wall with a spectral movement of speed. One moment he was beside me, the second he had his fellow warder pounded against the brick. "I would never jeopardize any of your lives, even yours, Malic!"

The eyes lifted to rest on Ryan's face. "Even mine?"

He stepped back only to move the bigger man off the wall and ram him back into it again. Malic smiled instead of crying out. It should have hurt. The force exhibited, how the wall shuddered from the impact, it would have cracked my ribs, broken things inside my body.

"Are you seriously considering taking your hearth with you to kill verdant demons tonight? Is that wise?"

"I'm not his hearth yet," I corrected him.

"Oh, the fuck you're not." He dismissed me as Ryan stepped away from him, turning his back on him to cross the room. "You're accepting of us being warders, seeing creatures get sucked into small black holes didn't flip you out, and you like fucking Ryan—I can still feel the heat in this room. Tell me, Julian Nash, how are you not his hearth?"

I had no answer. He was a snotty, snarky asshole, and also completely correct. The idea of being Ryan Dean's touchstone was a hundred percent appealing. I liked to matter. I wanted to matter, and I had a chance to really mean something to a man I found intoxicating. I very much wanted to sign on for the hearth gig.

"You're right."

Ryan's head snapped up, and his eyes met mine. "You mean it?"

I smiled at him. "Yeah, come live with me. It's what Cash is expecting, anyway."

He took a step forward. "But your whole life will change."

"I like change, keeps your life from getting stagnant. And besides, once you live here, you can make the apartment safe, right? I own it, so seal it up or whatever. Later, when we find a house, you can seal up the new one too."

"Julian, I—"

"Being a warder's just one part of you. It's not all you are. I like the rest of you a helluva lot, always have. We can work out the new avenging angel of the night part."

He leaped at me, and I was laughing as I grabbed him. He wasn't that much smaller than me, and trying to hold him and still keep my balance proved much too difficult. We fell back onto the bed, a tangle of arms and legs.

I lifted his face, bent, and kissed him. The deep, husky moan tore through me as I slanted my mouth over his. My tongue slid between his lips as I took possession of the kiss, letting him know that he was mine.

There was the sound of a throat clearing, and it took every drop of willpower I possessed to break the kiss and look up at the ice man towering over the bed. But he wasn't looking at me.

"I ask again, is he going out with us to hunt demons tonight?"

"Yes." Ryan caught his breath. "He is."

"And what if he's killed, what will you do then? You just found your precious hearth. If he dies, who will you fuck then?" The tone of the question was aggressive. He sounded like a jilted lover more than anything else.

"I'll protect him," Ryan promised. "I'll ask Leith, see if he can come help me, or Jackson or Marcus. I know you won't help watch him, but one of them will."

"I'll watch him. I would no more allow your hearth to be harmed than any of the others. You insult me by suggesting I would be anything but vigilant."

Ryan grunted as he rolled off the bed to his feet in one seamless movement. It was like he was boneless.

"This is the one man you've found that you can fuck and not kill. Why would I let you lose him?"

I saw Ryan deciding whether he was going to take offense at the other man's wording. After several moments, he nodded. "I'll meet you at midnight down by the marina."

"I'll meet you there," Malic agreed, walking out of the room, slamming the bedroom door after him.

"Hey." Ryan turned around to face me. "What's with you and him?"

"It was years ago," he admitted, no game playing between us, no making me dig. "Malic and me, it didn't work, and two warders together is so much more than simply a bad idea."

I let out a deep sigh. "I don't think he's over you."

"We're different men," he told me. "And we want different things. Maybe as more time passes, Malic will find his own home and hearth, but for now, he has no one and does not seem all that interested in finding one."

"I thought it was dangerous for warders not to have hearths?"

"It is, so we all watch him, but even Jael can't force Malic to love someone if he doesn't or can't. We may be scary warriors fighting against supernatural forces, but we're still guys, ya know? If you don't feel it, you don't feel it."

I squinted at him. "So with me, it's there, right?"

He swallowed hard, looking overwhelmed suddenly.

I opened my arms, and he moved fast to fill them, his head down on my shoulder, hugging me tight. "Can I ask you a small favor?"

It was funny how he leaned back slowly and peered up at me.

"I promise it's not a big deal."

The disbelief was all over his face, and my smile helped nothing. "Oh God, what?"

I softened my request by kissing him so hard and long that he had to shove me off of him so he could breathe. I took advantage of the moment, and he agreed before he realized he'd made a deal with the devil… well, with me.

# VI

"HOW come I don't have a sword?" Cash asked, looking from Ryan to Malic and back again. Malic did the slow pan to Ryan, who let out a deep breath before looking at me.

"What?"

"Remind me to kill you."

"Why?" I chuckled, trying not to laugh, but the absurdity of the entire situation was simply too much for me. I was going to start giggling any second, and I never giggled. I was a grown-up, for heaven's sake.

If Ryan wanted me for his partner, he got Cash too. There was no way around it. I would not keep the biggest event in my life from my best friend. I explained to Ryan that it was like having a bigger safety net, now he had Cash, and Phoebe, who was not along but dying to know what happened. She was pregnant; she did not get to see demons being killed. Ryan and Malic were stunned at how easy it was for my best friend and his wife to wrap their brains around the fact there were actual things that went bump in the night that had to be destroyed. And Phoebe, like me, who watched every single scary show on the CW and FOX and every horror movie that came out, was very excited to be in on their whole big secret. She was all ready to help make fake IDs, spread salt around doorways, or banish angels back to heaven. She watched way too much *Supernatural*.

"Jules?"

I turned to look at Ryan.

"This is the one and only time you and Cash are allowed here with us. Do you understand?"

I had already made the same promise at least ten times, but I understood that the arrangement was giving him an ulcer. It was really very sweet. "Yes, Ry."

"Could we all please fuckin' focus?" Malic growled beside me.

My eyes moved to him. We were all crouched behind some stacked pallets at the wharf, looking at the empty space in front of us through the slats.

"What?" he asked irritably.

"Jael calls Ryan 'Rindahl', but it's like his call sign or something, it's not his name. What's your real name, Malic?"

"It's just Malic," he said between clenched teeth.

"It is." Cash nodded, bumping my shoulder. "Remember? He owns that strip club that Ben and Carlene did the grand opening for, like, six months ago. I thought at the time that Malic was a cool-ass name."

Malic's cold eyes flicked to Cash, but instead of looking away, Cash stared right back. My money was on my best friend, and it turned out I was right. Malic could not hold his gaze long.

"There," Ryan said suddenly, his voice guttural and icy.

Before I could caution him to be careful, he stood, and from that standing position, bent his knees and leaped straight up into the air and over the stack we were hiding behind.

"Jesus," Cash breathed as Malic followed right behind him.

I had expected, from many seasons of *Angel* and everything else, demons with horns, big heads, scaly skin, or fangs. What I saw were men, or things that looked like men, all in black, looking more like assassins than creatures from the pit. The eyes, though, their bleeding eyes, under the glow from the streetlamps, were a dead giveaway.

I heard Ryan growl low in his throat, and in a blur of movement, he pulled his two swords from the twin scabbards on his back and rushed toward the demons.

Cash roared out a warning as Ryan was quickly surrounded, but he was already moving. As I watched, I was frightened for the man who had become more important with every passing second I spent with him, but it was beautiful at the same time, the synchronization, more a dance than war.

"I'll cut out your heart," one of the creatures snarled at Ryan.

"Try, servant, try," Ryan baited him, the swords spinning in his hands as he lunged forward.

I was breathless watching him. His sword cut through the air in arches and circles, whirling fast, like a fan, sweeping from side to side, moving in studied steps, intricately executed, each maneuver able to cause instant death if contact were made.

I looked for Malic, found him, and watched as he rolled, leaped, froze still as stone, and then dove into a somersault and landed light on his feet once more. Swords struck one another hard, steel ringing against steel, the only sound on the empty dock. Malic and his adversary stopped suddenly, frozen together in statuesque form. Malic's body in an arch above the ground, one hand on the dock, splayed fingers gripping the wood, the other holding his sword straight up to ward off the death strike. His adversary was poised above him, driving down with his stroke, his legs braced apart, the other hand filled now with a dagger no one else had seen. He had thought to deliver the last blow, but Ryan's yell turned the demon's head at the last moment. The moment of fractured focus was taken full advantage of. Malic collapsed to the ground and somersaulted to his feet in a seamless movement that was like watching a dancer.

I turned to look for Ryan and watched as he sprinted past where Cash and I were and ran up the side of a building with a demon not more than a breath behind him. I watched as the demon flew after Ryan, both arms outstretched like wings, each wielding a razor sharp weapon meant to take my lover's life.

Ryan spun in mid-air, whipped around, and beheaded the demon instantly. The ground opened up, and just as it had done before in my apartment, there seemed to be a yawning, blowing black hole that sucked the headless corpse down into it. And I saw suddenly where Ryan would complete his leap as well as what he didn't see: the two demons there.

Charging out from behind the pallet with Cash right behind me, I ran up on the creature as Ryan found himself at the end of his strike. The demon adjusted his stance and drove forward, the honed edge of the sword down, ready to cut through Ryan's heart and sever him in two.

I swung hard with the bat I had brought along, catching the demon in the chest, driving him back. Before I could turn, he recovered and charged forward. The sword would have driven through my abdomen, but it was knocked sideways by a three iron. Cash had brought a gold club, and with it, he saved my life.

I watched as he swept the demon's feet out from under him, but before I could be impressed, I gasped as I saw an ax arcing toward my best friend's neck.

Caught fast between twin swords, the ax was wrenched free of the demon's hand with such force that I heard a cry of pain. Ryan was there, between Cash and death, and I instinctively grabbed his arm and squeezed it tight.

"Run to the street," he growled at me.

I turned in time to see a flash of steel and watched, spellbound, as the edge of a hatchet stopped inches from my stomach. The flat side of the sword had intercepted the weapon, and as I followed the length of it up to the face of the demon, I found that there was no head to view as it was no longer there. I pushed the carcass away from me before it fell forward, and a stream of thick liquid coursed from the neck stem splattering the wooden dock at my feet. I was bumped sharply out of the way, and I saw beside me another vacuum of a black hole. Ryan had kept me from being sucked into it.

"Now run," he ordered, grabbing hold of Cash's jacket and shoving him forward in front of me.

As I bolted down the dock, Cash pounding after me, I saw Malic rush by me. A safe distance away, both of us turned to look. Malic leaped high in the air, spinning at the same time, and landed effortlessly on the roof of a restaurant before turning on the demons there. Looking for Ryan, I saw him hacking his way through one man after another with his savagely wielded swords, turning living beings to corpses before my very eyes. Those further away began to run instead of standing by, spellbound, to meet their fate. I understood their trancelike state, as I myself could not take my eyes from Ryan Dean, riveted, at the same time revolted, bearing witness to the carnage.

I heard a sound behind me, and turning, saw a demon. Bloody eyes swept over us before he lunged forward. I didn't have time to register Ryan's presence before he suddenly stopped just behind the creature, standing still and silent, his body frozen in position. He stood in a lunging stride, right leg forward, one sword held tight in both hands now against his left side, as though he had finished an arc of movement. It took me a moment to realize that he had not missed as I had thought at first.

When the demon tried to speak, blood gushed from his mouth, coursing over his lips and chin in gulping spasms, staining the entire front of his shirt bright crimson. His head fell back in agonizing slowness, opening a gaping wound before falling to the pavement with a sickening wet sound. The body stood for a moment and then lurched forward into a swirling black wind tunnel. My head lifted, and my eyes met Ryan's as Malic suddenly appeared at his side.

"Never again," Ryan said, releasing a deep breath. "But thank you for interfering on my behalf." The last part was spoken to not only me, but Cash, as well.

"Even though you interrupted a killing stroke," Ryan's fellow warder groused, glowering at Cash and me. "Neither he nor I ever take our eyes from one another in battle."

I looked back at Ryan.

"It's true," he said gruffly. "Now I want you and Cash to go home. As we had to intervene here to save you, others escaped, and we have to hunt them down. It's gonna take a while."

Malic growled, bumping my shoulder hard as he stalked by me.

"I'm sorry, Ry," I exhaled, "I just wanted to know what you did, but me being here put you in danger."

He didn't disagree, but I got a hint of a smile before he put his hand briefly on my cheek. "I'll call you tomorrow. Go home and go to bed, Jules. You have to work in the morning."

"So do you," Cash said.

"But I don't have to be at the museum to tape the date-night piece until nine," he sighed, brushing by me, following after Malic.

I watched him walk away, flicking his sword sharply so drops of blood flew off of it before he sheathed it across the other on his back. Malic turned to look at him before he took off running. Ryan broke into a sprint, and when Malic leaped high into the air, over the roof of the building he had been on earlier, Ryan followed right on his heels.

"They're amazing." Cash spoke my thoughts out loud.

I turned back to my best friend. "Why does Ryan need me if he has Malic?"

Cash pointed at my face. "You've got blood splatter on your glasses."

"Perfect," I groaned, taking them off to clean the lenses on my T-shirt.

I walked with Cash silently back to his Lexus. Leaning on the open door, one hand resting on the roof of the car, he looked at me.

"What?"

"It seems like Ryan's got backup when he's fighting, right?"

I shrugged.

"From what you said earlier about a hearth and what he said when I asked him, seems like the part that you're gonna do is to recharge his batteries. Just like when I come home from a shitty day at work, and my beautiful wife is there waiting for me with her own story about her own shitty day—I feel better just looking at her." He stared at me. "Isn't it your part to just love him and make everything better?"

I stared back. "You saw that... how do you feel better after that?"

"I dunno how it is with you guys, Jules, but just holding my girl in my arms fixes a helluva lot for me."

And hadn't Ryan said as much?

"I'll think about it."

"Well, that's what you do, Jules," Cash chuckled as he got into the car, "you think."

Now what the hell did that mean?

He let out a snort of laughter at the look I gave him once I was seat-belted in.

# VII

I GOT no sleep because I was worried about Ryan. I couldn't concentrate at our Monday morning meeting and finally had to excuse myself since I was climbing the walls. I had to go and make sure he was all right.

I was waiting at the elevator to go down, and when the doors swooshed open, found myself face to face with Peyton Wilson.

"Julian." He coughed, flushing bright pink, his ears turning red. "How are... you? I'm so sorry for Friday night and everything. It was a mess."

So much had happened in three days, and the guy I had been seeing having sex with the man in front of me didn't even register as important anymore. "It's fine," I assured him, getting on the elevator as he got off. "Honestly."

He took a breath. "Really?" The man sounded so confused.

"Yes, Peyton, we're good."

"Jesus, Julian," he said, catching the doors so they couldn't close. "You are seriously the coldest son of a bitch I have ever met in my life."

"Could you move?"

"Christ, if I lost a hot piece of ass like Channing Isner, I would feel like shit."

Since I had never had a piece of said ass, I had no idea what I was missing. Not that I cared. "Okay, can you move?"

"Julian, I—"

"How 'bout this: let's not talk ever again," I suggested as I pushed him back and the doors slid shut. I had never anticipated him giving me crap. I had figured him for scared and hopeful that our working relationship would not suffer. But in the big picture, as he worked for Cash, neither he nor Channing were any of my concern.

Only one thing mattered: Ryan Dean.

I took a cab to his apartment, and when the doorman saw me, remembering me from Friday night, he let me in immediately. I had my hand up to knock on his door when it opened.

"Hey." Ryan smiled at me, his eyes sparkling with all the kaleidoscope colors I loved, green, brown, and gold, holding up his BlackBerry so I could see it. "I was just gonna call you and—"

I lunged at him, hands on his face, kissing him hard and deep. His moan was hoarse, needy. "I was so worried."

"Why?" He smiled as I kissed his throat, his chin, his cheeks, his nose, and finally his mouth again, claiming his lips, his tongue. His hands fisted on the lapels of my cashmere trench coat. "You don't have to worry about me."

I sucked his bottom lip into my mouth, nibbling it gently.

"Jules, I… need… I hafta be somewhere, and you're making it really hard to—you're making me hard."

I could not get enough of him, knowing he was safe, the warmth of his body seeping through his clothes. I was rough and bruising as I prolonged the kiss, devouring his sweet mouth until I got the whimper I was after. His arms were wrapped around my neck, and I could feel his heart beating though his dress shirt. We stood together, in his doorway, wrapped around each other, kissing like lovesick teenagers until I finally had to breathe. My head was pounding as I lifted my lips from his.

"Forget what I said," he said, "you go ahead and worry."

"I want you to move in today. Hire movers, pack up your shit, and come home. I never want to sleep without you again—not that I did any sleeping."

He shifted his stance, easing back so he could look into my face. "Yeah, you look a little wrung out," he said gently, pushing my glasses up on my nose. "Those are hot, you know. Guys who wear glasses, brainy guys, do it for me, big time."

"Is that right?"

"Oh yes." He grinned, and I felt his fingers sliding up the back of my neck into my hair. "So how 'bout I pick you up after work, we'll grab some Chinese food, come here, and get in bed. How would that be?"

"I want you to move in."

"I'll do it tomorrow, for sure. Tonight, you hafta sleep over here with me. I need to make sure you're safe."

"Okay," I agreed, pressing wet happy kisses to his throat and jaw.

"God, I needed this," he sighed, "you coming over here all worried and hot for me."

"Watching you and Malic last night, I wasn't sure you—"

"Jules." He framed my face in his hands, making me still. "Me and Malic, me and all the others... we work great together, the killing is seamless, but that part is just training and ability. A sentinel can find his warders, knows them when he sees them, and when he trains us, it triggers the speed, the strength, the power. Jael finding me made me a warder, but that's all it is. The real part, the true part, is just about being a man and being loved. Having a hearth, a home, that's who I am, what I am."

Every doubt I had crumbled with his words. Being loved was the most important thing to Ryan Dean; I would not make him tell me again.

"You're gonna love me, Julian, sooner than you think."

I already loved him; I just wasn't ready to tell him. Pushing him back through the door, I locked it behind me.

"Mr. Nash, you—"

I grabbed him, pivoted, and shoved him face-first up against the front door.

"That's it... push me around." This, then, was Ryan's need, to feel my strength, my power exerted over him, to trust that I would be rough but never hurt him, my love his safety net. "Do whatever you want to me."

I loved him shaking with desire, the need there in his voice, his face, his heavy-lidded eyes and trembling lower lip. His sharp gasp of pleasure made me smile as I pinned him with my body, his inability to form words, only sounds from deep inside of him, his profile a study in anticipation.

"God, I love belonging to you," he moaned.

I loved it too. He was mine. "I'm not letting you go."

"Promise?"

"I do."

"Say it again."

So I did.

# Tooth & Nail

1

IT HAD been a good night, my favorite kind. Nothing planned—just the fun of being out with a few close friends and letting the night lead you wherever it wanted. Lack of a destination always made the journey fun. Planning was for amateurs.

"See," Rene Favreau said, smiling over his shoulder as he walked into the club ahead of me, "aren't you glad I talked you into coming out with us?"

And I was, up until I saw who we were meeting at our last stop. I never understood the need in some people to add others to the mix when what you had with you was working out fine. It was probably the same principle in action that made people cheat. If one guy is hot, two would be better. The mentality to want, need, to *have* more was lost on me. I liked small groups, a tight circle of friends, and one lover at a time. But Rene wanted to dance and have fun and to him, the more the merrier. He had gotten a text that Graham Becker and some of his other friends and acquaintances were at a dance club in the Castro, so he had routed us there to meet them. I was suddenly ready to call it a night.

"Wait." He slipped around in front of me, barring my path. "C'mon, Mal, just stay. You don't even have to talk to Graham."

But I would. He was there and I was there, and even in a large group, even with ten of us at a table being loud, I would get stuck at least acknowledging his presence and him mine. And then there would be trouble.

"Malic," Graham muttered after maybe five minutes of us all sitting down.

"Graham."

You could feel the ice blow over the table. I shot Rene a look.

He nearly spit out his Chivas and water.

"What's so funny?" Graham asked him.

He just shook his head, trying to breathe around the burn of having good Scotch go down the wrong hole.

Graham's dark green eyes were back on me, staring daggers. This was what came of telling the truth.

"How ya been?" I asked politely.

"What the fuck do you care?"

I didn't; I was making polite conversation, but if he was going to be a dick, I could easily ignore him.

A month ago we had been at a party together, and Graham had gotten really drunk. At one point in the night, he was in my lap, arms wrapped around my neck, nearly dry-humping my abdomen and whining for me to fuck his brains out. I had been more than willing to grant his request; he was tall, dark, and handsome, and his sexy green eyes made my cock hard. To cut down on drive time, I had suggested the bathroom. I was thinking of him. Fucking in the john, his face plastered up against the mirror, ass bared, was more comfortable than my car; it seemed like a good plan. I thought he'd be pleased. He was nowhere near it.

Apparently Graham Becker was not hot to be my hookup for the evening. He was not a one-night stand kind of guy; the man was looking for a relationship. I just wanted to get laid. He was upset that he had misinterpreted my interest as long term when it was merely immediate. And then he was embarrassed. And then he took it out on me again and again and again until just seeing the man made me cringe. He could hate me if he wanted, that was his prerogative; he just didn't need to be vocal about it.

"Lay off Mal," Rene told him. "Give it a rest."

"Why are you here?" Graham snapped at me. "Shouldn't you be in your closet?"

Christ.

"Well?"

He meant my club. My strip club. My straight strip club.

Ever since Graham had found out my club down on Mission was a girls-only venue, he had been giving me crap about it. Why did a gay man own a place where only women stripped? That made no logical sense. But it made perfect sense to me. At my strip club, Romeo's Basement, you could only watch beautiful women writhe out of elaborate costumes; there were no boys on stage. I had purposely made it a gentleman's club because hot men strutting around in nothing but G-strings would have been hard on me. Sleeping with your employees was bad for business as well as morale, so I made sure I was never tempted to do either. My explanation would not have interested the man who hated me. What he didn't know was that I took my sex casually for a very serious reason. I didn't want to hurt anyone.

I was not simply a cold-hearted bastard being a dick; I had nameless, soulless encounters in hopes that if they were fast, then the other person wouldn't suffer. Yes, I wanted to get laid, but also, because I was a warder, if you weren't my hearth and I screwed you, you could get hurt. Graham had no idea of the very real jeopardy he was in.

I was a warder; warders killed demons. I killed demons. I hunted them with others just like me, five of us in all, plus my boss, the sentinel of the city, Jael Ezran. Every city had a sentinel, every sentinel had five warders, and all of them hunted demons together either in pairs or in a group. I fought things that went bump in the night, which was the heroic part that probably would have excited Graham. The part that would not have excited him was that sleeping with me could not only hurt his feelings when I left in the middle of the night but could actually kill him.

The kiss, the touch of a warder, if you were not their hearth, could be deadly. There were a select number of humans who could be intimate with us, and when we found one of them, it was a cause for celebration. It wasn't like a hearth was the one and only mate of a warder; they were simply one of very few people that could handle being intimate with a warder.

Ryan, or Rindahl, as my sentinel called him, one of the other four warders I hunted with, had recently found his hearth, and I could not imagine him ever letting the man go. When a warder found a hearth, usually it was because they had finally taken the step and slept with someone they loved. When they had sex they hoped, prayed, that that person was compatible with them. Ryan had wanted Julian, and so he had gambled on a future with the man. When he found out that Julian was his hearth, could truly be his, I had never seen him so happy. He even allowed Julian to watch us hunt. And it had only happened once, but to so indulge another simply out of love was horrifying. The very idea made me crave lots and lots of air and wide open spaces. Love, in all its many forms, seemed more about control to me than anything else. I would fight to make sure it never got ahold of me.

"No snappy comeback?"

I looked over at Graham, unsure of what he was talking about.

"Malic?"

"Sorry, I stopped listening. What'd ya say?"

He threw up his hands, got up, and stalked away. I turned to look at Rene.

"You know you're an ass, right?"

My mind had drifted, that was all. I didn't try to piss people off deliberately, but it happened a lot nonetheless. I bored easily, as a rule; it was hard to keep my interest. Those that could usually became my friends. "So, what, are you picking up a fuck buddy or not?"

"We say make love to or sleep with," Rene corrected me, brows furrowed, scowl dark. "Why do you always have to be so goddamn crass?"

"Have the balls to say fuck, 'cause that's all it is," I said, yawning.

"Mal—"

"If it's hearts and flowers you really want, you should pick someone up at the library and ask them out for tea."

"You do not have a romantic bone in your entire body."

Which was probably true, but it didn't change the facts. "If it's romance you want, it ain't happening at a club."

He was still scowling at me, but I was right and we both knew it. "Malic, you know you're never gonna find someone to put up with your bullshit, right?"

I grunted, because that was simply a fact of life. I excused myself to go hit the head.

"I'm gonna get drinks. Whaddya want?" he called after me.

I yelled back for a Black and Tan and moved through the thick Saturday night crowd toward the bathroom. Once I reached it, I encountered something I never had before: a line.

"Something's going on," the guy in front of me said to my shoes.

"What?" I asked, annoyed. It would have been nice to have more people look me in the face, meet my eyes. But they didn't.

"I think some hustler's getting his ass beat."

I moved by him and several others, but no one said a word. The theory was that my perpetual scowl coupled with my height and wingspan, as well as my shoulders and chest, made most guys give me room. When I stepped around the corner, inside the bathroom, I realized how dark the red neon made it. Because the space was so big, there were dark spots everywhere, and at the other end of the row of stalls, there was a guy standing guard.

"No!"

The scream was from inside the stall, and I moved toward it. I didn't run, but it was easy to see that I was on my way down to have a word.

"Back off, man." The guard put up his hand. "This is shit you don't wanna be in."

"Get off me!" A second yell from inside.

I shoved the guard back hard, and when he moved further than he thought he would, I got a wary glance. Power exhibited over others is either seductive or scary. He was scared; it was all over his face.

"Let him out… now," I ordered, my voice low, cold.

He stared holes in me, but he turned and pounded on the door. "Greg, c'mon."

I waited. Not that I couldn't have picked the guy up and thrown him across the room. I was a warder, after all, I fought and killed demons, but it would have raised eyebrows and therefore questions if I put the man through the wall. I was solid and muscular, but the guy in front of me looked like he'd taken a few too many steroids. I might have been big, but the guy in front of me was bigger.

I heard another smack, that unmistakable sound of someone being hit, then a bang, and finally a guy stepped out who was almost as large as the one standing guard. The two of them could have easily passed for defensive linemen—massive muscle-bound guys with no necks.

"You gotta lotta balls, man," he said, shoving me back as the two of them moved by me.

I slipped inside the stall, and there on the floor was an angel. Literally. The guy was dressed all in white, dusted in glitter in a Lycra T-shirt, white leather pants, and white patent leather Doc Martens. The huge, white feather-covered wings he was lying on completed his outfit.

"Shit," I groaned, sliding down the wall beside him next to the toilet. His lip was split, there were big red blotches on his right cheek and throat, and his eyes were closed. He had either fainted or he'd been knocked out. "Hey, look at me."

There was no movement.

I leaned back, squatting, and got out my cell, sending Rene a text because there was no way he would either hear his phone ring in the club or be able to talk on it.

"What…."

I looked back down at the guy as he looked up… and was swallowed in big, warm, chocolate-brown eyes framed in the longest, thickest eyelashes I had ever seen in my life. I could barely breathe.

I hated feeling like that.

His hand reached for my knee.

I cleared my throat. "You all right?"

He nodded, just staring up at me with those huge anime eyes. I instantly changed my mind about his age. Not a guy, a boy. Very young. Maybe, if you were stretching it, just barely legal. He had thick mahogany curls that fell over his ears and down the delicate slope of his neck, fragile features, and full, pink lips that were made to be devoured. He looked about five eight, five nine, built like a gymnast with a tight lean body, defined muscles, and smooth skin. He was beautiful, much too pretty to be on the floor of a bathroom.

"What's your deal?" I asked him gently.

"You saved me," he said, lifting himself up, his body very flexible, sliding over my knee and down against my abdomen.

"Wait." I tried to stall him, but my balance was upset, so I ended up sitting on the floor with him in my lap.

"Why?" he asked, straddling my hips, tightening his legs as his hands went to my shoulders. "You saved me. You have to keep me now that you saved me."

He was warm on top of me, sliding his tight little ass over my groin, wriggling to get a better angle.

"Stop."

His eyes narrowed in half, and he bit his bottom lip, pressing, pushing.

"Baby," I said, because he was so young and so sweet. Tasting him would be heaven.

He leaned forward to kiss me, and when I lifted my head he came up short, his lips on my jaw.

"Stop. Stop," I said, taking his wrists in my hands, pushing him back so he had to look at me. "We're not gonna have this scene, okay? Are you hurt?"

He shook his head slowly, his eyes locked on mine. And it was then, after years of experience looking at and talking to men and women who came into my club, that I realized how drunk he really was.

"Why can't I kiss you?"

I doubted he could even tell me his name. He was sloshed out of his gourd.

"I wanna thank you for being my hero."

Christ.

I let him go and put my hands on his face, looking at his lip, moving his head, lifting his chin so I could check his throat, his neck. His hands went to my chest as he tried to push himself forward, get closer.

"Stop."

"God, you're beautiful," he whispered, his hand slipping around the back of my neck. I could not even fathom the amount of alcohol that had to be in his system for him to think I was anywhere near hot. The beer goggles were on good and tight.

"I have never seen eyes like yours."

Uh-huh. "They're blue," I said distractedly, checking him over. His neck was already darkening where he had been choked. Christ, who roughed up a guy this pretty?

"They're like ice," he said, shifting in my lap, sliding over my groin, notching his cleft over the bulge in my jeans. "They're really scary."

And he somehow made that sound good instead of bad. But that was hardly the point. The point was that he was trying to kill me. "Stop," I told him again, realizing that to stand from the angle I was at in the cramped space, he'd have to move first. Normally I could have stood with anyone in my lap, but the maneuver was out of the question from where I was beside the toilet.

"Mal!"

"Last stall!" I yelled back, and I heard Rene's shoes clip the floor as he came closer. "Listen, that's just my buddy Rene, okay? Nobody's gonna hurt—"

"You smell great." He inhaled, leaning forward, wrapping his arms around me as his head hit my collarbone. "And you feel amazing."

His skull was hard, and it hurt for a minute when he knocked it against me.

"Do I even wanna know?" Rene asked as he appeared above me, brows furrowed as he held up his phone. "And can I just say that this is the weirdest text message you've ever sent me?"

"What?"

"I need you in the bathroom?" He arched a brow for me. "For what?"

I shot him a look as the top of a wing nearly took out my left eye. "Shit."

"Okay, Cupid," Rene said, bending down to get his hands under the boy's armpits. "Let's get up."

"Wait," he protested, but Rene was too strong.

As he was put on his feet, I got up, and Rene and I stood there staring at the wobbly angel.

His thick eyebrows had a slight arch in the middle, which gave him a mischievous, almost wicked look, definitely alluring. He reminded me of those guys in paintings from the Renaissance, fragile-looking, with porcelain skin and big eyes. Because of all that, he was easily pulling off the angel costume.

"I'm Dylan." He smiled up at me, his eyes heavy-lidded, biting his bottom lip. "What's your name?"

"Malic." I smiled down at him. "What are you doing in the bathroom, Dylan?"

The decadent look I was getting, like I was candy, was adorable, and I had to remind myself that he was much—spell it out in neon—too young for me. And drunk. God, he was so drunk.

He took a quick breath. "I'm not a rent boy, if that's what you're thinking. I work at Epic Create and Copy down off Powell."

"I know where that is, we do some of our flyers and stuff there."

"Oh yeah?" His eyes glinted in the low light. "I don't remember ever seeing you come in. I would've totally remembered."

"Totally," Rene repeated, waggling his eyebrows at me.

"What do you do there?" I asked, ignoring both his compliment and my annoying friend.

"Assistant manager, I work second shift, sometimes graveyard."

Rene turned and looked at me.

"What?"

"At least this one's not a stripper," he said sarcastically.

"That guy didn't strip at my club," I said, defending myself.

"You have a strip club?" Dylan asked, way too interested in that bit of trivia.

"Not that you can go in," I assured him. "You're too young."

"I'm nineteen," he claimed.

"Which is way too young to be at a strip club," I said, sighing. Why couldn't he be older? Tougher? Or at least sober? "You know there are laws about serving alcohol to minors, right?"

"But I could just come to see you," Dylan said excitedly. "Right?"

"Wrong." I shook my head. "If you're not a dancer, then what're you doing in that outfit?"

"You think I look like a dancer?" He belched.

"Charming," Rene groaned.

I smiled, I couldn't help it. "What's with the costume?"

Big smile. "I have a second job from now 'til"—he hiccupped—"January at that Christmas boutique in Union Square. I'm an angel."

"No," Rene teased him, "really?"

"It's seasonal," he told my friend seriously, nodding.

He really was the cutest thing.

"I wish I was a stripper, how cool would that be?"

He was much too adorable to be stripping; no one should see him take his clothes off who wasn't planning on keeping him.

"Can I come home with you?" he asked, leering at me, his laughter bubbling up out of him like champagne.

"No," I said, even though I had the urge to grab him tight and hold him… just crush him up against me; I wanted to feel his skin next to mine. "What're you doing in here?"

"Oh, see, I was at a bar with some friends, and these guys came over and asked if I wanted to hit a club with them and then meet back up later with everyone else," he explained, taking hold of the hem of my sweater. "And so I said sure but I didn't know they thought they could… whatever."

I nodded, moving back so my sweater pulled free of his hands. "Well, listen, we're on our way out, so why don't you come with us to make sure you don't get in any more trouble tonight."

"Okay." He smiled up at me, stepping in close, arms wrapping around my waist.

"Oh for crissakes," Rene groaned.

"Hey!"

I looked up, and the guys that had left earlier were back. I shoved Dylan behind me and waited.

"I don't know who the fuck you think you are, man, but—"

Rene stepped in close to me. "Back up, man, we don't want any trouble."

And even though they were both bigger and younger than Rene and me, they backed off fast. I knew that had my friend been there alone, it was doubtful they would have left. He had a nice face and kind gray eyes with laugh lines at the corners. He was the guy that stopped for people stranded on the freeway in the rain—he wasn't scaring anyone. It was me. I scared them. I made them uneasy, caused them to fear for their continued safety. I was intimidating just standing still and I knew it. Even if I wasn't holding my spatha, the sword that gladiators used to use in the coliseum, I was still spooky. I was the guy you crossed the street to avoid having to walk by.

"Cocktease," one of the men called over to Dylan.

"Get out," Rene ordered them, and they moved a little faster.

"Big scary Rene Favreau," I teased him, and he smiled wide, his hand on my back.

"Let's go eat," he said, looking at Dylan. "You got friends you can call after?"

He nodded.

"Okay, c'mon, we're not leaving you here."

Dylan looked back and forth between Rene and me. "Are you guys—"

"What?"

"Together?"

"No," he said flatly. "Now, c'mon."

Dylan nodded, but turned to look at me, checking to see what I was doing, whether I was coming or not, to see which way I was walking.

"Go, already."

The way I was being looked at, what the hell was that about?

It was fun to watch the rest of Rene's friends when he and I joined them with Dylan. His pal Sean could not take his eyes off him, offering to go get him some ice for his lip. Dylan eased closer to me, and when I looked down at him, he smiled.

"What?"

"Will you buy me a drink?"

I gave him a look. "Sure. Whaddya want? Milk?"

He scowled up at me. "Hah, funny. I'm twenty-four, ya know."

"Really." I nodded because that was interesting. He had aged five years from the bathroom to the floor.

He cleared his throat. "Yeah."

"That's funny, because you already told me you were nineteen in the bathroom."

"I did?"

I nodded.

"Shit."

I smiled down at him. An angel swearing was funny. "How'd you even get in here?"

After a minute of staring at me, he answered. "The doorman knows me, we make their drink menus and coupons and stuff."

"I see. So he let you in here even though you're underage?"

"I'm barely underage. I'll be twenty-one in two years."

I grinned lazily. "Do you even know what you're saying at this point?"

He made a noise in the back of his throat. "Who cares, I'm legal to do what's important."

"Vote?"

"No, fuck."

"Oh," I said, chuckling. "That is important."

He grinned wide. "It is right this second."

"Stop flirting; it ain't gonna work."

"Why not?"

"Just—kill your motor."

"C'mon, let's have a drink together. I have a really good fake ID."

"No." I shook my head. "I'm gonna buy you some food instead."

"And take me home after?" he asked suggestively, his eyes all over me.

"No."

"Why?"

"'Cause you're too young for me," I explained.

"How old are you?"

"Thirty."

"That's it?"

I chuckled.

"Mal," Rene said, his hand on my shoulder. "I'll meet you at Dad's Diner on Folsom. Whoever gets there first gets the table."

"Yep."

"Hey, Malic, can I ride with you and Dylan?" Sean asked me.

"Sure," I agreed, what the hell.

So I had an angel and a guy that wanted to get into the angel's very tight leather pants hanging out with me. On the street I realized that Dylan was freezing. I immediately traded him his wings for my heavy leather jacket, and he wrapped himself up.

"Thanks, Malic," he said, smiling at me.

I took them to my silver Mercedes, and once Dylan was belted in the front and Sean in back, I pulled away from the curb. As I drove the streets of San Francisco I listened to them talk, Sean telling Dylan all about his job as an associate at a law firm. He was trying to impress the younger man; I knew the hard sell when I heard it.

"Malic, what do you do?" Dylan asked, and I could feel his eyes on me.

"I own a strip club, I already told you that," I reminded him. "Now tell me where you live."

"What kind?"

"What kind of what?"

"What kind of strip club?"

"The kind women strip at."

"Only women?"

"Yes, only women."

"Oh."

"I repeat… where do you live?"

"Why?"

"Just in case your friends don't show up and I might need to take you home."

"Malic, why don't I just come home with you instead?"

"You can come home with me," Sean volunteered with a leer.

Dylan's hand went to my thigh. "I wanna go home with Malic."

"Why?" Sean asked with a chuckle, patting my shoulder. "No offense, buddy, but I'm way cuter than you."

And he was. Cute was not a word that described me. I got "scary" a lot, and "cold" and "intimidating" and "mean." I heard "mean" the most.

"Don't you think I'm cute, Dylan?" Sean asked.

He didn't answer, which caused me to turn from the road so I could see him. Big, dark, liquid-brown eyes absorbed my face.

"I'm not looking for cute," Dylan said to Sean while he stared me right in the eye. "I'm looking for a man."

I just smiled as I turned the corner.

The restaurant was small and cozy, and I went first into the booth with Dylan in the middle between Sean and me. Rene was minutes behind me, taking a seat across from me. He had just started asking me what I was going to have when I realized that the angel was trying to wedge himself onto my lap.

"What're you doing?"

"I wanna be on the other side of you," he said, rubbing his cheek against my bicep, leaning into me.

"Why?"

"'Cause I do."

I looked over him and realized that Sean was much too close, and neither of his hands was on the table. Since I didn't want my angel to be molested—it would annoy me—I agreed. I shifted back and he went over my legs, ass sliding over my crotch provocatively as he wriggled against me and dropped down on my left side. Wedged between the wall and me, he was in heaven.

"Stop," I chuckled, as his hand slid over my thigh.

I felt him shiver against me.

"What're you gonna eat?"

He focused on his menu even as he pressed himself into my side from shoulder to hip.

After the late-night, early-morning snack, Sean had to go with Rene after we ate; there was no more stalling. They had a BDSM club to hit. Dylan was all hot to go, he wanted me to tie him up, but I assured him that he was going home because he was, for the hundredth time, too young. So I was alone as I walked him toward his apartment. It turned out that all Dylan's friends were out partying, and he didn't feel like meeting up with them after all. As I escorted him home, strolling through his neighborhood, I couldn't stop smiling. Hard to remember the last time I was in Haight-Ashbury.

"Why're you smiling?" he asked me.

"I just remember coming here when I first moved to the city. I feel so old right now."

"You're only thirty."

"Yeah, but compared to you, that's ancient."

He pointed and we went down an alley, around the back of a building, upstairs, and inside. It was like a maze, and inside it was no better.

He lived with three other guys in an apartment no bigger than five-hundred square feet. One of the rooms had a bunk bed in it, and the other had a futon against one wall and a mattress and box spring on the other. The kitchen had a stove with one burner and no oven. The microwave oven sat on top of the refrigerator.

"Seriously, why are you smiling?" he asked, turning to face me.

"I just remember living like this. My first roommate and me, I think our place was smaller. Our apartment was in the Tenderloin, and the refrigerator was outside on the fire escape and we opened it through the window."

"Shit."

"Yeah, small," I said with a smile, passing him the wings I was carrying for him.

"Oh, thank you."

"Can't lose those." I smiled at him.

"Where is he now?"

"Who?"

"Your roommate?"

I squinted at him. "I dunno, that was, like, a hundred years ago."

He snorted out a laugh, ending with a giggle. The food had helped a little, but he was still really wasted. "You're not that old."

I gave him a grunt.

He cleared his throat and took a breath. "Listen, I don't want you to think bad about me."

"No, baby," I told him, "I don't think anything bad." In actuality, I had thought nothing at all. I couldn't imagine I would ever see him again after I walked out of his apartment.

"'Cause I usually don't drink or do anything but work and go to school, but tonight when I got off and my friends asked me to come out and everyone told me to forget about taking the costume all the way home, that I should just leave it on and change my... oh shit."

"Oh shit what?" I asked because how pale he got suddenly was spooky.

"I left my bag in my friend's car."

"So what? You can get it tomorrow."

"But I need my books for school on Monday, and my wallet's in there and... shit."

He looked really upset.

So I had to fix it. "Let's try calling whoever you left your bag with. Where's your phone?"

It was wedged inside his back pocket. How, because of how tight the leather pants were, I had no idea, but he passed it over and told me who to call.

I spent another half an hour on his phone while he was trying not to hyperventilate, running down some guy named Tucker until I got him and he agreed to drop the messenger bag off the following morning before he went to work at eight. He would not forget, at least he sounded like he was sober.

"There," I told him, "catastrophe averted."

"God," he moaned, "this whole night was a fuckin' disaster… until you saved me."

The long-drawn-out sigh would have made me laugh if anyone else had done it. But there was something about Dylan that made it sexy beyond words. And he was cute and hot and everything else, but there was more. Pretty only went so far, especially with me. I saw evil practically every day of my life. What was on the surface was easy to look past. With Dylan there seemed to be an innate goodness that drew me more than anything else. He was so innocent.

"What would I have done if you weren't there?"

I didn't want to think about it.

"I just—I don't want you to think that I'm some fuckin' twink out there hitting the club scene every night and going home with anybody who asks, or shit like that, 'cause that ain't me, ya know?"

I wasn't sure what I was supposed to say.

"That guy and his friend, they—they thought I was a rent boy or something."

"Okay."

"But I'm not."

"I know you're not." I knew enough of them, saw them in clubs and on the streets, most of them strung out, losing their looks to the ravages of meth and other vices, trading their bodies for money so they could in turn trade the money for drugs. I knew a hustler when I saw one. There was no haunted look in Dylan's eyes; his were big and wide and baggage-free.

"I just don't want you thinkin' I'm trash because I'm not and I really like you."

"You don't even know me."

"I know enough," he said, his breath catching as he took off my leather jacket I had given him to wear. Instead of passing it to me like I thought he would, he turned and dropped it on the threadbare couch. "You probably saved me from getting raped or at least really hurt, and then you and your friend protected me afterwards. I'd say I know a little bit about your character."

"I see."

"Would you stay?"

"What about your roommates?" I teased him, moving to step around him to get my coat.

He barred my path, his hands on my abdomen. "They're not coming home."

"Dylan," I said gently. "I'm very flattered, but we both know that you are very drunk."

"So what?"

"So you'll regret it."

"I won't," he assured me. "I swear I won't."

"Baby," I sighed, "I don't wanna hurt you, you're too sweet."

"Hurt me? How the fuck would you hurt me?"

Having sex with a man who was not my hearth could be potentially lethal; I would not put the angel in danger.

"Malic?"

"Just—"

"You won't hurt me, I promise."

It was only then that I realized that the very pretty boy trying to talk me into his bed was on his knees in front of me. When had he done that?

"Please, Malic, lemme take care of you."

But he was too young.

What if it took a week to heal the damage I inflicted? He had work, he had school. There were practical, real-life, real-world problems to consider. Older men had grown-up jobs and they could miss work, call in, or take a vacation. He was a poor, struggling college student with a job working at a copy store. If I slept with him and he needed to heal, how would he manage that and still get to class? There was no possible way he was my hearth, so was I going to drain some years off him just because I wanted to bury my cock in his sweet, tight little ass? It was beyond selfish, and even though I was, on most occasions, a self-centered prick, even I had limits. If he was over thirty, I would have thrown him down on the couch and pounded him into the floor. As it was, I took his hands in mine, moved them off my belt buckle, and brought him back up to his feet.

"Baby, this is not gonna happen."

He gave me the most wounded look I'd seen in a while. "So you would never want me, huh?"

I shook my head. "That's not what I said. You come see me when you're twenty-five, and we'll talk. If you still want me, I'm all yours."

He nodded fast before he looked up into my eyes. "I don't wanna wait." One hand went flat against my chest; the other went up the side of my face and then back into my hair.

"Again, I'm very flattered," I told him, reaching for his hands, moving them off me. "But no."

He nodded. "You have the most beautiful eyes I have ever seen. I could drown in them."

Which was a very cheesy thing to say, but he was just a baby, after all. I remembered talking like that when I was young and dramatic too. "Well, yours aren't bad either." I grinned at him, moving to the couch to grab my jacket and pulling it on before I turned around. "So you take care, Dylan, and try an' be a little more discriminating about who you say yes to in clubs, all right?"

"Could I maybe call you sometime?"

"Sure," I told him, because it was all I could do for him.

"Can I get the number?" he asked me as he pulled out his cell phone.

After I gave it to him, he stood there looking up at me, his hands shoved down into the pockets of his leather pants. He never took his eyes off me.

"Can I call you anytime, Malic? Day or night? Whenever I want?"

I nodded and squeezed his shoulder before I put my hand gently on his cheek. He was so sweet; I was worried about him.

He pushed his cheek into my hand like a cat does when you pet it, and I saw him shiver hard. I wasn't helping. I was giving out mixed signals, and that was a shitty thing to do. I just needed to go already.

"Malic." He swallowed hard. "I could just—"

"I'll see ya," I said gently, turning to leave.

"Oh."

You had to be made of much stronger stuff than flesh and bone not to respond when someone made a noise like that. Halfway between a moan and whimper, he sounded like he was going to cry. I twisted back and caught him in a tight hug, where he ended up with his face in my chest and his arms wrapped around me. He was tiny, all five nine of him, maybe a hundred and forty pounds, and as my chin rested on the top of his head, I realized that he fit really well against me.

"Listen, we don't hafta have sex to be pals, Dylan. Gimme a call, and we'll get some food, all right? Anytime you like."

He nodded, lifting his head so his face was against my throat. He let out a deep breath.

"Okay?"

"Okay, Malic."

I let him go and he stepped back from me, his eyes flicking up to mine, locking there. "So I'm gonna call you, all right?"

"Yeah."

"Malic?" he said when I got to the door.

"Yeah?"

He rushed across the room and threw himself at me so fast that I had to scramble to get ahold of him.

"Dylan," I said gently as he whimpered and twisted in my arms, pulling his shirt off, his hands suddenly on me, on my cashmere sweater, under the T-shirt underneath, tugging it up before I could grab him, pressing his smooth skin to mine.

"Malic," he breathed out, moaning as he shoved me back against the wall, his fingers fumbling on my belt buckle. "Jesus, your skin is so hot."

"Baby," I said softly, cupping his face in my hands, lifting his chin so I could look down into his eyes. "Baby, stop, this isn't going to make us close. Being friends is gonna make us close."

His eyes filled, and I sighed deeply before I grabbed him tight and hugged him again. I put my face down onto his shoulder and rubbed his back. The boy was just starved for physical contact, and though I didn't need it, he really did. I doubted that there was anyone in Dylan's life that would just hold him. Wherever home was, he maybe needed to visit and have some family time. He needed his mother to love on him a little.

"You okay?"

He nodded against my chest, but when I went to move, he clung to me. I let out a deep breath and held on. At that moment there was no one who needed me more.

The sobbing came fast, and he clutched at me and tried to breathe. I held him until he was drained and sat down with him on the couch. He wanted to sit in my lap, but I sat on the floor beside him and stroked his hair.

"Malic what?" he asked softly, his eyes heavy-lidded as he stared at me.

"Sunden. You?"

"Shaw."

I nodded. "Dylan Shaw, I got it."

He closed his eyes as I massaged his scalp.

"What kinda name is Sunden?"

"Swedish."

"I like it. I could be Dylan Sunden."

He was really just edible. It was too bad he was so completely off-limits.

"Would you sleep with me when I'm twenty?"

"No."

"Twenty-one?"

I chuckled. "No."

"But for sure when I'm twenty-five?"

"Yes," I said, placating him.

"I can't believe you're just sitting here with me, not wanting anything."

I leaned over close to him. "Don't be so jaded; you're too young."

He shivered, and I couldn't resist kissing his temple.

"Please don't go."

"Just rest."

"I'm gonna call you, don't think I won't," he promised, reaching out to take hold of my jacket. "I will have you, Malic."

I smiled as his eyes drifted closed. When I left, he was sleeping. I hoped his hangover wouldn't be too horrible.

# II

I COULD tell just from how the man was looking at me that he was confused about why I was there.

"What exactly is it that you do, Mr. Sunden?"

I turned my head, looking for Detective Tanaka, not in the mood to talk as I was still raw physically, mentally, and emotionally from fighting earlier in the day. I had gone alone to battle a demon possessing a lovely coed, and it had gone bad like it always did when I was alone and never did when I had backup. Everything always went perfectly when there was someone else there to watch. But because I was by myself, I ended up exorcising the demon, yes, but not without getting sliced to ribbons in the process. It would easily take a week to heal the damage. And then I got the call from Tanaka.

I was really hoping that I would not need to call for help now, because then I'd be in trouble. If one of my fellow warders saw me and told Jael, I doubted that I would be any use to anyone for a month. It would take that long to convince my sentinel to let me out of my own house.

"Hello?" The man snapped his fingers in front of my face.

"Sir," Detective Tanaka barked, walking up beside me, putting out a hand to move the man back. "What's going on, Mr. Everett?"

"I want to know who this man is," he said, his voice rising as he pointed a finger at me. "I want to know why he's in my house."

"He's a specialist in this area," Detective Tanaka's partner, Detective Curtis, said as he, too, joined us, moving Mr. Everett back away even further. "He finds people."

"Oh." His voice broke suddenly, and I looked up. There was a hand thrust out to me, and my eyes settled on the father of the missing girl. "I'm sorry—if you can help me find my baby... I'm sorry, Mr. Sunden.... Jason Everett."

I took the offered hand. "Call me Mal."

He forced a smile, nodding. "Please, Mal, come take a look around my house."

It was so much easier when they invited me than when Tanaka and Curtis had to lie to get me in places.

A year ago Detective James Tanaka had found strange symbols at a murder site. When he had gone to the county museum to research what he thought were Celtic runes, the assistant curator of antiquities, Joshua Black, had sent him to see me at my club. He and his partner had been way more than hesitant; I owned a strip club, a high profile, lucrative strip club, and they were uncomfortable being there.

Unease turned to flat-out disbelief when I informed them that they were not looking at symbols but demonic writing. Tanaka and his partner, Detective Curtis, had both thought I was nuts. But a week later when we discovered the lair of a demon together, along with Marcus, a fellow warder, they both became converts. The four of us saved a kidnapped mother of three and in the process sent the creature back to hell. Since then, if whatever they were looking at seemed odd to them, I got a call.

I was at the home of Jason and Kellie Everett because their six-year-old daughter had been taken from a crowded room. The lights had flickered momentarily, and when the power came back on, Sophie Everett was gone, having disappeared in plain sight. It made no sense, and after finding no trace of the little girl anywhere—no tracks, no forensic evidence, nothing—they called me.

Walking into the house, I was overwhelmed by the too sweet smell of flowers.

"Christ," I groaned, turning to look at Tanaka. "Don't you smell that?"

"What?" he asked me seriously, his dark black eyes squinting at me, broad shoulders hunched like they did when he was nervous.

"The flowers," I told him, smelling magnolia and honeysuckle and gardenia. Normally I liked the smell, but not under the circumstances. The scent was meant to mask other, harder, scents.

"So I told Mr. Everett you were with the FBI," Curtis said as he joined us, "since I didn't think he'd be too excited to learn that you own Romeo's Basement."

"Probably not," I sighed, walking into the girl's bedroom, having toured the rest of the house with Tanaka. I noticed her stuffed animals instantly. "Look."

Both men turned to look where I was pointing.

"What?" Tanaka asked me, annoyed, unsure what he was supposed to be seeing.

I crossed to the bed, looked at the toys, and then turned, following their blind gazes to the closet door. "She was afraid of whatever's in here. All her animals are watching it for her."

"Please, all kids are freaked out about their closets."

"Not like that," I assured him, pointing at the animals. "Can't you see this?"

"I don't get why the animals are important," Curtis told me.

"A child believes in the power of their totems," I told him, picking up a stuffed German shepherd. "The dog is not a dog but a friend ready to rip out the throat of whomever or whatever would come to hurt her. The animals are like a ring of protection; the demon wouldn't have been able to touch her on the bed."

"You're serious," Detective Curtis said, picking up a fluffy black-and-white wolf with big blue glass eyes. "This is scary?"

"Not to you, but to the little girl he would be her protective spirit."

He grunted, dropped the wolf back on the bed, and tipped his head at the closet. "I'm gonna tell you again that all little kids get creeped out by their closets."

"And again I say, not like that," I disagreed, walking to the door and putting my hand flat on the wood. "She was afraid of whatever is in there." The touch sent a sliver of ice straight to my stomach. It felt like when you drink cold water when you're hungry and you can feel it go all the way down, illustrating how empty you are. "Shit," I groaned, taking a step back.

"What?"

"I'm pretty sure I found your missing girl. I just hope she's in one piece when I go in there." I took a breath.

"In where?" Curtis asked me. "In the closet?"

"It's not a closet."

"What is it?"

"A passage."

"Like in *Poltergeist?*"

I looked over my shoulder at him. "Movie references?"

"I'm just tryin' to get a handle on this shit, Malic. I still have trouble processing half the shit I've seen."

I understood that. "Okay, listen, I'm gonna go in here, but you guys need to find the person in this house who is trafficking with a demon. They're doing it in trade for something... money, power, love... I dunno, but the demon was called and allowed to take the child, which is why we have a doorway. You allow it in, you have a passage to its lair; that's how it works."

"Okay, I'll hafta take your word for that."

The look I was getting, the trust, I appreciated it.

"And so what?" Curtis asked me. "Do we pull our guns and go in there with—"

I shook my head, reached over my left shoulder, and pulled the spatha, the straight sword with a long point that I needed for fighting in close quarters, from the sheath strapped to my back. Under my heavy leather jacket, it had gone unnoticed when I walked in. I had a greatsword, or Zweihänder, that I used as well, but I would have never smuggled it into the house. That sword was for when stealth was not important.

Tanaka smiled at me. "That is some cool shit, man."

The gladiator sword never failed to impress once it was drawn.

"I wouldn't want to mess with you."

But I was being stupid and I knew it. It was one thing to fight a lower-class demon alone, but whatever had the little girl... and I was hurt from earlier and I was going into its lair... but I didn't have time to wait. She didn't have time for me *to* wait. I opened the door.

"Hold on," Detective Tanaka said, hand on my shoulder. "Mal, we're not gonna let you go in there by—"

"You can't come with me," I assured him. "You're not strong enough. But while I'm gone, find the person responsible for trafficking with the demon. It has permission to be here, a deal was made…. I just need to see if I can reason with it or if I have to kill it."

"Of course you kill it," Tanaka said, his grip on my shoulder tightening. "Don't be stupid."

"Tell everyone in the house that you found a summoning stone."

"What the hell is that?" Curtis squinted at me.

"My guess would be it's what you use to call a demon." Tanaka gave him a look that spoke volumes about his brain process.

I watched Curtis scowl at his partner.

"Just be careful," I said, squeezing the man's shoulder. "Whoever called the demon will want to protect that secret. Watch your backs."

"Same to you," Curtis told me. "Be careful."

It was easier said than done. The second I stepped into the closet and closed the door behind me, I saw stairs, saw a light flickering in the distance, and heard words chanted in Latin. I heard the whimpering as well, that was not to be missed. Taking a breath—this was what I did, after all, what I had been chosen to do—I rushed forward, taking the stairs by twos.

The descent was endless; my hands on the wall were slimy with wet mold, sliding on the goo, my feet stumbling occasionally because the stairs were ancient and worn. I was no longer in the house in Marin, and I knew if Curtis or Tanaka opened the door now, I would be gone, having completely disappeared to where they could neither see nor hear me. If they opened the door, all they would see would be whatever was normally in the closet: clothes, shoes, toys. When I heard the crying, I sped up.

I found Sophie alone in a huge hall. The little girl was in a daze, I could tell that as soon as I saw her. I couldn't see what she was looking at for a minute, but then I concentrated, took a breath, and the empty walls filled in with her memory. I was looking at the night she had been abducted. She was walking through the dining room in her home, but where there should have been noise, party sounds, there was only silence. No clinking glasses, no music, no low buzz of conversation, no one calling her name. Everyone but her was frozen, people like statues poised to speak to one another with no one moving. She looked around the room and saw men and women silent and still, suspended in time. All was stopped but for her and now me.

"Sophie?"

The sound of her name being called out startled the child, and she whirled around to face me.

"Hi," I said softly, squatting down, holding out my hand for her to take. "How're you?"

Her face scrunched up, dirty, wet with tears, she was so scared, so exhausted, and there were scratches where the demon's claws had gotten her without even trying. Her party dress was in disarray with drooping bows, soiled skirt, and ripped lace. She was terrified and I was tall. Even down on the ground, I was much bigger than she was, and I was armed. I wished I had remembered to bring her stuffed wolf. But I had… what did I have I could give her?

I searched the pockets of my jeans and my leather jacket and… a feather. I had one of the white feathers from Dylan Shaw's costume on me. I had found it in the passenger seat of my car and shoved it, for whatever reason, in my pocket.

"Look." I held it up for her. "You know what this is?"

Quick shake of her head, short red curls falling into her dirt-smudged face, huge baby-blue eyes absorbing me, wanting so much to trust and so terrified to at the same time. It was heartbreaking.

"It's an angel feather," I assured her. "I got it from an angel."

She was unsure.

"I promise. He's an angel."

"What's the angel's name?"

"Dylan."

She took a quivering breath. "Dylan's a funny name for an angel."

"I think it's a really good name, actually."

Her eyes were studying everything about me, not missing a thing.

"You want it?"

Quick nod.

"Is it okay if I bring it to you?"

Second nod.

I rose to my full height, which was not short on a good day but to her had to be huge. I was careful with how I moved, and when I was a few feet from her, I knelt down and held out the three-inch white feather dusted with gold glitter. Why in the world I had held onto it was beyond me, but it was perfect that I had.

She took the feather and stayed close, which was a start.

I made a face. "It stinks in here, huh?"

She nodded.

"Maybe we should go?" I asked, tilting my head and smiling at her.

She took a big breath, like she was jumping into the deep end of a pool, and then flung herself at me. Trust was just like that; you had to take the leap of faith.

"Oh, there's my girl." I smiled, holding her, rubbing her back as she trembled against me. "My name's Malic, but you can call me Mal."

"Mal," she repeated, clutching me with her skinny arms. "Did you bring that sword to fight the scary man?"

She meant the spatha. "Yes."

"He wants me to stay here, and I think he wants to eat me."

I grunted. "He's not going to eat you. I won't let him."

"Promise?"

I moved the spatha so she could really see it, how long the blade was. "I promise."

She nodded fast.

I stood up with her tucked against me. "Okay, cute stuff, let's take a look at this memory of yours and see who took ya."

Small whimper.

"Oh no, sweetheart," I sighed, pointing. "See, it's a dream, yeah? This is all over. It's all happened already. None of this can hurt you; we're just looking at it together, me and you."

"Okay."

She didn't question me. She was six, so her mind could accept a hell of a lot more than an adult could. I said it was a dream and she calmed because that meant it wasn't real, none of it, and *that* made sense. She could accept the Twilight Zone; it was being away from Mommy and Daddy that was freaking her out.

I walked slowly, and the longer we strolled, the calmer she got. We moved in between and around people frozen in action, some looking as though they should have fallen over, so incapable of holding the pose they now held. Out of the corner of my eye, I saw something flutter, move, shift, but instead of stopping I increased my stride, feeling the weight of my weapon in my hand.

"There, see?" I pointed, and Sophie was suddenly looking at herself.

We came to a stop, both of us staring.

"Look." I pointed again, and the little girl's eyes went to where I guided them.

She saw, just as I did, the woman lifting her up into the arms of what looked like a huge, hooded bird. It was like a vulture cloaked in a cowl, and it had talons, which was how Sophie's chubby little arms got scratched up.

"Watch."

Sophie stared as the creature slowly flew, frame by frame, like a movie we were fast-forwarding through. The dark wings flapped and the robe blew back, as though air were rushing by. Sophie's hands were over her face and she was fighting, twisting, sobbing, absolutely terrified because the woman had given her to the creature.

"Who was the lady, honey?"

"My nanny, Nanny Lisa."

Nanny Lisa was going to jail if I didn't get to her first.

"She wants to kiss Daddy, but he said no. He said she had to go away."

And that fast I understood the whole scenario. The nanny wanted the husband, and he, in turn, wanted only his wife and child. So she was on her way to being fired for hitting on him when she came up with the plan to get rid of the little girl and make the demon give her the man of her dreams. And even as I wondered how regular people even knew how to traffic with demons, I also thought, what a waste. Why hadn't the nanny just gone to one of those online dating services and gotten hooked up that way? Why did some people feel that they could just take what they wanted from others? Even I wasn't that selfish.

I continued to watch, and Sophie with me, as the demon flew her up the stairs to her bedroom and through the open door of her closet and in and down into the dark.

"I don't like it here."

It was the understatement of her young life. "No, me neither," I agreed, speeding up, back toward the stairs.

"Where do you run to, warder?" The eerie singsong tone, drawing out the word "warder" for an endless moment, made the hair on the back of my neck stand up. Just from the sound of its voice I knew what it was.

I hated all demons, but blood demons, the ones who centuries ago had given rise to vampire legends, those I simply reviled. The little girl knew what she was talking about—he wanted to eat her and drink her blood, but he wouldn't be satisfied with just that. He had to scare her first and hurt her. He would tear her limb from limb.

"I was waiting for the one who gave the child to me. I have to pay her too."

Apparently the nanny was not getting her reward; she was going to be a snack before the demon tore up the little girl. You had to be very careful when bargaining with demons; there was always fine print.

I tucked the little girl's head down into my shoulder. I had more history with demons than the nanny did. I didn't trust him. I had no idea if he was alone or not; they usually were, but there was no way to tell. If he was alone, I could put Sophie down and have her close her eyes, stick her fingers in her ears and sing "Jingle Bells" for me at the top of her lungs. But I couldn't be certain, so I needed her safe in my arms. There was no way he was getting her from me. None.

The demon went through its first shift, transforming into a monster; claws grew where hands should have been, and enormous vacant eyes with a jaw that was now hawklike, with a jutting beak filled with razor-sharp teeth that snapped open and shut. What looked like drool was actually blood that dripped into a small puddle at the creature's feet. It was disgusting, and even though Sophie could hear it, she also heard my whispered words of comfort and felt my hand on her head. She was holding onto me tight.

"I have her now," I told the demon, "and I'm going."

"I think not, warder." He smiled slowly, coming closer. "I think I will let the child see the blood run all out of you. I want you to remain here with me for a bit, and we shall see all there is to see. You need to find if there is an end to suffering. Do you imagine an end?"

If the demon got his hands on me, there would be no end. Caught here, kept here, undead in this limbo, I would learn what true terror was. I glanced around his hall and saw sights that were familiar. He was powerful, much more so than I had thought when I came down to bring Sophie home—he could kill me.

There was a bridge at one end of the huge room that ended at a wall, suspended in air as it touched the stone; it showed nothing unless stepped upon. It revealed where you belonged, where your acts on this plane said you deserved, either leading to a life after death of reward, repentance, or reincarnation, a bridge of renewal, offering comfort or... hell. It was a place, for all intents and purposes, that was hell, a realm of fear and fire and punishment. If I wanted to get out, I had to either roll the dice and cross over to another domain or go back up the damn stairs the way I had come. Since I was not ready to be judged on the bridge, and because both me and Sophie had a lot more living to do, I took a step back and slowly brought the spatha around in front of me.

"What do you hope to do with that, warder?"

"This child is mine, not yours," I said defiantly. "She's bound to this world, not yours."

"No," he said evenly, "you will stay, for her life ebbs even as you defy me. Soon she will be done, and you will have no way to return. As long as she lives, you can journey back; if she dies, so goes your passage."

"Her life is not ebbing," I assured him, "and I'm not a demon; I don't need to be tethered by a living soul promised as sacrifice to move between the planes. I'm a warder, and I have dominion over you."

He took a hissing breath and stepped away from me, but as he did, he yelled Sophie's name.

Her head snapped up, and she turned.

"No!" I ordered her, grabbing her head, shoving it back down fast. "You keep your eyes closed!"

I did not let her see the demon's true form.

He threw back the cowl he wore to reveal a face with empty sockets where his eyes should have been. The face was withered and drawn, gray and ashen. He looked as though he was decaying, and I winced with both revulsion and pity. The demon was in pain, it had to be, and I wondered, even in that second, what it had started out life as. Everything had a start; it didn't just blink into existence. What had it been?

"Warder!" His voice, when he spoke to me, was booming even as it came out of a rotting, decomposing face. "You will die because you are alone!"

I was thrown back hard into the wall, and for a moment, I couldn't breathe. My spine felt like it had shattered.

Sophie was crying hysterically as I clutched at the rock wall, trying hard to keep my balance, shielding her, having no choice but to drop either my weapon or her. I would not lose her, and I had to hold onto the stones at my back to remain vertical. I was scared for a second, because he was advancing and I was unarmed, before I felt the rush of cool air blow through the hall.

"Thank God," I groaned, taking a quivering breath. If I hadn't been sliced up earlier in the day, if I was at full strength, I would have been okay. It would have been hard, just his presence was draining me, but if I was healthy, I could have held him off long enough to make a run for it. Hurt, I was in trouble, and I had been on my way to being scared. But now I didn't have to be, because now I had help.

The thick fog rolled toward us. "I'm not alone," I yelled back.

"No!" The demon roared, advancing on me, raising a hand to strike me.

A low, menacing growl came from the direction of the fog before it was suddenly all around us, enveloping the demon, the child, and me. I released a deep breath even as I watched the demon shrink back away from me.

"Leith," I breathed out. "She has a wolf; it's black and white and it has blue eyes like hers."

"I can't," came the disembodied voice. "This is her house."

"No," I corrected him, "it's not. Look again. Change and look. You followed me and so you can't see it yet. Wait a second."

It didn't take even that long. My fellow warder was not as fast or strong a fighter as me or Ryan or Jackson, but he was more observant than all the rest of us put together—smoke and mirrors never tricked him.

"I see it now," he said, and all at once I had a huge wolf beside me, against my hip.

In the real world, in San Francisco, California, my fellow warders and I were guys that fought with supernatural creatures with our swords and fists. On alternate planes, in limbo, in between the living and the demons, we had other powers. Leith Haas, who was better at shifting than the rest of us, Leith who used his mind more than his sword, was at his strongest here.

I could never see myself as fog or a wolf or anything but me. I didn't have the breadth of imagination. I was thankful that Leith did. He was everything I'd hoped he could be.

"Oh," Sophie cried, her eyes huge, the excited sound of her sucked-in breath making the demon cringe. She wasn't scared, she was happy, and demons had a rough time processing joy.

I let her slide down my side, and she tripped forward against Leith. He looked like she knew her stuffed wolf did in real life. He was huge. His head, his paws, the tulip-shaped ears, and his teeth. His teeth looked downright vicious. But not to Sophie. To Sophie he was salvation and safety and just… hers. She saw a wolf; she believed it, had the absolute faith that only a child can have. Her face was buried in his neck, her little hands in his thick fur, and she squealed out her happiness. I was a good protector; he was better.

"Take her," I ordered him, bending as the smell assailed me, the demon's breath as he came at me.

I caught him by the throat, holding him off, shoving him away.

He drew back, gathering his strength for the next charge. I lifted the little girl.

"Hold tight," I ordered, barking out my command.

"No," she wailed suddenly, and I realized what a dear sweet girl I had on my hands. With her own safety imminent, she didn't want to go without me.

"Go!"

She clung, and Leith flew forward to the stairs. He wasn't there for me, he was there for her, and that was all right. If I was done, it would be okay because she wasn't.

Knives drilled hard into my chest, and I was slammed back into the rock wall, sharp edges punching through my jacket, sweater, and T-shirt.

"You die now, warder, and you will bide with me!"

Not knives, *talons*, his long, sharp, barbed claws driven deep, so deep into my flesh and muscle. All I could process was heat and pain.

My girl was gone, so I could use my barroom vocabulary. "Fuck you!" I yelled back, wrapping both hands around his throat and choking him hard.

He yanked free and the barbs tore out pieces of me. I felt the rush of fluid, blood, but I dove down for my weapon, grabbed it, and rolled to my feet. I twisted around, the spatha extending out in front of me the way I had been taught.

"I am stronger than you, warder; you will not see another day. I will take you to hell with me."

And that was okay, but then I saw the stupid feather. Sophie must have dropped it when she fell in love with her wolf all big as life in front of her. The white angel feather was lying in the dirt, trampled but still in one piece.

"Shit," I groaned, realizing that for whatever idiotic reason, I could not get the stupid boy... kid... man, barely man, definitely kid, out of my head. I really wanted to see those big dark-brown eyes again.

When the demon bashed me into the wall the second time, I felt my skin open, my bones crush, and everything get soggy. It was terrifying. But his howl of pain, in the same moment, comforted me.

In his haste to eviscerate me, he had missed that I had changed my grip on the spatha and driven it up like a dagger.

I ground the point in deep, and since demons had hearts just like everything else, me piercing it and shredding it left him just as dead and bleeding at my feet as anything else.

I collapsed beside him, our blood mingling in the dirt. I couldn't even make it to the bridge to see where I was off to, heaven or hell.

"You fuck," I was growled at, "don't you dare die."

I opened one eye to see Leith standing above me. "Funny," I gasped. I coughed, and it hurt. "With a name like Leith—shouldn't you be, like, Irish or Celtic or something?"

He scowled at me as he knelt down beside me. "Shit, how am I gonna move… shit."

I outweighed him by at least fifty pounds. "I betcha wish you were bigger right about now, huh?"

With a name like Leith, you expected some highland laird. What you got was a surfer from Malibu, Zuma, who had actually had to live on the beach for a time in his life. Now he was a welder during the day, an artist in his free time whose media of choice was wrought iron, and at night…at night he did what all the rest of us did: he hunted demons. He was amazing and he didn't know it, and I liked that about him best of all. I was also a fan of the wavy, sun-bleached mass of thick blond hair that fell to the middle of his back. It matched the blue-green eyes, his dark eyebrows, and pale lashes. He had freckles across his nose that made me think he was younger than thirty and a scar beside his right eye that gave him character. Leith was closest to me after Marcus, so if anyone had to watch me die, this man with his quiet strength would do.

I let out a deep breath, and my eyes fluttered shut. I was falling asleep.

"No. No," he barked at me. "Open your eyes."

"In a second."

"Mal—"

"Shhh," I soothed him. "Be still."

"I don't know if… oh, no, I can." He was talking to himself and I found that comforting. "You're such an idiot, if no one can go with you, you don't go, you stupid fuck."

He was talking about earlier.

"Okay," I said, hoping to shut him up.

The sound of thunder, and I let out a deep breath. Warders, could, in emergencies, travel in funnels of wind, wormholes, where we basically moved from one place to the other, following the path of other warders. It felt like falling with a tornado whirling around you. I hated it: the cold, the icy rain that came with it, how loud it was. I tried never to use it, and now Leith was moving me that way. It was how he had followed me, but he wasn't sure he could use it again; it took a lot of energy to wield. But he apparently had it in him for one more shot. Not that I would be awake for all of it.

"Malic!"

Everything went dark.


"LOOK at me."

The tone, the father tone… fuck.

"Shit," I growled, opening my eyes just enough to see my sentinel, my leader, Jael Ezran, hovering above me. The man was huge, easily seven feet tall and built like a tank. He was massive, and he looked even bigger as he squatted down beside me, leaning in, looking at me, hand on my chest. I was stretched out on a bed in his enormous guest bedroom that had been decorated in early Middle Ages chic. You would have thought, glancing around, that I was in a castle in Scotland or something, but I was actually at his mansion in Sausalito. I hated his big gloomy house and had never, ever, wanted to be there, especially wounded and unable to leave.

"When you're well, I'm going to beat you," he assured me.

I let out a breath, my body starting to shake. I was really cold.

"Only you, Malic, have no regard for your own safety. If you had a hearth, you would."

The man was consistent. He never missed an opportunity to tell me that I needed to find a hearth, someone to love, to return to at the end of the day, to make a home for me, to be my anchor. With

Ryan having found his hearth, I was the only one who didn't have one, and apparently that fact was grating on my sentinel.

"You need a home."

But I didn't. Home equaled jail. What I said was, "Okay," because I hurt too much to argue with him.

"Leith spoke to the detectives," he soothed me, hands open above me, fingers splayed out, tensed.

"Wait," I pleaded, because it was going to hurt like a son of a bitch. When Jael knit you back together, it always did. Finesse was not the man's strong suit.

"No," Leith rasped, pacing behind him, "do it now. He's way too pale even for him."

I would have flipped him off if I'd had the strength. I was Swedish, first generation born in the United States; my parents moved from Stockholm three months before I arrived. It didn't change anything that we lived in California; I was never going to be the guy that tanned. "Sophie...."

"Is fine. She told her parents about her wolf protecting her, and they feel better thinking that she missed the real horror and focused on the dream part. Her nanny was arrested for kidnapping and giving the child to others to hold hostage for ransom."

"That's what—" I gasped because it felt like something rolled inside me and broke, down deep. "Leith told them?"

"Yes," he said, and I saw the faint glow around his hands.

"No, oh God," I muttered. "Jael, can't you just—"

"Everything's fine, Malic: the girl is safe, the demon is dead, the detectives are appeased, and the family thinks you're a hero. Now shut up and let me heal you!"

But the bone knitting and everything else hurt so goddamn bad, and it was like jumping off something high: there was nowhere to go but down.

Leith tried to take my hand, but I pulled free, annoyed. I didn't need him to comfort me like a child.

"Stubborn asshole," my friend Marcus Roth, Marot, said as he charged across the room and dropped to his knees beside the bed I was laid out on. Dark sepia eyes locked on mine, and he grabbed my hand and held tight. It looked cool, his dark-brown fingers wrapped around my pale ones. When we patrolled together, people always stared at the picture we made: the tall, dark, African-American man and his blond-haired, blue-eyed... friend? Lover? No one had the balls to ask since he was big and so was I, both of us looking dangerous and combative. He, at least, was handsome. "Malic!"

I lifted my eyes back to his, realizing I'd closed them. The warmth of his hand was welcome.

"We're gonna do this now 'cause your lips are blue and you're turning a very unattractive shade of gray."

My groan of protest was loud. "I just needed to know everyone was okay."

"Fine, now don't be such a prick and hold Leith's hand. You know he's fighting with his hearth, so give him a break."

"Fuck you, Marcus," Leith growled.

It was the last thing I heard before Jael yelled at everyone to shut the hell up and he leaned over and put his hands on me.

It felt like he poured lava into my chest.

I wanted to die.

# III

"He's here again."

I looked up from the laptop on my desk where I was trying to make my brain click around the spreadsheet that my accountant, Frank Sullivan, Jackson's hearth, had sent me. "What?" I asked the woman standing in the doorway.

"I'm sorry, what word didn't you understand?"

I groaned loudly. It was too late in the day—technically night—for her to be this snarky.

"Mal?"

Claudia Duran, the woman I trusted more than any other in the world, my manager, my right hand, was standing there, hands on hips, looking at me and scowling. "I don't know what we're talking about."

She tilted her head like women do when they know you're a dumb-ass but you're too stubborn to ask for help. "Would you like me to help you read the—"

"No," I barked at her. "I can figure it out. I've looked at a spreadsheet before, I'm just—who's here?"

"The"—she waved her hand dismissively—"boy."

"What boy?"

"The boy, the boy," she said, exasperated with me, "and Christ, it must be nice to be you, huh? Just take off whenever you frickin' feel like it?"

I had been healing. Muscle, bone, skin, all of it knitting back together had taken me seven days on my back. A normal man would have been dead. A normal man would not have lived through the first demon attack; the second was not even an option. As it was, Marcus and Leith had taken turns visiting me, bringing me supplies, as well as Ryan and his hearth, Julian Nash. I had to admit that Ryan cooked like a dream and Julian reading to me had been, well, really nice. The man had a deep, sultry voice that had been more soothing than I cared to admit. No one had read to me since both my parents died in a car accident when I was ten. I'd forgotten how much I liked it. Not that I told him or thanked him. I'd done a lot of grunting. Ryan had just smiled at me as he sat at my bedside.

"You can go," I had snapped at him, tipping my head at Julian. "You can leave him; I'll keep him."

I'd gotten an indulgent look. Ryan was keeping his hearth— that was plain to see. Watching Ryan Dean stare at the man he gave his heart to had actually made me wonder what I was maybe, possibly, missing. The way Ryan had to touch him, brush against him, the way Julian pushed Ryan's mane of hair back from his face to see his lover's eyes…. It was nice to see men touch each other gently, tenderly, and not just with heat and need and power.

"Hello."

I looked up at her, realized I had kept her waiting. "I'm the boss and I own this place, so, yeah, it's nice to be me, you giant pain in my ass."

She blew a long piece of hair off her forehead, and we both laughed. She didn't buy my bluster at all, never had, which was why when I did my thing—walked through the place and slammed doors so hard the walls vibrated—she was usually right behind me giving me hell. And then I'd have to poke my head out of my office and yell out the apology to my staff. They were all scared shitless of me except her. She kept me human.

"Shit," I said, grinning at her, "what boy?"

"I dunno, Mal, some guy—looks like he just graduated from high school, he's been haunting the front door for, like, two weeks, and Dante's like, fuck no, you ain't gettin' in no matter how great that fake ID is, but he totally slipped past Pete tonight and now he's at the bar."

I squinted at her. "Throw him out."

Her face scrunched up. "Yeah, but Mal, he's, like, the cutest thing I ever saw… he's got those big brown puppy-dog eyes and curly brown hair and… how can you be such a heartless bastard?"

I was at a complete loss. "What're you talking about?"

"Mal." She started talking with her hands, all animated and restless, dark eyes firing, the candy-apple-red lipstick glaring with the light behind her. "He just wants to see you. Just fuckin' see him already."

"Already?"

"Honey, he's been here every single damn night for two weeks. He stands by the door, in the cold, in that denim piece of crap coat he's got, in those ripped jeans that leave nothing to the imagination, and he waits... for you... and I think somewhere along the line he stopped eating."

I squinted at her.

"Sometimes he doesn't show because he has to work early and other times he hangs out until around ten because he has to work the graveyard shift at—"

"How do you know all this?"

"Because he told me," she said, annoyed, enunciating the words for me. "Like I said, he's been out there haunting the front door for a while."

"You were screwing with me." I squinted at her. "You knew who you were talking about the whole time."

"Yeah," she agreed, "and so do you."

Of course I knew. "And?" I asked her, shutting off my laptop, closing it up before I stood.

"And." She widened her eyes like I was the most irritating man on the planet. "What are you going to do about Dylan?"

"What do you want me to—"

"Malic Sunden!"

"Oh for crissakes," I grumbled, striding toward her.

"Poor little thing. He saw you leave with that guy last night and he was so sad."

I needed the release and I could tell that Mario... something... I either didn't get his last name or had forgotten it already, who knew? What I did know was that the man was not my hearth, but since I would have traded my soul to get laid, it hardly mattered. So I had gone home with the guy who had come with his buddies to my fine establishment. He had ditched the other members of the bridal party because he needed my dick up his ass.

"Come home with me," he had offered, leaning over to press a kiss to the side of my neck. "You can fuck me for hours."

Pushy bottom was what he was, but true to his word, I had fucked his brains out. And then slunk away the second he fell asleep, seeing in the fading light the streaks of white in his dark hair, his drawn, pinched face, and the lines around his mouth. I had taken maybe five years off him that would heal in a couple of days. He would think he had the flu; he would stay home because he felt like shit and looked like shit, and then, by the weekend, he would feel better again, he would look like himself and would return to his quest for the perfect top. I would be nothing but a memory.

"Claud—"

"I saw him, Mal; I watched his little face crumple all up when you put that guy in your car."

"Did you just say 'little face'?" I stopped from brushing by her to peer down into her pretty topaz eyes. "Are you kidding me with this?"

"Oh, c'mon, Mal," she said, hand on my chest. "He's adorable and so sweet... why not take the kid home and make a meal of him."

"You have lost your mind," I assured her, drawing out the word *lost* in case she missed it. "He's a baby. You know they imprint on the first adult they see."

She chuckled deeply before she suddenly caught her breath.

"What's wrong?"

She pressed her heavily coated lips together and took hold of the lapel of my suit jacket. "I just... you... thank you for opening up the 401(k) plans for all of us, Mal. I got my packet in the mail yesterday, and you're going to match up to ten percent of what I put in."

"It's not a big—"

"It is," she said flatly. "It's a huge deal, Mal, and way more than generous. Everybody, your entire devoted staff, we all got them and we all appreciate it."

"I just don't want you guys to think you're missing out if you work for me."

"No, dear, we're not missing out on anything. None of us think that."

I reached out and grabbed her, yanking her into my arms and holding her tight. Instantly she wrapped herself around me. I was always surprised at how fast women could mold their bodies to mine, and the deep purr of contentment that accompanied it.

"Just because I'm an ass does not mean that I don't intend to take care of you guys." They all had great health insurance that included dental and vision, and now they had 401(k) as well. "This is me."

"I know," she said, trembling, burying her face in my shoulder. "For a self-professed dick, you're an awfully nice guy."

I growled, shoved her off me, and swatted her hands away when she tried to hug me again before starting down the hall.

"I wish."

I stopped and looked back at her. "You wish what?"

"That people could see you the way I do."

I grunted.

"All they see is six feet four inches of scary-ass Swede, but that's not really you."

*The hell it isn't,* I thought as I walked away from her.

At the end of the hall, I opened the door and was instantly assaulted by driving techno music. There were men and women dancing at my club where you could drink, dance, and watch some of the most beautiful women in the city strip. I liked it; it was upscale, clean, drug-free, gangster-free, urban-yuppie goodness. No one messed with my club because no one wanted to tangle with me. As I made my way to the bar, I saw my angel standing at the end. Claudia was right, he looked like crap.

Pushing through the press of bodies, I made my way to him. You would have thought I was the Second Coming or something. Who got looked at like that?

"Hey," I greeted him, pushing up to the bar, wedging in between him and the guy beside him. "You can't be in here."

He reached out for the lapel of my suit jacket, fingering the material. "You look nice."

What I looked was normal. I always did.

I was tall, so that was why people saw me at all. But my eyes were set deep, the color too bright for my somber face, my nose had been broken many times, my eyebrows sat too close above my eyes, and I looked like I was tired most of the time. I kept my white-blond hair cut short because it was coarse and stuck up otherwise, and the stubble that ran over my jaw and upper lip was, for whatever reason, darker than my hair. The pieces of me, either pulled apart or lumped all together, did not add up to beauty. The boy in front of me did not have that problem.

Even with strippers in the room, he was still the most heavenly creature there. His enormous eyes, all innocent and pleading, the lush kissable lips and skin… God, his skin… he was just delectable. I needed to run.

"Go home," I snarled at him, turning away.

The whimper froze me.

Fuck.

"Malic," he said, slipping in front of me, hands on my chest, fisting the dress shirt I was wearing under the jacket. "Is it 'cause I'm poor and you think I want your money?"

"What?"

"I'm a starving college student," he said, stepping in closer, his head tilted back to look up at me, licking his lips. "Is that why you won't take me out?"

"Whaddya want?" I asked flatly, my eyes locked on his mouth. He really was the sweetest thing I had ever seen.

"Well, what I'd like is for you to take me to dinner and then ask to take me home with you," he said, his eyes all over my face.

"You need money?" I asked him instead.

It was strange, but beyond all his surface pretty was a warmth that just flowed off him. Just looking at him was soothing. He felt like home, and I had no idea why.

"Malic?"

I bristled with my need, the want in me. I hated it. "Just tell me what the fuck you want."

He shook his head. "I told you what I want; I need to go out with you."

I searched his face.

"For crissakes, Malic, I work for a living, I don't need money, and yeah, I'm a little short right now 'cause I just paid tuition, but I have enough to eat and—"

"Tell me what I can do for you."

He squinted at me. "I did, you're just not listening."

"Dyl—"

"Malic." His sigh was annoyed and I liked that, him being irritated at me. It was endearing. "I go to school during the day and I work the second shift, four to midnight, at Epic. I told you all that, remember?"

"Sure, I—"

"I go to the Art Institute; I'm getting my bachelor's degree in Graphic Design. I mean, I just started, but I should be done in four years just like most people."

He was so normal. He was just a poor starving college student who had a job and went to school full time. "Where are your parents?" I drilled him, wanting to know everything about him down to the last detail.

"They live in Atlanta. What about them?"

"I dunno," I said, shrugging, "do you see them, do they send you money—what?"

"No, they don't send me money. I have half a scholarship, and that's why I work. They gave me the option, stay there and go to school and they'd pay for everything, or come out here and do it on my own."

It was nice to listen to him talk about his parents. He was smiling just a little.

"They were really proud that I came out here to do it on my own, ya know? I mean, if I was gonna starve I'd break down and call my dad... maybe"—he grinned—"but I know he'd send a helluva lot more than I need and then both my folks would worry, and I just don't wanna have that whole scene, ya know? I'll see them at Christmas, and they can fuss over me then."

"They don't care that you're gay?"

He gave me a strange look. "They're my parents, why the hell do they care who I sleep with? What does that have to do with them and me?"

"You do know that some parents go so far as to disown their children when they find out that they're gay."

"No, I know, but that's not how it is with us. They love me no matter what. My dad says as long as I don't bring home a Democrat it's all good." He squinted at me. "What're you?"

"Never mind," I grunted, "you got brothers, sisters?"

"I have two of each, and a grandfather who is mean as spit who lives with us, them. You sort of remind me of him."

I reminded him of his grandfather? "You know what," I said, leaning away from the bar. If he had put up a billboard he could not have reminded me any more obviously of our age difference. "You need to go."

"Oh, c'mon, Malic, I didn't mean you reminded me of him 'cause he's old. You remind me of him 'cause you're a jackass just like he is."

That was so much better. I pointed at the door.

He grabbed my hand and pushed it down. "C'mon, it's noisy in here, will you take me to eat and we can talk?"

"No."

"Please, I wanna eat with you."

"You're just hungry," I muttered. "But you don't have to eat with me," I said, pulling my wallet from the breast pocket of my suit jacket. "I'll give you some money to—"

"Really?" He cut me off sharply, stepping back, eyes scrunched tight, hands balled into fists before he crossed his arms tight. "That's what you think? You think I have to trade a fuck for food?"

I was completely blindsided. I thought I was doing him a favor, and he looked like I hit him. "Dylan, wait a—"

"Fuck you, Malic," he shouted at me, which didn't have nearly the same effect, as he had done it in the middle of a loud, busy club.

But I heard him. His anger hit me like a sledgehammer before he pivoted around and charged toward the front. He was like a pinball bouncing off people on his way to the door.

It was best that he went. I doubted that he'd be back. It was over before it started, and I was glad.

Mostly glad.

Sixty-forty glad.

Shit.

I scanned the room and saw Claudia at the bar. She was pointing at the door, looking at me like I was the biggest idiot on the planet. And I probably was.

"Goddamnit," I growled, starting after him. I didn't want things to end like that between us. I wanted them over, but I didn't want him to be mad.

On the street, I looked both ways and saw him halfway down on the right. He was talking to himself, taking five steps forward and then two back. It was obvious that he was deciding on a course of action. Leave or return and fight with me. The way he turned sharply in the direction of the club made my stomach roll over. He was coming back to yell at me, I could tell, and honestly, if someone cared enough to fight with you, to try and make you see things their way, what other kind of proof do you need that they're in it up to their eyeballs?

He was ready to give me hell. I saw it in the set of his shoulders and the furrowed brows. When he looked up suddenly and realized I was there, staring back at him, the way his face lit up was really something to see. He had no right to look at me like that; I was annoyed and thrilled at the very same time.

"You're just grateful 'cause I saved your ass from gettin' beat," I yelled down the street to him.

He shook his head.

"You'd wanna fuck any guy that saved you."

"Nice." He threw up his hands. "Why don't you just take out ad space that I'm a whore!"

"No," I yelled back, "you're just beholden to me."

"I'm not," he corrected me, his voice carrying to where I was, the street empty but for the occasional cars. Thursday night was dead, not like the hustle of the weekend with its crowded sidewalks.

"You are!"

He flipped me off.

I liked him a lot.

And then he turned his head. Someone must have called out to him from the alley he was passing, and he was yanked suddenly off his feet sideways into darkness. I bolted down the street, went flying around the corner, and came to a skidding halt in front of the two men standing there.

"Such heroism," the guy on the left hissed at me.

My eyes searched all around them, but there was no sign of Dylan anywhere.

"Looking for this kitten?"

The voice came from the left, and when I turned, a woman with black hair and green eyes stepped from the shadows. She pointed behind her on the ground, and there, propped up against a dumpster, was Dylan.

"Let him go," I told them.

"As soon as he gets up, he can go," the woman assured me. "What makes you think we give a shit about the human... warder?"

"Shit," I growled under my breath, taking a step back.

I felt a rush of wind, and then there were hands on my shoulders, almost claws, holding me still. When I tried to move, whatever held me tightened its grip. I couldn't tilt my head back to look; I was afraid to take my eyes off the people, the *things,* in front of me. The pressure was like a vise, and I sucked in my breath.

"Here's the thing," the voice said, close to my ear, breath curling around me, hot and wet. "Killing warders is easier when they're all alone."

Shit again.

"You know how to break a sentinel's spirit?"

I kept quiet.

"You kill their warders."

I swallowed down my fear and took a quick breath. "I have no idea what the fuck you're talking about."

"Oh I think you do, warder of Jael, servant of the Labarum. I think you do."

What was I supposed to do? Just stand there and trade snappy banter with him? It? I rolled my shoulder, left the blazer with whatever had been holding me when it flexed its talons, and ran. I got halfway down the alley before I felt something rip at my back. Hurling myself to the ground, something flew over me and crashed into a dumpster. I got my feet under me and ran sideways, the scream from somewhere terrifying me even as I ducked under a fire escape. A creature, I wasn't sure what, hit the metal, and when I looked up all I saw was what appeared to be a giant bug. It was a cross between a cockroach and a wasp, and it had hit the metal hard enough to bend it. The buzzing, hissing noise it made had my stomach rolling as I dived to the right.

Caught fast in claws, I struggled hard even when I was hurled down onto the concrete. My back took the brunt of the impact, and I hoped it wasn't broken even as I had no air to breathe. There was a man, a *demon*, crouched over me, and with one slash of his talons, my shirt and the T-shirt underneath fell away.

"I love skin," he told me before his hand came toward my chest.

I grabbed his hand with both of mine, and his wail of pain startled me.

He tore his arm from my grip, and we both saw the burn on his withered flesh.

"Vienna!" he screamed.

I heard wings, saw the woman above me, and then a smell hit me hard, like molding oranges and mothballs and dirt. I couldn't help retching.

"Get off him!"

The voice thundered through the alley, filled the space, and had the demon above me recoiling, pushing back.

I rolled sideways and felt a knife in my right shoulder, buried deep and hard. I stumbled forward, onto my feet somehow, and hit the side of the building. My hand was there to brace me, hold me up, my fingers splayed on the brick.

I wasn't usually the one hunted; I was normally the one who did the hunting, which was why I wasn't armed. And I was a little slower as I was fresh from healing a lot of damage. It was my only excuse.

The shrieks turned my head, and I saw a man. At least he looked like a man. But the way he was fighting, moving so fast, *too* fast, let me know he was more than human. When he stopped suddenly, freezing in mid-strike, intent on beheading the insect-like creature I had seen earlier, I was amazed that his eyes were locked on mine. And then he smiled, and I registered the lengthened canines.

"Close your eyes, idiot."

And he was right; the splash would hurt if I didn't. It felt thick when it hit me. When I opened my eyes, I was covered in warm, viscous green slime. The man was in front of me, smirking, one eyebrow raised as he surveyed me. I trembled, falling back against the wall.

"Careful." He caught me, making sure my back never made contact with the wall. "You don't want that poison claw in any deeper."

I could barely drag air into my lungs. I saw the giant bug sheared in two behind him, beyond that a rising cloud of steam, or at least what looked like it, and then pieces of what I thought was a mannequin until I focused.

I turned and bent in half, dry heaving, retching hard, bringing up only bile from my stomach. He had disemboweled and eviscerated everything that had been in the alley moments before. I felt my body shudder with spasms, the smells making me gag over and over.

"Christ," he grumbled, giving me a hard slap on the back. "What kind of candy-ass warders does Jael Ezran have?"

I slid down the wall. "I just… I was hurt… still healing," I said from my knees.

"Shit," he growled at me.

I fought back a wave of nausea.

"Malic!"

I lifted my head and saw Dylan charge around the guy who had just saved my life. He was on his knees beside me seconds later, his hands all over me, and his eyes that I was crazy about were absolutely sick with fear.

"It's okay, baby," I soothed him.

"Oh God," he said, pulling out his cell phone, flipping it open. "I gotta get help."

"No," the man breathed out, taking the phone, kneeling down beside me next to Dylan, hands on my arms. "I'll take care of him."

"We need to go to the hospital!"

"You don't know anything," he said, and when he pulled his right hand up to look at it, I saw that it was covered in thick, dark blood.

"He's bleeding." Dylan sucked in a breath, his hand on my chest, on my bare skin. It felt amazing. I registered the heat because I was freezing.

"Warders don't go to hospitals, idiot, you know that!"

"Not my hearth," I managed to get out.

"Oh shit," the stranger breathed out, leaning back, staring at both of us.

I had a glimpse of his dark eyes, his chin, and then his boots. It was all there was as I fell forward.

I WAS warm. So warm. Opening my eyes, I immediately saw the man sitting on the edge of the bathtub beside me.

"Finally."

"Shit," I growled, shifting in the tub, feeling the electric currents of pain run through me just from even so slight a movement.

"Listen," he sighed, putting a quick hand on my chest, holding me still. "I purified the water, and it's pulling the poison out of your body. If you come out before it's done, you'll die—you know that."

I looked up at him and studied his face. "Who're you?"

"Raphael Caliva. Raph," he said.

"It takes a lot of energy to purify water," I said, studying his face. I couldn't do it; it was way above my pay grade. A sentinel could, but the power and then the drain of power was painful.

He grunted.

"Thank you for saving my life."

He smiled, and again I saw the elongated canines. "Do you know what I am?" he asked me.

"Yeah, you're a kyrie," I answered him, looking around the room for Dylan and spotting him across the room leaning against the door, slouching forward, obviously asleep.

"He pretty much passed out maybe fifteen minutes ago," he told me, obviously having followed my gaze.

I let out a painful breath.

"He's okay... Malic, right?"

I returned my eyes to his. "Yeah."

"He told me all about you, how you saved him from being raped, how you're like the second fuckin' coming."

"Sorry, he's young."

"Yeah, he is." His scowl got darker. "And so, what, warder? He's not your hearth, but you're gonna go ahead and fuck him anyway?"

"No, I'm not gonna fuck him," I assured him. "What if I killed—he's just a baby."

He grunted. "Awful strong-minded possessive-ass baby, if you ask me. The way he talks about you... does he know you're not gonna fuck him?"

"Yes, he knows."

"I dunno about that." The click in the back of his throat was judgmental at best. "Close your eyes, warder, so I can heal you."

I wondered vaguely why there wasn't blood in the water.

"Close your eyes," he ordered a second time.

"So... kyries," I began, "they're like bounty hunters, right? What were you paid to hunt?"

"The harpy that attacked you, Vienna. There's a witch that wants her dead."

"So you were tracking across planes."

He nodded, uninterested, apparently, in talking about himself. "From looking at you I'd say that you've taken quite a beating lately, warder. Your body is beat to shit."

We both heard the startled groan at the same time, and when I turned to look, Dylan had fallen forward and in the process woken himself up. He was adorable, all sleepy-eyed and out of it, his gaze sweeping the room before it landed on me.

"Malic," he gasped, voice cracking, breath hitching, as he scrambled across the room on all fours, getting to the bathtub as fast as he could. He nearly lurched forward and hit his head, but I was faster. Even though it hurt like hell to move even a little, when his forehead hit the back of my hand instead of marble, I smiled. The man was not coordinated at all.

His hands on the tub, he pushed up on his knees to stare at me. His eyes looked raw, like he'd been crying.

Reaching out, I put my hand on his cheek and watched as he leaned into my touch, turning his face to kiss my palm before he tipped his head back so my fingers slipped around his throat.

"You're sure he's not your hearth?"

I looked over at the kyrie. "Yes."

He shrugged like he didn't get me at all.

The whimper returned my attention back to Dylan.

"I wanna be that."

I squinted at him. "You wanna be what?"

"Please, Malic," he said, taking hold of my hand to hold it against the side of his face before moving my palm down under the collar of his cable-knit sweater.

"Dylan—"

He moved my hand to his collarbone. "Please, Malic, Raphael told me all about warders and their hearths. I wanna be that."

I looked up at Raphael. "You son of a bitch, what happened to lying your ass off? Isn't that the kyrie code? Lie?"

His smile was wicked. "Oh I like you; you're a dick just like me."

Pain shot up my spine, and the room went white for a second.

"You gotta move back, kid," Raphael told him. "I gotta submerge him."

"What?"

The room came back slowly, first colors and then soft, fuzzy shapes before it clicked over to sharp, clear focus. "Listen," I told Dylan. "Go home, okay?"

There was a heartbeat when I thought that he was resigned and going to get up and leave before his brows knit together and I knew better. The dark scowl was really something to see.

"Fuck you, Malic," he yelled at me. "I ain't leaving. No way in hell am I leaving."

"Go!"

He shook his head.

I looked to Raphael for help.

"Unless I can kill him, you're shit outta luck," he snapped at me. "Now close your eyes, warder, and let me heal you before you die."

"He can't die," Dylan told him. "I need him."

"Oh for crissakes," he growled at Dylan before he took my hand from him and took it in both of his. "Close your goddamn eyes, warder."

I did as I was told, squeezing his hand back for a second before I felt the pain crash over me again. I didn't note the exact moment I passed out.

# IV

MY EYES drifted open slowly, and I heard his deep exhale of breath.

"Christ," he groaned, leaning back, sitting beside me on the strange bed, one arm on one side of me, bracing him up, the other on the edge of the mattress. "I forget how fragile warders really are. It's a wonder any of you live."

I stared up at him with only one question. "Why am I naked?"

"Because your clothes were covered in duatin blood," he told me.

"Oh," I said, nodding, "that's what that flying thing was. I blanked it."

"You want some water?"

I nodded, tiring fast. Everything hurt.

He passed me a tall bar glass, and the room-temperature water in it was perhaps the best thing I had ever tasted in my life. After a minute I noticed him squinting at me.

"What?"

"Nothing, I was just wondering what an unarmed warder was doing out patrolling alone?"

"I wasn't patrolling," I said, glancing around the room. "Where's Dylan?"

"Christ, both of you have totally one-track minds."

"Where?"

"Right there, idiot."

Turning my head, I saw Dylan Shaw. He was passed out beside me, covers tucked around his shoulders, only his head sticking out from under the down comforter.

"Poor baby," I sighed.

"Oh, poor baby, my ass," he snapped at me. "He asked me so many fuckin' questions. I have never been interrogated like that in my life."

"What'd you tell him?"

He shrugged. "I don't know a helluva lot about warders, but what I do know, I told him."

"Shit." I groaned, trying to sit up.

"Careful," he said, hand on my chest. "You lost a helluva lot of blood."

I looked into his eyes. "You bathed me?"

"I stood you up in the shower." He tipped his head to my left. "He bathed you."

I looked back at the young man on the pillow beside mine.

"He is small but he is scary," Raphael chuckled, "and a fuckin' possessive-ass bastard."

I returned my eyes to his.

"But he's not your hearth?"

"He's nothing, actually."

"Does he know that?" He smiled at me. "'Cause he didn't let me do anything to you at all. If it involved touching your skin, he was doing it."

"Can you just take him home for me?"

"No." He yawned, indicating Dylan with a tip of his chin. "He's your problem."

"You made him my problem with your whole policy of full disclosure."

He chuckled. "Fuck you, warder. This is your clusterfuck, not mine."

"Why'd you put him in bed with me?"

"He got in bed with you, I had no choice. Like I told you before, unless I kill him, short of that, he's doin' whatever the fuck he wants. He's not scared of me and he's not scared of you. I just don't get him at all."

I groaned loudly; this was such a mess. "If I beg you can you take him home?"

"No. Hell, warder, if you don't want him I'll keep him."

"He's too young for you," I almost yelled. "He's too young for me. He's too fuckin' young for anyone but another college freshman. He needs to go home."

"Guess who stopped bleeding?" He smiled, changing the subject.

"Whaddya want to take him home?"

His eyes narrowed as he looked down at me. "What will you give me?"

"Fuck you," I growled at him, trying to sit up.

He wrapped his hand around my wrist, holding on. "Stop," he said softly, smiling at me, "I'm just fucking with you."

I settled back, staring up at him.

His dark eyes glinted in the light. His hair was buzzed short, like a military cut, and was just as black as his eyes. He had exotic features—long nose, full lips, dark brows, long lashes—not a handsome man, but very striking. If I saw him on the street, I would have moved out of his way. The teeth, those shiny, white, vampire teeth, didn't help make him look any less threatening.

"If you really want me to take him home, I will."

"Thank you." I sighed out my relief.

"Yeah, but when he does wake up he's gonna be pissed. And he looks all cute and sweet on the outside, but inside… he's seriously fucked-up. I think he's a little off. When he wakes up, he'll come after you. That one doesn't suffer from self-doubt; he knows who he is and he knows what he heard and saw."

"I don't care. If he comes to see me, I'll just tell him he's crazy," I said with as much conviction as I could dredge up.

"You want me to take him now?"

"I don't want him to wake up."

"Well, you've got to get up and go to the bathroom, then, because the displacement wave will make you sick. You're not strong enough not to feel it."

"I can't get up," I told him. "Just bring me a garbage can and I'll barf in that."

"And who gets stuck cleaning that up?" he groused at me.

"Scary-ass kyrie and vomit is gonna be too much for you?"

He smirked at me, but he got up and grabbed the garbage can. I was able to sit up, my back up against the headboard, and hold the small garbage can between my knees.

"Where the fuck am I going, warder?"

I gave him the address as he threw the quilt off Dylan. I saw that he had shed his denim jacket and hoodie, and only his long-sleeved T-shirt and jeans remained. He looked warm, and I had an urge to reach for him and hold him tight, happy to let his body heat my cold one.

"You change your mind?"

"No." My voice dropped lower. "Why? Did my smell change?"

"Little bit, yeah."

Kyries and their damned noses. Who needed a bloodhound?

I sighed deeply. "Don't forget his sneakers."

He muttered under his breath as he grabbed Dylan's shoes from where they were shoved under his bed. He tucked the rucksack under his arm, picked up Dylan in his arms, and just as the smaller man started to open his eyes, the room wavered, began to warp and shift, the shape stretching and pulling. My stomach lurched, and I tried really hard not to lose it, but in the end it was inevitable. I emptied the contents of my stomach, retching hard.

Warders moved through wormholes, but even the strongest of us could only do it once, maybe twice in one day. I had never been able to pull it off more than once. Ryan, and now Leith, could go twice. Your body told you if it was possible. You were silent for a moment and when you concentrated, your body either felt hot or cold. Cold meant that you were stuck wherever you were. If you were like Jael, a sentinel, it didn't matter how tired you got. Sentinels could use displacement to travel because they moved with their minds, just like kyries and most demons. Displacement sort of melted one place into another, and that *melting* sent out a wave of power that, if you got caught up in it, made you feel like you were being turned inside out. It was like food poisoning except it didn't last all day. Once whoever was traveling came back, it went away. Waiting through it, however, was horrible. After I threw up, I realized I had to pee. It felt like the night would never end.

A long time later, there was a knock on the bathroom door.

"You all right in there, warder?"

He couldn't just use my fucking name? "Fine," I growled back as I hung on for dear life to the side of the sink.

I had crawled off the bed, dragging the stupid metal wastebasket with me. After flushing the contents down the toilet, I managed to put the garbage can in the shower to rinse it out. And that was all I could do. I had to sit on the floor and gather my strength for a few minutes. Moving again, I crawled to the sink, which is hard to do in a sheet, and got first to my knees and then slowly, awkwardly, finally, to my feet. I splashed cold water on my face and used the hotel toothbrush and toothpaste to brush my teeth, rinsing away the taste of vomit. I felt better after that for a second before I slid back down to the floor.

"Can you walk?" he asked through the door.

"Can you?"

"Barely."

"Get in bed; I'll be there when I can."

"Sounds hot, I wish I had the energy to fuck you."

Fuck me? Nobody fucked me. "I do the fucking," I yelled back, correcting him.

"Whatever, just hurry the hell up, I'm freezing."

His body temperature was dropping. I had asked a lot of him. He had purified water to drain poison out of me, which took a lot of strength, and then I had asked him to move Dylan. It had been selfish, but I had no alternative. Dylan needed to have a monster-free life, and I was going to make sure he got it.

I wanted to walk back into the room, but I ended up crawling. Once I made it to the bed, I collapsed beside Raphael, who was facedown and not moving. He was naked, and I noted the dark bronze color of his skin. He was strong and muscular, with a carved physique that came from using his body as a weapon on a daily basis. I had no doubt he was a formidable fighter even if I had never seen him in battle.

"Can you move?"

"A little," he sighed. "Why? What do you have in mind?"

"If you can let me hold you then I can wrap the blanket around the both of us."

He lifted up, slid over, and slipped his leg over my thigh, draping it between my two, before he put his head down on my shoulder, pressing his face into the side of my neck. Like we had been lovers for years, we notched into position with the easy slide of skin over skin, warmth jumping between us immediately. I pulled the thick down comforter up and tucked it around the both of us.

"Christ," he groaned. "You smell good."

I grunted. "So you dumped him and he was okay?"

"He was sleeping when I left."

"Good. Thank you."

"He's gonna be mad as hell when he wakes up," he grumbled, nuzzling in tighter.

I had no doubt. "Did you kill the harpy?" I asked quickly. Now that Dylan was gone I was able to focus on other things.

"No, and she's gonna be really pissed when she resurrects in a few hours. I know you saw her in pieces, but I would have to burn her alive to kill her. Chopping her up into pieces only slows her down."

"I don't know anything about the demons I fight; I'm not the brains of the operation, that's more Leith and Marcus."

"Just kill the bad guy, that's all warding really is."

"So you killed all the others?"

"I killed the duatin and the woral, but Vienna got away."

"The guy talking was the—"

"Woral," he said, shivering.

I wrapped my arms around him and tucked his head under my chin. "I'm not trying to—"

"You think I care if you lie here naked next to me?" he asked gruffly. "I don't give a shit. I've had plenty of men in my bed over the years."

"Women too?"

"Yes."

"How 'bout those bug things?" I teased him, which wasn't like me at all. I might have been a little more out of it than I thought.

The silence made me smile.

"You did not just say that," he growled at me.

I coughed so I wouldn't laugh. I was definitely in a strange mood.

"Listen," he said after several long minutes, stirring me from the almost sleep I had fallen into. "When you get up and you're rested... would you give me some blood?"

"Sorry?"

"I need blood."

"Why?"

"I don't heal like you do, and the fight and purifying the water and then taking care of your boy... I'm drained."

"And my blood will help?"

"Yes."

"I thought you weren't a vampire," I teased him.

"I'm not."

"But you wanna bite me."

"Very much," he said, lifting his head to look down at me, eyes flashing dangerously in the low light of the room.

I smiled, letting out a deep breath.

"I would love to sink my teeth into your throat. Like I said— you smell fuckin' great."

"You saved my life," I said, my voice husky and soft, "thank you."

"You're changing the subject."

"I wanna help you, but...." I trailed off.

"Trust me, I won't take enough to hurt you."

I studied his face. I owed him my life.

"Why would I want to kill you, warder? I just saved you."

His argument seemed logical.

"Please."

I exhaled deeply. "Okay, but do it now. That way I can just rest and not have that to look forward to when I wake up."

"Are you certain?" he asked even as he bent and opened his mouth on my throat, licking the salt from my skin. "You have to be sure."

I pressed my neck into those lengthened canines of his. "I'm sure. I owe you this."

"Tell me I can, give me the words," he said, his voice thick as he sucked in his breath.

"You can, I pay my debts."

He sucked hard, then licked again and sighed deeply.

"Will it hurt?"

"Only for a moment."

"Okay."

"Willingly, you give me your blood." He shivered hard. "Warder... Malic... I think perhaps I will take you with me to the pit. You're extraordinary."

Stupid was what I was, and I got that a second later when his teeth skewered into my skin. Maybe, just maybe, this wasn't the best idea I ever had.

It hurt for a second, he hadn't lied, but the pinprick was followed immediately by a rush of heat that swept through my body. I heard him swallowing as I felt my body get heavy, sinking down, down, into the bed. I was so tired. One of his hands slipped over my heart, the other was on my chin, holding me still. I took a last breath and fell through the floor.

There was only black.

# V

WAKING up to a glowering Ryan Dean was a mixed bag. The man was very easy on the eyes, and seeing him in nothing but jeans, leaning over me, hand on my forehead, the other on my heart, was nice. Close up or far away, he really was a treat to look at. On the other hand, he annoyed the crap out of me. And just as I suspected, the minute he opened his mouth he was an annoying dick.

"Are you stupid or are you new?"

I groaned and closed my eyes.

"Open your eyes!" Marcus roared at me.

I opened them slowly because they were really heavy as Marcus climbed onto the bed from wherever he'd come from and crawled across to reach me. Once there, he dropped over me, his head on my heart.

"I'm obviously breathing, asshole."

The pinch to my hip hurt like being branded. He had the five-second pinch that my grandmother used to have. It was a twist of skin and then he let go, and you thought for a minute that it wasn't going to hurt and then came the burn.

"Fuck," I growled at him, rubbing it fast. "Marcus, you shit."

He leaned up, hovering over me, and I saw the pain in his eyes. The others would be worried and annoyed, he was worried and hurt. Because he was the best friend I had, and it went both ways. We didn't spend as much time as we wanted together—his hearth, Joseph Locke, was the reason for that, as we were like oil and water—but....

"Hey, that's funny," I said, thinking of something.

Cognac-colored eyes settled on my blue ones.

"All Jael's warders are gay. That's funny, right?"

"Jael isn't gay."

"I didn't say Jael was, I said his warders are."

Marcus just stared at me.

"What'd I do that you're lookin' at me like that?"

"You almost died," Ryan said after several minutes of silence where Marcus just kept staring. "What in heaven's name would make you submit to a kyrie? You know better'n that."

I did? "Is it bad?" I was guessing it was bad. From the look he was giving me, I was guessing it was very bad. "Why don't you have a shirt on?" I noticed then that Marcus didn't, either. "What the hell?"

"We've all been taking turns lying in bed with you for the last three hours," Ryan barked at me. "All of us except Jackson. Your heart remembered to beat because hearing ours reminded you that it was supposed to. The skin on skin was needed so your body remembered that it was supposed to warm itself—shit, Malic, you know this."

I did.

"If you have a fuckin' death wish, it would be better if you just let us know so we would stop trying to fuckin' save you!"

I reached up, pulled the pillow out from under the back of my head, and covered my face with it. Maybe I could pay him to go away.

"Malic—" Ryan began.

"No." Jael's voice filled the space. "Malic, look at me."

I lifted the pillow so I could see my sentinel.

"Leave us," he said softly.

Marcus got off the bed and Ryan stalked out of the room. I noticed as he was leaving that there was blood on his jeans.

"What happened?" I asked Jael, tucking the pillow back behind my head.

He took a seat on the edge of the bed, squinting, staring down at me and studying my face.

"I don't have a death wish," I defended myself. "I had no idea that—"

"If you had a hearth, you would allow no other man to put his fangs in you."

It was a weird thing for him to say. "If I had a hearth, I doubt he would have fangs."

He nodded slowly. "The point being that you are made loyal to one man at a time, Malic Sunden, and if there were one man in your heart, no other could claim it or trick you or almost kill you."

"I—he, Raphael, he asked me to let him drink, and since he had just saved my life and he was lookin' a little shot I figured that donating a pint or so would be a good thing. I figured it would help him out and—"

"Blood demons and kyries are separated only by what side of the plane they appeared on!" he yelled at me. "There is a balance with everything and so for every blood demon that springs from the pit there is a matching kyrie that rises in limbo. They both drink blood, Malic, one from a desire to kill and the other from the desire to enslave. A kyrie is not good. A kyrie is inherently evil just like a blood demon. They are not to be trusted, and they are not your friends."

I never doubted Jael, he was my sentinel, but really… did he know all the facts in this instance? "He saved me. He could have let them rip me apart but he saved me instead. And he took a friend home for me. He helped me."

"Are you sure he took your friend home?"

I thought about that, thought about the bored way I had been answered at the time, Raphael's interest in me over Dylan. "Yeah, I'm sure."

He scowled at me. "Rindahl went to you because his hearth wanted to invite you to dinner and found the kyrie there with you."

Any warder could find any other of the warders in his clutch, or group, by standing still, thinking of them, and concentrating. If a warder had not traveled through their wormhole that day, had not been whipped through the tunnel, that vortex of wind, then they could go to wherever their fellow warder was. It looked cool, simply appearing in a new place, but it took a lot of concentrated effort. Ryan must have really wanted to find me if he had done it. I wondered why. We were not close, far from it. Why had he come looking for me simply at Julian's request? Unless….

"You're having Ryan watch out for me, check up on me."

"Not just him."

"So I need babysitting now?"

"Obviously."

"That's not fair. I'm a good warder."

"You are, there's no argument," he agreed. "You above all the others balance when you do and do not use your abilities."

"Well, then."

"You fight well, you carry yourself well, but your regard for your own safety… that piece is missing, and so until I see that self-discipline in you, until then we all watch you."

I shook my head.

"You have no say."

But I opened my mouth to give him hell.

His raised hand shut me up. "When Rindahl arrived and found the kyrie draining your blood, he got him off you and called for Marot and Jaka."

It explained why Marcus was there, but where was Jackson Tybalt, Jaka? And it was funny how Jael instinctively used their warder names. He just thought Marot, Rindahl, and Jaka, and I thought Marcus, Ryan and Jackson. Funny.

"Jaka went to get us all dinner, but when he returns… you remember that his parents were victims of a blood demon."

Great. So now I had given my friend a new nightmare. "I'm sorry."

"He was incensed. Rindahl had to hold him down while Marot got the kyrie off you."

"You know," I said, thinking of something, tired and irritable and thus not having my usual stop-block in my head, "why do we have to have the whole warder name and regular name? Why can't we just get rid of the warder names and just use the ones we were born with? I mean I say Jackson, and you say Jaka, 'cause you're the sentinel. I think Ryan, and you think Rindahl. That's stupid, right?"

He squinted at me. "As you know, some warders, like Ryan and Jackson and Marcus, lead very public lives. As we have to interact with people while still being discreet, other names, warder names, are necessary. You and Leith own your own businesses and so are relatively unknown. The use of warder names for you is not vital and so you use your warder names for all facets of your lives. But Malic and Leith are not the names either of you was born with."

I knew that. I was born Alexander Sunden; Jael made me Malic. And Leith was born Edward Haas. Jael gave him the name Leith. But when I became a warder, I became a different person, and as my parents were gone, so was Alexander. Leith was the same. Even though the others didn't have families either—except for the clutch and their hearths— they still held onto their former lives. As Jael said, being in the public eye in one form or another, they needed their regular names. I was glad I could just be Malic and not have to worry about answering to two separate names.

"Are you done trying to divert me?"

"I wasn't trying to… I was just thinking about it."

He nodded.

"How did Ryan get all the blood on him?"

"When he first got to the hotel room and pulled the kyrie off you… the kyrie took half your throat with him."

But my throat was where I left it when I fell asleep.

He sighed deeply, beyond exasperated. "I healed you. Again."

I noticed then how bad he looked. "Shit, Jael, I really am—"

"You didn't know, I understand"—he cut me off with a raised hand—"but, Malic, you need to realize now that the kyrie has a taste of your blood."

"What does that mean?"

"The kyrie drank from you and you lived, and now he will crave it, crave your blood, until he dies. Now he is in thrall to you."

"Is that a bad thing?"

He nodded slowly. "There is a temptation in that because a kyrie can go places and retrieve items, relics, things from the abyss and other planes that you cannot. If you ask him to search for something or someone, find a treasure for you, then he must, but then you must pay in blood."

"How much blood?"

"Malic!"

"I'm just saying that if we really needed something, then—"

"Eventually he'll want it all, do you understand? He'll want every last drop and maybe your body and soul along with it! Don't be an idiot! Never, ever call him again."

"How would I even do that?"

He growled at me. "You think I'm some novice to give you the key to your own destruction? Do not take me for a fool!"

"No, c'mon," I soothed him. "I don't wanna die, I swear to God. I just—"

"Don't care if you live," he rasped. "You have never understood your value. Never! You alone make me want to tear out my hair and have you tied up and flogged. I thought when you and Rindahl... I thought he would make you understand, but both of you need grounding, both of you are high-strung and volatile. That match could have been disastrous. I was happy when it first began because I knew no better, but then ecstatic when it ended," he said brokenly, angry and sad at the same time.

I watched him stand and pace beside the bed. I was back in his guest room again. I wondered how long he'd keep me before I could go home and sleep in my own bed.

"I'm sorry about almost dying."

"I know, Malic, you're always sorry."

Which made me feel about *that* big. I stared up at him. "Who wants to hurt you by hurting your warders?" I asked him.

"Pardon?"

"The woral that attacked me, he knew I was your warder. How come he wanted to hurt you?"

His scowl was back from earlier. "Malic, I am the sentinel of this city. Every demon out there knows who I am and who my warders are. Just because this is the first one who has apparently called you by name, make no mistake. You are known and so am I. And every demon with a brain in its head knows that killing warders weakens a sentinel. When Grayson died, I... he took a piece of me with him."

And now I'd managed to remind him of the death of one of his warders. I was like the plague.

"Malic!"

I cleared my throat, my focus back on him. "Sorry... again."

He released a sharp breath. "Listen, when I met Julian, when we all did, I saw that Rindahl had found in him a man that would be his omphalos, his center. I want the same for you. A man... perhaps a woman who—"

"A man," I corrected him. I adored women, but the idea of being in bed with one left me cold.

"Fine, then," he told me almost sadly. "I feel that you will continue to take chances and do things that you know are ill-advised unless you find your hearth."

Ill-advised, near suicidal. God, I was driving him nuts. "I don't do—"

"No." He cut me off hard. "It takes seconds to make a call on your cell phone. Even better," he said sarcastically, "stand still and silent, think of me or the others, and we'll feel it, feel the call, and then we'll check with each other and figure out who's in need."

"Yeah, I know, I just didn't think."

"You... never... think. You just do!"

"No, I—"

"You fought one demon alone and then went blindly into the lair of another. All you had to do was call one of us, any of us. But you almost died, and I felt it and I called to see who could go. In the middle of my own fight, I had to stop and leave Jaka alone to call someone to check on you! What if Jaka had died? What if there had been no one to go to you? Everyone else but Leith was fighting. If he had been engaged as well, you'd be dead! Do you understand? Are you hearing me, Malic?"

"Jael—"

"No, Malic," he yelled, "tell me why you needed a kyrie to save you? Why not call one of us? Why let a kyrie drink from you? You knew it was stupid when you agreed to it."

And I had, a little, but it seemed basically harmless. Mostly.

"You care nothing for yourself!"

"Is he up?" I heard Jackson yell from the other room.

"Fuck," I muttered under my breath.

"Perhaps I should send you to speak to the Labarum council. They will determine if—"

"Jael," I crooned, making my voice low and soft, "please, I'm not a basket case. I just... I didn't think. The little girl, she—she needed me, and by the time I realized I was in over my head, it was too late. And Dylan got grabbed by—"

"Who's Dylan?"

"The guy, the angel, he—"

"Angel?"

"No, he's not an angel, he—"

"Who is this man?"

"He's not a man, he's just a boy, and—"

"How old is he?"

Why in the hell were we suddenly discussing Dylan? "He's nineteen."

"He's a man, Malic, not a boy."

"Fine"—barely a man—"but something grabbed him and—"

"Your first instinct was to save him."

"Well, yeah."

Jael nodded. "Where is he now?"

"Home, school, work, I dunno."

"And you've slept with this man, and he's not your hearth?"

"No, I haven't slept with him," I snapped. "He's just a baby."

"Nineteen is not a baby."

I scowled at him as Jackson came striding into the room, pointing at me.

"You stupid fuckin' son of a bitch! How dare you let anything take blood from you!"

What was I supposed to say? "Sorry" would not fix it.

He barreled up to the side of bed, bent over, and put his hands down on both sides of my head. "Goddamnit, Malic! I don't wanna lose anyone else!"

Anyone else? What was he....

"When we lost Grayson two years ago, it nearly fuckin' killed me. I never thought I'd get over that shit, and then Leith came and it was better and now he's a friend too, but... Malic! You and me... Ryan... Marcus... and Jael... please." He pleaded with me, his voice cracking, softening almost to a whisper, his eyes squinting hard so he wouldn't shed a tear, "Malic, please."

But I was the asshole they all hated.

"I can't... I lost my parents and then I lost my sister and then Grayson, and if—" He swallowed hard, and I heard him take a shuddering breath before he straightened up and started walking away.

"I'm sorry!" I yelled after him.

"Fuck you, Malic!" he roared back.

I stared after him, and Ryan stuck his head into the room and gave me a thumbs-up.

I flipped him off.

"Brilliant," he said, and then I saw his eyes do the thing that hazel eyes did and darken and change color. They went from a sort of light brown to deep dark green. "Maybe tomorrow you can play in traffic or something."

I let my head roll to the side so I was looking out the window instead of at him.

"Hey, where's the man with the death wish?" I heard Leith yell from the other room.

"In here," Ryan called back cheerfully. "But he's sorry."

"He's always fuckin' sorry!"

Christ. It was going to be a long-ass night.

# VI

I RECUPERATED, and after three days of staying with Jael, the man finally let me go home. I was excited about the prospect of solitude. After eating with all of them, running with all of them, training, and just lying around watching TV with all of them, I thought my brain was going to explode. I would have never made it in the armed services, and my hat was off to the men and women who did. To constantly have other people underfoot and around, to never, ever be alone, would have slaughtered my sanity. I never wanted to see any of them again for the rest of my life. But it was not to be.

I had to promise to check in with someone, anyone, once a day every day. It was humiliating, but I agreed just so I wouldn't have to see the wounded look on Jackson's face again. I was actually astounded that they cared as much as they did. Who knew that even if you were a prick to everyone they would actually still like you?

"If you see the kyrie again, Malic," Jael had said, "you call immediately. He disappeared when Rindahl pulled him off you and he might think you're dead, but if he checks back he'll know you're alive and he'll try and contact you. Do not meet him or speak to him alone. Promise me."

And I had promised because there was nothing else I could do. I didn't have a death wish, but apparently conversing with kyries alone constituted suicide. I wasn't so sure. Raphael had seemed all right to me, but it was too much to ask anyone to trust my judgment at that point.

By the weekend I was back to work, and the second I walked in the door I received a stack of pink messages from the pad by my receptionist's desk. Apparently Dylan had called every day twice a day for a week. And someone had given him one of my business cards, so my e-mail and voice mail had messages as well. He was persistent, I would give him that.

When the week rolled over to the next, the calls stopped, the messages stopped, it all just stopped. And I was glad, but I wasn't, but that was okay. I had looked for him over my shoulder, Raphael over my shoulder, and between the nightly patrolling and work and spending time with the other warders as well as my very human, very normal friends, I was too busy to think. I went out with Rene in a fog, going through the motions, but not really myself. He told me I should get laid, but the idea was not appealing. I was lifeless, and it was hard to figure out why. My head was so much in a different place that when Claudia sent me to pick up posters promoting a change of venue, I didn't even think about it. Everyone else was busy; I was the only one who had nothing to do, who could even go home if I wanted. So I walked into the copy shop at ten after nine at night and there at the front counter, talking to a customer about God knows what, was Dylan.

I stood behind the man and waited.

"Be right with you," he said without looking up.

I kept quiet.

"Can I help you?" the girl who had walked up to the counter beside Dylan asked me.

"Yeah," I said, smiling at her. "I'm here to pick up some color posters for Romeo's Basement."

"Oh." Her bored smile got huge. Promotional materials for strip clubs tended to perk people right up. "Sure thing, lemme go grab 'em."

I stood there not even daring to look sideways to see if Dylan had noticed me. If he ignored me, that would hurt; if he was smiling expectantly, that would hurt too. I was erecting the wall between us for him, but the distance, being forced, was hard to maintain. I just wanted to talk to him.

When the cute little girl with the side-pony came back, I thanked her, didn't bother to check what I was paying for, grabbed the bag, and left. Walking to the car, back around the building to the parking lot, I took my first breath in easily ten minutes. Once inside, I just sat there in the car as it began to rain.

I had no idea how long I listened to the drops in the dark interior of the car. It was sort of peaceful. I was finally ready to go, feeling that I had completely closed the book on Dylan Shaw, when I saw the back door open and he came out.

He was standing under the awning in the circle of light, just waiting. He could not have been there for me; for all I knew he hadn't even seen me. When I saw the sleek little Acura roll up, I understood. He didn't move, just stood there, leaning on the wall. After a few minutes, the driver left the car running but got out and ran around the front to reach him. He stepped in front of Dylan and his gestures said it all. What the fuck was he waiting for; he needed to get in the goddamn car. It was all there in the sharp, exaggerated motions. He wanted to know what the hell was going on. Dylan shook his head, and then did the head tip for him to go. The stranger didn't leave; instead he grabbed hold of Dylan's chin, forcing his eyes up to his face, and yelled. I couldn't hear the volume, but you could tell there was shouting.

Dylan yanked free and immediately started across the parking lot in the rain to my car. Little shit. He'd known I was there the whole time. When he reached the passenger side, I reached over and opened it for him. I could have just clicked the button, but in the downpour, he would have no idea it was open. And I wanted him to see he was welcome.

"Get in the car," I snarled at him. "You're gonna catch fuckin' pneumonia."

He shook his head, which sent water all over the car.

"What the hell are you—"

"You didn't leave," he sighed deeply, moving fast, throwing his courier bag in my backseat, pulling off his fleece-lined denim jacket and the heavy hoodie underneath, stripping down to the thick fisherman sweater before he pulled that off as well. I saw smooth skin for a second as the T-shirt pulled up, but then he tugged it back down when he tossed the sweater with the rest of his clothes past my head into the back.

"What're you doing?" I growled, turning to face him. "And who was—" I began, but I glanced back into time to see the Acura screech from the parking lot. The guy was pissed, that was obvious. "What—"

"I was hoping," he said breathlessly. "I was praying, I thought if I stopped stalking you then maybe you'd come around."

"I had to pick up some posters, you deluded—"

"No." He cut me off, grabbing my face, shutting me up, climbing over the emergency brake, moving over into my lap. "I don't care why the hell you came to the store. I only care that you didn't drive away."

I scowled at him as he wiggled around on my lap until he found the position he liked, his ass pressed to the hardening bulge in my pants. He did wild, wicked things to my libido just seeing him, and my body craved him even as a warning buzzer went off in my brain.

"Jesus, Malic, you're hard for me already," he gasped, pushing forward, the low moan torn from his lips.

I sighed deeply. "I'm too old for you."

He arched an eyebrow for me. "I'm done with boys, I told you. I'm ready for a man."

"Dylan," I said, swallowing hard. "Lemme take you home and—"

"I wanna go home with you," he said, hands on the side of my neck before he sighed deeply, savoring the sensation of his hands on my skin. "Please, Malic, what do I hafta do? Raphael told me if I'm not your hearth that it's gonna hurt me and drain me a little, but I… don't care…." He bent forward so his lips were hovering over mine, our shared breath hot, wet. "Malic, please… you gotta let me have you."

The eyes looking at me full of need, the hopeful expression coupled with the way he licked his lips, nervously bit them… there was just no way to say no. And I was tired, so tired, of fighting with myself and him at the same time.

"Okay." I relented for the moment, my hand sliding up the back of his neck. "How 'bout I feed you and we can talk about it?"

He trembled, and groaned, his eyes fluttering as he pushed his groin into my abdomen.

"But you gotta move," I said, because I was really uncomfortable. My cock was rock hard in my pants, straining against him, and as much as I wanted nothing between us, wanted to be buried inside him, it would wait and had to. There were things that needed to be said, boundaries drawn, and rules to be set down. So he needed to get up. "Now."

"Why?"

"'Cause you're killing me."

"I have lube and a condom in my bag. Fuck me right here holding my ass. I'd love to ride your cock."

I felt my brows furrow and the smile that spread across his face, the way he lit up, was just ridiculous. He had no right to be that happy. "Get. In. Your. Seat."

He scrambled off me, crawled back over the emergency brake, and flopped down into the passenger seat. I shook my head when I heard the seat belt snap.

"Ready," he announced.

He was way too cheerful. I looked over at him. "Can you imagine what your mother would say if you took me home for Christmas?" I asked him. "She'd be horrified."

"She'd be impressed," he assured me. "She wants me to have someone serious about me. If she met you, Malic, she'd be fuckin' thrilled."

I couldn't even get him to be rational.

"I'm starving, feed me."

And he was damn bossy.

"Please, honey."

Christ.


I TOOK him for Italian food in North Beach at a small café I loved that was open late. I tried to steer the conversation toward generally safe topics, but he wasn't having it. As we ate, he wanted to know about me being a warder and that was all. The questions came fast and furious between bites of lasagna and garlic bread and the wine that I could have but that he couldn't. His mineral water actually looked pretty good, though.

"God, enough already," I snapped at him. "Don't you wanna know about anything else?"

He thought about that a moment. "Sure, whaddya want me to make you for breakfast."

"Funny," I said, smirking at him.

"You can cook if you want. Can you cook?"

"Listen," I snapped at him, leaning forward, "you need to understand that—"

"Malic."

The sneering tone was not lost on me. Looking up, I was not surprised to find Graham Becker standing beside the table. His suit must have cost a small fortune, and the very beautiful man standing beside him, obviously his date, looked the same.

"Graham." I said his name, tipping my head at the guy beside him. "Who's your friend?"

"This is Nathan Chase. Nathan, this is Malic Sunden."

We shook hands, and I immediately introduced both men to Dylan. I watched Nathan's eyes slide over him, and my blood went cold.

"Thanks for coming over." I cut the conversation off, leaning forward to see if Dylan had liked his lasagna.

"I loved it," he said, smiling at me, his eyes locked on mine. "Every last bite."

I heard them drift away and then was aware, because my peripheral vision was good and I was paying attention, that I was being talked about when they reached their friends. They were only separated from us by two other tables, and it was obvious that Dylan and I were the butt of many jokes. I was going to get up when Dylan reached across the table for my hand. When I looked up, I was caught in his milk-chocolate gaze.

"Who cares?" he said, shrugging, lacing his fingers into mine. "They think I'm some twink, but you know I'm not. They think you're too old for me, but we both know we're probably about the same age emotionally."

"What?"

He was laughing at me.

"God, you're a pain in my ass."

His smile was out of control. "C'mon, Malic, you know I'm serious and into you, and that if you let me I could make you so happy... if you just fuckin' let me already."

"Already," I muttered, "you don't even know me."

"Pay the bill, and let's go home."

Home? "Dylan, you and I don't live at the same—"

"We will," he assured me. "But c'mon, take me home, Malic."

"You mean let's go to my house," I corrected him.

"Yeah." He shrugged. "That's what I said. Let's go home."

"Dyl—"

"Just stop fighting with me." His eyes settled on mine. "God, aren't you tired of fighting? Malic? Aren't you?"

I just looked at him. It was like he could read my mind. "I don't know what to do."

"Take me home with you. We'll figure everything out in bed."

I shook my head.

"Pay the bill, I wanna go."

I was waiting at the front door for him to catch up—he had to run to the bathroom—when Graham stepped in front of me.

"You're making a fool of yourself with that little boy," he said before I could even get a word out of greeting.

I released a deep breath. "It's not what you think."

"What do I think?" he asked snidely.

"That I'm screwing him."

"And you're not."

"No," I sighed wistfully, "I'm not."

The smug look on his face changed as he stared at me. "You're really not, are you? You're not fucking that boy."

"Not yet," Dylan said cheerfully, walking up beside me and slipping his hand in mine. "C'mon, I wanna see your bed."

I opened my mouth to say something, but the daring grin I got back made me mute. "Gotta go," I told Graham, squeezing Dylan's hand and yanking him after me to a lusty squeal of delight. It was an extremely uncouth exit that made everyone around us smile. Except Graham. Graham's look should have killed me. Fortunately for me, warders were made sturdy.


I LIVED in Pacific Heights, close to the Presidio. My place was small in comparison to most of the others on the hill, but I loved it and it was comfortable. I liked quiet; it was a sanctuary away from the noise and crazy of my business. If I wanted, I could drive down the hill and be in the Marina District, which I liked to walk around at night. Mostly I stayed home, sat out on my deck, and had a drink. There was no way a nineteen-year-old would like it there even for a night.

"Oh my God, I love your house," he said with a smile, looking around, his eyes wide, dropping his things everywhere like it was understood. Like he lived there too.

"You—"

"Where's your bedroom?"

"Come over here, lemme talk to you."

He moved fast and leaped at me. Even unprepared, I was bigger than him, stronger, so I easily caught him and sat down on the couch with him in my lap, straddling my thighs.

"See?" He beamed at me, tightening his legs on either side of my hips. "Man."

I chuckled, hands on his face, pushing his hair—and there was so much of it, big wild unruly curls—back from his face. "What're you talking about now?"

"You're a big strong man, Malic, and I don't wanna be in bed with skinny, scrawny guys like me anymore. I wanna be loved hard and held tight after. That's what I want."

But I was a cold, miserable…. I could not be the warm man he wanted, craved. "Dylan, honey, listen to me. You need—"

"I know what I need," he said, scrambling off my lap to walk over to where he had dumped his courier bag onto a chair.

He bounced back over to me, and I was smiling, I couldn't help it, when he sank back down into my lap. I was passed a brand-new tube of lubricant.

"I have this in my nightstand," I told him.

"Yeah, but it would be just like you to tell me that you didn't have any so that's why we couldn't do it," he said, squirming in my lap until I had to clench my jaw to fight the urge to devour him.

"You're driving me nuts," I told him, swallowing hard.

"Good," he said, passing me a box of condoms.

I let out a snort of laugher. "This I most certainly have as well."

"Same reason," he said, and then he coughed so that when he spoke his voice was low. "No, Dylan, we cannot have sex without protection. Step away from the penis."

I glared up at him, and he dissolved into peals of laughter.

"That's it," I said, dumping him off me, down onto the couch. "I'm takin' your ass home."

Before I could get up, he was back in my lap, arms wrapped around my neck, legs pressing against my hips, his lips on the side of my neck, nibbling up the side, kissing and licking his way to my ear.

"Knock it off," I grumbled as I put my hands on his ass and shoved his groin against mine. I couldn't help it; he was like candy. He felt so good in my arms, and a lot of it was simply the fact that he was young and hot, but that wasn't all. He wasn't afraid of me even a little, and because of my size, my strength, just for a moment, sometimes I instilled fear in others. Most of the men I took to bed were apprehensive about relinquishing their control, worried about what I could do if I wanted. And I could hurt Dylan if I wanted, but that thought didn't even enter his mind. "Hey."

We were eye to eye, and again I pushed the unruly curls back from the face I was so crazy about.

"You should be more careful, you know. If you're into big scary men, then one of these days, one of them might hurt you."

He squinted at me. "For starters, just to put your mind at rest, I never go to anyone's house that I don't know. Those guys that pick people up in bars... like you... and take them home and fuck them and then have to spend the next day doing laundry, washing some stranger's jizz off their sheets—yeah, that ain't me. I've slept with a total of two other guys in my life, and that's two too many, if you ask me."

"Oh shit," I groaned, trying to move him out of my lap.

But his legs held me tight and his wrists were locked behind the back of my neck. "And now you're worried that I haven't fucked enough other people to know if fucking you will be enough." He laughed softly, leaning his forehead against mine. "For crissakes, Malic, could you maybe give me a chance to become disillusioned with you myself instead of thinking up reasons for me to leave you?"

He was so young, he would leave. And if he actually turned out to be my hearth and then he left... it would destroy me.

"Here, look," he said, unfolding a piece of paper he had also retrieved from his courier bag and passing it to me. It was, as far as I could tell from the quick glance I gave it, a printout of some kind. "I had to get shots for school and I thought since I was there I'd get tested, just so you could see that I am free and clear of any and all communicable diseases."

"You're just carrying around a piece of paper from—"

"The clinic on campus," he grinned at me, "yeah."

"Why?"

He looked confused. "Because I wanted to make sure I had it when I saw you again."

"If you saw me again."

"No," he shook his head, "when."

"Oh for Christ's—"

"I'm ready for my lovin' now," he announced. The brown eyes looking at me were so soft, so warm, and so full of everything anyone could ever hope for that, of course, my first instinct was to growl at him. What the hell was wrong with him?

"Why the fuck didn't you run away that night as soon as you came to?"

"Why would I run?" he asked, restless hands going to work on the buttons of my shirt.

"What're you doing?"

"I'm being nice," he assured me. "Instead of ripping this off you and ruining a shirt that probably cost more than my rent, I'm being careful, but it needs to come off because I need to touch you."

"Dylan," I said, stilling him, surprised at how much my shirt gaped open—he already had a lot of buttons undone. "I'm a warder. I kill demons."

"Yeah, I know," he said, shaking my hands off. "Hey, you're gonna like having my legs wrapped around your hips when you're buried in my ass."

"Dylan," I groaned, my hands on his thighs, loving the feel of the hard muscles under the denim.

"Malic." He sighed out my name, pushing forward. "Tell me, why would I run?"

"Because you should," I told him. "You have your whole life to live, and to be burdened with my secrets... it's not fair, and I don't wanna do that to—"

"God," he grumbled, cutting me off, leaning back to whip his T-shirt off over his head. He wadded it up and threw it at his courier bag. "Is there a reason to not do me that you haven't thought of, 'cause I'm going with no."

I had a moment to look, to see the defined chest, the dark nipples on hard pecs, the flat, cut stomach, before he pressed all his warm, sleek skin to mine.

I jolted under him, closing my eyes for a second as the sensations roared through me, and when I opened them to look at him, I found his face inches from mine.

"What're you doing?"

"Where's your bedroom?"

"It's at the top of the stairs on the right," I lied.

He rolled his hips forward, put his hands on my face, and stared down into my eyes. "Don't lie, where is it?"

"How the fuck do you know I'm lying?"

"I can read it on your face," he said, shrugging. "That's how I know you want me bad but you really, truly, are worried about hurting me."

I just gazed back at him, loving the way he was staring at my mouth. He was drunk with the sight of me, and that had never happened to me before. He was the only one who had ever wanted to not only fuck me, but keep me. It was all over him, in every glance, every movement, the desire to stay, to be asked to stay. I had no idea what to do.

"Even if I'm not your hearth, Malic Sunden, I am something, and, yeah, it'll fuckin' kill me if I'm not the guy for you because I wanna belong to you so bad and you want me to be so bad, but if I'm—"

"I never said I wanted you for more than a night."

His snort of laughter made me smile. I couldn't help it. We both knew I was full of shit. He was laughing at me and he was laughing hard.

"Shut up," I muttered, shoving him off me, getting up and walking toward the stairs that led to the second floor. My house wasn't big—more like a summer cottage in South Florida than anything else. The porch in back—half of it enclosed, half open, the French doors for windows, small fireplace—had an airy feeling with lots of light. At night, in the summer, I left everything open. Now, in fall, it was warm once I got a fire going. Since I had just gotten home, it was a little chilly, but my bed would be cozy under the down comforter.

I felt him hit my back and wrap arms and legs around me, and I lifted him up, carrying him easily. His lips grazed my ear, and then he sucked the lobe into his hot mouth.

"Quit," I said, pinching his ass as he shoved his hardening cock against the small of my back.

"Malic," he breathed out, which put goose bumps all over my body. "If you fuck me and I age, you can use that wormhole thing and get me home and away from you before you do any real damage. How long does it take to see if you hurt me?"

I had told him far too much about the ins and outs of being a warder. It had been a mistake to arm him with knowledge.

"Answer me."

"What, oh, I dunno, right away," I said, walking by the first bedroom, the guest one, on the right and passing by my office and the bathroom to move on to my bedroom. Once there, I dumped him down on the mission-style bed and walked through the room to snap on the light.

"Oh, I love this room," he said, smiling as the green and brown tones of the room became visible to him. It was still light, but darker than the rest of the house: the colors, the décor. The stained teak furniture, the cherry wood armoire, the large mirror, and the wingback chair in the corner with the matching ottoman. "I would have known this was your room, Malic, it feels like you in here."

"Like what?" I asked from the doorway that led from the bedroom to the connecting bathroom.

He looked over his shoulder at me. "It's warm, just like you."

I strode back to the bed and towered over him. "I am not warm. I have never been—"

"Yes you are," he said, lying back down on the bed, unzipping his jeans, and wiggling out of first them and then the underwear underneath.

My first look at his beautiful penis made my mouth go dry. It jerked as I stared at it.

"It likes you," Dylan said huskily, and when my eyes caught his, I saw how heavy-lidded and hot they were. He was turned on just from me looking at him. "Come suck me."

"I—"

He rolled to his knees, looking boneless as he moved, and had one hand on my belt buckle and the other on my hip. "Lemme take this off and suck you, then. I've felt you against my ass, but I would love to see your dick, Malic. I bet it's just as big and gorgeous as the rest of you."

He thought I was gorgeous? How? "We should talk about—"

"I'm sick of talking," he said hoarsely, moving away from me, giving me a perfect view of his firm, round ass as he crawled back up to the top of my bed and got under the covers. "And it's cold in here. Get in bed, Malic."

I stood beside the bed and kicked off my dress shoes before unzipping my pants. The catch of breath made me look over at him.

"Christ, Malic, it's like you're carved out of granite or something."

I was a big, strong, muscular guy. My physique was all I had going for me looks-wise.

"Come here."

Once I had everything off and had thrown my cufflinks and watch on my nightstand, I got under the covers. It was cold for a moment before he wiggled up against me, his thigh sliding up over my hip as his hard cock pressed into my abdomen.

"You want me out of this bed, you're gonna have to throw me out."

"I just don't want to hurt you."

"You won't," he promised me, his hand sliding over my cheek. "God, Malic you have the most beautiful eyes I have ever seen in my life. Whaddya call that color, ice-neon blue?"

"Dylan, fucking you would be—"

"Is that what we're gonna do?" he whimpered, pressing into me, hands on my face as he eased me down closer. "Please say that's what we're gonna do."

My heart was pounding so hard, so fast, and his touch was just making it worse.

"Malic." He shivered. "Finally."

I felt his hands on my chest under the covers, fingers splayed out, circling my pebbling nipples before he pinched them. A hard throb of desire washed through me.

"Quit that."

He made a noise in the back of his throat. "Malic, I wanna be yours, make me yours." His hands slid up to my throat. I couldn't stifle the soft moan of anticipation; his fingers caressing my skin felt so good. "You're all big and scary, but you love to be touched."

Not by everyone, I didn't.

"Most of all, you want me to touch you."

He was guessing, he couldn't have simply known. "Dylan, you—"

"Why're you fighting me so hard?"

I couldn't tell him for the five thousandth time, I just didn't have it in me. "I think about you all the time," I confessed to him; my voice was a raspy, choked whisper.

"You do?" It was easy to hear the surge of happiness in his voice.

"Yes."

"Me too," he said with a smile, letting out a deep sigh.

I had been looked at a lot of different ways in my life, but never, ever, like I was a goddamned gift. I had him spellbound, and I had no idea how. He was so young and innocent and sweet, and it would kill me to see anything but trust in those big melting eyes.

"Malic," he groaned, lifting his mouth to mine at the same moment he eased me down. "Is kissing all right? Could I please... just... kiss you?"

I could have said no. I could have. But I caught my breath when his lips touched mine. He tasted even sweeter than he looked, and the whimper of need washed heat all over me. My lips parted on instinct.

His mouth was hot, and I kissed him hard because in that moment, he was mine. I could kiss him all night, kiss him until his lips were raw and swollen, kiss him as he begged me to never stop, kiss him as he writhed under me. When his tongue swept inside, I felt my body shudder. There came the quick tensing, the warmth, and my need for his touch. He tasted so good; I pressed and rubbed against him. I felt his hands roaming all over, sliding down my chest, my abdomen, and finally to my cock. When he fisted me gently and pulled, I moaned into his mouth.

"Christ," he gasped, his voice husky and low, "Malic, you're so strong and there's so much power in you and heat and... and I could, I want... Malic."

I rolled over on top of him, pinning him down to the bed, and ordered him to wrap his legs around me. Tight.

"Oh Malic... yes...."

"I'm not gonna be gentle," I told him, making my voice gruff, hard, trying to scare him. "You're gonna be fucked and claimed and—"

"Oh thank God," he almost cried, climbing me, molding his small body to mine, trying to get closer, to transfer his need to me.

The heat in his eyes, the darkness, his want... I loved it. All that hunger was directed at me and no one else. I realized that I didn't want him to look at anyone else that way, ever.

"Please stop thinking," he begged me. "Stop worrying... just fucking stop. You're not gonna break me! I'm not too good for you! I am your hearth. I know it in my heart, and if you don't take a chance you're never gonna know if I'm the one who is gonna make your life a fuckin' joy to live, you grouchy-ass bastard!"

Grouchy-ass bastard?

"Malic! Just stop!"

I stopped.

I pulled out of his embrace and kissed my way down his chest, over the flat stomach to his hard, leaking cock. It really was just as pretty as the rest of him. I smiled up at him, which made him catch his breath, before I bent and swallowed him down the back of my throat.

"Malic!"

I licked and sucked, loving the feel of the velvet hardness sliding over my lips, my tongue, coating him from head to balls before I wrapped my hand around the throbbing shaft.

He jolted under me, drawing his knees up, lifting, the whimpering and the long, aching whine telling me what he needed much more articulately than any words could.

Releasing his shaft, kissing it before I moved, I lifted over him to reach into my nightstand for the lube.

"Malic, when was the last time you got tested?"

"Why?" I asked, grabbing a condom from the pile in the drawer, putting it between my teeth as I brought the lube with me.

"'Cause I want you without anything between us," he confessed.

"No," I told him quickly around the foil packet in my mouth.

"Please, Malic." He caught his breath. "I know you get tested, it's how you are, where's the fuckin' piece of paper? I wanna see it."

He was so damn bossy, and I liked it more than I would ever tell him. I reached again and came back with the sheet of paper from Jael's doctor that showed that as of a month ago I was healthy as a horse.

His face lit up like it was Christmas.

"Oh for crissakes, that doesn't mean we're gonna—"

"Mine is from two weeks ago, yours is from four... holy shit, Malic, we can fuck like bunnies and we're both good."

"Maybe," I said, "we'll see, but tonight... I wear a condom or we're done."

"Why?" He sounded so pained.

I sat up slowly, straddling the lean hips. He was a vision and I was frozen, admiring the line of him. His body was sinewy, defined, and when I bent to kiss his abs, his torso quivered under my attention. "Because what if I got something in the last two weeks or—"

"How?" he gasped. "You've been hurt, right? Recovering? You didn't fuck anybody."

He had sounded so damned sure. "I could've."

The look I got, full of understanding, was annoying as crap. "You didn't."

"Dyl—"

"So you want us both to get tested again?"

"Just me," I told him.

He rolled his eyes like I was stupid, and I was going to tell him off, but the way he was looking at me changed, heated, and made my heart beat funny.

"You must really like me since you're so worried about me being safe and all."

I didn't want anything to hurt him. Ever.

"Let me put the condom on you."

He took the foil packet from me, and while I watched him, his hands started to tremble. I found that just as endearing as I found the contour of his hip erotic. Everything about him was spellbinding. I told him so as I reached out and fisted his cock in my hand, my grip gentle but firm.

"Malic," he whined, his foot on my thigh, pushing. "I need you."

I stroked him, using the leaking precome to coat the end of his shaft.

"Guys think 'cause I'm small they hafta be careful… no one ever trusts me or believes me, so I never get what I need. I never get it deep enough or hard enough… I never do."

With two whole other lovers he didn't get what he needed? I knew a prepared speech when I heard it. I snapped open the tube and squeezed more than I needed onto my palm. "You will," I promised him as I ran my fingers across his entrance.

"Oh," he gasped, shivering, "Malic…."

I swirled a finger around the puckered hole before I slid it deep inside.

"I don't need you to… I'm ready now."

But he wasn't, no matter what he would have me believe. When I pulled out and then pressed two fingers inside him, spreading them, opening him up slowly, gently, I realized that the words, just as I thought, had been for me and not him.

"You think 'cause I'm big and strong that I need it mean and rough," I said, working my fingers in and out, deeper, stroking his cock harder, faster, watching him come apart in my hands. "You think that if you let me hurt you that I'll want you."

He was panting, back bowed, thighs quivering, biting his bottom lip hard.

"But it's not true," I said, curving my fingers forward, inside him, feeling for the spot even as I jerked him off at the same time.

My name had never sounded like it did at that moment, deep and sexy and so very hot.

When I withdrew my fingers, his yell of outrage made me smile. My name went from one extreme to the other.

"Malic!" He railed at me. "I need you now! You've gotta—"

"I know." I cut him off, chuckling at his anger, grabbing his thighs, lifting them up and then pressing them back against his chest as I buried myself in his ass in one smooth stroke.

His voice went back to being infused with bliss, and my name was again a prayer.

I pulled out partway and then sheathed myself inside him a second time, harder on the second plunge, deeper. I had taken my time getting him ready, and from the way his muscles held me, tightened around me, I understood that he was teetering on the edge, his orgasm seconds away.

I lifted his knees, sliding first one, then the other over my shoulders, bending forward, arching my back.

"You feel so good, Malic, so fuckin' good. Please, I won't break... I won't... fuck me. Oh God, please fuck me."

The seductive pleading nearly killed me. I drove inside harder, feeling the sizzling heat pooling down low, my balls tightening, the rise and swell that signaled my impending climax. His hands gripped my shoulders tightly.

"Malic," he gasped, his voice giving out on him. "I can't take––I need you, I wanna come, make me come."

His response to me was so honest and open, his ragged breathing and small shudders letting me know how much he wanted me.

"Baby, please—I... please."

He was eager and begging, his body throbbing with heat, and I leaned over and kissed him, letting him taste himself on my tongue, on my lips, and his frustrated growl let me know how turned on he really was.

My kiss combined with my movement, the thrust forward, me burying myself inside him, undid him. He clutched the sheet, his hands balled into fists, and he pushed himself up into me and yelled my name.

"Harder! Malic, just—fill me up, do it hard, do it now!"

I buried myself in him, in his heat, loving the feel of him wrapped around me, his muscles squeezing me tightly, milking my shaft.

"You feel so fuckin' good," I groaned, pushing in deeper and harder with every stroke. "God, I hope you can be mine."

"Yours already," he rasped, his body flushed, so hot and so wet. "From the second I opened my eyes... since then."

Love at first sight was romantic bullshit, but he was a baby so he didn't know it yet. I was kind of glad.

"Tell me!" he yelled at me. "Malic!"

"Mine," I growled, my hands on his hips, lifting him before I buried myself in him, cognizant of my angle, watching his body convulse as he roared my name, spurting thick come over his beautiful, quivering stomach.

All his muscles tightened at once, bearing down on me, and watching him, seeing his desire there in his eyes, on his face, raw and open, I came, hard, filling the condom. My heart stopped for one perfect frozen moment in time. This man was it. How the hell it had happened I had no idea, but somehow, someway, he had taken hold under my skin, and I wanted him more than I had ever wanted anyone else in my life. If I could not spend the rest of my life with him, it wouldn't be any kind of life at all. There was only one response to such an epiphany.

"Fuck," I growled at him.

His deep throaty laughter made me scowl down at him. "Kiss me, you dick."

There were no better words.


I WOKE up and he was gone. I sat up, my back against the headboard, and felt his spot on the bed. It was still warm, but that didn't mean anything. Maybe he was somewhere hurting. I threw the covers off me and was ready to get out of bed when the door opened.

"Do not get up," he ordered me.

My eyes filled with Dylan and the tray of food he was carrying. He was in his jeans and nothing else, and the tousled curls, sleepy eyes, and swollen lips were enough to make me hard all over again.

"You're hungry, right?"

"Put that down and come here," I grumbled, because I was so happy to see him.

He smiled widely; he made sure the tray was steady on the nightstand and then crawled across my huge king-size bed to me. He didn't stop when he reached me but climbed into my lap, straddling my thighs, rubbing his ass over my groin.

"Stop that," I muttered, hands on his face, checking him over.

"I'm fine," he assured me, unsnapping the button of his jeans, working the zipper down. "And after you're done eating, I wanna do it in the shower."

I opened his eyes with my fingers, examining his pupils as he giggled. "This is serious business, idiot. You could die from letting me fuck you."

"Nope," he told me, rolling sideways, shucking out of his jeans, kicking them off before returning to my lap. "But I could die from not letting you fuck me. That would be the real tragedy."

"Could you just—"

"Malic," he said, his breath touching my face before his lips claimed mine. He kissed me like he owned me instead of the other way around. He tilted my head back, and his tongue was all over mine, tangling, sliding, stroking as he whimpered for attention. I liked it when he got pushy and bit my lip.

I took pity on him and took his cock in my hand.

"Oh," he gasped, shivering in my grip, breaking the kiss to let his head fall back as he levered up off my lap, pushing in and out of my fist. "Malic… could you… oh."

I took hold of his beautiful, tight little ass and pulled him forward into my lap, lifting up and carrying him to the edge of the bed.

"What're you doing?"

I put him on his feet and sank to my knees in front of him.

"Malic—"

"Come on, baby, let me suck you dry."

The whimper let me know it was the greatest idea I'd ever had in my life. When I swallowed him down, his hands were instantly in my hair, threading through, tugging, holding tight. My gag reflex being nonexistent, I took in the length of him and sucked and licked and rolled him in my hands. I tugged gently and then with increasing force as his breathing became panting and the begging, pleading, turned to loud, adamant demands. When I slid a finger into his still slippery crease, he gave me quick warning.

"Malic, I'm gonna come," he gasped, his breath hitching.

I sucked harder, added another finger to the first, and then the back of my throat was coated in thick, salty come. I swallowed hard and fast, working my tongue over and around him, continuing to suck until I had it all. Not until he was limp and soft in my mouth did I let the sated cock slip from my lips.

"Feel better?" I asked him.

He sagged against me, and I threw him over my shoulder and stood up. I dumped him back down onto the bed and stared at him. He looked like he belonged there.

"Come here," he sighed, gesturing me to him.

He took my face in his hands as I bent to kiss him.

"You're amazing and I get to keep you."

My head snapped back as I stared down at him.

"Don't be scared," he crooned, "I'll take good care of you."

I stood up, and he couldn't keep hold of me as I moved fast around the bed, putting it between us. I had to think.

"Oh, you are scared," he teased me.

I scowled at him.

He waggled his eyebrows at me. "C'mere, lemme feed you and fuck you."

I ran my fingers through my hair, yanking hard. What the hell was I going to do? Yes, he could be my hearth, but... that didn't change the fact that he was just a baby. "I'll fuck up your life."

"Okay, that's one option," he said, laughing at me. "There is maybe another."

"Don't—this is serious now."

"It's always been serious, you big stupid jerk, now it's permanent."

"What?" My voice went up way higher than it should have.

His laugh was goofy, the grin stupid. "You squealed like a little girl."

I cleared my throat. "You—I'm still too old for you. What would your father say?"

He looked me up and down, finally coming to rest on my shaft. "Who cares? Let's ask instead, how did I feel wrapped around your cock?"

I made a noise, pulled up from my gut, I couldn't help it. He had felt like heaven.

"Malic," he said, rolling up to his hands and knees, presenting me with his perfect ass. "You want romance; you need bullshit words and a fuckin' sonnet?"

"Jesus, Dylan," I moaned, feeling the sensation of a wickedly smiling angel looking over his shoulder at me with his heavy-lidded, bedroom eyes.

"I wanna ride you. Come lie down."

"Please," I managed to get out, my tongue sticking to the roof of my mouth.

He patted the bed.

I sank down beside him, stretching out so my feet were on the floor, knees bent over the side of the mattress. Instantly he was up and back with the lube from the nightstand.

"This time there's no condom, Malic. There doesn't need to be, and safe, unprotected sex is the gift you get when you're monogamous. You don't have to worry about me, I will never, ever, get in bed with anyone else. I finally have the man I always wanted."

I was going to protest, tell him I wasn't his, but when I felt his slippery hand fist my cock, I forgot who I was and therefore had no idea what we were talking about.

He lifted up, and I saw my shaft glistening with the lube he had coated me with before he sank slowly down, inch by inch, letting me feel his muscles clench around me, engulfing me, holding me tight. I had no idea how such a small man could take the length and width of me so easily, so completely, but the reason was unimportant, only the fact that he could and apparently loved doing it.

"Made for you," he told me as if he was reading my mind. "I was made for you, Malic Sunden... just you."

Head back, eyes closed, he shivered hard as I was fully seated inside him. I wrapped my hand around his shaft, milking it as he started to move, rising and lowering, letting me slide in and out of his tight, hot channel.

"Don't wanna hurt you," I said, feeling my cock go deeper with each downward plunge.

"I can't get... I need more," he whined, pushing forward into my fist and back to push himself down on my cock. "Malic!"

I lifted him off me and smiled as he yelled his outrage. "Shut up," I growled in his ear, before I put him down on the bed on his hands and knees.

"Oh yeah," he whispered as I shifted him off balance so he went facedown onto the big soft bed. I slid over him, pinning him under me, letting him feel my weight, before I kissed a trail down his spine, watching the goose bumps appear over his silky skin.

"Malic, I—" he began, his voice sounding like dried leaves.

"Tell me I can do whatever I want."

"God, you sound sexy as hell." His voice with the catch of desire made me ache.

"Say it."

"Malic—yes, whatever you want."

I moved down his body and kissed the taut flesh of his ass, first one cheek and then the other before my tongue slid between them. He writhed under me.

"You can't do that," he gasped, trying to move away from me. "Malic, don't—"

But it was just him and me, us mixed together, and he tasted like sweat and come, and the lube was there too but I didn't care, couldn't be made to. I loved the musky smell of him, the feel of his puckered hole under my tongue, all of it making me groan with my own need.

"Nobody's ever… oh."

All the sounds he was making, the moans and the whines, all muffled in the pillow he had buried his face in even as the small tremors shook him, it all ran right to my cock, made it swell and harden. I slipped my tongue in deeper, in then out, continuing the rimming that I could tell was driving him wild. I stroked gently over his hip with one hand, the other slipping under him. The begging started, and I kissed a wet line up his spine then down again. When I returned to his ass, nibbled on it, unable to resist, my mouth sucking and licking at the same time, I thought maybe he was going to come right there. I pushed my tongue deep inside the fluttering hole, bathing him in saliva, tasting him, feasting, until he was panting and finally demanding that I fuck him.

I lifted up, grabbed hold of his hips, and breached him in one driving forward plunge. He howled my name.

I froze, terrified that I'd hurt him.

"Malic," he yelled, pushing back against me, sliding off my throbbing cock before slamming back against me. "Fuck me. Please… oh, baby, please."

I rode him hard. I fisted my hand in his hair, yanked his head back hard, grabbed hold of his hip with my other hand and slammed into him over and over, deeper and deeper, as he got louder and louder.

"Malic, I can't… you feel so good… .so fuckin' good."

He was so tight, so hot, so slick, and so vocal. I had never been wanted more and knew that I truly never would be again if I was stupid enough to let this man go. But did I have any right to keep him tethered to me and my secrets and the uncertainty that was my life? Yes, he was my hearth, or could be my hearth, but was that any reason just to make him mine?

"Malic!" he screamed, pushy little bottom that he was. "I need you, drill me through the goddamn floor!"

I buried myself to my balls in his ass again, and he spattered the sheet below him with semen. It was thick and messy, and seeing his body contort in ecstasy brought my orgasm roaring through me seconds later. I froze, only my hand moving, massaging his head where I had yanked on his curls.

He slid off the end of my cock, lurched sideways so he wouldn't hit the come-splattered sheets, and rolled over on his back. I stared down at my wicked man, and he arched one mischievous eyebrow for me.

"You wanna do it again?"

I flipped him off.

"Can't do it, old man?"

I gave him both fingers. "I need food and water and sleep."

"I can do that with you." He grinned at me, motioning for me to go to him. "First we'll eat, then we'll shower and change, and then you can fuck me again when you're all rested."

"It's the middle of the night."

"Like I give a shit."

"Why you gotta be so crass?" I said even as I realized it was probably the most hypocritical thing that had ever come out of my mouth.

"Maybe someday you can make love to me," he sighed, "but for now, I want you to hold me down and tie me up and do whatever the hell you want to me. I just wanna be the only guy in your bed, sucking your cock, making you come."

"Dylan, you gotta slow down, you've got to think about what you really want and—"

"Malic, you're lying your ass off if you say you want any other guy's dick in me. Go ahead; tell me it's okay for other guys to fuck me."

Shit. "I didn't say I wanted any—"

"If you don't wanna keep me, then other guys will get to fuck me. If you tell me that's okay with you, then I'll go."

Pain-in-the-ass conceited smirking self-righteous son-of-a-bitch brat from hell!

"Malic, kiss me 'til I come again," he moaned, licking his lips. His feet, his beautifully arched, fine-boned, feet started sliding up and down my thighs.

He was insatiable. I arched over him but didn't sink down, and his hands wrapped around my neck as his back bowed up off the bed to try and slide across my chest and abdomen.

"Malic... I've never come that hard in my life. Just your hands on me and your mouth... your eyes get so dark and your skin is... sit down and lemme get in your lap. My ass feels empty without your thick cock stuffed inside of it."

Jesus.

I sank down over him, pinning him to the bed, and kissed him to shut him up. He tasted so good, and his tongue swirling over mine sucking, drawing me down deeper, made me wonder if I could end up drowning in him if I wasn't careful. All of him, his entire body was wrapped around me, but instead of feeling powerful and strong, I felt nurtured and... loved. But surely he didn't feel the same—

"God, I love you, Malic... don't ever lemme go."

I was so screwed.

# VII

WE WERE arguing as I walked him down the street toward the restaurant where we were meeting Ryan and Julian for dinner. Marcus was my best friend, but his hearth and I were not on good terms, so introducing Dylan to him first was out. Leith wasn't around or I would have called him next, and since Jackson was still mad at me, that left Ryan. To be fair, Ryan was okay, and I really liked Julian, so sharing a meal with them sounded like it just might work out. I had to introduce Dylan to the other warders eventually, even if I didn't end up keeping him.

The idea of not waking up beside Dylan every morning for the rest of my life had me breaking out in a cold sweat the night before. Watching him sleep next to me, in my bed for the fifth night in a row, it was hard to imagine him anywhere else. And the way he had taken over my house, accepting the spare key with a look like it was about fucking time, had made me growly and mean for the entire afternoon. He was driving me nuts, but even as I remained annoyed and on edge, I could not stop kissing him, holding his hand, grabbing him and hugging him. And each time, every caress, every display of affection was met with a surge of enthusiasm and him clutching me tightly. I thought of myself as rough and bruising without meaning to be, but to Dylan, with Dylan, I was gentle even when I squished him.

As usual, he was questioning me, which he did all the time, and it was always, consistently the same. "You're gonna keep me. Right?"

"You're too young," I replied, again, "you're gonna get bored."

"Bored of what? You? Your life?" The scowl I got had been adorable.

"You need to be careful of me," I told him for the millionth time as I walked beside him. "I'm not a good man, I'm not some big teddy bear, I'm a mean-ass war—"

"Malic!"

I turned to the sound of the squealing voice, turned in time to see the little girl tearing down the sidewalk as fast as her little six-year-old legs would carry her. Running toward me like it was life and death. I knelt and she was there, filling my arms, squeezing me as hard as she could.

"Malic," she cried, hugging me tight and kissing my cheek before turning her little head to lay it on my shoulder in complete and utter trust.

There was a noise above me, a sharp exhale of breath. I tilted my head up, and Dylan moved so I could see him.

"Oh yeah," he said, grinning wickedly, and I saw that he was on the verge of tears, moved by the cherub in my arms. "You're a very bad man."

This was not helping me make my case. I opened my mouth to say something.

"I lost the angel feather you gave me," Sophie Everett said as her father ran up, skidding to a halt beside Dylan before he doubled over, hands on his knees, heaving.

"You all right there, Mr. Everett?" I snorted out a laugh.

He lifted a hand as he panted, and held up a finger for me to give him a minute.

"I can't find the feather anywhere," Sophie whimpered, leaning back to look into my face. "Do you have another one?"

"I—"

"I looked and looked and no one believes me, but I know you gave me an angel feather and I need another one."

"Oh, baby, I don't have—"

"I do."

She and I both looked up at Dylan as he flipped open the flap of his messenger bag, felt around inside the smaller pocket, and then pulled out a pristine white feather. Her eyes went round, as did her mouth.

"Oh, thank you," she said, her eyes glowing as she looked up at him. "Do you know the angel too?"

"I do know the angel," he told her, stepping closer, hand on the back of my neck, stroking up into my hair. "And those come off his wings all the time."

It felt so good, his fingers petting me. I loved that he had to touch me all the time.

"Malic had the feather in his jacket; he said it was from an angel, Dylan from heaven."

Christ, I couldn't remember what I had for lunch but she could remember a month-old conversation?

"Did he." Dylan nodded. "From heaven." He smiled wide, leaning next to me so his hip was at my shoulder.

"Oh, thank you so much," she said, beaming up at him.

"Thank you for wanting it," he told her.

I let out a deep breath and so did Mr. Everett, his because he could finally breathe and mine because I finally gave up.

Turning fast, I buried my face in Dylan's abdomen, feeling it contract with the contact, the muscles there tightening. I lifted the T-shirt, kissed the warm skin hard, and pulled back, covering him up.

"Crap."

"Say it," he pressed as I rose above him until I was looking down at him.

"You're with me now," I told him, leaning in, pressing a kiss to the side of his throat before I eased back to look at him. "And I love you and that's it."

His breath caught as he stared at me with wide eyes, his mouth dropping open, and I wondered why he was....

"Awww, shit," I groaned, realizing what had just come out of my mouth.

"That's a bad word," Sophie reminded me.

Double shit.

He caught his breath. "I just wanted to live with you."

"Dylan—"

"It was all I was hoping for."

"Dylan—"

"I figured I'd wear you down eventually, get you to love me."

"Malic—"

"Shhh, honey," Mr. Everett said softly, shushing his daughter, "the adults are talking."

"Dyl," I began, "just forget I—"

"No." His hands went to my face. "Malic, you love me?"

What the hell was I going to say? The sweetest eyes in the world were staring up at me, waiting.

"Of course I love you, idiot," I growled at him. "What the hell?"

"Is hell a bad word?" Sophie asked her father.

Dylan's smile was luminous.

"But I fu—" Sophie was there. "Screwed it up," I grumbled, annoyed, disgusted. "I wanted to be—" I stopped myself, grabbed him, and shoved him a few feet down the street into an alcove, up against a wall. It was rough and I manhandled him, but the look on his face, the narrowed eyes, let me know it was okay. More than okay. "I wanted to be in bed with you and tell you how much I—"

"Malic." He cut me off, breathless. "You love me and you told me, and I could die happy right this second!"

I grunted, mortified with my delivery. "I just, I wanted it to be special."

"It was perfect," he said as tears slipped down his cheeks.

"Don't cry, baby," I soothed him, burying my face in the side of his neck, kissing gently. His breath quavered, almost stuttered, and I opened my mouth and ran my tongue over his collarbone. When I sucked hard, his hands went to my waist, burrowing under the shearling jacket, marled sweater, and beneath that to the T-shirt covering my bare skin.

"You've got too many clothes on."

"It's the middle of winter," I reminded him, defending my layers.

"Malic." He moaned my name, distracted now as he squirmed against me, pressing, pushing, rubbing, trying to get closer. "You feel... so... good."

I bit his shoulder, making sure I left a mark before I licked the bite, swirling my tongue over his skin, bathing it to take away the sting. The answering groan was full of absolute agony and shot racing heat straight to my groin. He loved it when I left marks on him with my mouth, would stand in front of the mirror in the morning and trace the raised bruises with his fingertips, a look of dreamy bliss on his face.

"Malic," he whimpered, shifting against me, hands moving over the skin he'd bared as he rubbed against my leg between his.

When I pulled back, I exhaled slowly, which put goose bumps all over him.

"Tell me again."

I watched him tremble, saw the jaw clench as he looked up at me. "I love you, you belong to me, and so that's it. I need you to move in, all right?"

"It'll be my house too?" He smiled up at me. "My home?"

"It already is."

His head bumped against my shoulder, his face buried there as his arms wrapped around me tight. "I knew it, you know, and I know you think it's stupid or not true or whatever, but I knew."

He was a mess. "What'd you know, honey?"

"I knew when I met you, when I looked up at you the first time. I knew you were the one... I just knew it. You were supposed to be mine, my man."

"Oh yeah?"

"It's all right, you don't hafta agree with me, but just look where you're standing."

I couldn't argue the point with him.

"And I know it's been weird 'cause it's been so fast but, Malic, I know this is it for me, I know you're it for me."

He didn't say, *I know it's been weird because you kill demons.* That part didn't come into play for him. He couldn't care less.

"You're the one."

"It's the same for me, D."

We stood like that for several minutes before he nodded and gave me a heart-stopping grin. He was all fixed up.

"Let's see if the angel and her daddy want to have dinner with you and me and Julian and Ryan."

But he was the angel; at least he was to me. Holy crap, how did I ever get so lucky to get an angel?

"Oh, is that her mom?"

Oh yeah, the whole Everett clan was there to witness my fall from badass warder to big romantic sap. Everyone was watching us from down the street. Mrs. Everett had teared up; Mr. Everett looked sheepish, uncertain what to do. Sophie zoomed up to me, eyes big, pointing at Dylan.

"Is he your boyfriend?"

Oh, good grief.

"Yes, I am," Dylan assured her.

"Yeah, can we go?" I growled even as I kissed his forehead.

The Everetts accepted the dinner invitation happily, and I called Ryan to get him to add more people to the reservation. I knew he was smiling on the other end.

"What?" I snapped at him.

"You're happy, Malic," he sighed into the phone. "Who knew you even had that emotion in you?"

"I—"

"So then what? This guy... he's your hearth, right? You're claiming him."

It was time just to say what I was certain he already knew. What everyone did. "Yeah," I said, trying to sound irritable and annoyed but failing miserably. I was too damn happy.

"You don't fool me a bit with this tough guy act of yours. I know you're in love, asshole."

"Nice."

"I can't wait to meet him, your hearth; I'm really looking forward to it."

And he was. He truly was. Christ.

Walking between Dylan and Sophie, each one holding a hand, I tried not to strut. It was hard, though, knowing that to the little girl, I was her hero, and to the man at my side, I was the reason for his joy.

I never thought I would mean anything.

"God, Malic," Dylan sighed beside me, "what would I do without you?"

He was never going to have to find out.

# heart In hand

I

I WAS working late, which had been happening a lot lately, but there was always some pressing employee problem that turned into a fire drill if it didn't get handled quickly without missing any steps in the process. Being as I was at the bottom of the human resources department food chain, a generalist not a manager, my desk was the first stop for everything, without fail.

Of course, the one night when I had somewhere else to be was when it took even longer than usual to send out all my e-mails and return voice messages. I was still done earlier than I thought I would be, and even though it was Friday and the traffic would be nuts, I was hoping I could still make the gallery opening. When I was finally ready to go, I was startled to look up from my laptop screen to find Eric Donovan standing in my doorway.

"Shit, Eric." I caught my breath. "You scared the crap outta me."

"Sorry. I asked at the front desk and they said you were still here."

I squinted at him. "Why are you here?"

"'Cause I wanted to talk to you."

"Why not call?"

He cleared his throat, raking his fingers through his thick brown hair. "Because I can never say what I want to on the phone."

"Okay." I nodded. It was strange but I let it go. "So what do you need?"

"Can you look at me?"

"Yep," I answered even though it took me a minute. I made sure my laptop powered down and then lowered the cover before I gave him my attention.

"It's so good to see you."

I nodded.

He crossed the room, and as he moved, I noticed the smile he was giving me was more leer than anything else. I hated it.

"I always love seeing you in a tie." He smiled at me. "Very hot."

I was annoyed but forced myself to smile. "What do you want, Eric?"

"Why are you mad?"

"I'm not mad," I told him. "I'm just trying to get out of here, so if you could just tell me what you want, that'd be great."

He cleared his throat. "So I saw you out the other night with a guy. Who—who was that?"

"You saw me when?"

He scoffed. "Can't you keep track of all the guys you go out with?"

"I have friends and family, Eric," I snapped at him, irritated by his presumption that I was sleeping around. "And if it was last Tuesday, I was out with my cousin Roger and—"

"The guy I saw you with has long blond hair."

"That's Leith." I smiled. "My boyfriend."

"What kind of name is Leith?"

"What's your question about him?"

"I just wanted to know who he was."

I squinted at him. "Which I just told you."

"Simon, I just—who is he?"

"My boyfriend," I repeated.

"Yeah, but I mean, is it, is he—"

"I live with him, it's serious… anything else?"

"It's only been six months since we broke up, and you're already living with somebody? How the hell is that supposed to make me feel?"

"Are you listening to yourself?" I asked. "C'mon, Eric, people move on. It's how things go when you break up with somebody. You both get on with your lives."

"But how do you think you're making me feel?"

"I don't really care," I told him. "We're not together anymore; I don't have to care how you feel."

"That wasn't my choice."

"But it was the one we mutually made," I reminded him.

"I didn't want to."

"But you did." I drove home the point because I wanted him to hear it.

"Simon—"

"C'mon." I cut him off, grabbing my messenger bag, flipping off the light on my desk as I herded him out of the room and locked the door behind me. "I'll walk you out."

"Wait," he almost whined, hand on my shoulder to stop me from moving away from him. "Just—Simon, please let me see you." His voice was soft, pleading.

I shook my head but didn't meet his gaze. I just wanted to be done with it.

He put a hand under my chin, turning my eyes to his. "Simon, please, I just wanna talk to you. You're killing me, here. I mean, I can't do anything, you know? I can't eat; I can't sleep; I'm anxious all the time; I pace everywhere, at home, at work... please. I need to see you. I need to talk to you just for a little while, all right? Please... please."

I lifted my chin out of his hand and stepped back. "Eric, it's not a good idea. We have nothing to talk about. Don't—"

"Don't what? Don't think about you anymore?"

"Yeah."

"Like if I could do that, I wouldn't. I really don't want to be thinking about you, Simon; I want to be in love with Rita."

"Good."

"No, not good, because I'm not. I want you. When I'm in bed with her, all I can think about is when I was in bed with you."

I turned around to walk away. His hand on my arm was tight and strong as he yanked hard to get me to stop. "Aww, man, c'mon, Eric," I groaned.

"No, Simon—shit! I'm out at dinner the other night and I see you with this guy! Did you even see me?"

I shook my head.

"'Cause you were all laughing and having a good time, and... he's got his hands all over you, and it's obvious from how he is, how comfortable he is, that... he's sleeping with you, and thinking about that is making me fuckin' nuts."

"Listen, I—"

"Don't just dismiss me," he said irritably.

"Sorry, wasn't trying to do that."

He took a breath. "I can't believe you just ended it like it was nothing."

"It wasn't nothing, but it wasn't enough," I said, starting down the hall toward the elevator.

"Wait," he groaned, rushing around in front of me, giving me no recourse but to stop or plow into him. "For fuck's sake, Simon, do you care at all?"

"About you?"

"Yeah, about me."

"Like I said before," I sighed heavily, "if you wanna be friends, we can—"

He cut me off. "Something happened."

"What's that?" I asked, more exasperated than concerned.

His eyes flicked to mine. "I figured something out."

"And?"

"I'm not gay," he said in a whisper, stepping closer to me.

I did not want to debate it with him.

He stared into my eyes. "I don't have to be anything I don't want to be. I can choose."

"That's right," I agreed.

"'Cause it wasn't any good."

"What wasn't any good?"

"I tried with another guy...." He trailed off.

But he wasn't gay. Christ.

"Did you hear me?"

"I did," I said instead of "go to hell." I so didn't want to be his therapist, but I'd been through this a lot in my life. It came with my job. "What happened?"

"It was awful."

I looked into his face, and the way his eyes were a little dead, the tone of his voice, the tense shoulders—I couldn't take it. I leaned forward and hugged him. He was stiff in my arms for only seconds before he grabbed me tight. I felt him shaking and heard his breath catch as he buried his face in my shoulder. "Aww, man, I'm sorry."

"I didn't know how patient you were with me... all those times I thought—I mean, I figured it would be the same with anybody... feel the same."

I sighed heavily. What a mess. "Everybody's different. You should try and—"

"You always went so slow, made sure I was ready and—"

"It's okay." I didn't want to get into what I had or hadn't done.

"It didn't hurt."

Jesus.

"The way you do it, it's not fucking. Why didn't you tell me it wasn't gonna be like that?"

I gave him a final squeeze and tried to pull back. He held on.

"It was so different when we—with us."

"Eric, it's okay." I patted his back, hugged him as tight as I could. "What are you going to do?"

He eased back to look at my face. "I'm gonna marry Rita."

"Good." I nodded.

"But can I see you?"

"When?" Now I was confused.

He just looked into my eyes and then started to lean. I got it.

I smiled gently, easing him away. "No, man, that ain't gonna work."

"Why?"

"'Cause I need more than that. I'll never be something you do on the side."

"Why?"

"I need more."

"How much more?"

"Just the same as everybody else. I won't share."

"So, what—you're gonna get married?"

"I might." I smiled because he just didn't get it. "Someday."

He let out an exasperated breath, rubbed his forehead, and cracked his knuckles one by one. It would have been funny at any other time. "Simon, c'mon, don't—just, can't you just—"

"I gotta go. I have somewhere to be."

"You gotta go meet your guy," he said, his voice hard and flat.

"Yes, I do."

"But I need you, and this new guy, whatever the fuck his name is, can't possibly want you more than I do."

I wasn't listening. Instead, I stepped around him to walk down the hall toward the elevator.

"Simon!"

I kept walking, and again he was suddenly in front of me, barring my path.

"You need to listen to me."

"No," I sighed deeply. "You need to listen to me. All the reasons we broke up are still there, and if you think about it a second, think about it logically, then you'll get it."

"He's trash, Simon!" he yelled at me, grabbing my arm, holding on tight. "I'm the—"

"You don't know him." I ripped my arm free of his grasp. "And you're not allowed to have an opinion, anyway."

I never got mad, it took so much energy, but he couldn't talk about Leith Haas. No one who didn't love the man got to talk crap about him. I would not allow that.

Wanting to burn off the anger and frustration, I decided to take the stairs instead of the elevator. Ten flights would work off some tension.

"Simon!"

"Go to hell, Eric," I yelled, starting down.

"Stop."

"Can't," I called out to him, ready to take the second flight down.

"Simon, stop and look at me."

When I looked up at him, I realized he had a gun, and it was pointed straight at me. "Oh, Eric, what the hell?"

He closed the distance between us fast. "I want you to just stop and listen to me."

I was silent, waiting.

He took a settling breath, holding the gun on me as he advanced. "Okay. Here's what I want. You go home and tell your new guy, whatever the hell his name is, that you don't wanna see him anymore, and then tonight after I drop Rita off, I'll come by and see you."

"Okay."

"And it'll be just like it was before you broke up with me."

"Sure, Eric," I said, trying to remember everything I had ever seen on TV about living through someone holding a gun on you.

"'Cause here's what I think," he said, close enough now to reach out and put his hand on my cheek. "If you could just stop moving, stop talking, just sit and be still—I think you'd realize that there's no one that can take better care of you than me. I mean, I see you and I look at you and I just want you back. Sometimes when I'm screwing Rita, I have to think about your skin so I can come."

I just looked at him.

"It's so hard, 'cause usually you break up with someone, or they break up with you, and it hurts or whatever, but you get over it, ya know?" He raked his fingers through his hair. "But with you, I can't seem to get my head clear."

"Huh," I breathed, and then I grabbed his wrist, slamming it as hard as I could against the railing.

"Simon!" he screamed.

I slammed it again, and the gun dropped out of his hand. I didn't let go fast enough, and he caught me in the face with his elbow and then his fist. There was blood everywhere. I kicked him in the knee as hard as I could, and when he fell forward, I swept his feet out from under him and he bounced down the flight of stairs. I took the steps in threes to get to him. I was terrified that the fall had killed him. But he got up so fast, I didn't even have time to stop before he grabbed me and threw me up against the wall.

I thought he was going to break my arm, but he punched me in the kidney instead. All I had free was my head, so I hit him with the back of it as hard as I could. I felt him let go and fall against me. I dropped my shoulder, and he went down hard against the floor, the fall knocking him out cold. I walked backward until I was sitting on the steps. I put my head forward and pinched my nose to stop the bleeding. It was over so fast, taking only seconds, and with my adrenaline pumping, I still couldn't feel anything. When my heart stopped pounding in my ears, I flipped open my phone and called Eric's sister, Chloe. I had met her and the rest of her family through Eric. He had introduced me as a friend, and no one had suspected anything different. Before she could start talking, asking me questions, I interrupted and asked for her father. It was all I could think of to do.

Twenty minutes later, Mr. Donovan threw open the door and joined me and his unconscious son in the stairwell. He reached Eric fast. He was still sprawled out on the landing.

"Ohmygod!" he gasped, checking his son for signs of life.

"He's fine," I told him, having checked to make sure he was breathing. His pulse was strong and steady; I had just knocked him out cold.

He looked at me holding the sleeve of my dress shirt against my nose. "What happened?"

I held up the gun for him, which I had retrieved from the bottom floor, holding it with my other sleeve, making sure to put no prints on it.

"What's going on?" he asked, walking over to me, taking the gun carefully. "Why is my gun here?" He checked it. "It's loaded."

I shrugged. "I have no doubt it's loaded," I said, sounding nasally since my nose was filled with blood.

He took a seat beside me on the stairs. "What's going on, Simon?"

"I have no idea."

Mr. Donovan turned and looked at me. "You want to try again?"

I sighed. "No, sir."

"Tell me the truth."

"It's not my place to tell you the truth," I said, dabbing at my nose, testing for wet blood.

He looked at me, and I knew the moment he understood. His eyes got wide, and then the most defeated look I had ever seen came over him. My dad had never looked like that. The night I told him I was gay, he had listened a long time before he went for a long drive alone. When he returned, he came into my room and hugged me and told me it was fine. He wanted to know what my life was going to be like, wanted me to be careful in and out of bed, and told me that if I decided it was just a phase that he'd understand that too. Mr. Donovan was devastated; I wanted to kiss my father at that moment. A traditional Korean man, who had emigrated from Seoul when he was a boy, understood that family came first no matter what, and this rich, educated man had missed that lesson completely. I got up and went to the stairs, stepping over Eric on the way.

"Simon, I appreciate you not calling the police. You could have embarrassed my family, but you chose not to. I won't forget that. What can I do for you?"

"Just take him home and keep him away from me, so I don't have to get a restraining order, Mr. Donovan," I told him coolly, staring him down. "I don't want to see him anymore."

He looked away, unable to hold my gaze. I heard Eric moving, asking his father where he was, as I descended the stairs down to the next level and reentered the building. I couldn't take the stairs; I needed to leave fast. I was on the elevator minutes later.

Outside, I ran around the side of the building and threw up in the alley. Not one of my finer moments, but with the adrenaline gone, I was suddenly terrified. I debated long and hard whether to call Leith, but he was at the gallery opening of his latest show. I wanted him to enjoy his night, not leave to come and see me bleed.

When I could, I jogged down the street to a drug store and grabbed a bottle of water before using their bathroom to wash my face. I looked a little better when I came out but would not pass undetected under my boyfriend's careful scrutiny when I showed up at the gallery opening of his latest show. I needed to figure something out.

# 11

MY PHONE rang after I got out of the shower.

"Hey," I sighed, checking the clock on my nightstand. "I'm sorry I'm late. I had to come home and change."

"Oh, so you're still coming?" He sounded so hopeful.

"Absolutely," I assured my boyfriend, rubbing my hair dry. "I just needed to make a quick stop"—because there was blood on my clothes—"but I'm on my way back out."

"Okay, then, hurry up, 'cause I wanna go to dinner after."

"You bet." I smiled into the phone, wincing when I accidentally bumped my lip.

"Simon?"

"Yeah?"

"You all right? You sound stuffed up."

"No, I'm fine; I'll be right there."

"You're at home, you said?"

"Yeah."

He cleared his throat. "Maybe I'll come get you, and we can ride back together."

"Oh, no, don't leave, stay there and schmooze. You need to sell something." I chuckled. "I want an elaborate Christmas gift this year."

He snorted out a laugh. "You don't give a crap about that kind of stuff."

And I didn't, but I was trying for chatty.

"I've been mingling all night, trying to be charming and—"

"You're always charming."

"Am I?"

I laughed at him. The man really had no idea how very appealing he was. "Yes, dear."

He gave me a less-than-convinced grunt.

"Okay, so I'll be—"

"Are you sure you're okay?"

"'Course, just gimme, like, twenty minutes, okay?"

Silence on the other end.

"Leith?"

"What's wrong?"

"Whaddya mean?"

He took a breath. "I mean I can hear it in your voice that something's up. Please tell me."

I sighed heavily. Never, ever, had I been with a man who could tell just from the sound of my voice, from my silences, even, that something was amiss. But then, I had never been in love with a man who killed demons before, either.

The man in my life, Leith Haas, was a warder, which meant he killed demons as his night job. He was a welder during the day and an artist whose chosen medium was wrought iron on the side, and at night... at night he hunted and killed the creatures that preyed on men, women, and children. He was one of five warders who were led by the sentinel of San Francisco, Jael Ezran. As I was Leith's hearth, I was one of only a handful of people who could ever go to bed with him and come away unscathed. And all of it had been a revelation and a burden, and exciting and frightening, all at the same time. My personal life had been on a giant roller coaster since the blond-haired, aqua-eyed man had caught me in his heated gaze. I had been unable to resist him, and I was happy about that every single day. Not that it had been a picnic. We were navigating a relationship that was, by turns, normal and out-of-the-park weird, but he had given a little and I had given a little, and we were, we both agreed, on track to do great things.

"Simon?"

I cleared my throat. "I don't want to ruin your night with my stupid bullshit."

"Baby," he said gently, softly, "you don't have any bullshit; it's one of the many reasons I can't live without you."

"Oh yeah?"

"Yeah."

I took a deep breath. "Okay, so I had a visit from my ex tonight, at work, and we sort of got into it."

"Got into it how?"

I made a noise in the back of my throat. "He hit me and—"

"Hit you?"

"Yeah and—"

"Simon, how did you let him hit you?"

He was right; it wasn't like I was some small, fragile guy. I was six one, I worked out, ran, I was in good shape; I could have kept him off me, but there had been the whole gun situation added to the mix.

"Simon?"

The gun thing would make him nuts.

"Simon? Did he jump you?"

"No."

"Then what?"

"Shit."

"Simon?"

I coughed. "He had a gun."

"I'm sorry?"

"He had a gun," I said, louder that time.

The phone went silent, and I couldn't think of anything to say that wouldn't sound stupid.

"He had a gun?"

"Yeah."

Silence.

"Leith?"

"Stay right there."

I groaned loudly. "No, honey, just—"

"Simon, goddamnit! Are you hurt?"

"Just a little."

His shaky breath was followed by the slightest, smallest whimper, and I could hear in his voice everything I was to him.

I had to make a decision, and I was finally going to have to use words. I was terrible at that. Showing the man what he meant to me in bed was easy. Giving voice to those feelings was a whole other story.

"Simon."

"I need you," I confessed, almost moaning, because I did, and he had to know, or he was going to fly apart, broken at the seams. He was vulnerable after hearing that I was hurt, and I responded in a way I normally never did. Revelations about myself, anything about me, about what I could or could not survive, did or did not need, were not something I did. Spilling my heart, I felt, served no one. Leith had enough people depending on him—victims, his fellow warders, his sentinel; he didn't need to carry me as well. The last thing I ever wanted to be was a burden, but it seemed like maybe he didn't see it the same way that I did. "But I don't want to be—"

"What are you so scared of?"

"I'm sorry?"

"Simon." His breath hitched. "Tell me what you're thinking."

I cleared my throat. "I just don't wanna be one more thing you hafta deal with."

He was silent.

"Leith?"

"For crissakes, Simon, you're the only thing I have that's mine. Everything else is just...." He trailed off. "But you, I chose you."

And he had and I finally got that. His whole life, everything, all of it except me, had been thrust upon him. "Okay."

"Okay?"

"Yeah, so can you come home and take care of me?"

He sucked in his breath. I didn't think it was that big of a deal.

"Please?"

"Yes," he said, voice cracking with relief, grateful for my admission. "I'll be right there. Don't go anywhere."

"Where would I go?" I teased him, trying to lighten the mood. "I'm already home."

He hung up and I sighed deeply. I was so glad I didn't have to finish getting dressed. After I pulled on a pair of sweats and an old T-shirt, I walked into the kitchen and looked out at the pouring rain. It was nice because I loved rain, how soothing it was, but it also reminded me of Leith, and thinking about him was always good.

Six months ago I had been on my way home and it had been raining, so I ducked into an art gallery until it cleared up. Since I was expected for drinks with a big group, I had no intention of staying, but I was immediately struck by what I saw. The wrought iron sculptures were dark and almost angry, and as I strolled the exhibit, *Transgressions*, it was called, I found myself enjoying the gothic, masculine feel of the creations. I had been in many galleries in the city, but this one was new to me, and I was suddenly very glad that I'd found it.

"What do you think?"

I turned, and there was a man, just slightly taller than me, broad shoulders, lean waist, and long legs. He was muscular but not overly so, toned, defined, with sharp features and an angular face. His curly hair drew my eye; it was long and dirty-blond, thick and messy, and tumbling past his shoulders down to the middle of his back. It looked wet, like he had been outside in the rain.

"You just get here?" I asked, smiling at him.

"No." His deep-blue-sea eyes got wide. "Why?"

"You got caught in the rain." I gestured at his hair.

"Oh no." He shook his head. "I was at work before I got here, so I had to clean up and make myself presentable."

He was fresh from the shower, which was why he smelled so good, like soap combined with some sort of citrus scent. I wanted to inhale him and see if his skin was still warm underneath his clothes.

"Do you like them?" he asked, licking his lush bottom lip almost nervously.

I had no idea what we... were... talk....

"Do you like the sculptures?"

The way he was looking at me was making it hard to concentrate on anything else. There was hope there, and innocence, and interest, and it was a little overwhelming two seconds after you met a person. I needed to get ahold of myself.

"Do you?"

"I-I think they're actually sort of spooky," I told him honestly, getting my bearings. "And yeah, I like 'em a lot."

Those eyes of his, framed with dark-blond lashes, searched mine. I noticed the freckles on his nose and dimples covered by the fine stubble on his cheeks. "You think the sculptures are scary, but you still like them?"

"I do," I confessed, stepping around him, moving to the next piece of art and the next, following the trail down the hall and through the maze. I wanted to see how creepy it was all going to get, take the full tour.

"Which sculpture do you like best?" he asked from behind me.

"Why?" I smiled, looking over my shoulder at him.

"I'll give it to you."

"Why would you do that? Isn't the point of this for you to sell your work?"

"How'd you know I was the artist?"

"Because you just offered me anything I wanted," I said, watching him as he walked around in front of me.

"Oh yeah." He grinned sheepishly.

"And even if you hadn't, usually only the artist walks up to total strangers and asks them what they think. It's like your art is your kid, you want to know what everyone thinks."

"Yeah, it's pretty lame; we're all a little too externally motivated."

I shrugged. "Who doesn't like to hear praise?"

"But what if people hate it?"

"That's the risk you take if you put it out there."

"It's still stupid."

"It's human," I corrected him, moving on, looking at the next piece, watching as they got more twisted, more sinister. "Christ," I breathed out when I entered the next room. It was dark, with strange, red-dappled lighting, and I had the feeling I was at the aftermath of a gory battle.

"You keep walking away," he said, and I felt his breath on the back of my neck.

I turned, and he was close, right behind me, eyes glinting in the darkness. He was just slightly taller than my own six one, so our eyes met and locked.

"I wanted to see how it turned out."

"What?"

"The fight," I told him, turning back to the pieces. "You said you came here from work. What do you do besides the art?"

"I'm a welder," he said, moving to stand beside me. His hands were shoved down in the pockets of his jeans; the sweater vest over the dress shirt looked strange on him, like he should be in board shorts instead, checking out the swells. I wondered what a surfer was doing so far up the coast.

"A welder," I repeated, glancing around before looking back at him. "You're not a soldier? This strikes me as fighting, as good versus evil, that sort of thing."

He nodded and reached out and took hold of the lapel of my suit jacket. "There's no way you're gonna believe this, but I swear it's the truth," he said as his eyes flicked to mine. "I never talk to anybody at these things, I don't, it's not me, but... I.... When you came in and you were really looking at the art, not just here to get out of the rain or—"

"I did come in to get out of the rain," I told him honestly.

His shrug was cute. "Yeah, but then you started looking around, and I could tell when you started getting into it."

More than just the man's artwork had me interested.

"Would you maybe want to have dinner with me?"

There was vulnerability in him, so that I didn't doubt him for a minute. He didn't pick up men; he wasn't the type. He was shy and quiet but there was strength there too. I liked that.

"I'm actually supposed to be meeting friends," I told him regretfully.

"Could you maybe not meet them?" he asked, curling a long piece of hair around his ear to keep it out of his eyes so he could see me.

"Why?"

His eyes studied my face. "I'm Leith," he said, ignoring my question. "What's your name?"

"Simon."

"Simon." He repeated it, and the sound from the back of his throat, achy, needy, was surprising. I stepped forward, into his space, and heard his breath catch.

"Tell me what you want."

He swallowed hard and I saw it, saw the veins in his neck cord and watched the muscles in his jaw clench. I had never seen such raw, exposed need. I was surprised he wasn't shivering with it.

"Or just tell me what I can do," I said, my voice dropping low, the shudder that finally ran through him making me smile.

The strangled sound he made flipped my stomach over before he lunged at me. His lips sealed over mine, and I immediately felt his tongue pressing for entrance. I opened for him, and I heard his sharply drawn breath before he devoured my mouth. Heat tore through me, and I bucked forward into him when his hand suddenly groped me through my dress pants.

I pulled back because I couldn't breathe and saw the aching desire all over his face.

"This your thing? You attack guys at your gallery openings?"

"I—"

"You're a twisted piece of work, man." I grinned slyly.

He shook his head. "No, listen… I'm not ever like… I'm not sure what's happening."

Lust was what was happening, and since he was plainly not thinking straight, I fisted my hand in his sweater vest and yanked him after me. There was no protest given as I dragged him behind one of the movable partitions of the exhibit and shoved him up against a wall. He moaned as I pressed the painfully hard bulge in my dress pants against the crease of his ass.

"Please," he whimpered, squirming against me.

"What do you want?"

He shuddered hard, flattened his hands on the brick wall, and spread his legs. It was all the invitation I needed. I immediately went to work on his belt and had his jeans and briefs shucked down around his ankles seconds later. As my hands slid over his right cheek, he caught his breath.

His ass was gorgeous, firm and round and muscular with appealing divots in each side. When I knelt behind him, spreading the cheeks so I could see his already fluttering pink hole, he moaned deep and loud.

"What're you... no, wait, you—God!"

When my tongue licked over his opening, he jolted under my touch. Clearly he had not expected the deep rimming he was in for.

"You shouldn't do—"

"Shut up," I said, my voice full of gravel and heat. As I suspected, his sleek skin was still warm from the shower he had taken recently, and he smelled like soap but also, here, musky, earthy, and that was a great big turn-on. When I leaned in, licking and sucking, pushing my tongue in deeper with every stroke, tasting, the other hand moving around front to fist his cock, I heard a low groan of unmistakable, up-from-his-gut pleasure.

"No one ever... ever... oh please."

I wished I had lube so there would just be the slip and slide, but what was on the condom in my breast pocket was all there was. So I pushed more saliva into his clasping channel and then added a finger. The ring of muscles was tight, but between my tongue and my persistent press inside of him, it slowly loosened. When I curled my finger forward and stroked over his gland, I heard the cry of longing.

"Please." His breath hitched, and I felt the surge of power wash through me. I was driving the beautiful, sensual man right out of his mind. "I'm gonna come if you don't stop."

The threat had no effect on me whatsoever. I added a second finger that slid in easily, and as he levered back and forth against me, I began gently scissoring them apart inside him.

Watching my fingers disappear into his tight round ass, over and over, was making it hard to breathe. I felt his muscles contracting, felt the velvety walls clenching around the invasion of my flesh inside his, and knew he was moments away from release.

"I wanna come with you buried inside me," he gasped. "Please... fuck me."

He was lucky I never left home, or my office, without a condom. I took some grief from friends, keeping a box of condoms in my top desk drawer, but you never knew where you could end up after work. I would never second-guess myself again.

Letting him go, I moved fast, unbuckling my belt, working the zipper, and pushing my pants down just enough to let my hard, dripping cock out. I almost came just sheathing myself in latex, but the promise of his ass was too great. I wanted to be buried to my balls in him.

"Please," he whimpered, the begging so sweet from a man who had been mostly self-possessed when we were discussing his art just a short time before. Watching him come apart from my attention had me shaking.

Hands on him, I lined up my dick with his hole, spread his cheeks, and shoved forward in one long, hard thrust, impaling him in a brutal plunge.

"Simon!"

That sounded good. My name torn from the man's chest sounded very good.

"Oh God, please."

The begging was not necessary. One hand in his thick, curly hair, I yanked hard, bowing his back as I pulled out only to pound back inside seconds later. He felt so good, so slick, so hot, so tight, and I hammered into him as hard as I could.

"Fuck!" he growled, "Simon... oh God, baby, please."

I liked the "baby"; it was nice. Seeing my long, thick cock slide in and out of his ass, watching him take all of me and moan for more, rolled my stomach, sending a sizzling pulse through me.

"Simon! Don't stop, please don't stop. I'm gonna come... I wanna come."

Good to hear, good to know, and as I drove in and out of the saliva-slicked, fluttering hole, I bent forward and bit down into his shoulder.

"Harder." His voice was sexy and low and dark, like maybe it had never occurred to him that being manhandled and marked during sex would do it for him. "I wanna feel you deeper."

But I knew he was close, and so when I leaned forward, changing my angle, dragging my throbbing cock over his prostate, grasping his dripping shaft at the same time, he shot his load over my fingers, my wrist, and onto the dark red bricks. It was hot and so was the man.

He chanted my name as I rode out the orgasm that tore through him, my balls slapping against his ass, feeling his rippling muscles contracting around me, squeezing me tight. When I came, seconds later, I filled the condom and wished, for the first time in my life, that I was filling the man's channel instead. The idea of my semen coating his insides, of having my come dripping down his thighs, was the most erotic thing I could think of.

As we stood there together, heaving, panting, him with a final shudder as he leaned his head against the brick and me bracing myself against the wall, I eased gently, tenderly from his body.

"I miss you already," he whispered.

I smiled as I slid the condom from my cock, tied it off, and tossed it into the huge empty garbage can someone had hidden behind the movable wall. It was probably there for cleanup later on but served perfectly at that moment.

Leaning back, adjusting myself, pulling up my briefs and dress pants, belt buckle jingling, I was surprised to feel his hands on my face. I lifted my eyes and found him staring.

"What?" I smiled at him, not sure how comfortable I was with the scrutiny being leveled at me.

"You're fine." He breathed out long and deep, his face breaking into the most beautiful smile I had ever been gifted with.

I was touched by the depth of his happiness. "Why wouldn't I be fine?" I tried to tease him but only succeeded in having him step forward, into me.

He looked at my hair and my face, could not stop staring deeply into my eyes, and let his hands linger on the sides of my neck.

"Am I all inventoried now?" I teased even though it was nice, his overwhelming interest. "Why the concern about my well-being?"

"Come home with me and I'll tell you."

But I needed to give him his out. "Oh, no, you don't have—"

"Simon." His breath caught. "I want to eat with you and talk to you and take you home and take you to bed and sleep with you. Please let me. Please."

It should have been scary, how adamant he was, how insistent, how passionate. But instead it just made me feel wanted, and I liked that. I tended to pick men who were either in the closet or who only wanted me for the night. I wondered, oddly, if my luck had just finally changed with a chance encounter with a stranger.

"You should stay here," I told him, raking my fingers through my hair. "And hope to God no one heard us way back here."

"No one's even really here yet," he told me. "And besides, I put a sign across the entrance before I followed you in here."

"Really? I looked easy, did I?"

He coughed nervously before I got a shy smile. "I was actually just hoping to talk to you."

I nodded. "Do you think maybe I could get your number?"

"No."

"No?" Frankly, from how he was looking at me, his response surprised me. I had thought he'd be up for seeing me again. "Are you—"

"No, I mean, don't go," he pleaded softly.

It was his eyes, again, that had me. They were so liquid and dark and the color of the deepest, bluest part of the ocean, a sort of heated aqua, and they were on me, swallowing me, and I was held there and caught without hope of release. As if I wanted any, as if I wanted to be free. I had never been looked at the way he was looking at me, like I was special, like he would not take me for granted.

So I agreed not to leave by myself but to instead go with him and blow off my friends. When we were on the street, he took hold of my hand. He laced his fingers into mine and spoke low and soft, telling me about his favorite Italian restaurant and the smooth bossa nova they played there. It was in North Beach, and his friend Malic had been the first one to take him.

At dinner he watched me and listened and told me that my charcoal-gray eyes were the color of solder when it heated.

"Is that good?" I asked, smiling at him.

"Yes," he said, his voice low and husky.

I studied him: his finely cut features, the high cheekbones, how strong his hands were, the roped veins in them. I liked the bracelets he was wearing, leather and hemp, another made of a metal I couldn't place that I later learned was recycled material. They were artistic, like him.

"You're very perceptive."

I snorted out a laugh. Never had I been given that compliment.

"You are," he said with a chuckle, signaling the waiter to bring me another beer. "You knew exactly what you were seeing at the gallery."

"Did I?"

"Yes, sir."

I nodded, and he tipped his head, studying me.

"What?"

He confessed that he had never seen hair so dark black that there were actually blue highlights in it. I started to say something dumb, because self-deprecation came easy for me, but his hand on my cheek stopped me, silenced me, and his fingers slid around the back of my neck and up into my hair. I liked the possessive yank forward as he made sure I was really looking at him.

"I can't wait to get you home."

The way he said it, staring at my mouth, his eyes heavy-lidded with need, had me wanting it just as bad. And it wasn't that he was so gorgeous—I had met more beautiful men in my life—but when he looked at me, eyes flicking to mine, staring, there was an intensity there that took my breath away. He wanted me and no one else would do. I liked that. I liked it a lot.

I stayed all weekend, in his bed, and when Sunday night rolled around, I told him that I had to go home. I couldn't actually just wear his sweats and his T-shirts forever; I had to get ready for Monday, get ready for work, and go back to my life.

But that wasn't what he wanted. He needed me to move in, and so I was made to wait as he made a call.

It got weird after that, off-the-chart strange, and I would have run from anyone else. But for him I stayed.

Twenty minutes later, I met the biggest man I had ever seen in my life, the sentinel Jael Ezran. I fell into a world I never even suspected existed except on TV and in movies. I was scared at first, overwhelmed, and it took me a week after the man stopped talking and I finally left to process everything.

Demons? Warders? It was insane.

Leith fought creatures from hell and he expected me to simply accept that it was real, take it on faith. It was too much to ask.

And not.

It was the way he had looked at me while his sentinel was speaking, with hope and desire all rolled up together. How could I not believe him?

In the end, it was Leith, with his persistence and his absolute belief and need, that won me over. He stalked me in his sweet, cheerful way, showing up wherever I was, waving, grinning, always the happiest man in the world just to see me. I had never been wanted like he wanted me. He had to have me be his hearth, his home, the grounding, centering presence in his world. I was *necessary*.

I understood what I was truly being asked for: to share his life, his secret, to be both his present and his future. His hope was to never open his front door at the end of the day and not have me there, or at least to have the promise of me there soon. As I was already kind of crazy about him myself, I agreed to move in.

And it was fast, scary, crazy fast, but when he was there, waiting for me after work, oozing happy like a kid at Christmas, ready to start his life with me in it, I was sold. He wanted to meet my family, my friends, and dive right into the deep end, because he was absolutely sure I was it.

I liked being *it*. I had no regrets.

The light caught the blade of a sword, Leith's sword, where it rested on the rack whenever it wasn't in use, and that visual brought me back to the present. It was a beautiful, elegant weapon, a Turkish kilij. The saber was both deadly and decorative, and when my boyfriend slid it into the scabbard whenever he left our home to patrol, I shivered every time. He was a powerful man but with the sword, he took my breath away. I crossed the room to look at it and realized that just seeing it there soothed me.

Exhaling deeply, I found that I really needed to lie down. My head hurt and I was exhausted. I had no idea how Leith and the others squared off against demons on a daily basis. Fighting took a hell of a lot out of you. Once I crawled into bed, I inhaled my boyfriend's scent on the sheets. I didn't even think I'd closed my eyes.

# III

IT WAS raining outside, and I was warm in bed, and something more... something better... and then I felt the soft lips slowly trailing up my spine. It felt so good.

"Finally," I griped as I shivered under him, smiling.

"I should have been worried about you first, but I was annoyed that you were late, and then I was pissed that I had to call you, and then you said what happened and.... Shit. I'm so scared that you're gonna leave me, and now I'm just so ashamed, Simon. I'm so sorry."

It was an avalanche of words from him; usually he didn't ramble.

Wait. Leave him? "What the hell are you talking about?" I asked, trying to roll over.

He held me still with a hand on the small of my back. "You've been gone so much lately, and I hardly see you, and when I do see you, all I do is complain, and then you get mad and we fight and—"

"I'm working on fixing that problem," I soothed him. He was right; it was turning into a vicious cycle that could be fatal if something didn't give. If I didn't give. "I promise."

"Really?" He sounded surprised.

"'Course. I miss you as much as you miss me, idiot. Why wouldn't I? I love you."

The choked whimper made me smile. "I love you too, more than you know."

"So I'm glad you're home," I said lightly. "You wanna fool around?"

"Shut up," he growled, and I felt his hair brush over my shoulders, felt his lips, again, on the small of my back.

"Leith," I breathed out.

His hands slid up both sides of my body, his mouth on my skin. The kisses were light but searing, and I felt every single one. When he sucked, mouth open, tongue licking, I gasped.

"Forgive me for doubting your feelings," he breathed over my skin. "I'm an idiot and I don't deserve you."

"Yes, you do," I said, shifting because my cock was hardening, moving under his hands. "It's me... I'm the—"

"You're honest, Simon. You always tell me exactly what you can and cannot do. You have no idea how great that really is. I never have to guess where I stand."

"Good," I said, still sleepy. I could hear the sand in my voice.

He laid his cheek between my shoulder blades and let out a deep breath. "God, I was so scared," he told me, and his breathing sounded shaky.

"It's okay, I'm okay." I rolled over, and he reached for the light on the nightstand at the same time. I wanted to get naked, but the look on his face was suddenly not conducive to sex. He was horrified.

"Oh God, honey... Jesus, look at your eyes and your lip and...." His hands were all over me, yanking at my clothes, lifting the T-shirt. It should have hurt, but even as scared as he sounded, he was gentle, so gentle and careful with me because I was the man he loved.

"I'm fine." I chuckled because my relief that he was there, with me, was great. I didn't realize until that moment that the whole event was more traumatic than I had yet to process.

"Oh shit," he cried, his hands pushing the T-shirt further up, his fingers trailing over my skin. When they touched the bruises, I shivered hard. There was no mistaking that I had been attacked. Anyone could see that. "Simon... baby—" He pulled the T-shirt up and over my head.

I couldn't contain my smile.

"Christ."

I took his face in my hands, which stilled him completely. "I like you all worried about me," I said, easing him down to brush my lips over his. "It's very nice."

He trembled under my hands, and I smiled, seeing the reaction. The man had it bad for me, and the way he closed his eyes when I kissed him, wrapped his hands around my wrists, and whined in the back of his throat let me know that the sight of me roughed up was kind of doing it for him.

"You're getting off on seeing me manhandled," I teased him.

"No," he corrected me, his eyes opening to only slits, glazed and dreamy. "What I like is you confessing that you needed me… finally."

"Finally? What?"

He stared deeply into my eyes. "You're so strong all the time, so independent, and sometimes I'm not sure if I'm important to you at all."

"You just told me I was honest and you always know where you stand so—"

"That's not what I mean. You want me—sexually. I know that 'cause you show it, but needing me to be with you and then telling me is a whole other thing."

"Leith—"

"But tonight you finally said you did. Tonight…." His breath caught. "Simon… I was necessary."

When I rolled him over on his back, his moan of pleasure could not be missed.

"Which doesn't mean that I'm so happy that I'm not gonna kill this guy… your ex… Eric something."

"Baby—"

"Nobody puts their hands on you except me."

And the way he said it, the way his eyes hardened, was very sexy.

I rubbed against him, pressing my groin to his as I covered his face with kisses—his eyes, his nose, his throat, and finally his lips— I kissed everywhere, wanting him badly.

"Oh God," he groaned, arching up into me. "You gotta stop, you're hurt."

I wasn't hurt enough not to jump him.

"Simon," he whined.

I moved a hand to his belt buckle to begin the process of getting him out of his skintight jeans, and he tried to protest, worried about me, even though he was panting and breathless. When I slanted my mouth down over his, he went boneless under me.

The kiss was scorching and wet. I missed nothing, sucking, licking, tasting, biting, and making sure he felt the overwhelming desire mixed with love. My tongue tangled with his, teasing, pushing, and his deep whimper of need, pulled from his soul, made me smile against his silky, supple lips. The man had the softest lips I had ever kissed, and he tasted like honey.

"Simon, please," he begged me when he tore his mouth from mine so he could breathe.

"Please what?" I asked, having unbuckled his belt and gone to work on his button-fly jeans.

"I need... I...." His eyes fluttered shut as he was assaulted by the sensation of my hand slipping under the waistband of his briefs, slipping over the velvet length of hot flesh.

"Leith," I whispered, pressing kisses to the base of his throat.

"I need you."

And I knew that even as I fisted my hand around his hard, leaking shaft.

He bucked up off the bed, trying to lift up higher, wanting to be closer to me. "Please, Simon, fuck me so hard that I come screaming your name and then hold me after all night long."

I kissed him again, slowly, sucking on his tongue, stroking his dripping cock at the same time. "You want me bad."

"Yes." His voice cracked as his glazed eyes drifted open. He lifted his hips up off the bed so I could slide the stubborn jeans over his beautiful, round ass. I smiled when lube was shoved at me. He had pulled it from under his pillow, left there from the morning. He liked to start his day with me bending him over the bed. I never argued.

I smiled down into his dark, wet, hungry eyes. "Take off your T-shirt. I wanna feel your skin on mine."

He pulled it roughly up over his head, his breath hitching as he looked up at me. Gently, I eased his legs down flat. The look of confusion that came over his face made me smile. When I climbed over him, straddling his thighs, his eyes got huge.

"Simon, you—"

"Stop." I quieted him, flipping open the cap on the lube, squeezing it into my palm. When I fisted his cock in my hand, he bucked up into me.

"What're you doing? Why're you—"

"You know what I love about us?"

All I got was a raw groan of whimpering need.

"I love that we can be whatever the other guy needs whenever he needs it." Rising to my knees, I lined his cock up with my entrance. "And tonight I need you inside me." It was not his favorite thing, to top, and I didn't normally ask it of him, but there were times, like this one, when I needed to be claimed instead of the other way around.

"Simon," he gasped, and his hand clenched on my thigh stilled me. "I don't want to hurt you or—"

"Do I hurt you?" I asked him, my voice low and husky.

"No, but—"

"Please." My voice bottomed out as I slowly, gently lowered myself onto the long, hard, thick length of him. Leith had a beautiful cock, which I never failed to mention to him whenever I took him inside or down the back of my throat. "Oh yes," I whispered.

"Simon," he gasped, hands clawing into the bedsheet, struggling so hard not to move, not to drive up into me.

There came the slow burn that accompanied the stretching and filling, always there at the beginning, before it slowly subsided to first a dull ache and then, when I lifted and slid back down the second time, to that surge of sizzling heat. I leaned forward and kissed him, tasting him, my tongue tangling with his.

Strong hands, callused hands, gripped my thighs, holding me tight, his hard, muscled body shuddering under me as I again lifted up off him only to plunge back down, fully seating him deep inside me.

He tore his mouth from mine. "Oh God, Simon, you're so tight and hot, and I fuckin' love being inside you."

I smiled around the flickering orgasm that was beginning to roll through me. In the position I was in, his cock was rubbing over my prostate, which was making it hard to think. "You love being inside me? Since when?"

"Since forever," he moaned, and I saw the muscles in his jaw cord. "Whatever we do, you in me, me in you, kissing you, holding you... for crissakes, Simon, I get a boner just hearing your voice on the goddamn phone!"

His confession made me want to make him come so hard he saw stars. "Oh yeah? You want me all the time?"

His answering whimper was adorable.

"You love me, huh?"

"Oh God, yes."

I leaned back, feeling his balls against my ass.

"Simon," he whispered, reaching beside him for the lube, popping open the cap, lubing his fingers and then tossing it aside, caring only that he could touch me, feel me, and slide his slicked fingers over me from base to head in long, tight strokes. "Gonna come, baby, and I want you to go first."

Always he considered me; there was never a time when he had not. "I'm so close," I confessed as he started to thrust from the bottom, pushing in and out as my eyes fluttered shut. It felt too good; I didn't even care that he stopped jerking me off; I just let my head fall back on my shoulders, braced myself on his thighs, and let him thrust up into me.

"Fuck, Simon, you're so beautiful, and I can feel your body wrapped around me so tight, holding me, squeezing me.... Baby, please... come."

He was going to leave bruises, he was holding me so tight, and when he cried out my name, possessive and primal at the same time, I instantly felt the flood of hot semen fill my channel. As he drove up into me, I came, loud and messy and chanting his name.

I WOKE up in the early morning and realized I was alone. I smiled in the darkness, hearing him in the other room, walking around as I knew was his habit, checking the front door just to make sure it was locked. Making sure our home was secure.

"Come to bed," I called out to him.

He was there in the doorway seconds later.

"Why're you up?"

He was silent, just staring through the dark at me.

"Tell me."

"I dunno," he answered, his voice low, full of gravel. "I'm just happy, I guess."

And I understood. Simple things like his keys and wallet on the shelf with mine, his leather jacket hanging beside my peacoat on the wall rack, his messenger bag on the coffee table, mine on the floor, spoke of two people living together. We had a home together, Leith and I, and I liked it, craved it, and so did he.

"I know this is stupid, but I just feel like everything is okay because I can come in here and see you sleeping."

"It's not stupid," I said softly, smoothing my hand over his pillow. "Now come to bed."

He crossed the room fast, and when he leaned over, I reached up and put a hand on his cheek. "Lemme hold you."

"I love you, Simon."

"I love you too, baby. Get in bed."

He crawled in under the covers and molded his body to mine, spooning me, his arms around my waist. I took a deep, settling breath and closed my eyes. I fell asleep smiling.

# IV

I WISH I had been able to stay happy. But by Tuesday morning, I was just foul. For starters I was away from home, having to fill in at the last moment for one of the other HR generalists in my department. Leith and I had gone from bliss on Saturday to a hellish Sunday after my boss called that morning. My boyfriend wanted me to say no; I asked him when I had become independently wealthy.

He was angry.

I was defensive.

It didn't get any better after that.

Sunday evening was even worse than the day had been, like navigating a minefield, and we were both happy when it was over and we could go to bed. I was surprised on Monday that he was up before I was and making me breakfast.

"I don't want you to leave and us be pissed at each other," he told me as I wandered into the kitchen that overlooked a cramped patio.

I took a seat at the table and watched him move around the room. Already there was a mug of steaming coffee and glass of orange juice waiting for me. "You're mad at me," I said when he put a plate with what looked like a Denver omelet down in front of me. His looked similar except it was covered in salsa.

"I'm not mad at you," he sighed, taking a seat across from me. "I'm mad that you have to go, is all."

"You think I wanna go?"

He shook his head. "Just, I don't wanna fight—please."

The *please* killed the last bit of spite in me, and I rose out of my chair and leaned across the table. He met me halfway, hand on my cheek, his breath catching as I kissed him. Every single time I pressed my lips to his, the man received my attention like a gift. And because of that, I was putty in his hands. His long sigh made me smile.

"I just like knowing you're home," he said, kissing the side of my throat.

And I liked being home for him, but I had no choice.

One of my coworkers had been chosen to attend the conference instead of me, but his wife ending up giving birth two weeks early, so suddenly, because the spot was paid for, I had to go. The call came from my boss, and the look on Leith's face had been painful to see. It was hard for him when I wasn't there to come home to. The hearth of a warder was a precious thing. Knowing I was home was good; having me there when he got home was even better. To walk in and be able to grab me, that was the very best part for him.

So it hurt not to be home, and the training itself was going to be tedious, and to top it off, I seemed to be the only one that found the situation we were in, when Tuesday rolled around, to be in the least bit odd. As I stared out the window at the blanket of white, I took a breath and tried to breathe.

"Simon?"

I turned to look at my boss, Dan Brenner. There were four of us from the office there together; along with him and me, there was Jess Turner and Kenny Boyd.

"Jess said you were kind of freaking out." He gave me an indulgent smile. "You don't think you're taking this whole snowed-in thing to *The Shining* level for no reason?"

I loved Stephen King as much as the next guy, but really this had less to do with anything but the fact that no one but me saw the nightmare we were in.

He clapped me on the shoulder. "Mr. Saudrian, the hotel manager, has advised me that this sometimes happens this time of year."

"They get snow."

"Yes."

"In November," I said dryly.

"Yes," he insisted.

"Are you kidding?"

He shrugged. "I guess where we are, close to the California-Oregon border, that—"

"We're close to the camping grounds in Merrill," I told him. "My sister and I camped there once when I was—"

"It's just snow," he said with a chuckle, "and you're freaking out."

I cleared my throat. "Dan, we got here yesterday afternoon and it was clear, and in a matter of a twelve-plus-hour period, we are completely snowed in. That doesn't strike you as odd?"

His scowl was dark. "It's weather, for crissakes."

It wasn't; there was no way. Even though I was not a meteorologist, I knew the difference between what was possible and what was not. And maybe somewhere in the Midwest you got freak snowstorms that buried you from Monday afternoon to Tuesday morning, but this was northern California, and it was, as I'd pointed out to my boss, November.

"Simon?"

I forced a smile, because having a debate with the clueless man was not going to get any of us any closer to the truth of our strange situation. "Okay, Dan, you're right. I'm just bein' stupid. Where's Jess?"

He squinted at me. "I think she went to her room to change before we start the afternoon session."

I nodded and left him alone in the sitting room on the second floor where he had found me.

It was a huge hotel, very nice, very high-end, with polished wood floors and imported Italian fixtures and a whole sort of Casablanca-type feel to it. There was a fountain in the entryway and black-veined marble, and the staff looked crisp and clean in their spotless ivory uniforms. There was nothing wrong at all with the inside, the piano bar and the sports bar; the French restaurant was heaven—it was the outside that was the problem, where the strange built-up overnight snow was. It could not be there, not logically, not naturally occurring. If you could forget about the fact that we were basically trapped, it was fine. My problem was that I couldn't just put it out of my head.

Halfway down the long hall, I heard my name called. Turning, I found one of the other members of my human resources department, Kenny Bond. He jogged fast to catch up with me.

"What's wrong?" I asked, because his face was all scrunched up.

He held up his iPhone for me. "I just—I can't get anybody. I'm tryin' to call my wife, and I have no reception up here. All the lines at the hotel are down, too, and the Internet and everything else. I just fuckin' hate this."

"Yeah, I know," I sympathized. "I'm on my way to get Jess. Come with me."

He nodded, falling into step beside me. It wasn't like him to be quiet, so I knew the whole isolation thing had him really bugged. As he walked with me, I felt the tension rolling off him.

At Jess's door, I knocked quickly.

Nothing.

I had tried again, thinking she was in the bathroom or something, when the door suddenly flew open. I jumped back, startled.

"Christ," Kenny barked at her. "What the hell?"

She lunged at me, wrapping around me tight and hard. I realized only then that she was shaking and panting.

"What's wrong?" I asked, hands on her face, tipping her head back so I could look down at her.

"Let's go," she gasped, squirming free, grabbing my arm and trying to pull me after her.

"Honey"—I pointed into her room—"where's your purse and laptop and—"

"Fuck it. Let's just go to your room and—"

"Jess." I cut her off, worried. She was frantic, panicked, her breathing shallow and fast. "You need to get your—"

"I don't need shit," she told me. "I'll wear one of your T-shirts or—"

"Stop," I said, soothing her, wrapping her in my arms again, holding her close to me, rubbing circles on her back.

She was close to hyperventilating. It took several long minutes for her to calm down. Once she had returned to her normal, composed self, I leaned back to look down at her. "Talk to me."

Deep breath. "I was lying down on the bed, and something breathed on me."

I squinted at her. "Breathed on you?"

"Yeah, like an animal."

"You're kidding."

"You were dreaming," Kenny chimed in.

"I wasn't," she told him. "And I'm not," she answered me.

I agreed with him. "Honey, you had to be."

She shook her head and then pointed into the room. "I'm not going back in there. Last night I didn't sleep a wink, and you know that ain't like me."

It wasn't. The woman could fall asleep anywhere, anytime. According to her husband, there had been a few very inappropriate times when she had nodded off when they were in the middle of things.

"Why couldn't you sleep?"

"I felt like something was watching me, looking at me." Her breath hitched. "I just... I hate that fuckin' room, and I'm not going back in there."

"But, Jess—"

"And right before you knocked, I couldn't get the door open."

"Oh that's crap," Kenny barked at her, pushing by us and striding into the room.

We watched from the doorway as he walked to the center and stood there.

"What now?"

She pointed at the bed. "Get all my stuff. I'm sleeping with Simon."

He squinted at her.

"Oh, you know what I mean! Grab my crap and c'mon."

He rolled his eyes like she was being ridiculous, got her garment bag and her messenger bag, and brought those both to me before walking back in to retrieve her purse and her princess coat. Those were passed to Jess.

"Seriously?"

She just stared at him as he stood there, him in the room, us out in the hall.

"Do you—fuck!" he yelled as his body jerked backward toward the bed.

"Oh God!" Jess screamed.

I bolted forward, grabbed my friend's hand, and nearly plowed into him. He had stopped moving so abruptly that the force I had exerted to reach him was overkill.

"Fuck." He clutched at me, eyes wide, looking all over.

"What happened?" Jess demanded, standing at the door, gesturing for us to come out. She was not about to step one foot back into the room.

"Fuck if I know," he said hoarsely, shoving me forward, fast, across the carpet and out into the hall.

The three of us stood together, clustered close.

"What was that?" I asked him.

His eyes were locked on mine. "I dunno. It felt like somebody grabbed me, like I was yanked into the room—did you guys see anything?"

I shook my head.

"No," Jess's voice cracked. "Goddamnit, I am freaking out."

"You felt like there were hands on you?" I needed to clarify.

"Yeah," he said, pushing up the sleeve of his sweater to reveal his forearm, "and now my whole arm fuckin' hurts."

"Oh shit," Jess moaned.

The skin that stretched from above his wrist to his bicep was covered in dark, angry red splotches. It was going to turn black and blue and looked like someone had given him the Indian burn from hell.

"What the fuck!" Kenny almost yelled, fisting a hand in my sweater, holding tight. "If you hadn't—I mean, Simon, I felt like I was gaining speed, ya know, and it hurt like a son of a bitch, but the second you grabbed me, it stopped. I mean, just stopped."

I nodded. It was weird, because they were both acting strange, and the snow outside was eerie, but everything else felt fine. Everything looked fine. Nothing was out of the ordinary.

"Okay, well, let's go to my room, Jess, and put away your stuff."

"And we'll stop at my room on the way and get mine," Kenny told me. "I'm moving in with you too."

His announcement was not appealing in any way. "Why? What's wrong with your room?"

"It was cold."

"Cold?" I squinted at him. "Ever heard of a thermostat?"

"Just... it gave me the heebie-jeebies."

I rolled my eyes at him.

"Just c'mon, Simon."

I wasn't in the mood to argue.

THERE was nothing more boring than a conference about things you already knew. Refresher, they called it, but it was busywork, plain and simple.

We were there to take classes, brush up on our listening skills and conflict management while we interacted with other HR managers/trainers from across the country. Our company, Ellis Pharmaceuticals, put a lot of money and resources into its people, and the four-day seminar/conference was for our benefit as well as all the employees of the company.

After the three of us collected Kenny's things, both he and Jess moved into my room. There were a lot of products in the bathroom suddenly, but the counter was huge, so we were fine; cramped, but fine. The towel situation would have to be addressed, but Kenny was smart and grabbed his on the way out. We were late for the afternoon session, but the instructor, Mrs. Aoki, didn't give us much more than a stern look as we tiptoed in.

As class droned on, the feeling of unease left me. Hard to be scared or worried when you're bored to death. When we were dismissed for the day with homework for the following morning, we left quickly.

There were supposed to be drinks before dinner, and everyone was scheduled to report for a mixer around five thirty. Once we were back in the room, I watched Jess fall down onto the California king.

"You all right?" I asked her.

She rolled to her side to look at me, draping her hourglass frame over the quilt. "Simon, honey, your room is awesome." Deep indrawn breath. "It's warm and light and just... I love it."

"It's different," Kenny said from the window, and I looked over at him. "I mean last night, my room... I just I gotta tell you, it was weird."

"You ass," Jess snapped. "You were giving me shit and your room was weird too?"

He made a face. "I thought you guys would be, like—" He raked his fingers through his thick brown hair. "I dunno, thinkin' I was stupid or something. It was fucked up. I haven't been scared of the dark since I was five years old, but last night... I turned on the light and I could swear—"

"That something was there right at the edge of the light," Jess finished for him.

"Yeah," he told her, his face draining of color. "What the fuck was that?"

"Did you sleep in the middle of the bed, afraid to get up?" she asked.

"No." He shook his head. "But I got up in the middle of the night and turned every light in the room on." He took a quivering breath. "Did you do that?"

"I was too scared to get off the bed," she confessed as she got up and walked over to stand beside me.

"You okay?" I asked when I realized she was trembling.

She leaned into me, wrapping her arms around my waist, her head against my heart. "I am now. I can probably even sleep tonight. Your room isn't spooky at all. There's no sort of dark places in here, and it's not cold. My room must have been like a meat locker."

Kenny nodded. "It was fuckin' freezing."

I had been warm all night, and I was crazy about my room. I had watched a movie, gotten cozy in bed, and fallen asleep.

"But it feels great in here," Kenny said, flipping on the TV. "Let's just hang here instead of going to the mixer after we do the bullshit homework."

"If you guys want." I yawned, ready to stretch out on the bed for just a minute.

It was funny how I lay down in the middle and both of them leaned against my legs. I muttered a thank-you when Kenny pulled off my shoes.

That night we had room service and watched movies and played cards. When I woke up at three in the morning, I realized that the lights were finally off and both my friends were in bed with me. Kenny was sleeping facedown beside me, and Jess was next to me on the other side. I was in the middle on my back with her wrapped around me. I shifted, and she tightened her arm around my waist.

"I knew the moment I met you that I'd get to sleep with you someday," she murmured, snuggling against me.

"Go to sleep," I muttered, tightening my arm around her back. It was funny, but I would have wagered that everyone at Ellis Pharmaceuticals in San Francisco thought Jess and I had slept together at one point in time. We were just too close, the rumor mill said, for it to be anything but sex. As Kenny let out a snort, I had to chuckle. Seeing the three of us like we were would just have made the stories that much better. I hoped Leith was too busy to worry about me, since I had not called like I promised.

# V

I STAYED awake the following morning even though the session was enough to make me want to slit my wrists. The afternoon one was worse, and I was surprised at how many people didn't show, as well as the fact that a lot of others nodded off. And it was boring, yes, but normally, as adults, we didn't actually fall asleep sitting up. Looking around, I realized how exhausted everyone looked, like no one was getting any rest at all. Our trainer cut the afternoon session short because she felt that everyone needed to recharge their batteries.

As I sat at the bar having cocktails with Kenny and Jess, I realized I had not seen our boss all day.

"We should go check on him," I suggested.

"Sure, you do that." Jess smirked at me, coughing into her hand. "Brownnoser."

"Really? Is that necessary?"

"Yeah," she drawled, laughing at me. "But whatever, go look for him, and me and Kenny'll go check with the concierge again about Internet service and a phone line."

"Sounds good," I agreed, getting up and starting out of the bar to go find my boss.

"Meet at your room in an hour, and we'll get dinner!" she called after me.

I waved but didn't turn back around. Halfway to the door, I moved sideways to let a woman pass and ending up stepping into the path of someone else. I would have been plowed into by the stranger if another hand had not gripped my bicep and yanked me sideways.

"Careful."

My head turned, and I found there in front of me a very handsome man. "Oh, hey, sorry."

He let me go immediately. "My mistake."

"Oh, no, that's okay, thanks for saving me from gettin' run over."

"It's my pleasure," he assured me.

I offered him my hand. "Simon Kim, San Francisco office."

His smile was strained as he clasped mine. "Chale Diaz, New Mexico."

"Nice to meet you," I sighed, pulling back my hand. "Are you comin' in or going out?"

"Fuck if I know," he muttered under his breath, but I heard him, saw him shiver.

Reflexively I reached out and put a hand on his shoulder. "You okay?"

His head snapped up, and his eyes locked on mine. "Sorry, I didn't, I just, I can't—I need to call my... partner... and I can't"—he cleared his throat—"reach him."

I gave him a warm smile. "I can't reach my boyfriend, either, and it's gettin' old."

Seeing the wave of relief that washed over him made me feel really good. "Yeah, it is."

"I'm off to check on my boss, and then I'm gonna have dinner with a couple of my friends. Would you like to join us?"

He nodded. "I would really like that."

As we walked we got to know each other, and I found out that he and his partner had been together for six years. It had been rough going at first, as his boyfriend, Wade, had been a big-time player before he had fallen head over heels for Chale.

"You haven't lived until you've had to screen booty calls at two in the morning," he said with a snicker.

I enjoyed listening to him, and when he asked why there were bruises on my face, I explained about my ex.

"Oh shit." He scowled at me. "What did your guy say?"

"I'm not sure what he's going to do, but one of our friends is a lawyer," I said, thinking of Marcus Roth, or Marot, as Jael called him. Of the four other warders in Leith's clutch, or group, he was the one I had liked almost instantly. The man had the warmest brown eyes and a soft, resonant voice that soothed, I was guessing, everyone he met. He was deadly in combat, vicious in the courtroom, and yet always kind to me. I was always happy to see him. "And the last I heard, he was on his way to file a restraining order on my behalf."

Leith had called me when I was on my way up to the resort and told me that Marcus would be handling the legal piece of dealing with Eric Donovan and that his friend Malic Sunden would be handling the rest.

"What does that mean?" I had asked Leith.

"It means that if I go see Eric then he might not live. Malic is bigger and scarier than me, but because he knows he's powerful, he's really good about not exercising it over others. I might just go off; he'll just scare the crap out of him."

And I had no doubt. Of all of the warders in Leith's group, in his clutch, Malic was the one I most feared. The others were more refined, sleeker, but Malic was a bull. I had been stunned when I met his new hearth, Dylan Shaw. They were polar opposites, but maybe that made sense.

Malic was hard and scary and cold, Dylan soft and sweet and warm. Malic was not a handsome man, and Dylan was brown-eyed, smooth-skinned perfection. He was one of the prettiest boys I had ever met, and the way he looked at Malic, every time he looked at Malic, left no doubt in anyone's mind that the big, surly warder was absolutely loved and adored. I didn't get it, but we had all seen a change in Malic that we liked. He was suddenly part of the whole, like Dylan loving him had fixed whatever was broken. Finding his hearth had rendered the man necessary to the group. He was now needed and depended on, and the fact that Leith would purposely turn to him to help keep me safe spoke volumes. He trusted Malic to eliminate Eric as a threat but not kill him. It was a big step. Things had changed, and I was happy about that until Tuesday morning.

"I hate being here, learning crap I already know," Chale grumbled.

"I agree." I smiled at him.

"And this place…." He trailed off.

"This place what?"

"It gives me the creeps."

"The snow is strange too, right?" I asked him.

"Absolutely," Chale agreed with me, looking slightly panicked suddenly. "The snow, everything—it's spooky."

It was more than that.

We took the main staircase up to the second floor, and when we turned the corner, Chale almost walked into a man standing there in the long hall. I yanked him back because I thought I saw smoke.

It made no sense, thick, gray smoke blowing forward and then instantly gone, not even dissipating, just evaporating. And I was thinking I was seeing things because, even though I felt fine, everyone around me was edgy and freaked. The weirdness was starting to rub off on me, and I was ready to let it go, assure myself I was seeing things, when I realized Chale was trembling.

"What the fuck," he half yelled, stepping back, bracing himself, feet apart, ready to throw down.

"Gentlemen," the man said, but the end came out funny, like he gagged or choked.

I stared. Chale stared. Neither of us moved as the man stood there looking back at us. He looked pained suddenly, almost sad, and then his skin started to sag, stretch, and finally drip. I caught my breath at the first plink to the floor that wasn't water or even blood but was his skin dropping like he was made of wax and he was melting.

"Jesus Christ," Chale whispered.

I grabbed his arm and ran.

I was not the guy who thought long and hard or turned things over or didn't just act. So instead of standing there and figuring out what was going on, I bolted. Chale seemed to be of the same mind. Until we hit the end of the hall. Flinging ourselves through the door, we found ourselves on the other side in what looked like a condemned version of the same resort we were staying in.

"What the fuck is going on?" Chale roared at me.

I tugged him along after me, not wanting to get separated, and we ran in and out of gutted rooms that cold wind whistled through, past scorched walls, blackened, peeling paint, and over carpet that enormous holes had been burned in. There were those plastic tarps over spaces where windows had been, and they fluttered in the breeze. All of it, everything we could see, was ready to crumble and turn to dust.

"Simon?" he gasped, and his voice was high-pitched, scared, unhinged, and he clutched at my shoulder as we walked.

I had to get my bearings, but when something flickered on the opposite side of the room, I stopped fast.

"What?"

"Do you see that?"

"Hello."

We both turned to the voice, and there in front of us was a man. He was tall, classically handsome like a matinee idol from the forties or fifties, with slicked-back hair, dark eyes, and chiseled features.

"Welcome, gentlemen," he said, and his voice sounded hollow. "I'm Mr. Saudrian, the hotel manager."

I stared at him because he looked like he was made of plastic.

He smiled, and it was robotic as he reached for Chale.

My new friend screamed, and I grabbed the guy's wrist, intercepting him.

It was the stranger's turn to scream.

I didn't have time to even react before I was jolted, like the jolt you get when you fall in your sleep and it startles you awake. It was like I woke up and I was in a room that overlooked the now snow-covered courtyard.

"What the fuck was that?" Chale roared, staggering back, collapsing onto the overstuffed floral print chair behind him. He dropped down onto it, gripping the arms. "And how the hell did we get here?"

I moved fast, squatting down beside him, my hand on his knee, trying to figure out what was going on. "Are you okay?"

"Not at all." His voice rose and cracked, sounding frantic.

He was falling apart, and I was pretty sure the only reason I wasn't was because of Leith and what I knew about his life.

"Just—we'll figure everything out, okay?"

"Simon?"

I looked toward the door, and there was a man I had never seen in my life looking at me like he was waiting, watchful.

"Yes?" I asked as I slowly rose beside Chale's chair.

He gave me a slight smile, just a twist of the corner of his mouth, as he levered off the doorframe he had been lounging against.

Some people, the minute you met them, you knew they were wicked and wild. He was tall, strong, powerfully built, with military style, buzz-cut short chestnut-brown hair, dark tanned skin, and smoky topaz eyes. The man just oozed trouble.

"Who are you?" I asked him, wary, as he approached me.

"I'm Raphael Caliva," he told me as he stopped, close, but not close enough to make me uncomfortable. "And I was asked to check on you by Jackson Tybalt."

Jackson.

I wasn't sure I knew Leith's friend and fellow warder's last name, but how many Jacksons was I expected to know? And he had said the name like I should know whom he was talking about.

"Who?" I tested anyway.

He arched one thick brow as his eyes narrowed. The man was not handsome in a way that everyone would agree on, but there was something striking about him, something sensual and alluring and fiendish all at the same time. He looked, with his bedroom eyes and the swaggering walk, like the kind of guy who would bring nothing but heartbreak and pain... and heat and sex and lust. You saw him and thought about climbing into bed with him. I was immune, since I only got hot for one guy, but I clearly saw the man's appeal. Chale saw it as well, if his sucked-in breath was any indication.

"You don't know?"

I had no idea what we were talking about. "What?"

"How many do you know?"

"What?"

"Jacksons. How many do you know?"

"One."

He winked at me. "That's the one."

I nodded, cleared my throat, and then turned to look down at Chale. "I just need to talk to him for a second, okay?"

"Go ahead," he told me, pointing to the opposite corner of the room. "Talk over there, just don't—don't leave the room. I'm not going anywhere without you."

I patted his shoulder before walking far enough away from him that he wouldn't be able to hear every word I said to my visitor. If he really listened, he would get most of it, but as he was working through a meltdown, I figured he had more than just me on his mind. When I stopped and turned, I found myself faced with Raphael.

"Who are you?"

"I told you already."

I folded my arms across my chest. "What are you?"

"I'm a kyrie." He smiled, and I saw the extended canines from every vampire movie I had ever seen.

I nodded. "You're the kyrie who saved Malic, right? I heard about you."

"Did you?"

"Yes," I told him. "Leith said you drank Malic's blood."

"Only a little."

"And now you're supposed to be in thrall to him or something."

He tilted his head and smiled, which made his eyes glow a weird orange color, like he was sitting in front of a bonfire or something. "'In thrall to'," he scoffed. "Such antiquated terms your sentinel throws around and so infects his warders and their hearths. I am in thrall to no man."

"Then why are you here?"

"I was asked, as I said."

But not by Malic. He wasn't asked by Malic. "Jackson asked you to check on me. Why?"

"Because he could not come himself first, only second."

"I have no idea what that means."

He shrugged like he couldn't have cared less.

"So Malic has no pull with you, only Jackson."

"Only Jackson," he agreed.

"Why?" I pressed him, wanting to know.

"I will simply do the man's bidding and demand payment."

"Like what?"

"It's not necessary for you to know."

"It is if Jackson's taking care of a debt because of me."

"Again, you should not concern yourself with my bounty, only with your own safety."

"Why wouldn't Jackson just come himself, or Leith?" I asked, my voice cracking on my boyfriend's name. I had been missing the man before my world took a turn into the creature-feature nightmare, but now I felt like my skin hurt because he wasn't there to hold me.

The kyrie looked bored. He even yawned. "Warders can't cross over through façades, only demons and my kind. They can follow after I've found you, use the wormhole I create to reach you, but they can't punch through a dimensional door. It's harder than you think."

"Is Leith coming here?"

"I'm sure he's trying now even as we speak. He was frantic to reach you but I came alone since, as I explained, I was asked to come look in on you."

I took a breath and let the knowledge that Leith knew I was in trouble fill me with peace. I should have realized that the man I loved, my warder, would have been worried when he couldn't reach me.

"Simon?"

But I had more questions. "A kyrie is what, exactly?"

He yawned louder, and his eyes watered. "I'm a bounty hunter, a tracker. Other creatures pay me to find someone or something, and I either kill it when I find it, bring them back a piece to show that it's really dead, or just retrieve the whole thing still wiggling."

"What do you need money for?"

"Everybody needs money," he said with a shrug. "I need it to wave around when I require information. I used to threaten people's lives, bleed them, but it's way easier to just slide them over a fifty."

He was so cavalier about his job.

"But now to you. Shall we go?"

"Wait; make me understand what's going on."

"With?"

"Are you kidding?"

He scowled at me.

"With all this." I gestured around. "What the hell is going on?"

He scratched his head, then rubbed the back of his neck. "Okay, so this is a façade."

I waited.

"All this that you see"—he waved his hand in the air—"the walls, the floors, all of it is basically an illusion. It was all put up by a powerful demon to lure humans."

"But none of us were lured here. We came because we had training here. None of us would have picked this place if we'd had a choice."

"The lure was not for you, Simon Kim, but for whoever decided that your whatever-this-is would be here. Perhaps this hotel was chosen for the price or the fact that it was secluded, or that there were large rooms, who the fuck knows? But whatever the deciding factor was, that was the lure. Don't believe for a moment that this façade did not do precisely what it was meant to."

"Why?"

"Why what?"

"Why put up a façade to begin with?"

"Didn't I just answer that?"

"No, you didn't. What I wanna know is why? Why put up this trap? For what purpose?"

"Oh, well, demons put these up to lure people in," he said. "Once they come in, they can't get out. After a while, the façade peels, like this one is, and then it falls down onto a different plane with everyone inside."

"So you can come in, but you can never leave."

"Yeah." He smiled suddenly, waggling his eyebrows at me. "Just like that Eagles song."

I took a steadying breath, ignoring his attempt at humor. "So this hotel is going to plummet into the pit, into hell, and we're all gonna die."

"No, not into the pit; the pit is lower, that's the bottom of hell. This one is built over a hell dimension. Big difference, believe me."

"But we're all still going to die."

"Probably not die. More subjugation, slavery, degradation, that sort of thing."

He was much too matter-of-fact for my peace of mind.

"Jesus."

"Lemme see," Raphael told me as he sank down on one knee and looked like he was just staring at the floor, examining it. "Okay, so I'm right, this façade is built over a siphon world. So, yeah," he said, looking up at me. "It won't be death; you'll just wish it was."

"What does that mean?"

He rose in front of me. "That means that this was built by a demonic lord who needs soldiers, so he's recruiting."

"Now I'm really lost."

He exhaled deeply. "Okay, so like I said, a façade is what this is. Humans tumble into them, or get invited, and then they get stuck like you are now. When the façade has been depleted of all its energy, like this one is really close to being, then it peels like an onion, layer by layer, until you have what you and your buddy were running through earlier. What you saw before, that's what it looks like in here to me now."

I was stunned. "It looks burnt out and barren like it was gutted by fire."

"Yep."

"That's what you're seeing right now."

He nodded.

"Jesus."

Quick shrug from Raphael.

"How did you know Chale and I saw the façade all stripped?"

"I've been here for a bit."

"Why did you wait to contact me?"

"I was lookin' around. Plus, I can come in undetected, but when I leave everyone's gonna know."

"What does that mean?"

"Just listen," Raphael sighed tiredly. "You've got maybe an hour, maybe less, before this whole place is gonna fall like a runaway elevator and you're all gonna end up in a siphon world that looks a lot like Death Valley on crack. I'll bet you it's hot as hell during the day and freezing ass cold at night."

"God."

He grunted.

"And how long would we—how do we get back?"

Quick shake of his head. "You won't know that until you either find it yourself or you find someone that knows."

"Find what?"

"The way out, of course." He squinted at me like I was stupid.

He was really the most annoying man. "Am I looking for a door? A flashing neon sign? What?"

"Well, it won't be the sign thing, that's for sure," he said, grinning wickedly. "But there's really no way to tell. Sometimes you stumble onto the way out, sometimes you find a guide, there's no real way to tell until you're there. It can be words strung together that make something seen that was unseen, I've heard of it being an equation—you just don't know. Only runners have charts of all the hell dimensions and they don't share well."

"Is that a kind of demon, a runner?"

"Uh-huh."

I really couldn't be bothered with what would happen, though; I needed to know what my immediate future held. "Tell me what's going to happen once we fall?"

"Well, once you're there, you'll get attacked by demons, they'll bite everyone, and when they do, the true nature of each person will be revealed."

"I don't understand."

"That's what a siphon world is; it allows the hidden soul to come bubbling up to the surface. The bite of a lower demon there will either turn you"—he pointed at me—"into a demon yourself, or, if your humanity is strong enough, you'll remain you, and then you're dinner."

I shivered hard. I couldn't help it.

"But you don't have to worry about any of that, 'cause we're going."

"Why would demons want to turn people into demons?"

"We need to go!" he snapped at me.

"Tell me!"

"Fine. You wanna chat instead of run? We can do that."

"I need to know."

"Okay, for one, it's kinda their deal, right, the corruption of the soul, but mostly it's just for numbers. On the different planes of hell, there are territories, and demon lords fight battles for resources and land just like people do here on earth. It isn't any different."

"And these demon lords need soldiers."

"Exactly."

"Does this happen a lot?"

He shrugged. "It's harder to pull off nowadays, with technology, but c'mon, they still never found those people from the Roanoke colony, right?"

I sucked in my breath, and he winked at me.

"I don't...." I raked my fingers through my hair. "Shit."

"Now can we go?" he asked me. The wicked smile was back, and I realized I was being indulged.

"I have friends."

"No can do, ace. One passenger only." He yawned, rubbing his eyes again. "Just like warders, I can only move one at a time, and besides, the displacement wave I give off will probably peel the last layer and sink this thing into the siphon. That's why I've been hanging out. I can't just leave here unnoticed. You don't want to be here when I go."

"Why would you be noticed?"

"Kyries, like sentinels, and other travelers—"

"Travelers?"

"Any creature that can cross between planes is called a traveler."

"Can't warders cross planes?"

"They can follow, but they can't go themselves. If a traveler punches through a hole," he said, yawning, "then a warder can follow."

"That's what you meant earlier."

"Yes."

"Sorry, go on."

"Okay, so when I leave, I'm gonna create a displacement wave that, because this is a façade, everybody's gonna feel. How close this thing is to falling, it really might be the last straw."

"There was no wave thing when you come in?"

"No, the punch *in* implodes, backfills the hole it creates, but the punch out has nowhere to go but out so it sort of explodes. That one you'll feel."

I shook my head. "None of it makes any sense to me."

"Why would it?"

"I can't just leave my friends here."

"I don't see that you have a choice."

But Jess and Kenny and Chale were counting on me, and something else popped into my head. "Why did I hurt that man when he tried to grab me?"

"What man?"

"When Chale and I were running, we—"

"Oh, that wasn't a man." He yawned again.

"Are you bored or something?"

"Fuck you, man, I'm tired. I hunt for a living, you know."

He was so irritable it almost made me feel better, more normal. "Okay. Tell me why, when I touched a demon, it burned him."

"The touch of a warder scalds a demon, as does the touch of their hearth, as the hearth is their heart."

I absorbed that. "So I can hurt a demon?"

"Burn it with your hand, yes, but not fight it. Hearths don't fight demons."

"Sure."

"But if you ever wanna test if your man loves you or not, go grab hold of a demon. If it sizzles, you'll know you still got it."

"I—"

"Let's go," he said suddenly, almost whining, grabbing hold of my wrist.

"No. I can't just—"

But he was cut off when we all felt the earthquake, followed by the sounds of people screaming from downstairs.

"Okay, hearth," he growled at me, but he wasn't panicked, more annoyed. "We have to make the jump now. My idea of fun is not free-falling into a hell dimension."

When he finished, he yanked on my wrist, trying to pull me after him, but I planted my feet. It was only then that I noticed that I hadn't hurt him. He wasn't burned.

"I thought my touch would scald you." I was amazed.

He scoffed. "I'm not a demon, no matter what your deluded warder told you."

"All he said was that you tried to kill Malic."

"We've been over this. I needed some blood to heal; I was never going to hurt him."

I shoved him off me, and because he wasn't expecting it, I managed to free myself. "I can't leave my friends."

"Then you'll die," he assured me even as the room rocked.

Chale, who had run to the window when the first quake occurred—even if he hadn't told me I would have known he was not from California—slammed into my side, clutching at me.

"Simon, we gotta get out of here!"

I turned for the door and ran with Chale right behind me. We were joined instantly in our charge down the hall by the kyrie.

"This is madness, hearth of a warder," Raphael told me.

"I have to find Jess."

"Simon!"

I knew the voice. Stopping at the top of the stairs, I looked across the atrium and saw Leith. He was there with Ryan—or Rindahl—and Jackson—Jaka—both his fellow warders, but for me, he was the draw. And I knew everything would be okay. Leith would take me home, and Ryan and Jackson would take my friends. The kyrie could even take my new friend Chale.

"Run!" Leith commanded, and I yelled for Chale to follow me as I turned to charge around the terrace. I saw the people surge into the atrium, heard the screaming and yelling, the shrieks of fear. It was chaos, but Leith had come for me, had known intuitively that I was in danger. I simply wanted to reach him.

When I was almost to him, the ground beneath my feet fell away. It felt like the first downward drop of a roller coaster, the moment where you lift up off your seat and then realize that there is only air around you.

Chale screamed behind me, and there was a rush of air as we plummeted. The images rolled over each other, Ryan suddenly at the center of a swirling vortex, diving toward Leith, whose face was flooded with fear, Jackson leaping off the balcony only to be driven back hard as Raphael grabbed him, his claws sinking into Jackson's chest.

I fell faster and faster, my speed increasing. I couldn't see Leith or anyone, and all the voices became one horrible howl of pain as the speed and lack of oxygen overtook me, and all I saw was black.

# VI

THE shaking was insistent, and when I finally opened my eyes, I saw Jess's big brown ones staring down at me. Her face was dirty and scratched, but other than that, she looked unscathed. Sitting up, I wrapped my arms around her, crushing her to me.

"Oh, baby, are you all right?"

She was trembling hard. "Jesus Christ, Simon, what the fuck is going on?"

Why was she asking me?

"Oh God," she moaned.

I pulled back to look at her face. "Did you see Leith?"

"Leith? No. How would Leith be here?"

"Never mind," I said, taking a breath. "Did you see Kenny?"

She only nodded.

"Is he dead?"

She shook her head and started crawling away from me. It was only then that I realized that we were both covered in dirt. The two of us were in the entrance to what looked like a small cave. There were some rocks on one side, and I could see the furrow in the ground, which showed me how she had gotten me there. I had been dragged. But she wasn't big enough to—

"Simon!"

Even though my name had been whispered, it sounded like a yell. My head snapped around, and I saw Chale. He was banged up, his right eye was swollen almost shut, and there were cuts and scratches on his face and neck. I was so happy to see him.

He grabbed me tight and hugged me hard, ending up rolling over on top of me, as we were both lying down in the dirt. When he lifted up, I saw a tear roll down his bruised cheek.

"Thank you for helping Jess drag me here."

He nodded fast. "I'm not real sure where here is, but away from everyone else is better."

"What're you talking about?"

"Come here," Jess said softly, gesturing me to her.

When I rolled over on my stomach, my head swam for a minute before I got my bearings. I did the Navy SEAL crawl that they do in all the movies over to her, with Chale right behind me. We came up on either side of her and looked down the small hill at the craziness below.

I had never seen anything like it. There were creatures that looked like men but were definitely not. Some looked like Komodo dragons walking on two legs, like lizard men from some bad Saturday morning kids' show with guys in zip-up rubber suits. Except the suits looked real and terrifying and more like something out of Clive Barker's mind than Disney. Other creatures resembled bears, others like what I figured a werewolf would look like, but they were all doing the same thing: attacking the people in what resembled a giant corral. Off to one side there were two men who reminded me of Roman soldiers or gladiators in breastplates and those skirts made of leather strips. They wore guards on their forearms, but instead of sandals, both men wore boots made of fur that came to their knees. One had an ax strapped to his back; the other had a heavy broadsword hanging from a belt on his hip. They were enormous and primitive and scary as hell. The one with the ax kept gesturing to the other, and the creatures kept dragging woman after woman near them.

"I think," Jess said softly, pointing, "that the one with the ax wants the one with the sword to pick a woman, but the swordsman won't or doesn't like what he's looking at, so he passes."

"Unfortunately," Chale gulped on the other side of Jess, "every time he passes...."

And I saw what happened. The creature holding the last woman suddenly turned and bit down hard into her shoulder. I saw the blood roll down her shoulder a second before she fell to the ground, convulsing, foaming at the mouth.

And then she changed.

The seams split on her clothes; her hair sloughed off as her body ran with reptilian red skin. She came to her feet seconds later, leaping at the creature that had bitten her, trying to behead him. One of the wolf creatures pried her off, and she turned on him, screaming and shrieking, her arms and legs and tail wrapping around the wolf as she tried to dry-hump him. He stroked her tail and wandered out of the enclosure with her.

It was then, when I followed him with my eyes, that I saw it, the orgy that was going on off to the side. It had first looked like the fight that was raging in other areas, but my mind cleared, and I saw what I was really looking at. Creatures were falling on each other in a heated sexual frenzy.

Some of the women that were bitten did not change, instead remaining human. The bites bled, but shirts and sweaters stemmed the flow, and those women were herded toward another enclosure that looked like a barn from where I was. The whole thing looked like some medieval manor house, and I could see that there was an enormous outer wall that circled us. I couldn't see behind the cave, but as far as I could see to the left and right, there was a wall.

"The men have all been either changed or not." Jess's voice was shaky. "They did them first."

"Jesus," I groaned.

"Not all the women are shown to the swordsman," she told me, and I saw that several women were being bitten by werewolves. "I don't know why some are picked and some aren't, maybe it's a certain age he's looking for, or a type, but I haven't been able to figure out what it is."

Trying to figure out the reason was probably what was keeping my friend from going stark raving mad. Her brain, wrapping around a puzzle, was protecting itself from the total insanity of the situation.

"Maybe ax man has a preference and so he's showing only those to the swordsman... I really don't know."

"I'm sure you'll figure it out," I assured her.

Her eyes flicked to mine. "At least you woke up," she said, and her voice quavered. "I was so scared."

"How long was I out?"

"Three days," Chale told me, looking over Jess's head at me. "I mean, hard to tell, but I think it was three days."

"Yeah," Jess agreed, and I heard the sob in her voice. "You hit your head so hard."

I felt it then—the back of my head was tender. There was a large lump, but my mother always said, as it pertained to blows to the head, better out than in. She always preferred a big bump to no bump at all.

"I only started shaking you when I heard you moaning."

"You must've been dreaming," Chale chimed in.

"I seriously thought you were gonna die, but I kept putting water down you anyway," Jess told me. "Thank God you woke up. I was totally freaking out without you."

"Oh, sweetie."

"I feel so much better now that you're awake."

Her statement made no sense at all. How was I her touchstone?

"I missed you."

I reached for her and she grabbed me, pressing her body to mine, sighing deeply when Chale was suddenly at her back, the three of us wrapped together tight.

Jess sobbed silently, Chale was shaking, and I just held on. They had a three-day head start on me of horror, desolation, and hopelessness; I wasn't quite as freaked out as them yet.

When Jess and Chale finally let me go, I asked her where Kenny was.

She wiped at her eyes, leaving dirt smears on her face. "He got bit and turned into a wolf thing. I don't know which one; I can't tell them apart."

"I can," Chale told me. "They put a strange breastplate on him; the metal looked like bronze when it turns that green color if you don't polish it."

I nodded. "At least I can distinguish him."

"Why would you want to?" Jess asked me sadly.

I put my hand on her face. "We're gonna get out of here, and we're gonna get home. You'll see."

She pressed her eyes closed tight, and I saw the tears roll out from under her lashes.

"Tell me what else?" I prodded her, wanting her strong again.

Jess took a breath, wiped at her eyes, and then fanned her face with her hand. "Okay, well, some of the people they took into that big house. I think they went in to work, but I'm not sure. We'd have to go in to know. And the first day, there was only ax guy down there, and then yesterday—oh, you've been out four days," she gasped. "Because for one day, there was only ax guy, and then for the last three there's been sword guy too."

"Okay," I told her, realizing I was thirsty. "What are you guys doing for water?"

She pointed back, and to my wonder I saw, of all things, big bottles of Evian.

"What the hell is that?"

Her smile made my heart hurt. "I was in the room when I felt an earthquake. I threw everything from the minibar in a pillowcase, grabbed the comforter, and stood in the doorway. I grew up in Northridge, man. I know about earthquakes."

"You're amazing."

"I'm not, but you need to drink some now. There's six bottles there, that little round cheese, crackers, and some other stuff."

I crawled over to the bottles, which were deeper in the cave, picked one that was already open, and drained it. Just that little bit of liquid made me feel better. Sitting up made me slightly light-headed and nauseous, but after a minute, the feeling receded.

"Drink some more," Chale told me, "and eat a cracker if you can."

They went back to their lookout, and I opened a new bottle, sipped slowly, and ate a few Ritz crackers. My stomach couldn't take any more of either, so I made sure to twist the cap on extra tight and then crawled back over to them.

"So you guys have been camping up here all by yourselves, huh?" I asked when I was back at Jess's right shoulder.

"That's right." She shivered. "Camping."

"How did you guys meet?" I asked her, to try and infuse some sense of normal.

"I was trying to drag you," she told me, "and Chale was suddenly there, helping me. We met because of you, Simon, but Chale is my new best friend."

"Same here," he said, leaning into her, arms wrapped around her shoulders, squeezing gently. "We've had three days, no, four, you said."

"Four." She nodded, patting his cheek tenderly.

"We've had four days to bond.... She's the sister I never had."

"Okay." I exhaled. "So what's our plan here?"

"The plan is to stay hidden," she said softly. "I don't want to get bitten, and I have no idea what makes people change and what doesn't. I definitely don't want to be a slutty red reptile creature that wants to bang werewolves. It's one thing to read about hot guys who can shape shift, but all furry with the muzzle and the teeth does not sound like fun."

I had to agree.

"So what is—Jess!"

I saw it first, the stream of saliva or something that fell down onto her back. I rolled over, and there above us were two huge wolf creatures.

Jess screamed and bolted from the cave, but there to stop her, having snuck up on us, were three reptile creatures. I realized then that the cave was just up a small slope and could not have been that hard to find. They had just been busy before, four days of weeding through the crowd of people, and had finally gone looking for strays.

I rushed forward but was slammed to the ground and pinned under what was easily three hundred pounds of snarling werewolf. I heard Chale yelling as I was jerked to my feet. The three of us were dragged down the hill toward the corral.

The enclosure was muddy inside, and as we were shoved forward into it, I lost my balance and went down. Chale was screaming, and when I turned to look at him, I saw one of the wolves preparing to bite down into his shoulder.

I felt a surge of protectiveness, and because I had fallen, no one was holding me. Rising fast, I charged across the small space and hurled myself at Chale. I struck him hard and he crumpled under me, which kept him from the creature's jaws. The roar from the wolf creature was deafening, and I rolled over, hands up, to fend him off.

But he froze suddenly, still as a statue in his forward lunge, an enormous broadsword embedded in the middle of his chest as he sank to his knees. I hadn't seen it thrown, hadn't heard it whistle by me, it was just there, as though it had been summoned by magic. I scrambled backward as the creature fell forward from its kneeling position and slumped sideways into the mud. Jess was suddenly falling down into my lap, sobbing as she clutched at me, shuddering in my arms. Chale was plastered to my back, the three of us huddling together as lizard men and werewolves made a circle around us.

I heard a growl, low, menacing, and when I lifted my head, the swordsman was there, yanking his weapon from the wolf's fallen body and wiping the blade on the creature's fur before replacing it in the scabbard that hung from his hip. When he turned to me, I saw that his eyes were completely black. It was like the pupil had been broken like the yolk of an egg and the ebony color had filled the man's eyes. The way he was looking at Jess was terrifying, like she was food.

"Oh God," I moaned. "I think he found the woman he wanted."

"It's not her he wants," Chale said through chattering teeth.

I had a second of understanding before the big man bent, fisted his hand in my sweater, and lifted me free of the others. I was dragged up against him, crushed to the hard metal cuirass as he looked down into my face.

"Let go!" I yelled at him, trying to shove him off me, to no avail.

He grabbed a handful of my hair and yanked my head back hard. I gasped because it hurt and reeled in his arms as everything spun. The hand loosened, and he nuzzled my hair, inhaling deeply before he pushed at my cheek with his nose, tilting my head sideways. I struggled when he licked up the side of my neck, but when he just held me tighter, I stopped. He was massive and powerful, and as the top of my head only came to his shoulder, there was no way I was going to win a battle of strength.

"Please," I begged him.

And instantly, I was wrapped tight in his arms, held close, but tenderly, protectively.

"Simon!" Jess cried out.

I jerked in his arms, seeing a reptile creature grab her.

The barbarian roared and the creature froze, releasing her. And I understood: the man who had seemingly claimed me terrified the crap out of everyone else.

I moved slowly, wriggled free, and when I took a step back, he took one forward, wanting to stay close, his hand back to being fisted in my sweater. I stopped, smiled up at him, and reached a hand out to Jess. She moved fast, grabbing my hand, and he looked at her, his eyes narrowing.

I put a hand on the cuirass to show him that I wasn't going anywhere and heard him exhale sharply. When Jess reached for Chale, there was a snarl low in his throat. I lifted a hand to the barbarian's face and saw him lean into it and shudder.

"Jesus Christ, Simon, who the fuck is this guy?"

He dipped his head down so my hand ran up the back of his neck, and when he lifted his head, his eyes were back to being narrowed slits. He grabbed my wrist hard and dragged me after him. But I didn't let go of Jess, and she had a death grip on Chale. No one stopped us as he led me and the others from the enclosure and toward the manor.

The stench, the screams—it was overwhelming. I couldn't process all of it, and even when Chale was sick, he didn't stop, just threw up and kept walking behind us.

We reached a large, heavy, metal gate, and the monster reached under his breastplate and withdrew a long chain that had a key on the end. He opened the gate, pulled us all through, and then locked it behind us. Instantly I noticed a change.

"The meat smell," Chale said from behind me. "It's not in here."

"No one's screaming," Jess echoed him.

I looked around, and it was quiet. There were people dressed in togas, women and men, and they hurried forward to greet the man, bow low, and wait. The swordsman pulled Jess's hand from mine and shoved her and Chale at some of the people.

Jess started crying, but one of the women put an arm around her and tucked her into her side, stroking her face at the same time. The woman was clean, and so were the others, I noticed as I glanced around. It was definitely different behind the locked gate; it felt like a sanctuary.

"I think it'll be okay, Jess," I told her as two women stepped around Chale, their hands on his face, checking him over with eyes full of concern.

One of the women put her fingers together, motioning toward her mouth.

"She wants to feed me," Chale said, his voice cracking as he looked at me.

"Just go," I told them as I was jerked forward sharply by the man who had claimed me, nearly falling, stumbling before I regained my balance.

"Ohmygod, Simon," Jess moaned.

"Just be safe," I told her. "Don't leave here. It's safer in here than out there."

She nodded fast as I was pulled forward again, this time winding up in the dirt. The barbarian reached down and lifted me up, and I was thrown over his back, carried like a sack from the quad.

A door opened, and I heard a metal gate scrape the floor and the creak of the hinges that allowed it to swing open. It was dark, only torches on the walls lighting a long hallway that had empty, unlocked cells running the length of it. It looked like I was being walked into a jail from the courtyard that we had just left. I heard water a second before I was lifted and thrown.

I hit the warm water hard and was winded for a moment, disoriented, before I figured out what was happening. I had been hurled into some sort of enormous heated underground cistern. When I pushed off the bottom and rose to the surface, I realized that I was basically in the center of a giant bathtub with steps around it. I was not stupid. I knew what he wanted.

I stripped off my clothes, shoes, and socks and let them float free around me. When I was tossed a small cloth and a cake of soap,

I washed myself clean. Apparently the swordsman liked his food smelling good before he ate it.

When I was done, I stayed there, in the water, and watched him. Slowly, his eyes never leaving me, he started to strip out of his armor. The armguards were discarded, the enormous breastplate that covered a chest that should have been bronzed, and the leather-stripped skirt. His boots were last, and when he was naked, gleaming in the low light, I exhaled slowly. The man was a mountain of hard, rippling muscle, from the washboard abdomen to his roped thighs and calves. He was powerfully built and absolutely, stunningly beautiful. My breath caught just looking at him.

He gestured me to him, and I saw that his shaft was rock solid, precome already leaking from the tip. The man wanted me bad, and though he was gorgeous, though I could appreciate the sight of him, there was only one man I hungered for.

"Is this inevitable?" I asked him. "Are you gonna rape me whether I come out or not?"

He whimpered in the back of his throat, and that was surprising. I saw him reach behind him and lift a small wooden bowl off a ledge carved into the wall. He dipped his fingers inside, and when he lifted them, I saw them glisten in the torchlight. It was oil.

"At least you're not planning to dry-hump me," I said breathlessly, terrified just looking at his enormous cock. I wondered how it was going to fit inside me. I had only ever bottomed for Leith; he was the only man that had brought out in me the desire to submit.

Staring at the man whom I would not be allowed to say no to, I shuddered.

He grunted low in his throat, and the sharp gesture, the way his brows furrowed, showed me that he was done waiting; he wanted me out of the water.

I glided close, and he turned and pulled a cloth off a peg in the wall behind him. As I climbed out, he stepped forward and wrapped me up, hugging me tight, crushing me against him. I was dried off roughly, and when he was done, he smoothed my hair back from my face and looked down at me.

"Please don't hurt me," I pleaded with him.

He took my hand gently, lifted it, and placed it over his heart before covering it with his bigger, stronger one.

I sighed deeply. "That guy out there, ax guy, little did he know you weren't looking for a girl, huh?"

His eyes were dark pools of need, and when I lifted my hands to his face, he trembled under my touch. As I studied his face, his breath hitched, and he licked his lips. It was as if he knew what was going... to... happen. Like he knew what I would taste like because he knew me.

But how could he?

His eyes were all over my face, and the look was more than just lust. He reached out, cupped my face in his hand, and smoothed his large thumb across my lower lip slowly, seductively, his lips parting in anticipation.

I jolted in his arms, startling him, which made him clutch at me.

"It's okay," I soothed him, and I saw his eyes bleed from black to the deep, dark ocean-blue that I knew so well. "Oh shit," I breathed out, because my guess was correct.

The giant standing in front of me was my warder.

I was looking at Leith.

Whatever happened in a siphon world had changed the love of my life from his normal lean, muscular self into a battle-ready barbarian. And he knew me but didn't. He knew I belonged to him, but that was all.

"You need me, huh?"

Leith bent toward me, and I understood that what he wanted, what he had to have, what was hard-wired into him and primal, was to claim what was his. It was my place to give myself to him the way he always willingly gave himself to me.

Lifting up, I wrapped my arms around his muscular neck and pulled him down into a kiss. If I had not figured it out before, I would have known the minute our lips met. No one ever kissed me the way Leith Haas did. It was gentle and possessive at the same time, his tongue slipping between my lips, tangling with mine, rubbing, coaxing, as I whimpered in the back of my throat, pressing my now hard, leaking shaft into his thigh.

The minute I knew it was him, my desire had flared to life. I felt the electrical current that ran through his massive frame. When he tore his mouth from mine, he kissed everywhere, moaning out his aching need. Finally, at the base of my throat, he licked and bit, ravenous to taste me.

I was shoved back, turned, and thrown up against the wall. I heard the scrape of the bowl on the rock before his hot, oil-slicked fingers wrapped around my cock. I arched forward into his fist, pumping my shaft in and out of his grip. When he bumped my legs apart, I planted my feet and felt the head of his oil slicked cock press against my entrance.

It had started out as something unknown and frightening but had become, just as quickly, that which I hungered for. And it wasn't gentle—he wasn't going to take his time, and that desperate, hungry, violent need sent heat rushing through me. I was going to be taken, and I shivered in expectation.

He pushed inside of me, past the tight ring of muscles, the pain overwhelming and white-hot as he thrust hard into my clenching channel. I breathed through the burn and willed my body to relax, open for him, take him in because this was Leith, the man I loved. Even as outwardly changed as he was, his need for me, his desire, his want, was absolute.

As my slippery hole swallowed him, I felt a hand on the small of my back, and then his engorged penis slid over my gland. He squeezed my cock tight at the same time, and I cried out in pain and ecstasy.

I heard a deep, rumbling moan from him as he eased out almost completely before pushing back in slowly, inch by inch. His hand moved, and as he withdrew again, I felt his thumb slide inside me with his cock.

It hurt and felt incredible at the same time. I whimpered in the back of my throat, wiggling on the shaft now buried inside me.

He hissed out words I didn't understand, and I knew he was watching the length of him slide in and out of me, and it was driving him mad. He growled hungrily before he withdrew, hands clamping down on my hips before he rammed back into me, his balls against my ass as he began pumping in and out of me as hard as he could.

The unrelenting pace brought on deep, shuddering tremors, the sizzling heat from my quickly building orgasm starting to fill me up.

He grabbed my ass, spread my cheeks, and plunged in deeper and deeper, each hammering thrust more jarring than the last. I was stretched and pounded, and when I could hold on no longer, I roared his name with abandon and came so hard I thought I would pass out.

Even as my legs buckled, he grabbed me and held me tight, driving in and out of me, pistoning inside as my muscles clamped down, squeezing him tight, my body collapsing around him in a velvet vise of heat.

He bit down into my shoulder, muffling his scream in my flesh as I felt hot come fill my ass and overflow. His hand cupped my face, and then he turned my neck sharply so that my lips could be claimed and ravaged. He bit, licked, suckled, and stroked my tongue with his own. The kiss was as brutal and devouring as his lovemaking, and I found that when he eased from my body, I was suddenly cold and shaking.

He turned me around and wrapped me in his arms, holding me gently, rubbing circles on my back. When he lifted me and walked me back down into the warm, caressing water, I didn't protest. As he held me, I understood what it was to be cherished. All the words he could have ever said to me would never compare with the truth he had just shown me. No matter who he was or what he was, I was still his, and he loved me.

# VII

HIS bedroom was huge, with animal pelts on the floor, a pallet for a bed, and an enormous fireplace. When the sun set, I was startled by the drop in temperature. Sitting in front of the fire on a thick fur, wrapped in another, I waited for him to return. He had led me to the room from the bath and carried me to the place I had not moved from. People—servants? I wasn't sure; I had ever seen them before—brought me fruit and bread and a dark red meat that I didn't touch. It could have been lizard man, for all I knew.

When the door opened, I was shocked to see a very ordinary-looking man walk into the room. His clothes stunned me because they were so completely out of place. He was wearing a three-piece cashmere Ralph Lauren suit. I had one very much like it back in the real world where I worked and lived and went to Starbucks. It would have made sense at home, in the office, but here... here he was completely out of place. In the hell dimension, perfectly coiffed and accessorized down to a pocket square and wingtips, he was an anomaly. My mouth opened, but no words came out.

He sneered at me. "I had no idea that the hearth of a warder could be a man. I knew the only reason he was here, trapped, was because he had followed his hearth, and so I've been looking, searching... I brought woman after woman before him, had others hold them, and if he had shown even the slightest interest, I would have had their handler kill them instantly. The only way to truly change a warder, turn him into a beast, is to kill the hearth. And of course, for the trespass of killing their hearth, the warder would have slaughtered the handler, but that was a price I was willing to pay."

I just stared at him as I remembered who he was and where I had seen him before.

"I told my slaves that there had to be a hearth in among the filth somewhere, but never in my wildest dreams did I think to look for a man."

"Why not?"

"Why not indeed. I will learn from my mistake."

I pulled the soft fur cloak tight around me. "You're Mr. Saudrian."

"It is actually just Saudrian. No 'mister' needed."

I nodded. "You're a demon."

"I am more than a demon. I am a demon lord."

"What do you want?"

He shrugged. "I want power, land, all that any demon lord craves, as well as souls. Many, many souls." He sighed deeply, his eyes glinting in the flickering flames. "I wish I could fill a bathtub with them and soak, but alas, I cannot, only breathe them in one at a time."

It was an over-the-top declaration and somehow calmed me, annoyed me.

"I have done well, but unlike others, I have no warriors. I used to have them—I used to train them and beat them and watch them be slaughtered or slaughter others in the coliseum, but millennia come and go, and fortunes change. I have had no champion in ages until now." He breathed out, and I almost shivered with the sound of sinister happiness in his voice. "When the warder toppled into my trap, I was astounded. How? It's unheard of. No warder would ever allow himself to be trapped in a façade and fall into a siphon. It simply would not happen. But when I saw him, held down by ten of my slaves, his eyes just aglow with hatred, I was overcome. I turned him myself, bit into him, drank his blood, his essence, and even though he killed many of my slaves, in the end, he changed and was mine."

I shivered thinking of Leith pinned down and attacked. His was such a gentle soul, even though he killed demons. It had to have been a horror for him.

"Along with looking for his hearth, I have been sending woman after woman to him," he told me. "You need to feed and train your champion but you must also see to his sexual needs, make certain he's sated in every way. I sent sirens and nymphs, and nothing. I even sent my own mate, the dark witch Moira, and she too was rebuffed. I have had to have her chained in her quarters since that day, her desire to bed him almost as great as her desire to drive her dagger into his heart."

I watched him closely, waiting for the attack.

"I never thought to tempt him with beautiful men. I was shortsighted."

But I knew better. No matter how pretty the guy, Leith only wanted me.

He made a sound in the back of his throat. "I gave him the old ludus—"

"What's a ludus?"

"It's where you are now, where a lord trains his gladiators for the ring, or his men for combat, it's where you house them."

"It's a prison."

"It's an area in my home," he said snidely, "where I used to lock my fighting men, yes, but I gave it to the warder for his own use as he is to be my champion."

I nodded.

"But there are tunnels that he does not know of."

Which explained his presence in the room.

"What do you want?" I asked again.

"I want you dead, hearth, but now that you are claimed, now that he knows you're here, if you were to die within my walls, he would slaughter everyone here, including me."

I saw the dread in his eyes for only a fleeting moment.

"So now you will play your part, or I will have your friends raped and dismembered limb from limb. The pain, I can promise you, will be horrific."

I sucked in my breath and felt the rage welling up inside of me.

"You have no idea the torture I can inflict; I've had centuries to perfect my technique."

He presumed that I would let that happen.

"And I don't mean your friends who are now safe behind the locked gate; I mean your friend who now ruts like a stag in heat outside these walls, your man who is now a wolf. I mean your boss and more…. Do not think for a moment that I cannot leave here and travel to your pitiful human realm and bring people here or drop them lower into the pit. Your parents, your sweet sister—I can choose who I—"

"Fuck you," I snarled at him, feeling the anger flood me as I got to my knees. "You think Jael, Leith's sentinel, is just sitting there doing shit about finding him? You don't think that he's watching my friends and family?" I stood up fast, and when I did, he took a step back. "I'm not afraid of you, you asshole. You think we're gonna be here forever—fuck you! I will figure out a way to get out, and I will take my warder with me, and if you ever, ever, threaten me again, I will have him rip out your fuckin' lungs!"

"You are not allowed to speak to—"

I grabbed his forearm, and instantly he screamed from the contact. He shoved me back hard, and I fought for balance, hitting the wall hard, stunned for a moment. When my vision cleared, I saw him holding his injured arm; saw the blisters on his skin, the welts on the palm of this other hand, which he had used to push me off him.

"I may not be able to touch you, hearth, but I can pierce your heart with a sword, sever your head from your shoulders with my ax."

And I watched in amazement as he morphed from his magazine perfection to the ax-wielding barbarian. He roared as he came at me, and I ran. Halfway across the room, my wrist was yanked hard, and I was pulled into what felt like a closet. It was small and cramped, and I was suddenly face to face with Raphael the kyrie.

"Hiya," he said as he smirked at me.

"Holy shit," I gasped, looking at him, my face inches from his. "What're you... how?"

"It's called the tomb of Osiris," he told me, pointing away from him.

I jolted, realizing that the demon was right there beside me, and my hands fisted as I prepared to defend myself.

"Calm down," the kyrie said, his tone patronizing.

I realized then that even though I could see the demon, he could not see me. I watched with huge eyes as he walked around us, sniffed, and reached through me before roaring out his frustration and charging out of the room. "How?" I exhaled sharply, turning back to Raphael.

"It's why it took Isis so long to find her dead husband. Their brother Set, he put all the pieces in one of these and spread 'em all over every plane of hell he could get to."

I just stared at him.

"What?"

"You're telling me that that myth, that myth is real?"

"Pieces of every myth are real," he said, squinting at me. "You know that."

"I don't know that."

"How come?"

"Because I don't live in your world with demons and strange worlds and—"

"Don't you?" he challenged me, arching an eyebrow.

I went mute as I realized he was absolutely right.

"I never get you hearths. You go around thinking that somehow or other you can pretend like everything is how it's always been, all normal, even after you know all about the things that go bump in the night. Why do you do that?"

"To stay sane."

"Isn't it better to be ready? To know what could happen? Be prepared?"

"I don't know."

"Maybe you should figure it out."

He had a point.

"But this is cool, right?" Raphael waggled his eyebrows at me. "The tomb of Osiris is the shit."

The man was astounding.

"You wanna know how it works?"

He enjoyed his own power, that was obvious. "Sure."

"Well, see, you come in one door, and if we open the one behind us, we're in limbo. So we're not gonna do that."

"How long can we stay in here?"

"Only a few minutes before the door just sort of dissolves by itself and we'll be transported to purgatory."

"Is that bad?"

"It's not *bad* bad; it's where I was created, after all, but there's nothing to do there but wait, and most people go nuts just hangin' out."

"How did you leave?"

"I'm made to get out," he said, like I was stupid. "I'm a kyrie; we hunt across planes, dimensions, rings. It's what we're designed for."

"So if you're here, does that mean warders can be here?"

"Yeah, no." He shook his head. "Only demons and kyries in siphon worlds."

"That makes no sense, Leith is here."

"Sorry, lemme rephrase, no warders that still know they're warders. Your boy is changed, he has no idea what he is or who he is beyond this place."

"He knows me."

"He knows what's primal; he knows you belong to him, but that's all. He has no idea who he is or even what his name is, and that's why he can be here. He's a creature of the pit now, not your warder."

"He's still mine."

"Fine, whatever."

"How are we going—"

"Shit," he groaned, shoving me forward.

I felt wind on my back before I was suddenly in the room again, standing on a large fur.

"I have to pay closer attention," he said as he exhaled, grinning at me. "That could've been bad."

My eyes found his. He was unbelievable. My savior was a five-year-old boy in a man's body. "Do you have a plan to get us out of here?"

"Kinda."

"Kinda?"

"I have an option for you."

I threw up my hands. "And what is that?"

"I know where the cliff is, but you've got to get everyone to it."

"I'm sorry?" Talking to him was exhausting.

"Cliff," he repeated like I was impaired.

"Cliff?"

"Yeah, cliff."

"What cliff?" I snapped at him.

"Why're you yelling?"

"Just—what cliff?"

"The edge of this dimension, the jumping-off point." He grinned at me. "I found it."

He really was much too cheerful for my peace of mind. "Do you ever take anything seriously?"

The way he went silent led me to believe he was actually contemplating my question.

"Well?"

He tipped his head. "I have something I want that helping you will get me closer to, so yeah... I can be serious."

"What do you want?"

His eyes narrowed.

"Tell me."

Quick puff of air from him. "I want a warder."

"Do you have one in mind?"

"Why, yes, I do."

I swallowed hard. "My warder?"

His face scrunched up like he'd bit into a lemon. "Are you kidding? There's no evil in that man, no blackness. How could I want him?"

"Malic," I said, because he was the hardest, angriest man I knew.

He snorted. "Have you seen Malic with his hearth? That man is as tame as a kitten."

I would take his word for it. Malic Sunden still scared the hell out of me. Though after my day trip to the siphon world, I would have to re-evaluate what really gave me chills.

"I don't—Jackson," I said softly, because I suddenly remembered our conversation from four days ago. "I saw you grab him, save him from falling in when the façade fell. He's the one who asked you to find me."

His eyes glazed, and I saw the wicked grin. "Yes."

"But he has a hearth."

"Does he?"

Didn't he? I had met Frank Sullivan many times myself. "You can't kill his hearth."

"I don't need to." He shook his head. "Warders are hard to keep and even harder to love. A hearth must be strong to the core, and Frank Sullivan is weak. I cannot take what is freely offered."

"I don't understand."

"And you don't need to," he told me. "Just listen, because I can't stay. It's hard to remain here and keep my baser nature in check."

I saw it then, the beads of sweat on his forehead, talons where his fingers should have been. "You're changing."

"I am." He nodded, but he gave me a smile that showed off his extended canines that somehow were not scary in the least. "Now, ten miles east of here is the edge of this dimension. You must leap from the cliff within two weeks' time, and that will take you back to the hotel."

"What? I don't—how can going down be up?"

He cleared his throat. "Have you ever gone scuba diving?"

It was the weirdest subject change ever. "Yes," I sighed, really annoyed and trying hard not to let him hear it.

"Okay, you know how sometimes when you're out far from shore and there are no markers, no reef, just you and the deep blue sea, and you think you're swimming up, but you're actually swimming down?"

"Sure. You just have to stop and watch which way your bubbles go."

"Precisely. This is the same thing. You're actually upside down, and you just can't tell."

"And so leaping down will actually be leaping up."

"Yes, but this world isn't stagnant like yours. It will change, fold in on itself, and then there will be no out, just a jump to another plane and then another and another. You'll be lost if you don't get home soon. The window to your home is very small."

"Two weeks is not a definite timeline."

"It's all I can give you."

"So what you're really saying is that we should go as soon as we can."

"I would."

I absorbed what he was telling me. "Okay."

"Keep in mind, as well, that the longer you remain here, the harder it will be for you to convince others to leave. Even now, your friend, what's-his-name, the one who was changed into a wolf, he's gone. He can't come back from that change. You'll have to leave him here."

"But why did he change to begin with?"

"It's his nature. Whatever truly lives in the heart will come forth with the demon's bite. Your friend Chale—had he been bitten, you don't know what would have happened."

"But all the people who were bitten and didn't change—"

"Their humanity is strong. It doesn't make them saints; they just know who they are."

"Like when a hypnotist tries to put you under but you remember your name so they can't."

"Sure," he grunted.

"Ten miles east," I reiterated, because I heard the raspy sound to his voice. His eyes were darkening, his smile changing from friendly to carnivorous. "Edge of a cliff."

"Yes."

"You've been here a while, watching me," I said, because from everything he knew, everything he'd commented on, no other conclusion could be drawn. "Thank you."

"I wish I could move you, but you're too far down for me to wormhole you out. Even Jael couldn't bring you out from this depth."

"That's okay; you gave me the way out, now I just have to convince everyone to go with me."

"Use your gifts, Simon, your natural gifts."

I had no idea what those were.

"And Leith, make him follow you," he said, as he winced with pain.

"I'm gonna try my best. Is there going to be a displacement wave when you leave, will Saudrian know you were here?"

"He saw me before the façade fell, and my scent is in this room now; he'll know I was here."

"He'll hunt you down."

I got a flashing grin. "He'll try."

"But, is there gonna be a wave or whatever? What'll happen?"

"No, there's no wave in a hell dimension, only on your plane. I can just leave from here like demons can come and go from your world."

"That's not comforting," I told him.

"But that's why people have warders," he said with a grimace, "to protect them."

"Go, go, go," I urged him, seeing the pain on his face. "Hurry."

The muscles in his jaw corded, and I saw the veins in his neck bulge before he closed his eyes and disappeared. I wondered for a second what a kyrie wanted with a warder before Leith stepped through the door wearing what looked like a mink coat with a huge collar. I rushed across the room and flung myself at him.

He clutched me tight, head in my hair, rubbing his cheek on the top of my head.

"I missed you," I told him.

He rumbled deep in his chest, speaking words—maybe Latin, maybe ancient Greek; I wasn't sure—and slowly removed my cloak.

I looked up into his face and wrapped my arms around his neck. He bent to kiss me, and I felt his hands on my ass, cupping me before I was lifted up, held tight to his chest as he crossed the room to his bed.

He lay down, stretching languidly under me as I straddled his thighs. In either form the man took, the lean, toned, sinewy-muscled man I was used to or this new buffed-out Adonis, he was the same when he touched me: gentle, reverent. His hands wound into my hair, pushing it back from my face, and I saw the awe as he looked at my eyes. He was speaking to me softly, his voice deep and growly as I leaned down to kiss him.

He opened for me, moaning urgently into my mouth, and I felt his huge, throbbing cock pressing against me. I tried to lift my mouth from his to ask where the oil was, but he caught my bottom lip between his teeth and nibbled, holding me there. When I felt his hands on my ass cheeks, spreading them slowly, and then a finger slide into my cleft, I realized that the oil was somewhere beside his bed.

Leith pushed inside me with his slippery digit, rubbing, pressing, before adding a second that came with more oil. Tenderly, he prepared me, stroking deeper each time until he bent his finger forward and eased over my gland. It felt amazing, as did the strong hand he wrapped around my lust-hardened cock.

I leaned forward, away from his fingers, only to push back down onto them, driving them further inside me. The second time I rose up, when I lowered myself, a third finger was added, filling me and coaxing a choked whimper from him as my hands dug into his chest.

"Leith," I barely got out his name, moving away from him, pushing his hands away so that I could take hold of his long, hard, thick shaft. I lined it up with my clenching hole and eased down inch by inch. He filled me, stretched me, and it hurt and didn't at the exact same time. He pushed up into me, unable not to, arching up off the bed, head back, eyes closed.

My slick, hot channel squeezed around him, held him tight, and as I levered off him only to plunge back down, his hands clasping my thighs made me groan with my own need. He felt so good. When he opened his eyes to look up at me, I saw it clearly there in his passion-clouded gaze: he loved me.

"Do you like being buried inside me?" I asked him, pushing down hard, impaling myself on his shaft.

"Simon," he gasped, and I saw his eyes in that second of clarity.

I felt the smile explode out of me. "Yes."

He knew me. And even though his understanding was gone a moment later, it gave me hope nonetheless and made my heart swell.

He whined in the back of his throat, and I lifted up off of him, rolling over on my back in his enormous bed.

I laughed at how fast he moved and lifted my legs for him. Reverently, he eased them over his shoulders, leaning forward and curling around me before he pushed gently against my entrance.

"No," I ordered him, my voice low and filled with gravel. "Fuck me hard."

He stared down into my eyes, and I pushed up so he would understand.

The first plunge took my breath away. He drove inside of me deep and fast, his cock buried to the base. It was always astounding to me that from Leith, and only ever from Leith, I craved this domination. I had never allowed anyone else but him to see me lose control, lose composure, watch me abandon all my careful restraint and lay myself bare for the taking.

He rocked into me, thrusting deeply into my clenching passage, holding my hips tight, not allowing me to move. When he changed his angle, sending the length of him rubbing over my prostate, my back bowed as I came off the bed. I heard his rumble of satisfaction as he fisted my shaft. The moment he tugged, his slick fingers gliding over my sensitized flesh, I yelled his name.

My orgasm tore through me, and semen erupted over his fingers, his wrist, and across his magnificent sculpted stomach. He fucked me through my release and then came as my muscles rippled around him, clenching him tight.

He collapsed on top of me, pinning me to the bed, his weight taking all the air from my body. I laughed in spite of the fact that I couldn't breathe, and he whispered into my hair before he started to kiss me.

My mouth was savaged as he lifted up off me, kissing me hungrily, breathlessly, until I had to push him off me to suck in air.

"God, you're gonna kill me."

He tucked me tight against him, lifting my leg and pulling it over his hip, stroking my ass, his right arm sliding under me, curling around my back. He always liked to cuddle. On lazy Sunday afternoons, cold and rainy outside, I would be sprawled out on the couch reading a book, football on in the background, and he would suddenly be stretched out on top of me, head on my chest, eyes closed, content. The man enjoyed being close, and I would need to remember that, remember that I didn't need to be so careful and correct and hold things in instead of sharing. I had to trust him more, and now that he was in the position to make me accept his affection, I understood how much he craved being demonstrative. I needed to thaw a little, and I would. When we got home... things would change.

As I heard the heavy sigh come up out of him, I realized how replete with happiness the man was. And while I was thrilled to be the cause, I knew that to get everyone where I needed them to be, I was going to have to scare the hell out of him. But there was no choice.

# VIII

THE next morning, after Leith dressed in his armor, I asked him if I could see my friends. He didn't understand at first, but when I took his hand and put the other one out, holding it like I had been the day before, he nodded. He left me in the room alone, petting me first, stroking my hair. Minutes later, Jess appeared with a tray of food.

"Oh God." She broke down when she saw me, dumping the platter on wooden table and rushing across the room to me.

She flung herself at me, and I caught her, tucking her onto my lap.

"I know the way home," I told her.

She twisted around to look at my face. "How?"

"We have to get to a cliff."

"What?" she gasped.

"You have to really listen to me now."

The way she was looking at me, vulnerable and scared but trusting, was almost overwhelming. I had her whole life in my hands, and just for a second, I was terrified. What if I wasn't up to the challenge?

"Simon?"

I had to try.

So I explained about Leith and who he was and what I was to him. I explained about what I knew and where we had to go and how I knew the only way for us to get home. As I watched her, studied her face, it hit me what Raphael had meant. My natural gift was this: I was honest. Everyone knew that if I could help it, I didn't lie. They knew that if I was their friend, I would do whatever I could. So when I changed everything for Jess Turner, between where she was and what she knew of me, she accepted instead of screamed. I watched her shudder, saw her make up her mind to trust me, saw her nod, and felt her warm hand clutching mine.

"I want to see my kids." She sucked in her breath. "Promise me I can see my kids."

"If you listen to me, you can see your kids."

"What do I have to do?"

"We have to make a plan, and we've got less than two weeks to bust out of here if we want to get home."

"Simon," she said shakily, "honey, I don't think I can last even a week here."

But she would have to, because we had to watch and plan and figure things out. There were items to collect and people to talk to. Nothing could be done overnight. "You have to be strong, Jess."

She nodded fast.

I was counting on her to inform the others, tell them we were making a break for it. She said she knew where Chale was. She would talk him into coming with us, though she didn't think it would take much convincing on her part.

"When we get home, I want to talk to Leith myself, all right? I want to thank him for saving me from that horror out there."

"Yes, honey."

She took a deep breath. "Okay."

"Okay. You trust me?"

"Of course, Simon, always."

And as she walked away from me, I had time to think about that. Why did people always end up trusting me?


I HAD the freedom that no one else had, so it fell to me to use that power wisely. During the day I wandered the ludus that belonged to Leith. I slipped outside with Saudrian's servants when they came to bring food for the champion, and even when I was found and chased back, no one dared raise a whip or a hand to me. They knew who I belonged to, and their fear of Leith was greater than my transgression.

I checked every room, watched all the comings and goings, stood at the windows and looked out at night. I had worried about wild animals, but there were none. It was a vast, barren wasteland,

and the only thing that could kill in the desert was thirst. But ten miles was nothing, not really, easily done in an eight-hour period, or even faster, depending on the speed the others moved. I ran five miles a night three times a week at home; I was just worried about the people I was dragging along with me.

I found paper, a quill, and ink; I recorded events, made note of when guards changed, how late and early it was when people ate, drank, and went to bed.

Jess was ready to go, frantic to leave, her panic, more than anything, making the decision for me. When I told her it was time three days later, she had to clutch at my arm so she wouldn't fall. She was so thankful, and I realized that I could not be any more careful; there was only so much I could plan for.

We were all going to meet that night on the side of the manor house that led to the outer wall. I would lift the key from Leith and unlock the gate so we could run. Everyone had to bring their own water, and we would leave as soon as it got quiet and dark. We would be moving fast, but ten miles was a distance that was possible in one night for me and, the consensus had become, for most everyone else as well. I had tried to think of a better plan, but I really didn't think there was one. Waiting had given us the time to talk to everyone, spread the word to every human there of our escape plot. It also let me formulate a plan to try and save my friend Kenny.

I left Leith's room, as I did daily, wrapped in a toga that looked like it was made of raw silk and was not the dusky-brown color of everyone else's, but a pale red. The color afforded me a luxury that others didn't have: free rein to walk everywhere within the ludus. I still couldn't go out, only once having slipped out with Saudrian's food-bearing servants, but I could go anywhere else.

I found Chale, and he pointed out Kenny. The transformation was terrifying; he looked like a creature from a nightmare. But I had, I felt, one chance, and so I lingered, lounging in a chair under the shade provided by the second story of the manor house.

When I saw Leith crossing the courtyard from training all day—I had watched for a while from the upper balcony—I rose and sprinted toward Kenny. The wolf that he was turned on me, snarling, and I heard my warder yell at the same moment I grabbed my friend's arm.

Kenny howled in terror, and his fangs slashed at my bicep as he tried to twist free. I was afraid he was going to bite my arm off, but in the same second I prepared to release him, realizing that my plan had failed, he released a bloodcurdling scream.

We fell together in a tangle of limbs, rolling hard in the dirt, before my brain finally registered that it was a man who was wrestling with me and not an animal. I scrambled back and he twisted around, getting his knees under him, freezing seconds later as he blinked at me.

"Kenny," I said, seeing the armor hanging off his very human frame.

He was panting, chest heaving and eyes wide as he stared at me.

"Kenny, buddy," I soothed him, "you're gonna be all right."

His pupils were dilated, and he looked like he was feverish.

"This is all just a nightmare that we're living through. Come over here to me."

It took him only a second to make up his mind. He yanked everything off of him until he was naked. Moments later he was trembling in my arms.

Leith reached us, lifted Kenny by the back of his neck away from me, and hurled him away like he was throwing away a piece of trash. When he landed, dazed, winded, not moving, my warder went after him.

I ran at Leith, leaped, and landed on his back, arms and legs wrapped around him, and immediately started kissing up the side of his neck. He stilled in his lunge toward a terrified Kenny and took a step back. The onslaught of my affection, my hands under the breastplate on his sweat-dampened skin, my tongue in his ear, my teeth tugging on his earlobe, made his step falter. When I slid off his back, he turned on me. I walked backward, and he followed.

Others called to him, and he answered absently, hungry eyes locked on me as I began yanking at the toga, freeing myself from it. I should have been embarrassed, flaunting myself, but I was saving my friend, so it was worth it. Leith let loose a volley of words, and

Jess was there in seconds with three other women, one with the same piece of cloth everyone else wore, ready to wrap Kenny up.

Jess was crying as she grabbed hold of him, and he fisted his hand in her hair so they couldn't get separated.

"Keep him with you," I called out to her before Leith's towering frame cut off everything but him from my vision.

"I will," she yelled back. "I won't let him out of my sight!"

"Find Dan!" I directed her, my last order before I turned and ran.

I heard Leith growl behind me, and I sprinted down the dark, prison-cell-lined corridor toward the bath. As I rounded the corner, I felt his hand slide along my back, but I made it to the worn stone room and leaped, stretching my body out and hitting the warm water like a spear. I dove deep under the water, hit the bottom, and kicked off, breaking the surface half the length of the pool from my voracious lover.

He was tearing his armor away, hurling it into the wall, the door, uncaring where it hit and fell. When he was naked and heaving, he dove into the water, and I swam hard to the edge and climbed out. I saw his blond head bob up where I had been moments before. He pounded his fist into the water and yelled. I grabbed the cake of soap he had thrown at me a few days ago and threw it at him.

Silence.

The confusion was evident and endearing.

"Wash," I told him, shaking out my hair, grabbing one of the cloths from the pegs in the wall behind me and drying myself off.

We did not speak the same language at all, but he understood and so cleansed his massive frame from his hair to the soles of his feet. It took a while, and I was chuckling by the time he came out, his skin pruney and scrubbed clean. I pulled two cloths for him from pegs on the wall and led him from the room and down the long hall to his private quarters. He held my hand, his fingers laced in mine as I tugged him over to his bed. I dried his hair, which he really liked, from the rumbling purr that emanated from deep within his chest. I made him lie back, feet on the furs, and I wiped away all the water.

When I eased his thighs apart, on my knees between them, he lifted his head to see what I was doing.

"This is gorgeous," I told him, lifting his heavy cock in my hand, wrapping my hand around the base before I opened my mouth and licked the huge head.

His groan was deep and loud, and when I lowered my mouth over him, taking in as much of him as I could, I instantly felt his hand in my hair. I pushed it away, knowing he'd gag me if he was in control, and used my other hand to touch his balls. He jerked under me, and as I made everything wet with saliva, licking and sucking, using my hands, coating him, he came apart. Moments later he was shuddering with his climax, emptying into my mouth as I swallowed and swallowed, taking all he had to give me.

I rose over him after long minutes, when I was certain he was completely spent, and he watched me with narrowed eyes. Gently but insistently, I urged him to his hands and knees, and he let his head hang down as he shivered in anticipation.

The oil was beside the bed, but I wasn't ready for that yet. Instead, I leaned forward and parted his cheeks. His breath caught as I swiped my tongue across his puckered entrance, licking and sucking before I slid inside. His garbled words were raspy and broken as I plunged in and out, pushing saliva into his silky channel, before I added a finger.

His groan was fierce as he moved his knees further apart, inviting me, pushing back on my finger, trying to get it in deeper. I added a second and a third before withdrawing them to his stifled, desperate pleas. I leaned down, dragged my hand through the oil beside the bed, and then thrust the three fingers back inside of him to a gasp of startled pleasure. When I removed them, replacing them instantly with my cock, he dropped his face into the bed, muffling his yell.

His ass was big and firm and tight, not the one I was familiar with, but gorgeous just the same. As I thrust inside of him, I felt his muscles squeezing around the length of me, the pressure strong, pulling me in deeper. I leaned forward, my chest plastered to his back as I reached for his hand to guide it to his own hard, leaking shaft. Immediately he started jerking himself off, and I straightened behind him, fucking him hard as his yell filled the room. I felt the convulsion tear through him as I found my own release.

I stayed where I was, my groin plastered to his ass, and when I tried to ease back, he reached behind him to hold me there. I stroked over the small of his back gently, then down one taut cheek. He shivered with the contact.

"You don't remember, but your body does, and even though it's changed, it still knows me, knows my cock and loves having me buried inside," I told him, my voice gravelly as I gently slid from his body.

He flopped over on his side and looked up at me with heavy-lidded eyes.

I walked to the opposite side of the room, poured him a cup of what passed for water, and brought it back to him. He drained it in one gulp. When I took the cup from him, I turned to go get him some more, but his hand slipped around my wrist.

"What?"

He pulled me down onto the bed beside him and pressed my hand over his heart. He then covered it with both of his.

I nodded, bent, and kissed him. "I love you too, baby. Just remember that tomorrow when you wanna kill me, all right?"

He looked confused, and I had no doubt he was. I was not looking forward to breaking his heart.

# IX

THE first part was easy. I had checked with Jess and Chale the following morning, after Leith left, and found everyone in pretty good spirits. Kenny looked better; they had found our boss, who could not stop apologizing to me. I had been right after all—the hotel *was* weird—and we were all a go for that night.

It was maddening, the waiting, and that night after Leith had drifted off to sleep after we made love in the bathtub, I stole the key from my massive lover. I lifted the chain up over his head, untangled it from his mass of dirty-blond hair, and hauled ass back down the hall.

I found Jess, Chale, and Kenny crouched in the kitchen, and when we went outside, everyone, all the people who were still people, were kneeling along the edges of the courtyard in the darkness. I saw a lot of what looked like animal-skin wine flagons, but I knew they were filled with water. Jess wanted to head up to the cave to recover the Evian bottles, but I told her we couldn't risk it. Besides, even though Raphael had been right and it was hot, it was nowhere near desert hot. I had lived in Phoenix for a while, and the temperature was nothing compared to July in the Valley of the Sun. If the kyrie was right and ten miles was all it was, we would make it easily.

I used the key to get everyone out, a stream of people, and Chale went out in front, walking east, around the side of the manor house and out into the open. He was leading; I was bringing up the rear. When the last person was out, I followed, not locking the gate, putting the chain with the large key on it around the lock, making sure Leith could get out the second he realized I was gone, wanting him to see it there immediately. I had a terrible urge to go back in and wake him up, to get him to come with me, but I knew there was no way to make him understand.

I caught up with the others, unable to stop some from running, even as I saw Jess.

"What if they catch us?"

"What if there's something really scary out here?" I suggested to her.

"Oh for fuck's sake, Simon, I didn't even think of that."

"Yeah, I know," I told her. "Just keep moving."

"It's only ten miles," she reassured me.

"Which is, like, nothing," I agreed. "At home, we walk that easy, and probably walking though the Tenderloin is scarier than this is gonna be."

"Maybe."

"Maybe," I agreed.

She took my hand, and we began jogging.


THERE is no way to curtail the desire to run when you're scared. So we ran in bursts of frantic adrenaline that crested and ebbed the whole night. When we saw nothing, heard nothing, mile after mile, I got scared.

I was terrified that I had trusted a kyrie with my life. I became breathless thinking that Leith had not even noticed I was gone, would not at all, until it was too late, and I would end up abandoning him in a hell dimension. Worst of all was my terror that he wouldn't even care that I was gone and would simply take another man to his bed. That thought lasted a good hour and a half before Jess asked me if I had been sniffing glue.

I told her I probably still had a concussion.

She told me I was just stupid and that I couldn't blame head trauma.

"Maybe none of this is real, and I'm in a coma."

She shrugged. "Maybe we're all dead already and this is hell."

"This is hell," I assured her.

"I am so not up for some freaky existential debate about what's real and what isn't," she snapped at me. "Get it together, Kim, we've got people to lead to the Promised Land."

"Now I'm Moses?"

"An Asian version… yeah."

The banter was not helping.

Dawn broke and we stopped. Everyone sat down and drank water. Some of them lay down, and that was when we heard the horns.

Hunting horns.

I figured there would be dogs next, the baying that there was in every movie I had ever seen, but it didn't happen. But we were at the bottom of a hill, and up on the crest, we saw the chariots.

"Christ, it *is* like Moses," Jess said, exhaling sharply.

There were screams and cries as everyone got on their feet, running, terror pulsing through the crowd, propelling them all forward at the same time in a stampede of fear.

I saw Saudrian in one of the chariots and identified Leith beside him. Hard to miss them—they were both huge, both their heads covered in metal helms, the only difference being that one was carrying an ax and the other a sword. I shivered where I stood.

"Come on!" Jess yelled at me.

We started to run, and I saw the chariots begin down the hill as I checked them over my shoulder. They were leading the animal-people hybrids, wolves, lizards, and the bears that I had seen the first day but not since. They were apparently used for tracking and hunting.

"Ohmygod," Jess yelled beside me, realization hitting her. "Leith—he doesn't know you're you, doesn't know who he really is, and so right now he's thinking that you tricked him for the key."

"Yes," I agreed as we ran.

"Simon, he's gonna kill you!" She started to cry.

"Only if he catches me."

She screamed and rushed by me. I caught up to her, and we ran together fast. I heard Chale scream from up ahead and would have yelled at him to jump if he hadn't just gone ahead and done it.

I stumbled for a moment, overwhelmed at the trust, overwhelmed that he would just do something so ridiculous, so counterintuitive as to leap off a cliff into an abyss on just my say-so. Who the hell was I to inspire such faith?

No one stopped. They simply streamed over the edge like lemmings, and when I saw Kenny run as fast as he could and leap, arms stretched wide like he was free-falling into a pool, I went down.

Jess stopped, but I slapped her hands away and told her to run.

"No," she told me, grabbing my arm, lifting with all her strength. "Get the fuck up!"

It felt like one of those bad dreams, how sometimes you can't move, but I rose and shoved her forward. "I can't go without him anyway. Run!"

She hesitated.

"Your kids, Jess! Hurry the fuck up!"

She turned and ran. People streamed by me, and then I saw that the chariot was there, following them, streaking past me even as Leith leaped off, landing several feet away from me. His sword was drawn, his face was etched in pain, and the key on the chain was wrapped around the hilt of his sword.

"He's going to kill you, hearth," I heard Saudrian say from somewhere behind me.

"He's not," I promised him, and I turned and bolted for the edge.

I heard Leith's roar. Almost to the edge, I stopped and rounded on him. He lifted the sword fast instead of running me through. I saw the war going on inside, saw it raging all over his face, the betrayal, how much he hated me and loved me at the same time. He was shaking with his desire to kill me, the restraint costing him.

"Come to me," I demanded, gesturing him forward. "Trust me."

He was in misery, and I saw his eyes redden as tears welled up but didn't spill.

Saudrian screamed out words, and I knew without knowing them that Leith was being goaded to kill me. There were lies tumbling from the demon's lips, and I saw Leith react to them, saw him charge me, sword held high.

I did the only thing I could think of. I opened my arms and held them outstretched to receive him. "I love you," I told him.

He hit me hard. He was moving too fast, and he was much too big to slow his forward momentum. But there was no pain, only the arm that went around me, clutching tight, crushing me to his chest as he lost his balance and we went over the side.

"No!" Saudrian screamed, and as we spun sideways, I saw him lift his ax.

Leith saw it, too, and he flung his sword up. It caught the demon in his throat, and he fell back out of sight.

The wind was rushing by, and I held on tight, clutching at Leith, pressing a kiss to the side of his neck as we gained speed. I felt his arms around me, heard my name on the wind, and then the whistling became a scream. Then… nothing.

# X

I WAS wet, sitting in mud, coughing and choking on smoke. There were sirens and a voice on a bullhorn, and as my vision cleared, I saw the hoses and the firemen and the chaos around me. I looked for Leith but saw no sign of him. I tried to get up, but I had no power, not a drop of stamina to rise. I felt a hand on my shoulder, and when I turned, I saw Jess. She was covered in soot, but she was in the Donna Karan suit that she had been in last time I had seen her before we had all taken the plunge into the siphon world. Chale was on the other side of me, panting; he, too, was streaked in dirt and soot, coughing, but in his dress clothes as well. The three of us watched, as did Kenny and my boss Dan Brenner, as the hotel in front of us fell in stages to the ground. It was gutted by fire, smoking, burning, and slowly becoming ash.

"You people are lucky to be alive, as hot as that fire burned."

We all looked up as the fireman walked by us, and, stunned, I began sweeping my eyes in every direction to find my boyfriend. He was nowhere.

"Call home," Jess suggested, and when I looked at her, I saw that she had already dialed herself, ear to her phone, listening. "Hi, baby," she whimpered, and her tears were instant, making clean tracks down her dirt-smeared face. "You're not gonna guess what just happened to me. Put Daddy on, okay?"

I withdrew my phone from my pocket, amazed that it was there, and I would have dialed if I had not heard my name called.

Quickly I looked around and saw him coming toward me, my warder, moving fast through the debris. He was himself, long, lean, the carved features I knew, the shining eyes. I could barely breathe.

When he reached me, he came down into my lap, knees folded on either side of my hips, sinking into the mud with me, arms grabbing me tight. I hugged him back, face buried in his shoulder.

"Oh God, Simon, I'm so sorry." His breath caught. "I could've killed you. If you want me to go away and never see you again, I—"

"Are you kidding?" I growled at him, fisting my hand in his hair, yanking his head back hard so I could see his eyes. "You saved my life, you fuckin' idiot. Your love let me save everybody. Do you not get that?"

His eyes searched mine as I let him go.

"You—" I exhaled sharply, smiling wide, my hands cupping his face. "Jesus, Leith, do you get what we just did? You and me? Do you?"

He shook his head.

"Baby, we proved that we, we are way more than just good. I love you, you love me, and we're a fuckin' kick-ass team. I'm ready to do whatever with you. You wanna get rings, adopt kids, and buy a house? Whatever you want, sky's the limit."

His smile was huge. "Yeah? You're ready? Gonna be mine forever?"

"Forever and ever."

He was trembling suddenly as he leaned in and hugged me. "Finally."

I always was a slow learner.


HOURS later, at home, showered and changed, I was sitting on the couch while Leith finished up on the phone. He had been talking to Jael for close to an hour. I had been surprised that I was the only one who didn't buy the raging-fire story hook, line, and sinker. Even Jess had reported to her family that she had been lucky to make it out of the inferno alive. When Leith finally joined me on the couch, passing me a large mug of steaming tea, I just looked at him.

"What?"

"How can they not remember?"

"Why would you want them to remember?"

"But some of them were so strong."

"And some were weak," he reminded me.

I cleared my throat. "What about those that got turned into creatures?"

He squinted at me.

"Leith?"

"Honey, when you saved one, you saved them all. A demon lord can't keep one or a part; he keeps all or nothing, that's how it is. A façade traps everyone, and so everyone falls together or rises together. If even one stands strong, then everyone's saved."

"So everyone came out."

He nodded. "A façade is all or nothing. It's the gamble the demon takes."

"Why would they gamble?"

"The odds are pretty good most days."

"How come Raphael didn't know that if you save one person that you save them all? How come he thought I would have to leave Kenny after he shifted into a wolf?"

"Love, kyries don't know anything about sacrifice or faith. How would they? It probably never even occurred to Raphael that you would stay there and fight for your friends and not simply leave with him when you had the chance before the façade fell to begin with."

"Would you have let him bring just me out? When you got there to the hotel with Jackson and Ryan, were you there just for me or did you plan to save everyone?"

He squinted at me. "I would like to tell you that I was thinking of the others, but, Simon, all I saw was you."

"That's okay."

"It's not, my job is to save as many as I can, but in that instance I was selfish. I wanted my hearth safe first."

"Cut yourself some slack," I said, smiling at him. "It's human to want to save your own."

"But I'm not just human, I'm a warder too."

"And look what you ended up doing, you took care of everyone."

"You did, not me."

"It was us, make no mistake."

"I just didn't want to lose you."

I thought about that and then other things. After long minutes I spoke. "You killed him, didn't you? Saudrian?"

He scoffed. "With just a sword? Not likely."

"No?"

"Demon lords don't die that easy."

I nodded. "Will he come after you?"

"Maybe, but I'm never alone here, and he can't get into my home, so…. And now Jael knows who he is, and no matter how scary a demon lord is, they know better than to take on a sentinel."

"Jael's scary, huh?"

"Pretty much."

"Saudrian wanted you bad."

"But you wanted me more."

"Yes, I did."

His eyes were soft as he stared at me.

"Raphael helped a lot."

"Which will keep me from killing him the next time I see him," he assured me.

But I wasn't sure that Leith or any one warder could kill Raphael. I had a feeling he was stronger than they were giving him credit for. "Good, 'cause I kind of like him."

He squinted at me. "Kyries are not to be trusted, love."

"We'll see."

One of his eyebrows rose. "So now you're an expert on kyries?"

"No, just men."

I put my cup down on the table and listened to the rain outside.

He cleared his throat. "I have other news."

"What's that?"

"It seems small now in comparison but Marcus has that restraining order in effect against your ex. You need to call me and then the police if you see him anywhere near you."

"If Eric knew all about you, he'd be more frightened of you than the police."

After a minute, I realized that Leith had not responded and that he was moving beside me. Turning to him, I saw that he had put his cup on the table as well, and his eyes were suddenly wide, beseeching.

"What's wrong?"

"I am terrifying, aren't I?"

"What?"

"I am, you saw what's really inside me. I'm scary."

"Not to me, not ever."

"I… how did you know that was me when I was so different on the outside?"

"I know you," I told him, patting my chest. "And I love you."

He moved fast, stretching out, lying between my legs with his head under my chin, arms wrapped around me. "I love you too."

Which I knew. "What are you thinking?"

"That whatever I am is okay, as long as you're with me."

I smiled, turning to rest my cheek on the top of his head.

"I'm yours, Simon. I belong to you."

"I know." He liked belonging to me; it was all he wanted.

"And you said you were ready to make plans, so I know what we gotta do first."

I sighed deeply. Leith sounding happy and content made me smile. "What's that?" I asked, getting sleepy, the warmth of his body seeping into me.

"We need to get a dog."

"Okay," I agreed, realizing that the man I was holding in my arms was the one I would have for the rest of my life.

"I was thinking an Australian shepherd was just the ticket. I've done some research, and they get along with kids just fine."

I could not have been happier.

MARY CALMES currently lives in Honolulu, Hawaii, with her husband and two children and hopes to eventually move off the rock to a place where her children can experience fall and even winter. She graduated from the University of the Pacific (ironic) in Stockton, California, with a bachelor's degree in English literature. Due to the fact that it is English lit and not English grammar, do not ask her to point out a clause for you, as it will *so* not happen. She loves writing, becoming immersed in the process, and falling into the work. She can even tell you what her characters smell like. She also buys way too many books on Amazon.

# The GUARDIAN
## Mary Calmes

Also from MARY CALMES

http://www.dreamspinnerpress.com

Contemporary Romance from MARY CALMES

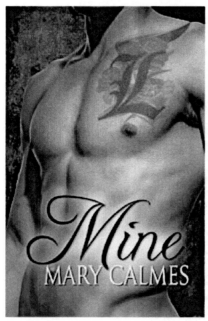

http://www.dreamspinnerpress.com

The *Matter of Time* series

 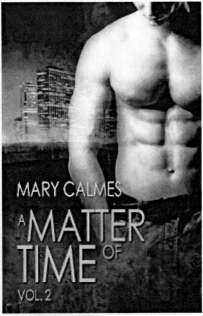

http://www.dreamspinnerpress.com

# Also from MARY CALMES

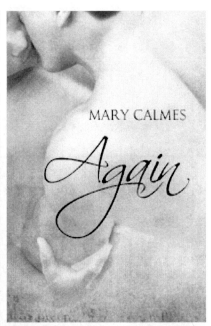

http://www.dreamspinnerpress.com

A novella from MARY CALMES

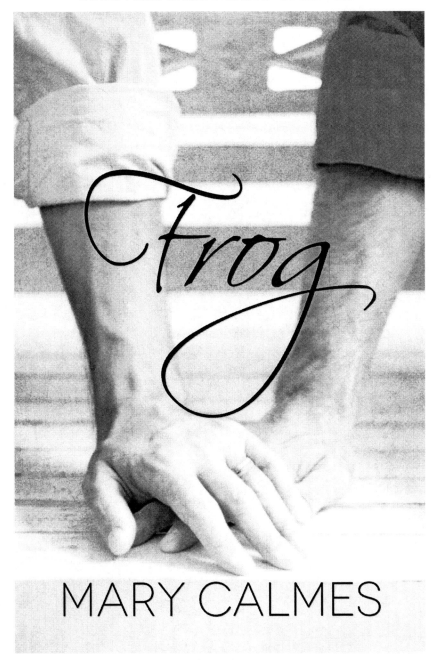

Frog

MARY CALMES

http://www.dreamspinnerpress.com

A novella from MARY CALMES

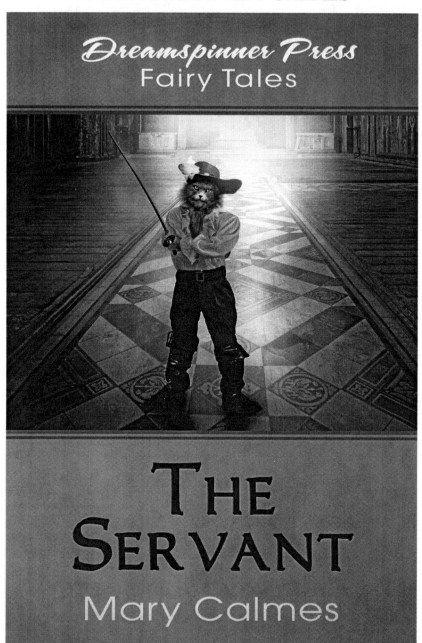

Dreamspinner Press
Fairy Tales

THE
SERVANT
Mary Calmes

http://www.dreamspinnerpress.com

A novella from MARY CALMES

# Romanus

## Mary Calmes

http://www.dreamspinnerpress.com

CPSIA information can be obtained at www.ICGtesting.com
Printed in the USA
LVOW07s0508110813

347255LV00003B/378/P